When Ben li *[text partially obscured]* **the wave and sa** *[text partially obscured]* **on the beach it was as if the past and the present had coalesced into one shining moment. A joy so unexpected it was painful flooded his heart.**

So here he was, against all resolutions, kissing her.

Her lips were warm and pliant beneath his; her body pressed to his chest. Her eyes, startled at first, had filled with an expression of bliss.

He shouldn't be kissing her. Starting things he could not finish. Risking pain for both of them. But those thoughts were lost in the wonder of having her close to him again.

It was as if the twelve years between kisses had never happened.

THE SUMMER THEY NEVER FORGOT

BY
KANDY SHEPHERD

Published in Great Britain 2014
by Mills & Boon, an imprint of Harlequin (UK) Limited,
Eton House, 18-24 Paradise Road, Richmond, Surrey, TW9 1SR

© 2014 Kandy Shepherd

ISBN: 978 0 263 91260 9

23-0214

Harlequin (UK) Limited's policy is to use papers that are natural, renewable and recyclable products and made from wood grown in sustainable forests. The logging and manufacturing processes conform to the legal environmental regulations of the country of origin.

Printed and bound in Spain
by Blackprint CPI, Barcelona

Kandy Shepherd swapped a fast-paced career as a magazine editor for a life writing romance. She lives on a small farm in the Blue Mountains near Sydney, Australia, with her husband, daughter, and a menagerie of animal friends. Kandy believes in love at first sight and real-life romance—they worked for her!

Kandy loves to hear from her readers. Visit her website at: www.kandyshepherd.com.

This is Kandy Shepherd's first book for Mills & Boon® Cherish™ and is available in eBook format from www.millsandboon.co.uk

Kandy Shepherd swapped a fast-paced career as a
magazine editor for a life writing romance. She lives
on a small farm in the Blue Mountains near Sydney,
Australia, with her husband, daughter, and a menagerie
of animal friends. Kandy believes in love at first sight
and a life-time of happiness ever after.

Kandy loves to hear from her readers. Visit her website
at www.kandyshepherd.com.

This is Kandy Shepherd's first book for ...
... Mills & Boon Cherish, and is available as ...
eBook format from www.millsandboon.co.uk

CHAPTER ONE

ON SANDY ADAMS'S thirtieth birthday—which was also the day the man she'd lived with for two years was getting married to another woman—she decided to run away.

No. Not run away. *Find a new perspective.*

Yes, that sounded good. Positive. Affirming. Challenging.

No way would she give even a second's thought to any more heartbreak.

She'd taken the first step by driving the heck out of Sydney and heading south—her ultimate destination: Melbourne, a thousand kilometres away. On a whim, she'd chosen to take the slower, scenic route to Melbourne on the old Princes Highway. There was time, and it went through areas she thought were among the most beautiful in the state of New South Wales.

Alone and loving it, she repeated to herself as she drove.

Say it enough times and she might even start to believe it.

Somewhere between the seaside town of Kiama and the quaint village of Berry, with home two hours behind her, she pulled her lime-green Beetle off onto a safe lay-by. But she only allowed herself a moment to stretch out her cramped muscles and admire the rolling green hills and breathtaking blue expanse of the Pacific Ocean before she got back in the car. The February heat made it too hot to stay outside for too long.

From her handbag she pulled out her new notebook, a birthday present from her five-year-old niece. There was a pink fairy on the cover and the glitter from its wings had already shed all through Sandy's bag. It came with a shocking-pink pen. She nibbled on the pen for a long moment.

Then, with a flourish, she headed up the page 'Thirtieth Birthday Resolutions' and started to scribble in pink ink.

1. Get as far away from Sydney as possible while remaining in realms of civilisation and within reach of a good latte.

2. Find new job where can be own boss.

She underscored the words 'own boss' three times, so hard she nearly tore the paper.

3. Find kind, interesting man with no hang-ups who loves me the way I am and who wants to get married and have lots of kids.

She crossed out 'lots of kids' and wrote instead '*three kids*'—then added, '*two girls and a boy*'. When it came to writing down goals there was no harm in being specific. So she also added, '*Man who in no way resembles That-Jerk-Jason*'.

She went over the word 'jerk' twice and finished with the date and an extravagant flourish. Done.

She liked making lists. She felt they gave her some degree of control over a life that had gone unexpectedly pear-shaped. But three goals were probably all she could cope with right now. The resolutions could be revisited once she'd got to her destination.

She put the notebook back into her bag and slid the car back onto the highway.

An hour or so later farmland had made way for bushland

and the sides of the road were lined with eucalypt forest. Her shoulders ached from driving and thoughts of a break for something to eat were at the front of her mind. When she saw the signpost to Dolphin Bay it took only a second for her to decide to throw the car into a left turn.

It was a purely reflex action. She'd planned to stop at one of the beachside towns along the way for lunch and a swim. But she hadn't given sleepy Dolphin Bay a thought for years. She'd adored the south coast when she was a kid—had spent two idyllic summer holidays at different resort towns with her family, revelling in the freedom of being let off the leash of the rigorous study schedule her father had set her during the school year. But one summer the family had stayed in Dolphin Bay for the first time and everything had changed.

At the age of eighteen, she'd fallen in love with Ben. Tall, blond, surfer dude Ben, with the lazy smile and the muscles to die for. He'd been exciting, forbidden and fun. At the same time he'd been a real friend: supportive, encouraging—all the things she'd never dreamed a boy could be.

Then there'd been the kisses. The passionate, exciting, first-love kisses that had surprised her for years afterwards by sneaking into her dreams.

Sandy took her foot off the accelerator pedal and prepared to brake and turn back. She'd closed the door on so many of the bittersweet memories of that summer. Was it wise to nudge it open again by even a fraction?

But how could it hurt to drop in to Dolphin Bay for lunch? It was her birthday, after all, and she couldn't remember the last proper meal she'd eaten. She might even book into Morgan's Guesthouse and stay the night.

She put her foot back to the accelerator, too excited at the thought of seeing Dolphin Bay again to delay any further.

As she cruised into the main street that ran between the rows of shops and the waterfront, excitement melted down in a cold rush of disappointment. She'd made a big mistake.

The classic mistake of expecting things to stay the same. She hadn't been to Dolphin Bay for twelve years. And now she scarcely recognised it.

Determined not to give in to any kind of let-down feelings, she parked not far from the wasn't-there-last-time information kiosk, got out, locked the car and walked around, trying to orientate herself.

The southern end of the bay was enclosed by old-fashioned rock sea walls to form a small, safe harbour. It seemed much the same, with a mix of pleasure boats and fishing vessels bobbing on the water. The typically Australian old pub, with its iron lace balconies was the same too.

But gone was the beaten-up old jetty. It had been replaced by a sleek new pier and a marina, a fishing charter business, and a whale-and dolphin-watching centre topped with a large fibreglass dolphin with an inane painted grin that, in spite of her shock, made her smile. Adjoining was a row of upmarket shops and galleries. The fish and chip shop, where she'd squabbled with her sister over the last chip eaten straight from the vinegar-soaked paper, had been pulled down to make way for a trendy café. The dusty general store was now a fashionable boutique.

And, even though it was February and the school holidays were over, there were people strolling, browsing, licking on ice cream cones—more people than she could remember ever seeing in Dolphin Bay.

For a moment disappointment almost won. But she laughed out loud when she noticed the rubbish bins that sat out on the footpath. Each was in the shape of a dolphin with its mouth wide open.

They were absolute kitsch, but she fell in love with them all over again. Surreptitiously, she patted one on its fibreglass snout. 'Delighted you're still here,' she whispered.

Then, when she looked more closely around her, she noticed that in spite of the new sophistication every business still sported a dolphin motif in some form or another, from a discreet sticker to a carved wooden awning.

And she'd bet Morgan's Guesthouse at the northern end of the bay wouldn't have changed. The rambling weather-board building, dating from the 1920s, would certainly have some sort of a heritage preservation order on it. It was part of the history of the town.

In her mind's eye she could see the guesthouse the way it had been that magic summer. The shuttered windows, the banks of blue and purple hydrangeas her mother had loved, the old sand tennis court where she'd played hit-and-giggle games with Ben. She hoped it hadn't changed too much.

As she approached the tourist information kiosk to ask for directions on how to get there she hesitated. Why did she need the guesthouse to be the same?

Did it have something to do with those rapidly return-ing memories of Ben Morgan? Ben, nineteen to her eigh-teen, the surfer hunk all the girls had had wild crushes on.

Around from the bay, accessed via a boardwalk, was a magnificent surf beach. When Ben had ridden his board, harnessing the power of the waves like some suntanned young god, there had always been a giggling gaggle of ad-miring girls on the sand.

She'd never been one of them. No, she'd stood on the sidelines, never daring to dream he'd see her as anything but a guest staying for two weeks with her family at his parents' guesthouse.

But, to her amazement and joy, he'd chosen *her*. And then the sun had really started to shine that long-ago summer.

'Morgan's Guesthouse?' said the woman manning the information kiosk. 'Sorry, love, I've never heard of it.'

'The old wooden building at the northern end of the bay,' Sandy prompted.

'There's only the Hotel Harbourside there,' the woman said. 'It's a modern place—been there as long as I've been in town.'

Sandy thanked her and walked away, a little confused.

But she gasped when she saw the stark, modern structure of the luxury hotel that had replaced the charming old weatherboard guesthouse. Its roofline paid some kind of homage to the old-fashioned peaked roof that had stood there the last time she had visited Dolphin Bay, but the concrete and steel of its construction did not. The hotel took up the footprint of the original building and gardens, and rose several floors higher.

Hotel Harbourside? She'd call it Hotel Hideous.

She took a deep, calming breath. Then forced herself to think positive. The new hotel might lack the appeal of the old guesthouse but she'd bet it would be air conditioned and would almost certainly have a decent restaurant. Just the place for a solo thirtieth birthday lunch.

And as she stood on the steps that led from the beach to the hotel and closed her eyes, breathed in the salty air, felt the heat shimmering from the sand, listened to the sound of the water lapping at the edge of the breakwater, she could almost imagine everything was the same as it had been.

Almost.

The interior of the restaurant was all glass, steel and smart design. What a difference from the old guesthouse dining room, with its mismatched wooden chairs, well-worn old table and stacks of board games for ruthlessly played after-dinner tournaments. But the windows that looked out over the bay framed a view that was much the same as it had always been—although now a fleet of dolphin-watching boats plied its tourist trade across the horizon.

She found a table in the corner furthest from the bar and sat down. She took off her hat and squashed it in her bag but kept her sunglasses on. Behind them she felt safer. Protected. Less vulnerable, she had to admit to herself.

She refused to allow even a smidgeon of self-pity to intrude as she celebrated her thirtieth birthday all by herself whilst at the same time her ex Jason was preparing to walk down the aisle.

Casting her eye over the menu, Sandy was startled by a burst of masculine laughter over the chatter from the bar. As that sound soared back into her memory her heart gave an excited leap of recognition. No other man's laughter could sound like that.

Rich. Warm. Unforgettable.

Ben.

He hadn't been at the bar when she'd walked in. She'd swear to it. Unless he'd changed beyond all recognition.

She was afraid to look up. Afraid of being disappointed. Afraid of what she might say, do, to the first man to have broken her heart.

Would she go up and say hello? Or put her hat back on and try to slink out without him seeing her?

Despite her fears, she took off her sunglasses with fingers that weren't quite steady and slowly raised her head.

Her breath caught in her throat and she felt the blood drain from her face. He stood with his profile towards her, but it was definitely Ben Morgan: broad-shouldered, towering above the other men in the bar, talking animatedly with a group of people.

From what she could see from this distance he was as handsome as the day they'd said goodbye. His hair was shorter. He wore tailored shorts and a polo-style shirt instead of the Hawaiian print board shorts and singlet he'd favoured when he was nineteen. He was more muscular. Definitely more grown up.

But he was still Ben.

He said something to the guy standing near him, laughed again at his response. Now, as then, he held the attention of everyone around him.

Did he feel her gaze fixed on him?

Something must have made him turn. As their eyes connected, he froze mid-laugh. Nothing about his expression indicated that he recognised her.

For a long, long moment it seemed as if everyone and everything else in the room fell away. The sound of plates clattering, glasses clinking, and the hum of chatter seemed muted. She realised she was holding her breath.

Ben turned back to the man he'd been talking to, said something, then turned to face her again. This time he smiled, acknowledging her, and she let out her breath in a slow sigh.

He made his way to her table with assured, athletic strides. She watched, mesmerised, taking in the changes wrought by twelve years. The broad-shouldered, tightly muscled body, with not a trace of his teenage gangliness. The solid strength of him. The transformation from boy to man. Oh, yes, the teenage Ben was now very definitely a man.

And hotter than ever.

All her senses screamed that recognition.

He'd reached her before she had a chance to get up from her chair.

'Sandy?'

The voice she hadn't heard for so long was as deep and husky as she remembered. He'd had a man's voice even at nineteen. Though only a year older than her, he'd seemed light years ahead in maturity.

Words of greeting she knew she should utter were wedged in her throat. She coughed. Panicked that she couldn't even manage a hello.

His words filled the void. 'Or are you Alexandra these days?'

He remembered that. Her father had insisted she be called by her full name of Alexandra. But Alexandra was too much of a mouthful, Ben had decided. He'd called her by the name she preferred. From that summer on she'd been Sandy. Except, of course, to her father and mother.

'Who's Alexandra?' she said now, pretending to look around for someone else.

He laughed with what seemed like genuine pleasure to see her. Suddenly she felt her nervousness, her self-consciousness, drop down a notch or two.

She scrambled up from her chair. The small round table was a barrier between her and the man who'd been everything to her twelve years ago. The man she'd thought she'd never see again.

'It's good to see you, Ben,' she said, her voice still more choked than she would have liked it to be.

His face was the same—strong-jawed and handsome—and his eyes were still as blue as the summer sky at noon. Close-cropped dark blond hair replaced the sun-bleached surfer tangle that so long ago she'd thought was the ultimate in cool. There were creases around his eyes that hadn't been there when he was nineteen. And there was a tiny white crescent of a scar on his top lip she didn't remember. But she could still see the boy in the man.

'It's good to see you, too,' he said, in that so-deep-it-bordered-on-gruff voice. 'I recognised you straight away.'

'Me too. I mean, I recognised you too.'

What did he see as he looked at her? What outward signs had the last years of living life full steam ahead left on her?

'You've cut your hair,' he said.

'So have you,' she said, and he smiled.

Automatically her hand went up to touch her head. Of course he would notice. Her brown hair had swung below her waist when she'd last seen him, and she remembered how he'd made her swear never, *ever* to change it. Now it was cut in a chic, city-smart bob and tastefully highlighted.

'But otherwise you haven't changed,' he added in that husky voice. 'Just grown up.'

'It's kind of you to say that,' she said. But she knew how much she'd changed from that girl that summer.

'Mind if I join you?' he asked.

'Of course. Please. I was just having a drink…'

She sat back down and Ben sat in the chair opposite her. His strong, tanned legs were so close they nudged hers as he settled into place. She didn't draw her legs back. The slight pressure of his skin on her skin, although momentary, sent waves of awareness coursing through her. She swallowed hard.

She'd used to think Ben Morgan was the best-looking man she'd ever seen. The twelve intervening years had done nothing to change her opinion. No sophisticated city guy had ever matched up to him. Not even Jason.

She'd left the menu open on the table before her. 'I see you've decided on dessert before your main meal,' Ben said, with that lazy smile which hadn't changed at all.

'I was checking out the salads, actually,' she lied.

'Really?' he said, the smile still in his voice, and the one word said everything.

He'd caught her out. Was teasing her. Like he'd used to do. With no brothers, an all-girls school and zero dating experience, she hadn't been used to boys. Never hurtful or mean, his happy-go-lucky ways had helped get her over that oversensitivity. It was just one of the ways he'd helped her grow up.

'You're right,' she said, relaxing into a smile. 'Old habits die hard. The raspberry brownie with chocolate fudge sauce *does* appeal.' The birthday cake you had when you weren't having a birthday cake. But she wouldn't admit to that.

'That brownie is so good you'll want to order two servings,' he said.

Like you used to.

The unspoken words hung between them. Their eyes met for a moment too long to be comfortable. She was the first to look away.

Ben signalled the waiter. As he waved, Sandy had to suppress a gasp at the ugly raised scars that distorted the palms of his hands. What had happened? A fishing accident?

Quickly she averted her eyes so he wouldn't notice her shock. Or see the questions she didn't dare ask.

Not now. Not yet.

She rushed to fill the silence that had fallen over their table. 'It's been a—'

He finished the sentence for her. 'Long time?'

'Yes,' was all she was able to get out. 'I was only thinking about you a minute ago and wondering...'

She felt the colour rise up her throat to stain her cheeks. As she'd walked away from the information kiosk and towards the hotel hadn't she been remembering how Ben had kissed her all those years ago, as they'd lain entwined on the sand in the shadows at the back of the Morgan family's boat shed? Remembering the promises they'd made to each other between those breathless kisses? Promises she'd really, truly believed.

She felt again as gauche and awkward as she had the night she'd first danced with him, at a bushfire brigade fundraiser dance at the surf club a lifetime ago. Unable to believe that Ben Morgan had actually singled her out from the summer people who'd invaded the locals' dance.

After their second dance together he'd asked her if she had a boyfriend back home. When she'd shaken her head, he'd smiled.

'Good,' he'd said. 'Then I don't have to go up to Sydney and fight him for you.'

She'd been so thrilled she'd actually felt dizzy.

The waiter arrived at their table.

'Can I get you another drink?' Ben asked.

'Um, diet cola, please.'

What was wrong with her? Why was she so jittery and on edge?

As a teenager she'd always felt relaxed with Ben, able to be herself. She'd gone home to Sydney a different person from the one who had arrived for that two-week holiday in Dolphin Bay.

She had to stop being so uptight. This was the same Ben. Older, but still Ben. He seemed the same laid-back guy he'd been as her teenage heartthrob. Except—she suppressed a shudder—for the horrendous scarring on his hands.

'Would you believe this is the first time I've been back this way since that summer?' she said, looking straight into his eyes. She'd used to tell him that eyes so blue were wasted on a man and beg him to swap them for her ordinary hazel-brownish ones.

'It's certainly the first time I've seen you here,' he said easily.

Was he, too, remembering those laughing intimacies they'd once shared? Those long discussions of what they'd do with their lives, full of hopes and dreams and youthful optimism? Their resolve not to let the distance between Dolphin Bay and Sydney stop them from seeing each other again?

If he was, he certainly didn't show it. 'So what brings you back?' he asked.

It seemed a polite, uninterested question—the kind a long-ago acquaintance might ask a scarcely remembered stranger who'd blown unexpectedly into town.

'The sun, the surf and the dolphins?' she said, determined to match his tone.

He smiled. 'The surf's as good as it always was, and the dolphins are still here. But there must be something else to bring a city girl like you to this particular backwater.'

'B...backwater? I wouldn't call it that,' she stuttered. 'I'm sorry if you think I—' The gleam in his blue eyes told her he wasn't serious. She recovered herself. 'I'm on my way from Sydney through to Melbourne. I saw the turn to this wonderful non-backwater town and here I am. On impulse.'

'It's nice you decided to drop in.' His words were casual, just the right thing to say. Almost too casual. 'So, how do you find the place?'

She'd never had to lie with Ben. Still, she was in the habit of being tactful. And this *was* Ben's hometown.

'I can't tell you how overjoyed I was to see those dolphin rubbish bins still there.'

Ben laughed, his strong, even teeth very white against his tan.

That laugh. It still had the power to warm her. Her heart did a curious flipping over thing as she remembered all the laughter they'd shared that long-ago summer. No wonder she'd recognised it instantly.

'Those hellish things,' he said. 'There's always someone on the progress association who wants to rip them out, but they're always shouted down.'

'Thank heaven for that,' she said. 'It wouldn't be Dolphin Bay without them.'

'People have even started a rumour that if the dolphins are removed it will be the end of Dolphin Bay.'

She giggled. 'Seriously?'

'Seriously,' he said, straight-faced. 'The rubbish bins go and as punishment we'll be struck by a tsunami. Or some other calamity.'

He rolled his eyes. Just like he'd used to do. That hidden part of her heart marked 'first love' reacted with a painful lurch. She averted her gaze from his mouth and that intriguing, sexy little scar.

She remembered the hours of surfing with him, playing tennis on that old court out at the back of the guesthouse. The fun. The laughter. Those passionate, heartfelt kisses. Oh, those kisses—his mouth hard and warm and exciting on hers, his tongue exploring, teasing. Her body straining to his...

The memories gave her the courage to ask the question. It was now or never. 'Ben. It was a long time ago. But...but why didn't you write like you said you would?'

For a long moment he didn't answer and she tensed. Then

he shrugged. 'I never was much for letters. After you didn't answer the first two I didn't bother again.'

An edge to his voice hinted that his words weren't as carefree as they seemed. She shook her head in disbelief. 'You wrote me two letters?'

'The day after you went home. Then the week after that. Like I promised to.'

Her mouth went suddenly dry. 'I never got a letter. Never. Or a phone call. I always wondered why…'

No way would she admit how, day after day, she'd hung around the letterbox, hoping against hope that he'd write. Her strict upbringing had meant she was very short on dating experience and vulnerable to doubt.

'Don't chase after boys,' her mother had told her, over and over again. *'Men are hunters. If he's interested he'll come after you. If he doesn't you'll only make a fool of yourself by throwing yourself at him.'*

But in spite of her mother's advice she'd tried to phone Ben. Three times she'd braved a phone call to the guest-house but had hung up without identifying herself when his father had answered. On the third time his father had told her not to ring again. Had he thought she was a nuisance caller? Or realised it was her and didn't want her bothering his son? Her eighteen-year-old self had assumed the latter.

It had been humiliating. Too humiliating to admit it even now to Ben.

'Your dad probably got to my letters before you could,' said Ben. 'He never approved of me.'

'That's not true,' Sandy stated half-heartedly, knowing she wouldn't put it past her controlling, righteous father to have intercepted any communication from Ben. In fact she and Ben had decided it was best he not phone her because of her father's disapproval of the relationship.

'He's just a small-town Lothario, Alexandra.' Her father's long-ago words echoed in her head. Hardly. Ben had treated

her with the utmost respect. Unlike the private school sons of his friends her father had tried to foist on her.

'Your dad wanted more for you than a small-town fisherman.' Ben's blue eyes were shrewd and piercing. 'And you probably came to agree with him.'

Sandy dropped her gaze and shifted uncomfortably in her seat. Over and over her father had told her to forget about Ben. He wasn't suitable. They came from different worlds. Where was the future for a girl who had academic talents like hers with a boy who'd finished high school but had no intention of going any further?

Underneath it all had been the unspoken message: *He's not good enough for you.*

She'd never believed that—not for a second. But she had come to believe there was no future for them.

Inconsolable after their summer together, she'd sobbed into her pillow at night when Ben hadn't written. Scribbled endless notes to him she'd never had the courage to send.

But he hadn't got in touch and she'd forced herself to forget him. To get over something that obviously hadn't meant anything to him.

'Men make promises they never intend to keep, Alexandra.' How many times had her mother told her that?

Then, once she'd started university in Sydney, Dolphin Bay and Ben Morgan had seemed far away and less and less important. Her father was right—a surfer boyfriend wouldn't have fitted in with her new crowd anyway, she'd told herself. Then there'd been other boys. Other kisses. And she'd been too grown up for family holidays at Dolphin Bay or anywhere else.

Still, there remained a place in her heart that had always stayed a little raw, that hurt if she pulled out her memories and prodded at them.

But Ben had written to her.

She swirled the ice cubes round and round in her glass, still unable to meet his eyes, not wanting him to guess how disconcerted she felt. How the knowledge he hadn't abandoned her teenage self took the sting from her memories.

'It was a long time ago...' she repeated, her voice tapering away. 'Things change.'

'Yep. Twelve years tends to do that.'

She wasn't sure if he was talking about her, him, or the town. She seized on the more neutral option.

'Yes.' She looked around her, waved a hand to encompass the stark fashionable furnishings. 'Like this hotel.'

'What about this hotel?'

'It's very smart, but not very sympathetic, is it?'

'I kinda like it myself,' he said, and took a drink from his beer.

'You're not upset at what the developers did on the site of your family's beautiful guesthouse?'

'Like you said. Things change. The guesthouse has... has gone forever.'

He paused and she got the impression he had to control his voice.

'But this hotel and all the new developments around it have brought jobs for a lot of people. Some say it's the best thing that's ever happened to the place.'

'Do you?'

Sandy willed him to say no, wanting Ben to be the same carefree boy who'd lived for the next good wave, the next catch from the fishing boats he'd shared with his father, but knew somehow from the expression on his face that he wouldn't.

But still his reply came as a surprise. 'I own this hotel, Sandy.'

'You...you do?'

'Yep. Unsympathetic design and all.'

She clapped her hand to her mouth but she couldn't take back the words. 'I'm...I'm so sorry I insulted it.'

'No offence taken on behalf of the award-winning architect.'

'Really? It's won awards?'

'A stack of 'em.'

She noted the convivial atmosphere at the bar, the rapidly filling tables. 'It's very smart, of course. And I'm sure it's very successful. It's just…the old place was so charming. Your mother was so proud of it.'

'My parents left the guesthouse long ago. Glad to say goodbye to the erratic plumbing and the creaking floorboards. They built themselves a comfortable new house up on the headland when I took over.'

Whoa. Surprise on surprise. She knew lots must have changed in twelve years, but this? 'You took over the running of the guesthouse?' Somehow, she couldn't see Ben in that role. She thought of him always as outdoors, an action man—not indoors, pandering to the whims of guests.

'My wife did.'

His wife.

The words stabbed into Sandy's heart.

His wife.

If she hadn't already been sitting down she would have had to. Stupidly, she hadn't considered—not for one minute—that Ben would be married.

She shot a quick glance at his left hand. He didn't wear a wedding ring, but then plenty of married men didn't. She'd learned that lesson since she'd been single again.

'Of course. Of course you would have married,' she babbled, forcing her mouth into the semblance of a smile.

She clutched her glass so tightly she feared it would shatter. Frantically she tried to mould her expression into something normal, show a polite interest in an old friend's new life.

'Did you…did you marry someone from around here?'

'Jodi Hart.'

Immediately Sandy remembered her. Jodi, with her quiet manner and gentle heart-shaped face. 'She was lovely,' she said, meaning every word while trying not to let an unwarranted jealousy flame into life.

'Yes,' Ben said, and a muscle pulled at the side of his mouth, giving it a weary twist.

His face seemed suddenly drawn under the bronze of his tan. She was aware of lines etched around his features. She hadn't noticed them in the first flush of surprise at their meeting. Maybe their marriage wasn't happy.

Ben drummed his fingers on the surface of the table. Again her eyes were drawn to the scars on his hands. Horrible, angry ridges that made her wince at the sight of them.

'What about you?' he asked. 'Did you marry?'

Sandy shook her head. 'Me? Marry? No. My partner… he…he didn't believe in marriage.'

Her voice sounded brittle to her own ears. How she'd always hated that ambiguous term *partner*.

'"Just a piece of paper," he used to say.' She forced a laugh and hoped it concealed any trace of heartbreak. 'Sure made it easy when we split up. No messy divorce or anything.'

No way would she admit how distraught she'd been. How angry and hurt and humiliated.

His jaw clenched. 'I'm sorry. Did—?'

She put her hand up to stop his words. 'Thank you. But there's no point in talking about it.' She made herself smile. 'Water under the bridge, you know.'

It was six months since she'd last seen Jason. And that had only been to pay him for his half of the sofa they'd bought together.

Ben looked at her as if he were searching her face for something. His gaze was so intense she began to feel uncomfortable. When—at last—he spoke, his words were slow and considered.

'Water under the bridge. You're right.'

'Yes,' she said, not sure what to say next.

After another long, awkward pause, he glanced at his

watch. 'It's been great to see you, Sandy. But I have a meeting to get to.' He pushed back his chair and got up.

'Of course.' She wanted to put out a hand to stop him. There was more she wanted to ask him. Memories she wanted to share. But there was no reason for him to stay. No reason for him to know it was her birthday and how much she would enjoy his company for lunch.

He was married.

Married men did not share intimate lunches alone with former girlfriends, even if their last kiss had been twelve years ago.

She got up, too, resisting the urge to sigh. 'It was wonderful to catch up after all these years. Please...please give my regards to Jodi.'

He nodded, not meeting her eyes. Then indicated the menu. 'Lunch is on the house. I'll tell the desk you're my guest.'

'You really don't have to, Ben.'

'Please. I insist. For...for old times' sake.'

She hesitated. Then smiled tentatively. 'Okay. Thank you. I'm being nostalgic but they were good old times, weren't they? I have only happy memories of Dolphin Bay.' *Of the time we spent together.*

She couldn't kiss him goodbye. Instead she offered her hand for him to shake.

He paused for a second, then took it in his warm grip, igniting memories of the feel of his hands on her body, the caresses that had never gone further than she'd wanted. But back then she hadn't felt the hard ridges of those awful scars. And now she had no right to recall such intimate memories.

Ben was married.

'I'm sorry I was rude about your hotel,' she said, very seriously. Then she injected a teasing tone into her voice. 'But I'll probably never stop wondering why you destroyed the guesthouse. And those magnificent gum trees—there's not one left. Remember the swing that—?'

Ben let go her hand. 'Sandy. It was just a building.'

Too late she realised it wasn't any of her business to go on about the guesthouse just because she was disappointed it had been demolished.

'Ben, I—'

He cut across her. 'It's fine. That was the past, and it's where it should be. But it really has been great seeing you again…enjoy your lunch. Goodbye, Sandy.'

'Good-goodbye, Ben,' she managed to stutter out, stunned by his abrupt farewell, by the feeling that he wasn't being completely honest with her.

Without another word he turned from her, strode to the exit, nodded towards the people at the bar, and closed the door behind him. She gripped the edge of the table, swept by a wave of disappointment so intense she felt she was drowning in it.

What had she said? Had she crossed a line without knowing it? And why did she feel emptier than when she'd first arrived back in Dolphin Bay? Because when she'd written her birthday resolutions hadn't she had Ben Morgan in mind? When she'd described a kind man, free of hang-ups and deadly ambition, hadn't she been remembering him? Remembering how his straightforward approach to life had helped her grow up that summer? Grow up enough to defy her father and set her own course.

She was forced to admit to herself it wasn't the pier or the guesthouse she'd wanted to be the same in Dolphin Bay. It was the man who represented the antithesis of the cruel, city-smart man who had hurt her so badly.

In her self-centred fantasy she hadn't given a thought to Ben being married—just to him always being here, stuck in a time warp.

A waitress appeared to clear her glass away, but then paused and looked at her. Sandy wished she'd put her sunglasses back on. Her hurt, her disappointment, her anger at herself, must be etched on her face.

The waitress was a woman of about her own age, with a pretty freckled face and curly auburn hair pulled back tightly. Her eyes narrowed. 'I know you,' she said suddenly. 'Sandy, right? Years ago you came down from Sydney to stay at Morgan's Guesthouse.'

'That's right,' Sandy said, taken aback at being recognised.

'I'm Kate Parker,' the woman said, 'but I don't suppose you remember me.'

Sandy dredged through her memories. 'Yes, I do.' She forced a smile. 'You were the best dancer I'd ever seen. My sister and I desperately tried to copy you, but we could never be as good.'

'Thanks,' Kate replied, looking pleased at the compliment. She looked towards the door Ben had exited through. 'You dated Ben, didn't you? Poor guy. He's had it tough.'

'Tough?'

'You don't know?' The other woman's voice was almost accusing.

How would she know what had gone on in Ben Morgan's life in the twelve years since she'd last seen him?

'Lost his wife and child when the old guesthouse burned down,' Kate continued. 'Jodi died trying to rescue their little boy. Ben was devastated. Went away for a long time—did very well for himself. When he came back he built this hotel as modern and as different from the old place as could be. Couldn't bear the memories…'

Kate Parker chattered on, but Sandy didn't wait to hear any more. She pushed her chair back so fast it fell over and clattered onto the ground. She didn't stop to pull it up.

She ran out of the bar, through the door and towards the steps to the shoreline, heart pumping, face flushed, praying frantically to the god of second chances.

Ben.

She just had to find Ben.

CHAPTER TWO

TAKING THE STEPS two at a time, nearly tripping over her feet in her haste, Sandy ran onto the whiter-than-white sand of Dolphin Bay.

Ben was way ahead of her. Tall and broad-shouldered, he strode along towards the rocks, defying the wind that had sprung up while she was in the hotel and was now whipping the water to a frosting of whitecaps.

She had to catch up with him. Explain. Apologise. Tell him how dreadfully sorry she was about Jodi and his son. Tell him… Oh, so much she wanted to tell him. Needed to tell him. But the deep, fine sand was heavy around her feet, slowing her so she felt she was making no progress at all.

'Ben!' she shouted, but the wind just snatched the words out of her mouth and he didn't turn around.

She fumbled with her sandals and yanked them off, the better to run after him.

'Ben!' she called again, her voice hoarse, the salt wind whipping her hair around her face and stinging her eyes.

At last he stopped. Slowly, warily, he turned to face her. It seemed an age until she'd struggled through the sand to reach him. He stood unmoving, his face rigid, his eyes guarded. How hadn't she seen it before?

'Ben,' she whispered, scarcely able to get the word out. 'I'm sorry… I can't tell you how sorry I am.'

His eyes searched her face. 'You know?'

She nodded. 'Kate told me. She thought I already knew. I don't know what to say.'

Ben looked down at Sandy's face, at her cheeks flushed pink, her brown hair all tangled and blown around her face. Her eyes were huge with distress, her mouth oddly stained bright pink in the centre. She didn't look much older than the girl he'd loved all those years ago.

The girl he'd recognised as soon as she'd come into the hotel restaurant. Recognised and—just for one wild, un-guarded second before he pummelled the thought back down to the depths of his wounded heart—let himself exult that she had come back. His first love. The girl he had never forgotten. Had never expected to see again.

For just those few minutes when they'd chatted he'd donned the mask of the carefree boy he'd been when they'd last met.

'I'm so sorry,' she said again, her voice barely audible through the wind.

'You couldn't have known,' he said.

Silence fell between them for a long moment and he found he could not stop himself from searching her face. Looking for change. He wanted there to be no sign of the passing years on her, though he was aware of how much he had changed himself.

Then she spoke. 'When did…?'

'Five years ago,' he said gruffly.

He didn't want to talk to Sandy about what the locals called 'his tragedy'. He didn't want to talk about it anymore full-stop—but particularly not to Sandy, who'd once been so special to him.

Sandy Adams belonged in his past. Firmly in his past. *Water under the bridge*, as she'd so aptly said.

She bit down on her lower lip. 'I can't imagine how you must feel—'

'No, you can't,' he said, more abruptly than he'd intended, and was ashamed at the flash of hurt that tightened her face. 'No one could. But I've put it behind me...'

Her eyes—warm, compassionate—told him she knew he was lying. How could he ever put that terrible day of helpless rage and despair behind him? The empty, guilt-ridden days that had followed it? The years of punishing himself, of not allowing himself to feel again?

'Your hands,' she said softly. 'Is that how you hurt them?'

He nodded, finding words with difficulty. 'The metal door handles were burning hot when I tried to open them.'

Fearsome images came back—the heat, the smoke, the door that would not give despite his weight behind it, his voice raw from screaming Jodi's and Liam's names.

He couldn't stop the shudder that racked his frame. 'I don't talk about it.'

Mutely, she nodded, and her eyes dropped from his face. But not before he read the sorrow for him there.

Once again he felt ashamed of his harshness towards her. But that was him these days. Ben Morgan: thirty-one going on ninety.

His carefree self of that long-ago summer had been forged into someone tougher, harder, colder. Someone who would not allow emotion or softness in his life. Even the memories of a holiday romance. For with love came the agony of loss, and he could never risk that again.

She looked up at him. 'If...if there's anything I can do to help, you'll let me know, won't you?'

Again he nodded, but knew in his heart it was an empty gesture. Sandy was just passing through, and he was grateful. He didn't want to revisit times past.

He'd only loved two women—his wife, Jodi, and, before her, Sandy. It was too dangerous to have his first love around, reminding him of what he'd vowed never to feel again. He'd resigned himself to a life alone.

'You've booked in to the hotel?' he asked.

'Not yet, but I will.'

'For how long?'

Visibly, her face relaxed. She was obviously relieved at the change of subject. He remembered she'd never been very good at hiding her emotions.

'Just tonight,' she said. 'I'm on my way to Melbourne for an interview about a franchise opportunity.'

'Why Melbourne?' That was a hell of a long way from Dolphin Bay—as he knew from his years at university there.

'Why not?' she countered.

He turned and started walking towards the rocks again. Automatically she fell into step behind him. He waited.

Yes. He wasn't imagining it. It was happening.

After every three of his long strides she had to skip for a bit to keep up with him. Just like she had twelve years ago. And she didn't even seem to be aware that she was doing it.

'You're happy to leave Sydney?'

'There's nothing for me in Sydney now,' she replied.

Her voice was light, matter-of-fact, but he didn't miss the underlying note of bitterness.

He stopped. Went to halt her with a hand on her arm and thought better of it. No matter. She automatically stopped with him, in tune with the rhythm of his pace.

'Nothing?' he asked.

Not meeting his gaze, swinging her sandals by her side, she shrugged. 'Well, my sister Lizzie and my niece Amy. But…no one else.'

'Your parents?'

Her mouth twisted in spite of her effort to smile. 'They're not together any more. Turns out Dad had been cheating on my mother for years. The first Mum heard about it was when his mistress contacted her, soon after we got home from Dolphin Bay that summer. He and Mum patched it up that time. And the next. Finally he left her for his receptionist. She's two years older than I am.'

'I'm sorry to hear that.'

But he was not surprised. He'd never liked the self-righteous Dr Randall Adams. Had hated the way he'd tried to control every aspect of Sandy's life. He wasn't surprised the older man had intercepted his long-ago letters. He'd made it very clear he had considered a fisherman not good enough for a doctor's daughter.

'That must have been difficult for you,' he said.

Sandy pushed her windblown hair back from her face in a gesture he remembered. 'I'm okay about it. Now. And Mum's remarried to a very nice man and living in Queensland.'

During that summer he'd used to tease her about her optimism. 'You should be called Sunny, not Sandy,' he'd say as he kissed the tip of her sunburned nose. 'You never let anything get you down.'

It seemed she hadn't changed—in that regard anyway. But when he looked closely at her face he could see a tightness around her mouth, a wariness in her eyes he didn't recall.

Maybe things weren't always so sunny for her these days. Perhaps her cup-half-full mentality had been challenged by life's storm clouds in the twelve years since he'd last seen her.

Suddenly she glanced at her watch. She couldn't smother her gasp. The colour drained from her face.

'What's wrong?' he asked immediately.

'Nothing,' she said, tight lipped.

Nothing. Why did women always say that when something was clearly wrong?

'Then why did you stare at your watch like it was about to explode? Is it connected to a bomb somewhere?'

That brought a twitch to her lips. 'I wish.'

She lifted her eyes from the watch. Her gaze was steady. 'I don't know why I'm telling you this, but right at this very moment Jason—my…my former boyfriend, partner, live-in lover or whatever you like to call him—is getting married.'

Sandy with a live-in boyfriend? She'd said she'd had a partner but had it been that serious? The knowledge hit him in the gut. Painfully. Unexpectedly. Stupidly.

What he and Sandy had had together was a teen romance. Kid stuff. They'd both moved on. He'd married Jodi. Of course Sandy would have had another man in her life.

But he had to clear his throat to reply. 'And that's bad or good?'

She laughed. But the laugh didn't quite reach her eyes. 'Well, good for him. Good for her, I guess. I'm still not sure how I feel about coming home one day to find his possessions gone and a note telling me he'd moved in with her.'

'You're kidding me, right?' Ben growled. How could someone treat his Sandy like that. *His Sandy.* That was a slip. She hadn't been his for a long, long time.

'I'm afraid not. It was...humiliating to say the least.' Her tone sounded forced, light. 'But, hey, it makes for a great story.'

A great story? Yeah, right.

There went sunny Sandy again, laughing off something that must still cause her pain.

'Sounds to me like you're better off without him.'

'The further I get from him the more I can see that,' she said. But she didn't sound convinced.

'As far away as Melbourne?' he asked, finding the thought of her so far away unsettling.

'I'm not running away,' she said firmly. Too firmly. 'I need change. A new job, a new—'

'Your job? What is that?' he asked, realising how little he knew about her now. 'Did you study law like your father wanted?'

'No, I didn't. Don't look so surprised—it was because of you.'

'Me?' No wonder her father had hated him.

'You urged me to follow my dreams—like you were following yours. I thought about that a lot when I got back home. And my dream wasn't to be a solicitor.' She shuddered. 'I couldn't think of anything less me.'

He'd studied law as part of his degree and liked it. But he wasn't as creative as he remembered Sandy being. 'But you studied for years so you'd get a place in law.'

'Law at Sydney University.' She pronounced the words as though they were spelled in capital letters. 'That was my father's ambition for me. He'd given up his plans for me to be a doctor when I didn't cut it in chemistry.'

'You didn't get enough marks in the Higher School Certificate for law?'

'I got the marks, all right. Not long after we got back to Sydney the results came out. I was in the honour roll in the newspaper. You should have heard my father boasting to anyone who'd listen to him.'

'I'll bet he did.' Ben had no respect for the guy. He was a bully and a snob. But he had reason to be grateful to him. Not for ruining things with him and Sandy. But for putting the bomb under him he'd needed to get off his teenage butt and make himself worthy of a girl like Sandy.

'At the last minute I switched to a communications degree. At what my father considered a lesser university.'

'He must have hit the roof.'

Sandy's mouth tightened to a thin line. 'As he'd just been outed as an adulterer he didn't have a leg to stand on about doing the right thing for the family.'

Ben smiled. It sounded as if Sandy had got a whole lot feistier when it came to standing up to her father. 'So what career did you end up in?'

'I'm in advertising.' She quickly corrected herself. 'I *was* in advertising. An account executive.'

On occasion he dealt with an advertising agency to help promote his hotel. The account executives were slick, efficient, and tough as old boots. Not at all the way he thought of Sandy. 'Sounds impressive.'

'It was.'

'Was?'

'Long story,' she said, and started to walk towards the rocks again.

'I'm listening,' he said, falling into step beside her.

The wind had dropped and now the air around them seemed unnaturally still. Seagulls screeched raucously. He looked through narrowed eyes to the horizon, where grey clouds were banking up ominously.

Sandy followed his gaze. She wrinkled her cute up-tilted nose. 'Storm brewing,' she said. 'I wonder—'

'Don't change the subject by talking about the weather,' he said, stopping himself from adding, *I remember how you always did that.*

He shouldn't have let himself get reeled in to such a nostalgic conversation. There was no point in dredging up those old memories. Not when their lives were now set on such different paths. And his path was one he needed—wanted—to tread unencumbered. He could not survive more loss. And the best way to avoid loss was to avoid the kind of attachment that could tear a man apart.

He wanted to spend his life alone. Though the word 'alone' seemed today to have a desolate echo to it.

She shrugged. 'Okay. Back to my story. Jason and I were both working at the same agency when we met. The boss didn't think it was a good idea when we started dating...'

'So you had to go? Not him?'

She pulled a face. 'We...ell. I convinced myself I'd been there long enough.'

'So you went elsewhere? Another agency?'

She nodded. 'And then the economy hit a blip, advertising revenues suffered, and last one in was first one out.'

'That must have been tough.'

'Yeah. It was. But, hey, one door closes and another one opens, right? I got freelance work at different agencies and learned a whole lot of stuff I might never have known otherwise.'

Yep, that was the old Sandy all right—never one to allow adversity to cloud her spirit.

She took a deep breath. He noticed how her breasts rose under her tight-fitting top. She'd filled out—womanly curves softened the angles of her teenage body. Her face was subtly different too, her cheekbones more defined, her mouth fuller.

He wouldn't have thought it possible but she was even more beautiful than she'd been when she was eighteen.

He wrenched his gaze away, cleared his throat. 'So you're looking at a franchise?'

Her eyes sparkled and her voice rose with excitement. 'My chance to be my own boss, run my own show. It's this awesome candle store. A former client of mine started it.'

'You were in advertising and now you want to sell candles? Aren't there enough candle stores in this world?'

'These aren't ordinary candles, Ben. The store is a raging success in Sydney. Now they're looking to open up in other towns. They're interviewing for a Melbourne franchise and I put my hand up.'

She paused.

'I want to do something different. Something of my own. Something challenging.'

She looked so earnest, so determined, that he couldn't help a teasing note from entering his voice. 'So it's candles? I don't see the challenge there.'

'Don't you?' she asked. 'There's a scented candle for every mood, you know—to relax, to stimulate, to seduce—'

She stopped on the last word, and the colour deepened in her cheeks, flushed the creamy skin of her neck. Her eyelashes fluttered nervously and she couldn't meet his gaze.

'Well, you get the story. I wrote the copy for the client. There's not much I don't know about the merits of those candles.' She was almost gabbling now to cover her embarrassment.

To seduce.

When he'd been nineteen, seducing Sandy had been all he'd thought about. Until he'd fallen in love with her. Then respecting her innocence had become more important than his own desires. The number of cold showers he'd been forced to take...

Thunder rumbled ominously over the water. 'C'mon,' he said gruffly, 'we'd better turn back.'

'Yes,' she said. 'Though I suppose it's too late now for my birthday lunch...' She hesitated. 'Please—forget I just said that, will you?'

'It's your birthday today?'

She shrugged dismissively. 'Yes. It's nothing special.'

He thought back. 'It's your *thirtieth* birthday.'

And she was celebrating alone?

'Eek,' she said in an exaggerated tone. 'Please don't remind me of my advancing years.'

'February—of course. How could I forget?' he said slowly.

'You remember my birthday?'

'I'd be lying if I said I recalled the exact date. But I remember it was in February because you were always pointing out how compatible our star signs were. Remember you used to check our horoscopes in your father's newspaper every day and—?'

He checked himself. Mentally he slammed his hand against his forehead. He'd been so determined not to indulge in reminiscence about that summer and now he'd gone and started it himself.

She didn't seem to notice his sudden reticence. 'Yes, I remember. You're Leo and I'm Pisces,' she chattered on. 'And you always gave me a hard time about it. Said astrology was complete hokum and the people at the newspaper just made the horoscopes up.'

'I still think that and—' He stopped as a loud clap of thunder drowned out his voice. Big, cold drops of water started pelting his head.

Sandy laughed. 'The heavens are angry at you for mocking them.'

'Sure,' he said, but found himself unable to resist a smile at her whimsy. 'And if you don't want to get drenched we've got to make a run for it.'

'Race you!' she challenged, still laughing, and took off, her slim, tanned legs flashing ahead of him.

He caught up with her in just a few strides.

'Not fair,' she said, panting a little. 'Your legs are longer than mine.'

He slowed his pace just enough so she wouldn't think he was purposely letting her win.

She glanced up at him as they ran side by side, her eyes lively with laughter, fat drops of water dampening her hair and rolling down her flushed cheeks. The sight of her vivacity ignited something deep inside him—something long dormant, like a piece of machinery, seized and unwanted, suddenly grinding slowly to life.

'I gave you a head start,' he managed to choke out in reply to her complaint.

But he didn't get a chance to say anything else for, waiting at the top of the stairs to the hotel, wringing her hands anxiously together, stood Kate Parker.

'Oh, Ben, thank heaven. I didn't know where you were. Your aunt Ida has had a fall and hurt her pelvis, but she won't let the ambulance take her to hospital until she's spoken to you.'

CHAPTER THREE

SANDY WAS HALFWAY up the stairs, determined to beat Ben to the top. Slightly out of breath, she couldn't help smiling to herself over the fact that Ben had remembered her birthday. Hmm… Should she be reading something into that?

And then Kate was there, with her worried expression and urgent words, and the smile froze on Sandy's face.

She immediately looked to Ben. Her heart seemed to miss a beat as his face went rigid, every trace of laughter extinguished.

'What happened?' he demanded of the red-haired waitress.

'She fell—'

'Tap-dancing? Or playing tennis?'

Kate's face was pale under her freckles. 'Neither. Ida fell moving a pile of books. You know what she's like. Pretends she's thirty-five, not seventy-five—'

Ida? A seventy-five-year-old tap-dancing aunt? Sandy vaguely remembered Ben all those years ago talking about an aunt—a great-aunt?—he'd adored.

'Where is she?' Ben growled, oblivious to the rain falling down on him in slow, heavy drops, slicking his hair, dampening his shirt so it clung to his back and shoulders, defining his powerful muscles.

'In the ambulance in front of her bookshop,' said

Kate. 'Better hurry. I'll tell the staff where you are, then join you—'

Before Kate had finished speaking, Ben had turned on his heel and headed around to the side of the hotel with the long, athletic strides Sandy had always had trouble keeping up with.

'Ben!' Sandy called after him, then forced herself to stop. Wasn't this her cue to cut out? As in, *Goodbye, Ben, it was cool to catch up with you. Best of luck with everything. See ya.*

That would be the sensible option. And Sandy, the practical list-maker, might be advised to take it. Sandy, who was on her way to Melbourne and a new career. A new life.

But this was about Ben.

Ben, with his scarred hands and scarred heart.

Ben, who might need some support.

Whether he wanted it or not.

'I'm coming with you,' she called after him, all thoughts of her thirtieth birthday lunch put on hold.

Quickly she fastened the buckles on her sandals. Wished for a moment that she had an umbrella. But she didn't really care about getting wet. She just wanted to be with Ben.

She'd never met a more masculine man, but the tragedy he had suffered gave him a vulnerability she could not ignore. Was he in danger of losing someone else he loved? It was an unbearable thought.

'Ben! Wait for me!' she called.

He turned and glanced back at her, but made no comment as she caught up with him. Good, so he didn't mind her tagging along.

His hand brushed hers as they strode along together. She longed to take it and squeeze it reassuringly but didn't dare. Touching wasn't on the agenda. Not any more.

Within minutes they'd reached the row of new shops that ran down from the side of the hotel.

There was an ambulance parked on the footpath out of

the rain, under the awning in front of a shop named Bay Books. When she'd driven past she'd admired it because of its charming doorframe, carved with frolicking dolphins. Who'd have thought she'd next be looking at it under circumstances like this?

A slight, elderly lady with cropped silver hair lay propped up on a gurney in front of the open ambulance doors.

This was Great-Aunt Ida?

Sandy scoured her memories. Twelve years ago she'd been so in love with Ben she'd lapped up any detail about his family, anything that concerned him. Wasn't there a story connected to Ida? Something the family had had to live down?

Ben was instantly by his aunt's side. 'Idy, what have you done to yourself this time?' he scolded, in a stern but loving voice.

He gripped Ida's fragile gnarled hand with his much bigger, scarred one. Sandy caught her breath at the look of exasperated tenderness on his face. Remembered how caring he'd been to the people he loved. How protective he'd been of *her* when she was eighteen.

Back then she'd been so scared of the big waves. Every day Ben had coaxed her a little further from the shore, building her confidence with his reassuring presence. On the day she'd finally caught a wave and ridden her bodyboard all the way in to shore, squealing and laughing at the exhilaration of it, she'd looked back to see he had arranged an escort of his brother and his best mates—all riding the same break. What kind of guy would do that? She'd never met one since, that was for sure.

'Cracked my darn pelvis, they think. I tripped, that's all.' Ida's face was contorted with annoyance as much as with pain.

Ben whipped around to face the ambulance officer standing by his aunt. 'Then why isn't she in the hospital?'

'Point-blank refused to let me take her. Insisted on seeing you first,' the paramedic said with raised eyebrows and admirable restraint, considering the way Ben was glaring at him. 'Tried to get her to call you from hospital but she wasn't budging.'

'That's right,' said Ben's aunt in a surprisingly strong voice. 'I'm not going anywhere until my favourite great-nephew promises to look after my shop.'

'Absolutely,' said Ben, without a second's hesitation. 'I'll lock it up safely. Now, c'mon, let's get you in the ambulance and—'

His aunt Ida tried to rise from the gurney. 'That's not what I meant. That's not good enough—' she said, before her words were cut short by a little whimper of pain.

Sandy shifted from sodden sandal to sodden sandal. Looked away to the intricately carved awning. She felt like an interloper, an uninvited witness to Ben's intimate family drama. Why hadn't she stayed at the beach?

'Don't worry about the shop,' said Ben, his voice burred with worry. 'I'll sort something out for you. Let's just get you to the hospital.'

'It's not life or death,' said the paramedic, 'but, yes, she should be on her way.'

Ida closed her eyes briefly and Sandy's heart lurched at the weariness that crossed her face. *Please let her be all right—for Ben's sake.*

But then the older lady's eyes snapped into life again. They were the same blue as Ben's and remarkably unfaded. 'I can't leave my shop closed for all that time.'

The paramedic interrupted. 'She might have to lie still in bed for weeks.'

'That's not acceptable,' continued the formidable Ida. 'You'll have to find me a manager. Keep my business going.'

'Just get to the ER and I'll do something about that later,' said Ben.

'Not later. *Now*,' said Aunt Ida, sounding nothing like a

little old lady lying seriously injured on a gurney. Maybe she was pumped full of painkillers.

Sandy struggled to suppress a grin. For all his tough, grown-up ways she could still see the nineteen-year-old Ben. He was obviously aching to bundle his feisty aunt into the ambulance but was too respectful to try it.

Aunt Ida's eyes sought out Kate, who was now standing next to Sandy. 'Kate? Can you—?'

Kate shook her head regretfully. 'No can do, I'm afraid.'

'She's needed at the hotel. We're short-staffed,' said Ben, with an edge of impatience to his voice.

Ida's piercing blue gaze turned to Sandy. 'What about you?'

'Me?' Was the old lady serious? Or delirious?

Before Sandy could stutter out anything more, Kate had turned to face her.

Her eyes narrowed. 'Yes. What about you, Sandy? Are you on holiday? Could you help out?'

'What? No. Sorry. I'm on my way to Melbourne.' She was so aghast she was gabbling. 'I'm afraid I won't be able to—'

'Friend of Kate's, are you?' persisted the old lady, in a voice that in spite of her obvious efforts was beginning to tire.

Compelled by good manners, Sandy took a step forward. 'No. Yes. Kind of... I—'

She looked imploringly at Ben, uncertain of what to say, not wanting to make an already difficult situation worse.

'Sandy's an...an old friend of mine,' he said, stumbling on the word friend. 'Just passing through.'

'Oh,' said the older lady, 'so she can't help out. And I can't afford to lose even a day's business.'

Her face seemed to collapse and she looked every minute of her seventy-five years.

Suddenly she reminded Sandy of her grandmother—

her mother's mother. How would she feel if Grandma were stuck in a situation like this?

'I'm sorry,' she said reluctantly.

'Pity.' Ida sighed. 'You look nice. Intelligent. The kind of person I could trust with my shop.' Wearily she closed her eyes again. 'Find me someone like her, Ben.'

Her voice was beginning to waver. Sandy could barely hear it over the sound of the rain drumming on the awning overhead.

Ben looked from Sandy to his aunt and then back to Sandy again, his eyes unreadable. 'Maybe...maybe Sandy can be convinced to stay for a few days,' he said.

Huh? Sandy stared at him. 'But, Ben, I—'

Ben held her with his glance, his blue eyes intense. He leaned closer to her. 'Just play along with me and say yes so I can get her to go to the hospital,' he muttered from the side of his mouth.

'Oh.' She paused. Thought for a moment. Thought again. 'Okay. I'll look after the shop. Just for a few days. Until you get someone else.'

'You promise?' asked Ida.

Promise? Like a cross-your-heart-and-hope-to-die-type promise? The kind of promise she never went back on?

Disconcerted, Sandy nodded. 'I promise.'

What crazy impulse had made her come out with that? Wanting to please Ben?

Or maybe it was the thought of what she would have liked to happen if it was her grandmother, injured, in pain, and having to beg a stranger to help her.

Ida's eyes connected with hers. 'Thank you. Come and see me in the hospital,' she said, before relaxing with a sigh back onto the gurney.

'Right. That's settled.' Ben slapped the side of the ambulance, turned to the ambulance officer. 'I'll ride in the back with my aunt.'

A frail but imperious hand rose. 'You show your friend around Bay Books. Settle her in.'

Sandy had to fight a smile as she watched Ben do battle with his great-aunt to let him accompany her to the hospital.

Minutes later she stood by Ben's side, watching the tail-lights of the ambulance disappear into the rain. Kate was in the back with Ida.

'Your aunt Ida is quite a lady,' Sandy said, biting her lip to suppress her grin.

'You bet,' said Ben, with a wry smile of his own.

'Isn't she the aunt who...?' She held up her hand. 'Wait. Let me remember. I know!' she said triumphantly. 'The aunt who ran off with an around-the-world sailor?'

Ben's eyes widened. 'You remember that? From all that time ago?'

I remember because you—and the family I fantasised about marrying into—were so important to me. The words were on the tip of her tongue, but she didn't—couldn't—put her voice to them. 'Of course,' she said instead. 'Juicy scandals tend to stick in my mind.'

'It *was* a scandal. For these parts anyway. She was the town spinster, thirty-five and unmarried.'

'Spinster? Ouch! What an awful word.' She giggled. 'Hey, I'm thirty and unmarried. Does that make me—' she made quotation marks in the air with her fingers '—a spinster?'

'As if,' Ben said with a grin. 'Try *career woman about town*—isn't that more up to date?'

'Sounds better. But the message is the same.' She pulled a mock glum face.

Ben stilled, and suddenly he wasn't joking. He looked into her face for a long, intense minute. An emotion she didn't recognise flashed through his eyes and then was gone.

'That boyfriend of yours was an idiot,' he said gruffly.

He lifted a hand as if he was about to touch her, maybe run his finger down her cheek to her mouth like he'd used to.

She tensed, waiting, not sure if she wanted him to or not. Awareness hung between them like the shimmer off the sea on a thirty-eight-degree day.

He moved a step closer. So close she could clearly see that sexy scar on his mouth. She wondered how it would feel if he kissed her…if he took her in his arms…

Her heart began to hammer in her chest so violently surely he must hear it. Her mouth went suddenly dry.

But then, abruptly, he dropped his hand back by his side, stepped away. 'He didn't deserve you,' he said, in a huskier-than-ever voice.

She breathed out, not realising she had been holding her breath. Not knowing whether to feel disappointed or relieved that there was now a safe, non-kissing zone between her and the man she'd once loved.

She cleared her throat, disconcerted by the certain knowledge that if Ben had kissed her she wouldn't have pushed him away. No. She would have swayed closer and…

She took a steadying breath. 'Yeah. Well… I…I'm better off without him. And soon I'll be living so far away it won't matter one little bit that he chose his mega-wealthy boss's daughter over me.'

She wouldn't take cheating Jason back in a million years. But sometimes it was difficult to keep up the bravado, mask the pain of the way he'd treated her. It was a particular kind of heartbreak to be presented with a *fait accompli* and no opportunity to make things right. It made it very difficult for her to risk her heart again.

'Still hurts, huh?' Ben said, obviously not fooled by her words.

She remembered how he'd used to tease her about her feelings always showing on her face.

She shook her head. After a lacklustre love life she'd thought she'd got things right with Jason. But she wasn't going to admit to Ben that Jason had proved to be another disappointment.

'You talk the talk, Sandy,' Jason had said. *'But you always held back, were never really there for me.'*

She couldn't see the truth in that—would never have committed to living with Jason if she hadn't believed she loved him. If she hadn't believed he would change his mind about marriage.

'Only my pride was hurt,' she said now to Ben. 'Things between us weren't right for a long time. I wasn't happy, and he obviously wasn't either. It had to end somehow....' She took a deep breath. 'And here I am, making a fresh start.' She nodded decisively. 'Now, that's enough about me. Tell me more about your aunt Ida.'

'Sure,' he said, glad for the change in subject. 'Ida got married to her wayfaring sailor on some exotic island somewhere and sailed around the world with him on his yacht until he died. Then she came back here and started the bookshop—first at the other end of town and now in the row of new shops I built.'

'So you're her landlord?'

'The other guy was ripping her off on her rent.'

And Ben always looked after his own.

Sandy remembered how fiercely protective he'd been of his family. How stubbornly loyal. He would have been just as protective of his wife and son.

No wonder he had gone away when he'd lost them. What had brought him back to Dolphin Bay, with its tragic memories?

He turned to face her, his face composed, no hint from his expression that he might have been about to kiss her just minutes ago.

'It was good of you to play along with me to make her happy. I just had to get her into that ambulance and on her way. Thank you.'

She shrugged. 'No problem. I'd like someone to do the same for my grandmother.'

He glanced down at his watch. 'Now you'd better go have your lunch before they close down the kitchen. Sorry I can't join you, but—'

'But what?' Sandy tilted her head to one side. She put up her hand in a halt sign. 'Am I missing something here? Aren't you meant to be showing me the bookshop?'

Ben swivelled back to face her. He frowned. 'Why would you want to see the bookshop?'

'Because I've volunteered to look after it for your aunt until you find someone else. I promised. Remember? Crossed my heart and—'

He cut across her words. 'But that wasn't serious. That was just you playing along with me so she'd go to the hospital. Just a tactic...'

Vehemently, she shook her head. 'A tactic? No it wasn't. I meant it, Ben. I said I'd help out for a few days and I keep my word.'

'But don't you have an interview in Melbourne?'

'Not until next Friday, and today's only Saturday. I was planning on meandering slowly down the coast...'

She thought regretfully of the health spa she'd hoped to check in to for a few days of much needed pampering. Then she thought of the concern in Ida's eyes.

'But it's okay. I'm happy to play bookshop for a while. Really.'

'There's no need to stay, Sandy. It won't be a problem to close the shop for a few days until I find a temporary manager.'

'That's not what your aunt thinks,' she said. 'Besides, it might be useful for my interview to say I've been managing a shop.' She did the quote thing again with her fingers. '"Recent retail experience"—yes, that would look good on my résumé.' An update on her university holiday jobs working in department stores.

Ben was so tight-lipped he was bordering on grim. 'Sandy, it's nice of you, but forget it. I'll find someone. There are agencies for emergency staff.'

Why was he so reluctant to accept such an easy solution to his aunt's dilemma? Especially when he'd been the one to suggest it?

It wasn't fair to blame her for not being aware of his 'tactic'. And she wasn't—repeat *wasn't*—going to let his lack of enthusiasm at the prospect of her working in the bookshop daunt her.

Slowly, she shook her head from side to side. 'Ben, I gave my word to your great-aunt and I intend to keep it.'

She looked to the doorway of Bay Books. Forced her voice to sound steady. 'C'mon, show me around. I'm dying to see inside.'

Ben hesitated. He took a step forward and then stopped. His face reminded her of those storm clouds that had banked up on the horizon.

Sandy sighed out loud. She made her voice mock scolding. 'Ben, I wouldn't like to be in your shoes if you have to tell your aunt I skipped out on her.'

His jaw clenched. He looked at her without speaking for a long second. 'Is that blackmail, Sandy?'

She couldn't help a smile. 'Not really. But, like I said, if I make a promise I keep it.'

'Do you?' he asked hoarsely.

The smile froze on her face.

Ben stood, his hands clenched by his sides. Was he remembering those passionately sworn promises to keep their love alive even though she was going back to Sydney at the end of her holiday?

Promises she hadn't kept because she'd never heard from him? And she'd been too young, too scared, to take the initiative herself.

She'd been wrong not to persist in trying to keep in touch

with him. Wrong not to have trusted him. Now she could see that. Twelve years too late she could see that.

'Yes,' she said abruptly and—unable to face him—turned on her heel. 'C'mon, I need to check out the displays and you need to show me how to work the register and what to do about special orders and all that kind of stuff.'

She knew she was chattering too quickly, but she had to cover the sudden awkwardness between them.

She braced herself and looked back over her shoulder. Was he just going to stay standing on the footpath, looking so forbidding?

No. With an exhaled sigh that she hoped was more exasperated than angry, he followed her through the door of Bay Books.

As Ben walked behind Sandy—forcing himself not to be distracted by the sway of her shapely behind—he cursed himself for being such an idiot. His impulsive ploy to placate Idy with a white lie about Sandy staying to help out had backfired badly.

How could he have forgotten just what a thoughtful, generous person Sandy could be? In that way she hadn't changed since she was eighteen, insisting on helping his mother wash the dishes at the guesthouse even though she'd been a paying guest.

Of course Sandy wouldn't lie to his great-aunt. He should have realised that. And now here she was, insisting on honouring her 'promise'.

The trouble was, the last thing he wanted was his old girlfriend in town, reminding him of what he'd once felt for her. What he didn't want to feel again. Not for her. Not for anyone.

Point-blank, he did *not* want Sandy helping out at Bay Books. Did not want to be faced by her positive get-up-and-go-for-it attitude, her infectious laugh and—he couldn't deny it—her lovely face and sexier-than-ever body.

He gritted his teeth and determined not to fall victim to her charm.

But as she moved through the store he couldn't help but be moved by her unfeigned delight in what some people called his great-aunt's latest folly.

He saw the familiar surrounds afresh through her eyes— the wooden bookcases with their frolicking dolphin borders, the magnificent carved wooden counter, the round tables covered in heavy fringed cloths and stacked with books both bestsellers and more off-beat choices, the lamps thoughtfully positioned, the exotic carpets, the promotional posters artfully displayed, the popular children's corner.

'I love it—I just love it,' she breathed. 'This is how a bookshop should be. Small. Intimate. Connected to its customers.'

Reverently, she stroked the smooth wooden surface of the countertop, caressed with slender pink-tipped fingers the intricate carved dolphins that supported each corner.

'I've never seen anything like it.'

'It's different, all right. On her travels Aunt Ida became good friends with a family of Balinese woodcarvers. She commissioned them to fit out the shop. Had all this shipped over.'

Sandy looked around her, her eyes huge with wonder. 'It's unique. Awesome. No wonder your aunt wants it in safe hands.'

Some people might find the shop too quaint. Old-fashioned in a world of minimalist steel and glass. Redundant at a time of electronic everything. But obviously not Sandy. He might have expected she'd appreciate Aunt Ida's eccentric creation. Just as she'd loved his family's old guesthouse.

She twirled around in the space between the counter and a crammed display of travel paperbacks.

'It even smells wonderful in here. The wood, of course. And that special smell of books. I don't know what it is—the paper, the binding.' She closed her eyes and inhaled with a look of ecstasy. 'I could just breathe it in all day.'

No.

His fists clenched tight by his sides. That was not what he wanted to hear. He didn't want Sandy to fit back in here to Dolphin Bay as if she'd never left.

He wanted her gone, back on that highway and heading south. Not connecting so intuitively with the magic his great-aunt had tried to create here. Not being part of his life just by her very presence.

How could he bear to have her practically next door? Every day she'd be calling on him to ask advice on how to run the shop. Seeking his help. Needing him.

And he wouldn't be able to resist helping her. Might even find himself looking in on the off chance that she needed some assistance with Aunt Ida's oddball accounting methods. Maybe bringing her a coffee from the hotel café. Suggesting they chat about the business over lunch.

That couldn't happen. He wouldn't let it happen. He needed his life to stay just the way it was. He didn't want to invite love into his life again. And with Sandy there would be no second measures.

Sandy threw herself down on the low, overstuffed sofa his aunt provided for customers to sit on and browse through the books, then jumped up again almost straight away. She clasped her hands together, her eyes shining with enthusiasm. 'It's perfect. I am *so* going to enjoy myself here.'

'It's only for a few days,' he warned. 'I'll talk to the agency straight away.' Again his voice was harsher than he'd intended, edged with fear.

She frowned and he winced at the quick flash of hurt in her eyes. She paused. Her voice was several degrees cooler when she replied.

'I know that, Ben. I'm just helping out until you get a manager. And I'm glad I can, now that I see how much of her heart your aunt has put into her shop.'

Avoiding his eyes, she stepped behind the counter, placed her hands on the countertop and looked around her. Despite his lack of encouragement, there was an eagerness, an excitement about her that he found disconcerting. And way too appealing.

She pressed her lips firmly together. 'I'll try not to bother you too much,' she said. 'But I'll need your help with operating the register. Oh, and the computer, too. Is all her inventory in special files?'

He knew he should show some gratitude for her helping out. After all, he'd been the one to make the ill-conceived suggestion that she should stay. But he was finding it difficult when he knew how dangerous it might be to have Sandy around. Until now he'd been keeping everything together in his under-control life. Or so he'd thought.

'I can show you the register,' he said grudgingly. 'The computer—that's a mystery. But you won't be needing to operate that. And, besides, it's only temporary, right?'

'Yeah. *Very* temporary—as you keep reminding me.'

This time she met his gaze head-on.

'But what makes you think I won't want to do as good a job as I can for your aunt Ida while I'm here? You heard what she said about needing every day of business.'

'I would look after her if she got into trouble.'

The truth was he didn't need the rent his great-aunt insisted on paying him. Could easily settle her overheads.

'Maybe she doesn't want to be looked after? Maybe she wants to be totally independent. I hope I'll be the same when I'm her age.'

Sandy at seventy-five years old? A quick image came to him of her with white hair, all skewered up in a bun on top of her head, and every bit as feisty as his great-aunt.

'I'm sure you will be,' he said, and he forced himself

not to smile at the oddly endearing thought. Or, by way of comparison, look too appreciatively at the beautiful woman who was Sandy now, on her thirtieth birthday.

'What about paying the bills?' she asked.

'I'll take care of that.'

'In other words,' she said with a wry twist to her mouth, 'don't forget that I'm just a temporary caretaker?'

'Something like that,' he agreed, determined not to make it easy for her. Though somewhere, hidden deep behind the armour he wore around his feelings, he wished he didn't have to act so tough. But if he didn't protect himself he might fall apart—and he couldn't risk that.

She looked up at him, her expression both teasing and serious at the same time. But her voice wasn't as confident as it had been. There was a slight betraying quiver that wrenched at him.

'You know something, Ben? I'm beginning to think you don't want me in Dolphin Bay,' she said, her eyes huge, her luscious mouth trembling. She took a deep breath. 'Am I right?'

He stared at her, totally unable to say anything.

Images flashed through his mind like frames from a flickering cinema screen.

Sandy at that long-ago surf club dance, her long hair flying around her, laughing as she and her sister tried to mimic Kate's outrageously sexy dancing, smiling shyly when she noticed him watching her.

Sandy breathless and trembling in his arms as he kissed her for the first time.

Sandy in the tiniest of bikinis, overcoming her fear to bravely paddle out on her body-board to meet him where the big waves were breaking.

Sandy, her eyes red and her face blotchy and tear-stained, running to him again and again to hurl herself in his arms for just one more farewell kiss as her father impatiently honked the horn on the family car taking her back to Sydney.

Then nothing. *Nothing.*

Until now.

He fisted his hands so tightly it hurt the harsh edges of the scars. Scars that were constant reminders of the agony of his loss.

How in hell could he answer her question?

CHAPTER FOUR

HE SAID *SHE* showed her emotions on her face? She didn't need a PhD in psychology to read his, either. It was only too apparent he was just buying time before spilling the words he knew she wouldn't want to hear.

For an interminable moment he said nothing. Shifted his weight from foot to foot. Then he uttered just one drawn-out word. 'Well...'

He didn't need to say anything else.

Sandy swallowed hard against the sudden, unexpected shaft of hurt. Forced her voice to sound casual, light-hearted. 'Hey, I was joking, but...but you're serious. You really *don't* want me around, do you?'

She pushed the rain-damp hair away from her face with fingers that weren't quite steady. Gripped the edge of the countertop hard, willing the trembling to stop.

When he finally spoke his face was impassive, his voice schooled, his eyes shuttered. 'You're right. I don't think it's a great idea.'

She couldn't have felt worse if he'd slapped her. She fought the flush of humiliation that burned her cheeks. Forced herself to meet his gaze without flinching. 'Why? Because we dated when we were kids?'

'As soon as people make the connection that you're my old girlfriend there'll be gossip, speculation. I don't want that.'

She swallowed hard against a suddenly dry throat, forced the words out. 'Because of your…because of Jodi?'

'That too.'

The counter was a barrier between them but he was close. Touching distance close. So close she could smell the salty, clean scent of him—suddenly heart-achingly familiar. After their youthful making out sessions all those years ago she had relished the smell of him on her, his skin on her skin, his mouth on her mouth. Hadn't wanted ever to shower it away.

'But…mainly because of me.'

His words were so quiet she had to strain to hear them over the noise of the rain on the metal roof above.

Bewildered, she shook her head. 'Because of you? I don't get it.'

'Because things are different, Sandy. It isn't only the town that's changed.'

His voice was even. Too even. She sensed it was a struggle for him to keep it under control.

He turned his broad shoulders so he looked past her and through the shop window, into the distance towards the bay as he spoke. 'Did Kate tell you everything about the fire that killed Jodi and my son, Liam?'

'No.' Sandy shook her head, suddenly dreading what she might hear. Not sure she could cope with it. Her knees felt suddenly shaky, and she leaned against the countertop for support.

Ben turned back to her and she gasped at the anguish he made no effort to mask.

'He was only a baby, Sandy, not even a year old. I couldn't save them. I was in the volunteer fire service and I was off fighting a blaze somewhere else. Everything was tinder-dry from years of drought. We thought Dolphin Bay was safe, but the wind turned. Those big gum trees near the guesthouse caught alight. And then the building. The guests got out. But…but not…' His head dropped as his words faltered.

He'd said before that he didn't want to talk about his tragedy—now it was obvious he couldn't find any more words. With a sudden aching realisation she knew it would never get easier for him.

'Don't,' she murmured, feeling beyond terrible that she'd forced him to relive those unbearable moments. She put her hand up to halt him, maybe to touch him, then let it drop again. 'You don't have to tell me any more.'

Big raindrops sat on his eyelashes like tears. She ached to wipe them away. To do something, anything, to comfort him.

But he'd just said he didn't want her here in town.

He raised his head to face her again. 'I lost everything that day,' he said, his eyes bleak. 'I have nothing to give you.'

She swallowed hard, glanced again at the scars on his hands, imagined him desperately trying to reach his wife and child in the burning guesthouse before it was too late. She realised there were scars where she couldn't see them. Worse scars than the visible ones.

'I'm not asking anything of you, Ben. Just maybe to be… to be friends.'

She couldn't stop her voice from breaking—was glad the rain meant they had the bookshop all to themselves. That no one could overhear their conversation.

He turned his tortured gaze full on to her and she flinched before it.

The words were torn from him. 'Friends? Can you really be "just friends" with someone you once loved?'

She picked up a shiny hardback from the pile to the left of her on the counter, put it back without registering the title. Then she turned back to face him. Took a deep breath. 'Was it really love? We were just kids.'

'It was for me,' he said, his voice gruff and very serious, his hands clenched tightly by his sides. 'It hurt that you never answered my letters, never got in touch.'

'It hurt me that you never wrote like you said you would,' she breathed, remembering as if it were yesterday the anguish of his rejection. Oh, yes, it had been love for her too.

But a small voice deep inside whispered that perhaps she had got over him faster than he had got over her. She'd never forgotten him but she'd moved on, and the memories of her first serious crush had become fainter and fainter. Sometimes it had seemed as though Ben and the times she'd had with him at Dolphin Bay had been a kind of dream.

She hadn't fully appreciated then what was apparent now—Ben wasn't a player, like Jason or her father. When he loved, he loved for keeps. In the intervening years she'd been attracted to men who reminded her of him and been bitterly disappointed when they fell short. She could see now there was only one man like Ben.

They both spoke at the same time.

'Why—?'

'Why—?'

Then answered at the same time.

'My father—'

'Your father—'

Sandy gave a short nervous laugh. 'And my mother, too,' she added, turning away from him, looking down at a display of mini-books of inspirational thoughts, shuffling them backwards and forwards. 'She told me not to chase after you when you were so obviously not interested. Even my sister, Lizzie, got fed up with me crying over you and told me to get over it and move on.'

'My dad said the same thing about you. That you had your own life in the city. That you wouldn't give me a thought when you were back in the bright lights. That we were too young, anyway.' He snorted. '*Too young.* He and my mother got married when they were only a year older than I was then.'

She looked up to face him. 'I phoned the guesthouse, you know, but your father answered. I was too chicken to speak to him, though I suspect he knew it was me. He told me not to call again.'

'He never said.'

Sandy could hear the beating of her own heart over the sound of the rain on the roof. 'We were young. Maybe too young to doubt them—or defy them.'

An awkward silence—a silence choked by the echoes of words unspoken, of kisses unfulfilled—fell between them until finally she knew she had to be the one to break it.

'I wonder what would have happened if we had—'

'Don't go there, Sandy,' he said.

She took a step back from his sudden vehemence, banging her hip on the wooden fin of a carved dolphin. But she scarcely felt the pain.

'Never torture yourself with *what if?* and *if only,*' he continued. 'Remember what you said? Water under the bridge.'

'It…it was a long time ago.'

She didn't know what else she could say. Couldn't face thinking of the 'what ifs?' Ben must have struggled with after the fire.

While he was recalling anguish and irredeemable loss, she was desperately fighting off the memories of how much fun they'd had together all those years ago.

She'd been so serious, so strait-laced, so under her father's thumb. For heaven's sake, she'd been old enough to vote but had never stayed out after midnight. Ben had helped her lighten up, take risks—be reckless, even. All the time knowing he'd be there for her if she stumbled.

He hadn't been a bad boy by any means, but he'd been an exciting boy—an irreverent boy who'd thumbed his nose at her father's old-fashioned edicts and made her question the ways she'd taken for granted. So many times she'd snuck out to meet him after dark, her heart thundering with both fear of what would happen if she were caught and anticipation of being alone with him.

How good it had felt when he'd kissed her—kissed her

at any opportunity when they could be by themselves. How his kisses, his caresses, had stirred her body, awakening yearnings she hadn't known she was capable of.

Yearnings she'd never felt as strongly since. Not even for Jason.

Saying no to going all the way with Ben that summer was one of the real regrets of her life. Losing her virginity to him would have been an unforgettable experience. How could it not have been when their passion had been so strong?

She couldn't help remembering their last kiss—with her father about to drag her into the car—fired by unfulfilled passion and made more poignant in retrospect because she'd had no idea that it would be her last kiss from Ben.

Did he remember it too?

She searched his face, but he seemed immersed in his own dark thoughts.

Wearily, she wiped her hand over her forehead as if she could conjure up answers. Why had those kisses been printed so indelibly on her memory? Unleashed passion? Hormones? Pheromones? Was it the magic of first love? Or was it a unique power that came only from Ben?

Ben who had grown into this intense, unreadable, tormented man whom she could not even pretend to know any more.

The rain continued to fall. It muffled the sound of the cars swishing by outside the bookshop, made it seem as if they were in their own world, cocooned by their memories from the reality of everyday life in Dolphin Bay. From all that had happened in the twelve years since they'd last met.

Ben cleared his throat, leaned a little closer to her over the barrier of the counter.

'I'm glad you told me you never got my letters, that you tried to phone,' he said, his voice gruff. 'I never understood how you could just walk away from what we had.'

'Me too. I never understood how you didn't want to see me again, I mean.'

She thought of the tears she'd wept into her pillow all those years ago. How abandoned she'd felt. How achingly lonely. Even the agony of Jason's betrayal hadn't come near it.

Then she forced her thoughts to return to today. To Ben's insistence that he didn't want her hanging around Dolphin Bay, even to help his injured aunt at a time of real need for the old lady.

It was beyond hurtful.

Consciously, she straightened her shoulders. She forced a brave, unconcerned edge to her voice. 'But now we know the wrong my father did maybe we can forget old hurts and... and feel some kind of closure.'

'Closure?' Ben stared at her. 'What kind of psychobabble is *that*?'

Psychobabble? She felt rebuffed by his response. She'd actually thought 'closure' was a very well-chosen word. Under the circumstances.

'What I mean is...maybe we can try to be friends? Forgive the past. Forget there was anything else between us?'

She was lying. *Oh, how she was lying.*

While her mind dictated emotion-free words like 'closure' and 'friends' her body was shouting out that she found him every bit as desirable as she had twelve years ago. More so.

Just months ago—when she'd still had a job—she'd worked on a campaign for a hot teen surf clothing label. Ben at nineteen would have been perfectly cast in the lead male role, surrounded by adoring bikini-clad girls.

Now, Ben at thirty-one could star as a hunky action man in any number of very grown-up commercials. His face was only improved by his cropped hair, the deep tan, the slight crinkles around his eyes and that intriguing scar on his mouth. His damp shirt moulded to a muscled chest and powerful shoulders and arms.

Now they were both adults. Experienced adults. She'd

been the world's most inexperienced eighteen-year-old. What would she feel if she kissed him now? A shudder ran deep inside her. There would be no stopping at kisses, that was for sure.

'You may be able to forget we were more than friends but I can't,' he said hoarsely. 'I still find you very attractive.'

So he felt it too.

Something so powerful that twelve years had done nothing to erode it.

Her heart did that flippy thing again, over and over, stealing her breath, her composure. Before she could stutter out something in response he continued.

'That's why I don't want you in Dolphin Bay.'

She gasped at his bluntness.

'I don't mean to sound rude,' he said. 'I…I just can't deal with having you around.'

What could she say in response? For all her skill as an award-winning copywriter, she couldn't find the right words in the face of such raw anguish. All she could do was nod.

That vein throbbed at his temple. 'I don't want to be reminded of what it was like to…to have feelings for someone when I can't…don't want to ever feel like that again.'

The pain behind his confession made her catch her breath in another gasp. It overwhelmed the brief flash of pleasure she'd felt that he still found her attractive. And it hurt that he was so pointedly rejecting her.

'Right,' she said.

Such an inadequate word. Woefully inadequate.

'Right,' she repeated. She cleared her throat. Looked anywhere but at him. 'I hear what you're saying. Loud and clear.'

'I'm sorry, I—'

She put up her hand in a halt sign. 'Don't be. I…I appreciate your honesty.'

Her heart went out to him. Not in pity but in empathy. She had known pain. Not the kind of agony he'd endured, but pain just the same. Her parents' divorce. Jason's callous dumping. Betrayal by the friends who'd chosen to be on Jason's side in the break-up and had accepted invitations to today's wedding of the year at St Mark's, Darling Point, the Sydney church famed for society weddings.

But the philosophy she'd evolved in those years when she'd been fighting her father's blockade on letting her lead a normal teenage life had been to refuse to let hurt and disappointment hold her back for long. She now firmly believed that good things were always around the corner. That light always followed darkness. But you had to take steps to invite that light into your life. As she had in planning to leave all the reminders of her life with Jason behind her.

Ben had suffered a tragedy she could not even begin to imagine. Would he ever be able to move out of the shadows?

'Honesty is best all round,' he said, the jagged edge to his voice giving a terrible sincerity to the cliché.

She gritted her teeth against the thought of all Ben had endured since they'd last met, the damage it had done to him. And yet…

From what she remembered of sweet-faced Jodi Hart, she couldn't imagine she would want to see the husband she'd loved wrapping himself in a shroud of grief and self-blame, not allowing himself ever again to feel happiness or love.

But it was not for her to make that judgement. She, too, belonged to Ben's yesterday, and that was where he seemed determined to keep her. He did not want to be part of her tomorrow in any way.

If only she could stop wondering if the magic would still be there for them…if they could both overcome past hurts enough to try.

She had to force herself not to sigh out loud. The attraction she felt for him was still there, would never go away. It was a longing so powerful it hurt.

'Now I know where I stand,' she said, summoning the strength to make her voice sound normal.

He was right. It was best to get it up-front. Ben was not for her. Not any more. The barriers he had up against her were so entrenched they were almost visible.

But in spite of it all she refused to regret her impulsive decision to return to Dolphin Bay. It was healing to meet up with Ben and discover that he hadn't, after all, heartlessly ditched her all those years ago. Coming after the Jason fiasco, that revelation was a great boost to her self-esteem.

She forced a smile. 'That's sorted, then. Let's get back on track. Tell me more about Bay Books. I'm going to be the best darn temporary manager you'll ever see.'

'So long as you know it's just that. Temporary.'

She nodded. She could do this. After all, she loved reading and she loved books—e-books, audiobooks, but especially the real thing. Added to that, the experience of looking after the bookshop might help her snag the candle store franchise. Maybe her reckless promise to Ida might turn out to benefit herself as much as Ben's great-aunt.

Yes, making that swift exit off the highway this morning had definitely been a good idea. But in five days she would get back into her green Beetle and put Dolphin Bay and Ben Morgan behind her again.

Five days of wanting Ben but knowing it could never be.

Five days to eradicate the yearning, once and for all.

But the cup-half-full part of her bobbed irrepressibly to the surface. There was one other way to look at it: five days to convince him they should be friends again. And after that who knew?

CHAPTER FIVE

BEN WATCHED THE emotions as they played across Sandy's face. Finally her expression settled at something between optimistic and cheerful.

He might have been fooled if he hadn't noticed the tight grip of her hands on the edge of the countertop. Even after all these years and a high-powered job in advertising she hadn't learned to mask her feelings.

He had hurt her. Hurt her with his blunt statements. Hurt her with his rejection of her friendship, his harsh determination to protect himself from her and the feelings she evoked.

He hated to cause her pain. He would fight with his fists anyone who dared to injure her in any way. But he had to be up-front. She had to know the score. The fire had changed him, snatched his life from him, forged a different person from the one Sandy remembered. *He had nothing left to give her.*

Her eyes were guarded, the shadows beneath them more deeply etched. She tilted her head to one side. A wispy lock of rain-damp hair fell across her face. He had to force himself not to reach out and tenderly push it aside, as he would have done twelve years ago.

She took a deep breath and again he couldn't help but appreciate the enticing swell of her breasts. She'd been sizzling at eighteen. As a woman of thirty she was sexual dynamite. Ignite it and he was done for.

Finally she spoke. 'Okay, so maybe promising to help your aunt wasn't such a great idea. But I crossed my heart. I'm here in Dolphin Bay. Whether you like it or not.'

Her lovely pink-stained mouth trembled and she bit down firmly on her lower lip. She blinked rapidly, as if fighting back tears, sending a wrenching shaft of pain straight to his heart.

She choked out her words. 'Don't be angry at me for insisting on staying. I couldn't bear that.'

'Like I'd do *that*, Sandy. Surely you know me better?'

She shook her head slowly from side to side. Her voice broke like static. 'Ben, I don't know you at all any more.'

A bruised silence fell between them. He was powerless to do anything to end it. Each breath felt like an effort.

Sandy's shoulders were hunched somewhere around her ears. He watched her make an effort to pull them down.

'If you don't want to be friends, where does that put us?'

'Seems to me we're old friends who've moved on but who have been thrown together by circumstance. Can't we leave it at that?'

Before she had a chance to mask it, disappointment clouded her eyes. She looked away. It was a long moment before she nodded and looked back up at him. Her voice was resolute, as if she were closing on a business deal, with only the slightest tremor to betray her. 'You're right. Of course you're right. We'll be grown-up about this. Passing polite for the next five days. Is that the deal?'

She offered him her hand to shake.

He looked at it for a long moment, at her narrow wrist and slender fingers. Touching Sandy wasn't a good idea. Not after all these years. Not when he remembered too well how good she'd felt in his arms. How much he wanted her—had always wanted her.

He hesitated a moment too long and she dropped her hand back by her side.

He'd hurt her again. He gritted his teeth. What kind of a man was he that he couldn't shake her hand?

'That's settled, then,' she said, her voice brisk and businesslike, her eyes not meeting his. 'By the way, I'll need somewhere to sleep. Any suggestions?'

Wham! What kind of sucker punch was that? His reaction was instant—raw, physical hunger for her. Hunger so powerful it knocked him for six.

He knew what he ached to say. *You can sleep in my bed. With me. Naked, with your legs twined around mine. On top of me. Beneath me. With your face flushed with desire and your heart racing with passion. Sleep with me so we can finish what we started so long ago.*

Instead he clenched his fists by his sides, looked somewhere over her head so he wouldn't have to see her face. He couldn't let her guess the thoughts that were taking over his mind and body.

'You'll be my guest at the hotel. I'll organise a room for you as soon as I get back.'

She put up her hand. 'But that won't be necessary. I—'

He cut short her protest. 'No buts. You're helping my family. You don't pay for accommodation. You'll go in a penthouse suite.'

She shook her head. 'I'm happy to pay, but if you insist—'

'I insist.' He realised, with some relief, that the rain had stopped pelting on the roof. 'The weather has let up. We'll get you checked in now.'

The twist to her mouth conceded defeat, although he suspected the argument was far from over. Like Idy, she was fiercely independent. Back then she'd always insisted on paying her way on their dates. Even if she only matched him ice cream for ice cream or soft drink for soft drink.

'Okay. Thanks. I'll just grab my handbag and—' She felt around on the counter, looked around her in panic. 'My bag!'

'It's at Reception. Kate picked it up.'

Kate, her eyes wide with interest and speculation, had whispered to him as they were helping Ida into the ambulance. She said Sandy had been in such a hurry to follow him out of the restaurant and onto the sand she'd left her bag behind.

Kate obviously saw that as significant. He wondered how many people now knew his old girlfriend was back in town.

The phone calls would start soon. His mother first up. She'd liked Sandy. She'd never pried into his and his brother Jesse's teenage love lives. But she'd be itching to know why Sandy was back in town.

And he'd wager that Sandy would have a stream of customers visiting Bay Books. Customers whose interest was anything but literary.

Sandy went to move from behind the counter.

'Sandy, before you go, there's something I've been meaning to tell you.'

She frowned. 'Yes?'

He'd been unforgivably ill-mannered not to shake her hand just to avoid physical contact. So what inexplicable force made him now lean towards her and lightly brush his thumb over her mouth where it was stained that impossibly bright pink? He could easily tell her what he had to without touching her.

His pulse accelerated a gear at the soft, yielding feel of her lips, the warm female scent of her. She quivered in awareness of his touch, then stood very still, her cheeks flushed and her eyes wide.

He didn't want her around. Didn't want her warmth, her laughter, falling on his heart like drops of water on a spiky-leaved plant so parched it was in danger of dying. A plant that needed the sun, the life-giving rain, but felt safe and comfortable existing in the shadows, living a half-life that until now had seemed enough.

'Sandy....' There was so much more he wanted to say. But couldn't.

She looked mutely back at him.

He drew a deep, ragged breath. Cleared his throat. Forced his voice into its usual tone, aware that it came out gruffer but unable to do anything about it.

'I don't know if this is the latest city girl look, but your mouth…it's kinda pink in the middle. You might want to fix it.'

She froze, then her hand shot to her mouth. 'What do you mean? I don't use pink lipstick.'

Without saying a word he walked around to her side of the counter and pulled out a drawer. He handed her the mirror his aunt always kept there.

Sandy looked at her image. She stared. She shrieked. 'That's the ink from my niece Amy's feather pen!'

It was difficult not to grin at her reaction.

Then she glared at him, her eyes sparking, though she looked about as ferocious as one of the stray puppies his mother fostered. '*You!* You let me go around all this time looking like this? Why didn't you tell me?'

He shrugged, finding it hard not show his amusement at her outraged expression. 'How was I to know it wasn't some fashion thing? I've seen girls wearing black nail polish that looks like bruises.'

'But this…' She wiped her hand ineffectively across her mouth. 'This! I look like a circus clown.'

He shrugged. 'I think it's kinda cute. In a…circusy kind of way.'

'*You!*' She scrutinised her image and scrubbed hard at her mouth.

Now her lips looked all pouty and swollen, like they'd used to after their marathon teen making out sessions. He had to look away. To force himself not to remember.

She glared again. 'Don't you ever, *ever* let me go out in public again looking weird, okay?'

'I said cute, not weird. But okay.' He couldn't help his mouth from lifting into a grin.

Her eyes narrowed into accusing slits. 'Are you laughing at me, Ben Morgan?'

'Never,' he said, totally negating his words by laughing.

She tried, but she couldn't sustain the glare. Her mouth quirked into a grin that spilled into laughter chiming alongside his.

After all the angst of the morning it felt good to laugh. Again he felt something shifting and stirring deep inside the seized and rusted engine of his emotions. He didn't want it to fire into life again. That way led to pain and anguish. But already Sandy's laughter, her scent, her unexpected presence again in his life, was like the slow drip-drip-drip of some powerful repair oil.

'C'mon,' he said. 'While the rain's stopped let's get you checked into the hotel. Then I have to get back to work.'

As he pulled the door of Bay Books closed behind him he found himself pursing his mouth to whistle. A few broken bars of sound escaped before he clamped down on them. He glanced to see if Sandy had noticed, but her eyes were focused on the street ahead.

He hadn't whistled for years.

CHAPTER SIX

SANDY SAT IN her guest room at Hotel Hideous, planning a new list. She shivered and hugged her arms to herself. The room was air conditioned to the hilt. There was no stinting on luxury in the modern, tasteful furnishings. She loved the dolphin motif that was woven into the bedcover and decorative pillows, and repeated discreetly on the borders of the curtains. And the view across the old harbour and the bay was beyond magnificent.

But it wasn't a patch on the charm of the old guesthouse. Who could have believed the lovely building would come to such a tragic end? She shuddered at the thought of what Ben had endured. Was she foolish to imagine that he could ever get over his terrible losses? Ever be able to let himself love again?

She forced herself to concentrate as she turned a new page of her fairy notebook. The pretty pink pen had been relegated to the depths of her handbag. She didn't have the heart to throw Amy's gift in the bin, even though she could never use it again.

She still burned at the thought of not just Ben but Kate, Ida and who-knew-who-else seeing her with the hot pink stain on her mouth. It was hardly the sophisticated image she'd thought she was putting across. Thankfully, several minutes of scrubbing with a toothbrush had eliminated the stain.

But maybe the ink stain had, in a roundabout way, served a purpose. Thoughtfully, she stroked her lip with her finger, where Ben's thumb had been. After all, hadn't the stain induced Ben to break out of his self-imposed cage and actually touch her?

She took a pen stamped with the Hotel Harbourside logo—which, of course, incorporated a dolphin—from the desk in front of her and started to write—this time in regulation blue ink.

1. *Reschedule birthday celebrations.*

No.

Postpone indefinitely.

Was turning thirty, with her life such a mess, actually cause for celebration anyway? Maybe it was best left unmarked. She could hope for better next year.

2. *Congratulate self for not thinking once about The Wedding.*

She scored through the T and the W to make them lower case. It was her friends who had dramatised the occasion with capital letters. Her so-called friends who'd gone over to the dark side and accepted their invitations.

She could thank Ben's aunt Ida for pushing all thoughts of That-Jerk-Jason and his lucrative trip down the aisle out of her mind.

Or—and she must be honest—was it really Ida who'd distracted her?

She realised she was gnawing the top of the pen.

3. *Quit chewing on pens for once and for all. Especially pens that belong to first love.*

First love now determined not even to be friends.
Which brought her to the real issue.

4. *Forget Ben Morgan.*

She stabbed it into the paper.

Forget the shivery delight that had coursed through her
when his finger had traced the outline of her mouth. Forget how he'd looked when he had laughed—laughed at
her crazy pink ink stain—forget the light in his eyes, the
warmth of his smile. Forget the stupid, illogical hope that
sprang into her heart when they joked together like in old
times.

She slammed the notebook shut, sending glitter shimmering over the desk. Opened it again. She underscored
the last words.

Then got on to the next item.

5. *Visit Ida and get info on running bookshop.*

She had to open Bay Books tomorrow and she didn't
have a clue what she should be doing. This was scary stuff.

She leaned back in her chair to think about the questions she should ask the older lady when the buzzer to her
room sounded.

'Who is it?' she called out, slamming her notebook shut
again in a flurry of glitter.

'Ben.'

In spite of her resolutions her heart leaped at the sound
of his voice. 'Just give me a second,' she called.

Her hands flew to her face, then smoothed her still-
damp-from-the-shower hair. She tightened the belt on the
white towelling hotel bathrobe. She ran her tongue around
suddenly dry lips before she fumbled with the latch and
opened the door.

Ben filled the doorway with his broad shoulders and impressive height. Her heart tripped into double time at the sight of him. He had changed into jeans and a blue striped shirt that brought out the colour of his eyes. Could any man be more handsome?

She stuttered out a greeting, noticed he held a large brown paper grocery bag in one hand.

He thrust the bag at her. 'For you. I'm not good at gift wrapping.'

She looked from the bag up to him. 'Gift wrapping?'

'I feel bad your birthday turned out like this.'

'This is a birthday gift?'

He shrugged. 'A token.'

She flushed, pleased beyond measure at his thoughtfulness. 'I like surprises. Thank you.'

Not sure what to expect, she delved into the bag. It was jam-packed with Snickers bars. 'Ohmigod!' she exclaimed in delighted disbelief.

He shifted from foot to foot. 'You used to like them.'

She smiled at him. 'I still do. They're my favourite.'

She didn't have the heart to add that when she was eighteen she'd been able to devour the chocolate bars by the dozen without gaining weight, but that at thirty they were an occasional indulgence.

'Thank you,' she said. 'You couldn't have given me anything I'd like more.'

She wasn't lying.

Ben's thoughtfully chosen gift in a brown paper bag was way more valuable than any of the impersonal 'must-have' trinkets Jason had used to choose and have gift wrapped by the shop. Her last present from him had been an accessory for her electronic tablet that he had used more than she ever had.

Her heart swelled with affection for Ben. For wounded, difficult, vulnerable Ben.

She looked up at him, aching to throw her arms around him and kiss him. Kiss him for remembering her sweet tooth. Kiss him for the simple honesty of his brown-bagged gift. Kiss him for showing her that, deep down somewhere beneath his scars and defences, her Sir Galahad on a surf-board was still there.

But she felt too wary to do so. She wasn't sure she could handle any more rejection in one day. His words echoed in her head and in her heart: *'I don't want you in Dolphin Bay.'*

'Thank you,' she said again, feeling the words were to-tally inadequate to express her pleasure at his gesture.

He looked pleased with himself in a very male, tell-me-again-how-clever-I-was way she found endearing.

'I bought all the shop had—which just happened to be thirty.'

She smiled up at him. 'The shopkeeper must have thought you were a greedy pig with a desperate addiction to chocolate.'

'Nah. They know chilli corn chips are more to my taste.'

She hugged the bag of chocolate bars to her chest. 'So I won't have to share? Because you might have to fight me for them.'

'That makes *you* the greedy pig,' he said. 'They're all yours.' He stood still, looking deep into her eyes. 'Happy birthday, Sandy.'

She saw warmth mixed with wariness—which might well be a reflection of what showed in her own eyes.

Silence fell between them. She was aware of her own quickened breathing over the faint hum of the air-condition-ing. Felt intoxicated by the salty, so familiar scent of him.

Now.

Surely now was the moment to kiss him? Suddenly she desperately wanted to feel his mouth—that sexy, sexy mouth—on hers. To taste again the memory that had lin-gered through twelve years away from him.

She felt herself start to sway towards him, her lips part-ing, her gaze focusing on the blue eyes that seemed to go a deeper shade of blue as he returned her gaze. Her heart was thudding so loudly surely he could hear it.

But as she moved he tensed and took an abrupt step backwards.

She froze. *Rejection again.* When would she learn?

She stepped back too, so hastily she was in danger of tripping backwards into the room. She wrapped her robe tighter around her, focused on the list of hotel safety instructions posted by the door rather than on him. A flush rose up her neck to sting her cheeks.

She couldn't think of a word to say.

After an excruciatingly uncomfortable moment Ben cleared his throat. 'I've been sent on a mission from Aunt Ida to find and retrieve you and take you to the hospital to meet with her.'

Sandy swallowed hard, struggled to make her voice sound light-hearted. 'Sounds serious stuff. Presumably an urgent briefing on the Bay Books project?'

He snapped his fingers. 'Right first guess.'

She smiled, knowing it probably looked forced but determined to appear natural—not as if just seconds ago she'd been longing for his kiss.

'Let me guess again. She's getting anxious about filling me in on how it all works?'

'Correct again,' he said. 'I promised to return with you ASAP to complete the mission.'

'Funnily enough I have no other pressing social engagements in Dolphin Bay.' She turned and started to walk back into the room, then stopped and looked back over her shoulder at him. 'Do you want to come in while I get dressed?'

His glance went briefly to her open neckline. He cleared his throat. 'Not a good idea.'

She blushed even redder and clutched the robe tighter. 'I mean... I didn't mean...' she stuttered.

'How about I come back to get you in half an hour?'

Her voice came out an octave higher. 'Twenty minutes max will be fine. Where will you be if I'm ready earlier?'

'Downstairs in my office.'

'Pick me up in twenty, then.'

He turned to go.

She swallowed against the sudden tension in her throat. 'Ben?' she said.

He swung back to face her, a question on his face.

'Thank you for the Snickers. I won't say I'll treasure them for ever, because they'll be devoured in double quick time. But...thank you.'

'You're welcome,' he said. 'It was—'

Afterwards she wondered at the impulse that had made her forget all caution, all fear of rejection. Before she could think about whether it was a good thing or not to do, propelled by pure instinct, she leaned up on her bare toes and kissed him lightly on his cheek.

Then she staggered at the impact of his closeness, at the memories that came rushing back in a flood of heat and hormones. The feel of his beard-roughened cheek beneath her lips, the strength of his tightly muscled body, the out-and-out maleness of him. She clung to him, overwhelmed by nostalgia for the past, for when she'd had the right to hold him close. *How could she ever have let go of that right?*

His hands grasped her shoulders to steady her. She could feel their warmth on her skin through the thick cloth of her robe. Swiftly, he released her. He muttered something inarticulate.

Reeling, she lifted her head in response, saw the shutters come down over his eyes—but not before she'd glimpsed something she couldn't read. It could have been passion but was more likely panic.

Bad, bad idea, Sandy, she berated herself. *Even a chaste peck is too much for him to handle.*

Too much for you *to handle.*

But no way was she was going to let herself feel ashamed

of a friendly thank-you kiss. She was used to spontaneous expressions of affection between friends.

She forced her breath to steady, tilted her chin upwards. 'See you in twenty,' she said, praying he didn't notice the tremor in her voice.

Ben stood back and watched as Sandy talked with his great-aunt in her room at the brand new Dolphin Bay Memorial Hospital. He might have known they would hit it off.

On doctor's orders, Ida was lying flat on her back in her hospital bed. She'd been told she had to hold that position for six weeks to heal her cracked pelvis.

Sandy had pulled up a chair beside her and was chatting away as if she and Ida were old friends.

Why, although they were talking about authors and titles of favourite books, did he sense this instant alliance could mean trouble for him? Trouble not of the business kind—hell, there was nothing he couldn't handle *there*—but a feminine kind of trouble he was not as well equipped to deal with.

Sandy was laughing and gesticulating with her hands as she spoke. His aunt was laughing too. It pleased him to see a warm flush vanquishing the grey tinge of pain from her face.

'What do you think, Ben?' Sandy asked.

'Me?'

'Yes. Who is the primary customer for Bay Books?'

He shrugged. 'People off the boats looking for something to read? Retirees?'

His aunt nodded. 'They're important, yes. But I sell more books to the telecommuters than to anyone else. They're crazy for book clubs. A book club gives them human contact as an antidote to the hours they spend working away on their computers, reporting to an office somewhere miles and miles away.'

Ben rubbed his hands together in simulated glee. 'All

those people fleeing the cities, making a sea-change to live on the coast—the lifeblood of commerce in Dolphin Bay. They're buying land, building houses, and spending their socks off.'

Sandy wrinkled up her nose in the way he remembered so well. It was just as cute on her at thirty as it had been at eighteen.

'That seems very calculating,' she said.

'What do you expect from the President of the Dolphin Bay Chamber of Commerce?' said Aunt Ida, her voice dripping with the pride all his family felt at his achievement. 'The town has really come on under his leadership.'

Sandy's eyes widened. 'You're full of surprises, Ben.'

On that so expressive face of hers he could see her wondering how he'd come from fisherman's son to successful businessman. Her father had judged him not good enough, not wealthy enough. He'd had no idea of how much land Ben's family owned. And Sandy didn't know how spurred on to succeed Ben had been by the snobby older man's low opinion of him.

'We have a lot to catch up on,' she said.

No.

More than ever he did *not* want to spend more time than was necessary with Sandy, reviving old feelings that were best left buried.

She was modestly dressed now, in a neat-fitting T-shirt and a skirt of some floaty material that covered her knees. But she'd answered the door to him at the hotel wrapped in nothing more than a Hotel Harbourside bathrobe.

As she'd spoken to him the robe had slid open to reveal the tantalising shadow between her breasts. Her face had been flushed and her hair damp. It was obvious she'd just stepped out of the shower and the thought of her naked had been almost more than his libido could take.

Naked in one of his hotel bathrooms. Naked under one of his hotel's bathrobes. It hadn't taken much to take the

thought a step further to her naked on one of his hotel's
beds. With the hotel's owner taking passionate possession.

He'd had to grit his teeth and force his gaze to somewhere above her head.

When she'd kissed him it had taken every ounce of his
iron-clad self-control not to take her in his arms and kiss her
properly. Not on the cheek but claiming her mouth, tasting
her with his tongue, exploring her sexy body with hungry
hands. Backing her into the room and onto the bed.

No.

There'd be no catching up on old times. Or letting his
libido lead him where he had vowed not to go.

He cleared his throat. 'Isn't this conversation irrelevant
to you running the bookstore for Aunt Ida?'

Sandy met his gaze in a way that let him know she knew
only too well he was steering the conversation away from
anything personal.

'Of course. You're absolutely right.'

She turned to face the hospital bed.

'Ida, tell me about any special orders.' Then she looked
back at him, her head at a provocative angle. Her eyes
gleamed with challenge. 'Is that better, Mr President?'

He looked to Ida for support, but her eyes narrowed as
she looked from him to Sandy and back again.

It was starting. The speculation about him and Sandy.
The gossip. And it looked as if he couldn't count on his aunt
for support in his battle to protect his heart.

In fact she looked mighty pleased at the prospect of un-
covering something personal between him and her temporary manager.

'You can tell me more about your past friendship with
Sandy some other time, nephew of mine,' she said.

Sandy looked as uncomfortable as he felt, and had trouble meeting his gaze. 'Can we get back to talking about Bay
Books, Ida?' she asked.

His aunt laughed. 'Back to the not nearly so interesting

topic of the bookshop? Okay, my dear, have you got something you can take some notes in? The special orders can get complicated.'

Looking relieved, Sandy dived into her handbag. She pulled out a luminous pink notebook and with it came a flurry of glitter that sparkled in the shafts of late-afternoon sun falling on his aunt's hospital bed.

'Sorry about the mess,' she said, biting down on her bottom lip as the particles settled across the bedcovers.

Ida seemed mesmerised by the glitter. 'It's not mess, it's fairy dust!' she exclaimed, clapping her hands with delight. Her still youthful blue eyes gleamed. 'Oh, this is wonderful, isn't it, Ben? Sandy will bring magic to Dolphin Bay. I just know it!'

Ben watched the tiny metallic particles as they glistened on the white hospital sheets. Saw the pleasure in his aunt's shrewd gaze, the gleam of reluctant laughter in Sandy's eyes.

'Magic? Well, it *did* come from my fairy notebook,' she said.

Something called him to join in their complicity, to believe in their fantasy.

Hope he'd thought long extinguished struggled to revive itself. Magic? *Was* it magic that Sandy had brought with her? Magic from the past? Magic for the future? He desperately wanted to believe that.

But there was no such thing as magic. He'd learnt that on a violently blazing day five years ago, when he had been powerless to save the lives of his family.

He would need a hell of a lot more than some so-called fairy dust to change his mind.

CHAPTER SEVEN

THE FIRST THING Sandy noticed on the beach early the next morning was the dog. A big, shaggy golden retriever, it lay near a towel on the sand near the edge of the water with its head resting on its paws. Its gaze was directed out to the surf of Big Ray Beach, the beach she'd reached via the boardwalk from the bay.

Twelve years ago she'd thought 'Big Ray' must refer to a person. No. Ben had informed her the beach had another name on the maps. But the locals had named it after the two enormous manta rays that lived on the northern end of the beach and every so often undulated their way to the other end. He had laughed at her squeals and hugged her close, telling her they were harmless and that he would keep her safe from anything that dared hurt her.

This morning there were only a few people in the water; she guessed one of them must be the dog's owner. At six-thirty, with strips of cloud still tinged pink from sunrise, it was already warm, the weather gearing up for sultry heat after the previous day's storm. Cicadas were already tuning up their chorus for the day.

Sandy smiled at the picture of doggy devotion. *Get dog of own once settled in Melbourne,* she added in a mental memo for her 'to do' list. That-Jerk-Jason had allergies and wouldn't tolerate a dog in the house. How had she been so in love with him when they'd had so little in common apart from their jobs?

She walked up to the dog and dropped to her knees in the sand. She offered it her hand to sniff, then ruffled the fur behind its neck. 'Aren't you a handsome boy?' she murmured.

The dog looked up momentarily, with friendly, intelligent eyes, thumped his plumed tail on the sand, then resumed his vigil.

She followed the animal's gaze, curious to see the object of such devotion. The dog's eyes were fixed on a man who was body-surfing. His broad, powerful shoulders and athletic physique were in perfect sync with the wave, harnessing its energy as it curled behind him and he shot towards shore.

The man was Ben.

She knew that even before he lifted his head from the water, a look of intense exhilaration on his face as he powered down the face of the wave. He was as at home on a wave as he had been when he was nineteen, and for a moment it was as if she were thrown back into the past. So much of her time with him that summer had been spent on this beach.

She was transported back to a morning like this when she'd run from the guesthouse to the sand and found him riding a wave, accompanied by a pod of dolphins, their grey shapes distinct on the underside of the wave. Joy and wonder had shone from his face. She'd splashed in to meet him and shared a moment of pure magic before the pod took off. Afterwards they'd lain on their backs on the beach, holding hands, marvelling over the experience. Did he remember?

Now he had seen her watching, and he lifted off the wave as it carried him into shore. She wanted to call out to him not to break off his ride on her account, but knew he wouldn't hear her over the sound of the surf.

He waved a greeting and swam, then strode towards her through the small breaking waves that foamed around his legs. Her breath caught in her throat at his near-naked magnificence. He was so tall and powerfully built that he seemed to dominate the vastness of the ocean and the horizon behind him.

His hair was dark and plastered to his head. The water was streaming off his broad shoulders and honed muscles. Sunlight glistened off the drops of water on his body so he seemed for one fanciful moment like some kind of mythical hero, emerging from the sea.

Desire, sudden and overwhelming, surged through her. Her nipples tensed and she seemed to melt inside. She wanted him. Longed for him. How could she ever have left him? She should have defied her parents and got back to Dolphin Bay. Somehow. Anyhow. Just to be with him.

That was back then. Now they were very different people who just happened to have found themselves on the same beach. But the attraction was as compelling as ever, undiluted by the years that had passed.

Why couldn't she forget that special time they had shared? What kept alive that fraction of hope that they could share it again? It wasn't just that she found him good-looking. This irrational compulsion was more than that. Something so powerful it overrode his rejection of her overtures. He didn't want her here. He had made that clear from the word go. She should just return his acquaintance-type wave and walk on.

But she ran in to the knee-deep waves to meet him. The dog splashed alongside her, giving a few joyous barks of welcome. She squealed at the sudden chill of the water as it sprayed her.

Remember, just friends, she reminded herself as she and Ben neared each other. Give him even a hint of the desire that had her so shaky and confused and he might turn back to that ocean and swim all the way to New Zealand.

'Good morning, Mr President,' she said. Ben as leader of the business community? It took some getting used to.

And yet the air of authority was there when he dealt with his staff at the hotel—and they certainly gave him the deference due to a well-respected boss.

'Just Ben will do,' he said as he walked beside her onto the dry sand. As always, she had trouble keeping up with his stride.

She was finding it almost impossible not to look at his body, impressive in red board shorts. Kept casting sideways glances at him.

'So you've met Hobo,' he said, with an affectionate glance at the dog.

'No formal introductions were made, but we said hello,' she said, still breathless at her physical reaction to him. 'Is he yours?'

She felt self-conscious at Ben's nearness, aware that she was wearing only a bikini covered by the skimpiest of tank tops.

'My mother helps out at a dog shelter. Sometimes she brings dogs home to foster until they find permanent homes. This one clapped eyes on me, followed me to my house and has been with me ever since.' He leaned down to pat the dog vigorously. 'Can't get rid of you, can I, mate?' He spoke with ill-concealed affection.

So he had something to love.

She was glad.

'He's adorable. And he guarded your towel like a well-trained soldier.'

Ben picked up the towel from the sand and flung it around his neck. *How many times had she seen him do that in just the same way? How many times had he tucked his towel solicitously around her if her own towel was damp?*

'What brings you to the beach so early?' he asked.

She pulled a face. 'Had to walk those Snickers bars off.'

'How many gone?'

'Only two.'

'One for dinner and one for breakfast?'

'Chocolate for breakfast? I've got a sweet tooth, but I'm not a total sugar freak.' She scuffed her foot in the sand. 'I couldn't sleep. Kept thinking of all I don't know about managing a bookstore.' *Kept thinking about you.*

He picked up a piece of driftwood and threw it for Hobo. The dog bounded into the water to retrieve it.

'You took a lot of notes from Aunt Ida yesterday.'

'It's just nerves. Bay Books is so important for Ida and I want to get it right.'

'You'll be fine. It's only for a few days.'

No doubt he meant to sound reassuring. But it seemed as if he was reminding her yet again that he wanted her out of Dolphin Bay.

'Yes. Just a few days,' she echoed. 'I guess I won't bankrupt the place in that time.'

Hobo splashed out of the shallows with the driftwood in his mouth, grinning a doggy grin and looking very pleased with himself. He dropped it between their feet.

Sandy reached down to pick it up at the same time as Ben did. She collided with his warm, solid shoulders, felt her head connect with his. 'Ouch!' She rubbed the side of her temple.

'Are you okay?' Ben pulled her to her feet and turned her to face him.

They stood very close, her hands on his shoulders where she'd braced herself for balance. He was damp and salty and smelled as fresh and clean as the morning. It would be so easy to slide her hands down, to tangle her fingers in his chest hair, test the strength of his muscles. Every cell in her body seemed to tingle with awareness where his bare skin touched hers.

She nodded, scarcely able to speak. 'That's one tough skull you've got there. But I'm fine. Really.'

He gently probed her head, his fingers sending currents of sensation coursing through her. 'There's no bump.'

'I think I'll live,' she managed to choke out, desperately attempting to sound flippant.

His big scarred hands moved from her scalp to cradle her face. He tilted her head so she was forced to look up into his eyes. For a long moment he searched her face.

'I don't want to hurt you, Sandy,' he said, his voice hoarse.

She knew he wasn't talking about the collision. 'I realise that, Ben,' she whispered.

Then, with her eyes drowning in his, he kissed her.

She was so surprised she stood stock-still for a moment. Then she relaxed into the sensation of Ben's mouth on hers. It felt like coming home.

When Ben had lifted his head from the wave and had seen Sandy standing on the beach, it had been as if the past and the present had coalesced into one shining moment. A joy so unexpected it was painful had flooded his heart.

And here he was, against all resolutions, kissing her.

Her lips were warm and pliant beneath his. Her breasts were pressed to his chest. Her eyes, startled at first, were filled with an expression of bliss.

He shouldn't be kissing her. Starting things he could not finish. Risking pain for both of them. But those thoughts were lost in the wonder of having her close to him again.

It was as if the twelve years between kisses had never happened.

He twined his hands in her shiny vanilla-scented hair, tilted her head back as he deepened the kiss, pushed against her lips with his tongue. Her mouth parted to welcome him, to meet the tip of his tongue with hers.

She made a small murmur of appreciation and wound her arms around his neck. His arms slid to her waist, to the smooth, warm skin where her top stopped, drawing her close. He could feel her heart thudding against his chest.

He wanted her. She could surely feel his arousal. But

this wasn't just about sex. It had always been so much more than that with Sandy.

The world shrank to just him and her, and the surf was a muted pounding that echoed the pulsing of their hearts, the blood running hot through his veins.

He could feel her nipples hard against him. Sensed the shiver of pleasure that vibrated through her. He pulled her tighter, wanting her as close to him as she could be.

But then something landed near his foot, accompanied by a piteous whining. Hobo. The driftwood. *Damn!*

He ignored it. Sand was dug in a flurry around them, stinging his legs. The whining turned to sharp, demanding barks.

Inwardly he cursed. Willed Hobo to go away. But the dog just kept on digging and barking. Ben broke away from the first time he'd kissed Sandy in twelve years for long enough to mutter, 'Get lost, boy.'

But when he quickly reclaimed Sandy's lips she was trembling. Not with passion but repressed laughter. 'He's not going to go away, you know,' she murmured against his mouth.

Ben groaned. He swore. He leaned down, grabbed the driftwood and threw it as far away as he could—so hard he nearly wrenched his shoulder.

Now Sandy was bent over with laughter. 'He wasn't going to let up, was he?'

Ben cursed his dog again.

'I know you don't really mean that,' she said, with a mischievous tilt to her mouth. 'Poor Hobo.'

'Back to the shelter for him,' Ben growled.

'As if,' said Sandy.

She looked up to him, her eyes still dancing with laughter. She looked as though she'd been thoroughly kissed. He didn't shave until after his morning surf and her chin was all pink from his beard. He felt a surge of possessiveness so fierce it was primal.

'That…that was nice, Ben.'

Nice? He struggled for a word to sum up what it had meant to him. When he didn't reply straight away, the soft, satisfied light of a woman who knew she was desired seemed to dim in her eyes.

'More than nice,' he said, and her eyes lit up again.

He reached out to smooth that wayward lock of hair from her eyes. She caught his hand with hers and dropped a quick kiss on it before she let it go.

'Why did you kiss me, Ben, when with every second breath you're telling me go away?'

Did he know the answer himself? 'Because I—'

He couldn't find the words to say, *Because you're Sandy, and you're beautiful, and I still can't believe you've come back to me, but I'm afraid to let you in because I don't want to love you and then lose you again.*

Her eyes were huge in her flushed face. She'd got damp from hugging him while he was still wet from the surf. Her tank top clung to her curves, her nipples standing erect through the layers of fabric.

She ran the edge of her pink pointy tongue along her lips to moisten her mouth. He watched, fascinated, aching to kiss her again.

A tremor edged her voice. 'It's still there, isn't it, Ben? That attraction. That feeling there isn't anyone else in this world at this moment but you and me. It was like that from the start and it hasn't changed.' She took a deep gulp of air. 'If only…'

He clenched his fists so hard his scars ached. 'I told you—no if-onlys. That—the kiss—it shouldn't have happened.'

'Why not?' Her eyes were still huge. 'We're both free. Grown-up now and able to choose what we want from our lives, choose who we want to be with.'

Choose to leave when we want to.

Even after that one brief kiss he could feel what it would

be like, having found her, to lose her again. He'd managed fine these past years on his own. He couldn't endure the pain of loss again.

She looked very serious, her brow creased. 'That time we had together all those years ago was so special. I don't know about you, but I was too young to appreciate just how special. I never again felt that certainty, that rightness. Maybe this unexpected time together is a gift. For us to get to know each other again. Or…or…maybe we have to try it again so that we can let it go. Have you thought of that?'

He shook his head. 'It's not that easy, Sandy.'

'Of course it isn't easy. It isn't easy for me either. I'm not in a rush to get my heart broken again.'

He noticed again the shadows under her eyes. Remembered her ex had got married yesterday. Typically, she wasn't letting on about her pain. But it was there.

'I can see that,' he said.

He was glad the beach was practically deserted, with just a few people walking along the hard, damp sand at the edge of the waves, others still in the surf. Hobo romped with another dog in the shallows.

Her voice was low and intense. 'Maybe if we gave it a go we'd…we'd burn it out.'

'You think so?' He couldn't keep the cynicism from his voice.

She threw up her hands. 'Who knows? After all this time we don't really know what the other is like now. Grown-up Sandy. Grown-up Ben. We might hate each other.'

'I can't see that happening.' Hate Sandy? No way. Never.

She scuffed the sand with her bare toes, not meeting his eyes. 'How do you know? I like to put a positive spin on things when I can. But, fact is, I haven't had a lot of luck with men. When I started dating—after I gave up on us seeing each other again—it seemed to me there were two types of men: nice ones, like you, who would ultimately betray me—'

He growled his protest.

She looked back up at him. 'I know now it was a mis-understanding between us, but I didn't know that then. If anyone betrayed me it was my father. By lying to me about you. By cheating on our family.'

He didn't disagree. 'And the second type of man?'

'Forceful, controlling guys—'

'Like your father?'

She nodded. 'They'd convince me they knew what was best for me. I'd be in too deep before I realised they had any-thing but my interests at heart. But obviously I must have been at fault, too, when things went wrong.'

'You're too hard on yourself.' He hated to see the tight expression on her face.

Her mouth twisted into an excuse of a smile. 'Am I? Even little things about a person can get annoying. Jason used to hate that I never replaced the empty toilet roll. It was only because the fancy holder he installed ruined my nails when I tried, but—'

Ben couldn't believe what he was hearing. 'What kind of a loser *was* this guy?'

'He wasn't a loser. He was smart. Clever. It seemed I could be myself with him. I thought at last I'd found Mr Perfect. But that was one of the reasons he gave for falling out of love with me.' She bit down hard on her lower lip. 'And he said I was noisy and a show-off.'

Ben was so astounded he couldn't find an appropriate response.

Her eyes flickered to his face and then away. 'When I first knew him he said I lit up a room just by coming into it. *Effervescent* was the word he used. By the end he said I embarrassed him with my loud behaviour.'

Her voice was forcedly cheerful but there was a catch to it that tore at Ben.

'But you don't want to hear about that.'

Anger against this unknown man who had hurt Sandy

fuelled him. 'You're damn right I don't. It's crap. That jerk was just saying that to make himself feel better about betraying you.'

She pulled a self-deprecating face. 'I tell myself that too. It made me self-conscious around people for a while—you know...the noisy show-off thing. I couldn't help wondering if people were willing me to shut up but were too polite to say so. But...but I've put it behind me.'

With his index finger he tilted her face upwards. 'Sandy. Look at me. I would never, ever think you were an embarrassing show-off. I never have and I never will. Okay? You're friendly and warm and you put people at ease. That's a gift.'

'Nice of you to say so. Kind words are always welcome.' Her voice made light of what she said.

'And I would never give a damn about a toilet roll.'

Her mouth twitched. 'It sounds so dumb when you say it out loud. A toilet roll.' The twitch led to a smile and then to full-blown giggles. 'What a stupid thing for a relationship to founder over.'

'And what a moron he was to let it.'

Ben found himself laughing with her. It felt good. Again, like oil on those rusty, seized emotions he had thought would never be kick-started into life again.

'I was just using the toilet roll as an example of how little things about a person can get annoying to someone else,' she said. Her laughter died away. 'After a few days of my company you might be glad to see the end of me.'

'And vice-versa?' The way he'd cut himself off from relationships, she was more likely to get the worst end of the bargain. He was out of the habit of being a boyfriend.

She nodded. 'Then we could both move on, free of... free of this thing that won't let go of us. With...with the past washed clean.'

'Maybe,' he conceded.

She wanted to rekindle old embers to see if they burned

again or fizzled away into lifeless ash. But what if they raged away like a bush fire out of control and he was the one left scorched and lifeless? *Again.*

She took hold of his arm. Her voice was underscored with urgency. 'Ben, we should grab this second chance. Otherwise we might regret it for the rest of our lives. Like I regret that I didn't trust in what we had. I should have come back to you to Dolphin Bay. I was eighteen years old, for heaven's sake, not eight. What could my parents have done about it?'

'I came looking for you in Sydney.' He hadn't meant to let that out. Had never intended to tell her.

Her brows rose. 'When?'

'A few months after you left.'

'I didn't know.'

'You wouldn't. My mates were playing football at Chatswood, on the north shore. I had my dad's car to drive down with them.' He'd been up from university for the Easter break. 'After the game I found your place.'

'The house in Killara?'

He nodded. It had been a big house in a posh northern suburb, designed to show off her father's social status. 'I parked outside, hoping I'd see you. Not sure what I'd do if I did.'

'Why didn't you come in?'

'I was nineteen. You hadn't written. Or phoned. For all I knew you'd forgotten all about me. And I knew your father wouldn't welcome me.'

'Was I there? I can't believe while you were outside I might have been in my room. Probably sobbing into my diary about how much I was missing you.'

'Your hat was hanging on the veranda. I could see it from outside. That funny, stripy bucket hat you used to wear.'

She screwed up her face. 'I remember... I lost that hat.'

'No, you didn't. I took it. I jumped over the fence and snatched it.'

Her eyes widened. 'You're kidding me? My old hat? Do… do you still have it?'

'Once I was back in the car my mates grabbed it from me. When we crossed the Sydney Harbour Bridge they threw *it out of the window*.'

'Hey! That hat cost a whole lot of hard-earned babysitting money.'

She pretended outrage, but he could tell she was shaken by his story.

'I didn't steal it to see it squashed by a truck. I wanted to punch my mates out. But they told me to stop bothering with a girl who didn't want me when there were plenty who did.'

Sandy didn't say anything for a moment. Then she sighed. 'Oh, Ben, if only…' She shook her head. 'I won't say it. You're right. No point.'

'That's when I gave up on you.'

He'd said enough. He could never admit that for years afterwards when he'd driven over that spot on the bridge he'd looked out for her hat.

'And there *were* other girls?' She put her hand up in her halt sign. 'No. Don't tell me about them. I couldn't bear it.' Her eyes narrowed. 'I used to imagine all those blonde surfer chicks. Glad the city interloper was gone. Able to have their surf god all to themselves again.'

He stared at her incredulously. 'Did you just call me a surf god?'

Colour stained her cheeks. 'Hey, I'm in advertising. I get creative with copy.' But when she looked up at him her eyes were huge and sincere. 'I adored you, Ben. You must know that.' Her voice caught in her throat.

Ben shifted from foot to foot in the sand. 'I… Uh… Same here.' *He'd planned his life around her.*

'Let's spend these four days together,' she urged. 'Forget all that's happened to us since we last saw each other. Just go back to how we were. Sandy and Ben. Teenagers again. Carefree. Enjoying each other's company. Recapturing what we had.'

'You mean a fling?'

'A four-day fling? No strings? Why not? I'm prepared to risk it if you are.'

Risk. Was he ready to risk the safe life he'd so carefully constructed around himself in Dolphin Bay? He'd done so well in business by taking risks. But taking this risk—even for four days—could have far greater complications than monetary loss.

'Sandy. I hear what you're saying. But I need time.'

'Ben, we don't have time. We—'

Hobo skidded at their feet, the driftwood in his mouth, wet and eager and demanding attention.

Sandy glared at the animal. 'You have a great sense of timing, dog.'

'Yeah, he's known for it.' Ben reached down for the driftwood and tossed it just a short distance away. 'I've got to get him back. Dogs are only allowed unleashed on the beach before seven a.m.'

'And you can't be seen to be breaking the rules, can you?'

Was she taunting him?

No. The expression in her eyes was wistful, and he realised how she'd put herself on the line for him. For them. Or the possibility of them.

He turned to her. 'I'll consider what you said, Sandy.'

Her tone was again forcedly cheerful. 'Okay, Mr President.'

He grinned. 'I prefer surf god.'

'I'm going to regret telling you I called you that, aren't I? Okay, surf god. But don't take too long. These four days will be gone before we know it and then I'm out of here. Let's not waste them.' She turned to face the water. 'Are the mantas still in residence?'

'Yes. More likely their descendants, still scaring the hell out of tourists.'

He remembered how she'd started off being terrified of the big black rays. But by the end of that summer she'd been snorkelling around them. She had overcome her fears. Could he be as brave?

She reached up and hugged him. Briefly, he held her bare warmth to him before she pushed him away.

'Go,' she said, her voice not quite steady. 'Me? I'm having my first swim at Big Ray Beach for twelve years. I can't wait to get into the surf.'

With unconscious grace she pulled off her skimpy tank top, giving him the full impact of her body in a brief yellow bikini. *Her breasts were definitely bigger than they'd been when she was eighteen.*

Was he insane not to pull her back into his arms? To kiss her again? To laugh with her again? To have her as part of his life again?

For four days.

She headed for the water, treating him to a tantalising view of her sexy, shapely bottom. 'Come see me when you've done your thinking,' she called over her shoulder, before running into the surf.

She squealed as the cold hit her. Water sprayed up over her slim brown legs and the early sunlight shattered into a million glistening crystals. *More fairy dust.*

He looked at the tracks her feet had made in the sand. After the fire he had felt as if he'd been broken down to nothing—like rock into sand. Slowly, painfully, he had put himself back together. But there were cracks, places deep inside him, that still crumbled at the slightest touch.

If he let it, could Sandy's magic help give him the strength to become not the man he had been but someone better, finer, forged by the tragedy he had endured? Or would she break him right back down to nothing?

CHAPTER EIGHT

EVERY TIME THE old-fashioned bell on the top of the entrance door to Bay Books jangled Sandy looked up, heart racing, body tensed in anticipation. And every time it wasn't Ben she felt so let down she had to force herself to smile and cheerfully greet the customers, hoping they wouldn't detect the false note to her voice.

When would he come? Surely he wanted to be with her as much as she ached to be with him?

Or was he staying away because she had driven him away, by coming on too strong before he was ready? His reaction had both surprised and hurt her. Why had he been so uncertain about taking this second, unexpected chance with her? It was only for four days. Surely they could handle that?

She knew she should stop reliving every moment on the beach this morning over and over again, as if she were still eighteen. But she couldn't stop thinking about the kiss. That wonderful, wonderful kiss. After all those years it could have been a let-down. But kissing Ben again had been everything she had ever fantasised about. In his arms, his mouth claiming hers, she'd still felt the same heady mix of comfort, pleasure and bone-melting desire. It was as if their twelve-year separation had never happened.

Although there was a difference. Now she wanted him with an adult's hunger—an adult's sensual knowledge of the pleasures that could follow a kiss.

She remembered how on fire with first-time desire she'd felt all that time ago, when they'd been making out behind the boat shed. Or in the back seat of his father's car, parked on the bluff overlooking the ocean. They hadn't even noticed the view. Not that they could have seen it through the fogged-up windows.

And yet she hadn't let him go all the way. Hadn't felt ready for that final step. Even though she had been head-over-heels in love with him.

Her virginal young self hadn't appreciated the effort it must have taken for Ben to hold back. 'When you're ready,' he'd always said. Not like her experiences with boys in Sydney—'suitable' sons of her fathers' friends—all grabby hands and then sulks when she'd slapped them away. No. Ben truly had been her Sir Galahad on a surfboard.

Would a four-day fling include making love with Ben? That might be more than she—or Ben—could handle. They should keep it to kissing. And talking. And lots of laughing. Like it had been back then. Carefree. Uncomplicated.

She refused to listen to that nagging internal voice. *Could anything be uncomplicated with the grown-up Ben?*

She forced her thoughts back to the present and got on with her work. She had to finish the job Ida had been in the middle of when she'd fallen—unpacking a delivery and slotting the books artfully onto the 'new releases' table.

Just minutes later, with a sigh of satisfaction, she stepped back to survey her work. She loved working in the bookshop. Even after just a few hours she felt right at home. The individuality and quirkiness of Ida's set-up connected with her, though she could immediately see things she'd like to change to bring the business model of this bricks-and-mortar bookstore more in step to compete with the e-bookstores. That said, if she could inject just a fraction of Bay Books' charm into her candle shop she'd be very happy. She must write in her fairy notebook: *Ask Ida about Balinese woodcarvers.*

But it wasn't just about the wooden dolphins with their enchanting carved smiles. The idyllic setting was a vital part of Bay Books. Not, she suspected, to be matched by the high-volume-retail-traffic Melbourne mall the candle people would insist on for their shop. It might be hard to get as excited about that.

Here, she only had to walk over to the window to view the quaint harbour, with the old-fashioned stone walls that sheltered it from the turquoise-blue waters of the open sea—only had to push the door open to hear the squawk of seagulls, breathe in the salt-tangy air.

This morning, in her hotel room, she had been awoken by a chorus of kookaburras. When she'd opened the sliding doors to her balcony it had been to find a row of lorikeets, the small, multi-coloured parrots like living gems adorning the balcony railing. On her way to the beach she'd surprised two small kangaroos, feeding in the grass in the bushland between the boardwalk and the sand dunes of Big Ray. It was good for the soul.

What a difference from fashionable, revitalised inner-city Surry Hills, where she lived in Sydney. It had more restaurants, bars and boutiques than she would ever have time to try. But it was densely populated and in summer could be stiflingly hot and humid. Driving round and round the narrow streets, trying to find somewhere to park her car, she'd sometimes dreamed of living in a place closer to nature.

And here she was back in Dolphin Bay, working in a stranger's bookshop, reconnecting with her first love.

It seemed surreal.

She paused, a paperback thriller in her hand. Remembered her pink-inked resolution. *Get as far away from Sydney as possible.*

That didn't necessarily have to mean moving to Melbourne.

But she had only ever been a city girl. Could she settle for small-town life and the restrictions that entailed?

The bell sounded again. She looked up, heart thudding, mouth suddenly dry. But again it wasn't Ben. It was red-haired Kate, the waitress from the hotel.

'Hey, nice to see you, Kate,' she said, masking her disappointment that the woman wasn't her tall blond surf god.

'You too,' said Kate. 'We all love this shop and the personal service Ida gives us. It's great you're able to help her out.'

'Isn't it? I'm getting the hang of things. Can I help you with a book?' she asked.

Kate smiled and Sandy wondered if she could tell how inexperienced a shopkeeper she was.

'Ida ordered some titles for me, but in all the drama yesterday I didn't get a chance to see if they were in.'

'Sure,' said Sandy, heading behind the counter to access Ida's computer. She had the special orders file open when Kate leaned towards her over the carved wooden counter.

'So, I heard you and Ben were kissing on the beach this morning.'

Sandy was so flabbergasted she choked. She coughed and spluttered, unable to utter a word in response.

Kate rushed around the counter and patted Sandy's back until her breath came more easily.

'Thanks,' Sandy finally managed to choke out.

'Don't be so surprised. News travels fast in Dolphin Bay.'

Sandy took another ragged breath. 'I'm beginning to see that.'

Kate's green eyes gleamed. 'So you *were* kissing Ben?'

Again Sandy was too aghast to reply. 'Well, I...' she started.

'She who hesitates is thinking of how to tell me to mind my own business,' said Kate with a grin.

Sandy laughed at her audacity. 'Well, now that you mention it...'

'Feel free to tell me to keep my big mouth shut, but... well, I love Ben to pieces and I don't want—'

Ben and Kate?

Sandy felt dizzy—not from lack of air but from the feeling that her heart had plummeted to the level of her ballet flats. 'I'm sorry, Kate, I didn't know… He didn't say…'

Kate's auburn eyebrows rose. 'I don't mean *that* kind of love. My mum and Ben's mum are friends. I grew up with Ben. It's his brother, Jesse, I have a thing for. Unrequited, unfortunately.'

'Oh,' said Sandy, beyond relieved that Kate hadn't marched into the bookshop to stake a claim on Ben.

Kate leaned closer. 'You *do* realise that for Ben to be kissing a woman in public is a big, big deal?'

Sandy took a step back. 'It was six-thirty in the morning on a practically deserted beach.'

'That might be private in Sydney, but not in a place like Dolphin Bay. Here, it takes one person to see for everyone to know.'

'I had no idea.' Sandy felt suddenly dry in the mouth. What kind of pressure did this put on Ben? On her?

'You and Ben together is big news.'

'Then next time—if there is a next time—I'll make sure we're completely alone.'

She spoke with such vehemence that Kate frowned and took a step back from her. 'I'm sorry, Sandy. But this is a small town. We all look out for each other. If you're not serious about Ben don't start something you're not prepared to see through.'

Sandy gripped the edge of the counter. She knew Ben had been to hell and wasn't yet all the way back. She didn't need anyone to tell her.

Pointedly, she scrolled through the special orders file on Ida's computer, looked up again at Kate. 'I don't see your order here, but your contact number is. How about I call you when it comes in?'

Kate shifted from foot to foot. 'You must think I'm the nosiest busybody you've ever met.'

Sandy didn't disagree.

'But I've only got Ben's interests at heart,' Kate continued, sounding hurt.

Sandy gentled her tone of voice. 'I appreciate that.'

She was gratified at Kate's smile as she said goodbye. Despite the redhead's total lack of tact, she thought she could get to like her.

But Kate's visit, with her revelation about the undercurrents of small-town life, had left her reeling. She'd had no idea that any reunion would be conducted under such watchful eyes. What had seemed so simple on the beach at dawn suddenly seemed very complicated.

It made her self-conscious when dealing with the customers who came in dribs and drabs through the doors. Were they genuinely interested in browsing through the books—or in perusing her? Her doubts were realised when two older ladies, hidden from full view behind a display of travel books, spoke in too-loud whispers they obviously thought she couldn't hear.

'She seems nice, and Ida likes her,' said the first one. 'That's a point in her favour.'

Sandy held her breath when she realised they were talking about her.

'It might be a good thing. Ben's been in mourning for too long. His mother's worried about him,' said the other.

'I wonder what Jodi's parents will think.' The first lady sighed. 'Such a sweet girl. What a loss. No wonder Ben's stayed on his own all this time.'

Sandy slammed her hand over her mouth so the ladies wouldn't hear her gasp. *Jodi.* Ben's late wife. The gentle woman Ben had loved enough to marry and have a child with.

She stared ahead without seeing. Noticed a poster promoting a bestselling new celebrity biography had come adrift at one corner. But she felt too shaken to do anything about it. Would there always be the memory of another woman coming between her and Ben? *Could she cope with coming second? With being just a disposable fling while his wife always held first place in his heart?*

She couldn't meet the ladies' eyes when they scurried out through the door without buying a book.

An old familiar panic had started to overwhelm her—the same panic she'd used to feel when she'd been faced with those big waves rearing up so aggressively as she'd stood dry-mouthed with terror on the beach. Ben had helped her conquer that fear and discover the joy of riding the waves—and she'd used the memory to help her deal with any number of challenges she'd faced in her career. But now what she'd thought would be smooth water ahead might be filled with swirling undercurrents. Did she have the strength to battle through the rough water?

Was it worth it for a four-day fling?

The bell on the top of the door jangled again. She jumped. More ladies to check her out and assess her suitability?

Ben shouldered his way through the door, carrying two large take-away coffee containers. The smile he gave her made her heart do the flippy thing—backwards, forwards and tumbling over itself. Her breath seemed to accelerate, making her feel light-headed, giddy.

Her surf god. In the flesh and hotter than ever.

He was back in shorts, and a blue polo shirt that hugged the breadth of his shoulders and brought out the blue of his eyes. She preferred the semi-naked beach look, but in true surf god manner he looked wonderful in anything he wore.

She smiled back in her joy at seeing him again. It was four hours and thirty-five minutes since she'd said goodbye to him on the beach.

She prayed no customers would intrude. More than ever she needed to be alone with Ben. To be reassured that the thing between them was worth taking the risks of which she'd been so blithely ignorant.

Kate's words had hit home. Made her all too aware of

the power she had to wound Ben. After all, she was the one who had left him all those years ago. Then he'd been young and untroubled, and still she had hurt him. Now he was anything but untroubled.

Could he deal with a walk-away-from-it fling?

Could *she*?

The expectations of her were frightening. But what if the reality of Ben didn't match up to her memories? What if they didn't have a thing in common and she wanted to run after the first twenty-four hours? What if he wanted her to stay and she hurt him all over again? Or if she fell hard for him again but couldn't match up to his wife? Then it would be her with her heart broken again.

She caught her breath in what felt dangerously like a sob.

Could she do this?

'You okay?'

His marvellous blue eyes were warm with concern for her. That sexy, sexy mouth was set in a serious line that just made her want to kiss it into a smile. Wordlessly, she nodded.

Could she not do it?

'Apparently we were seen on the beach this morning,' she said.

'Seen and duly noted. Makes you wonder what else people have to do with their time.'

'You're big news in Dolphin Bay.'

He put the coffee down on the counter. 'You're bigger news.'

'Tell me about it. The predatory city slicker hunting down the town's favourite son.'

She'd meant that to sound like a joke. But as soon as it came out she knew it was anything but funny.

Ben frowned. 'Did someone say that?'

'Yes. Well, not in so many words. Kate dropped in.' She couldn't help the wobble in her voice.

Why had Kate and those women come in and ruined

everything? Made her feel suddenly so self-conscious with Ben?

She just wanted to fall back into his arms and continue where they'd left off this morning. But the exchange she'd overheard had unsettled her.

She bit down on her lower lip and looked up at Ben, not certain what to do next. How could she tell him she was having cold feet because she was so terrified of hurting him? Could she find the courage to ask him about Jodi?

CHAPTER NINE

To BEN, SANDY looked as if she'd always stood behind the counter of Bay Books. The short hair he was still getting used to was tucked behind her ears. Just below her left shoulder she had pinned a round metal badge that urged people to get involved with a local literacy campaign. She looked smart, efficient—every inch the professional salesperson. Yet her yellow dress seemed to bring the sunlight right into the corners of the dark wooden carvings so favoured by Aunt Ida, and her vanilla scent brought a sweet new warmth.

She fitted right in.

Ida would be delighted.

But Sandy looked anything but happy—she was wary, guarded, with a shadow behind her eyes. She was chewing her lip so hard she was in danger of drawing blood.

Fear gripped him deep in his gut. What gave here?

'Hey,' he said, and went around the counter to pull her into his arms, expecting her warm curves to relax against him. Instead she stiffened and resisted his embrace.

Why the sudden cold change? Hell, he'd worked damn hard to pull down a chink in those barriers he'd built up. Had she now decided to put up a few of her own?

It didn't figure.

'What's going on?' he asked.

Sandy took a step back, her struggle to decide what to tell

him etched on her face. She picked up a waxed paper coffee cup, took a sip. Her hand wasn't quite steady and the froth on the top wobbled dangerously. She put it down and the foam slid over the lid of the cup and dribbled down its side.

'Leave it,' he said as she reached for a cloth to wipe it up.

'No. It might damage the wood,' she said.

She cleaned the spill too thoroughly. A delaying tactic if ever he'd seen one.

She put the cloth away, started to speak way too rapidly. 'Why don't we take our coffee over to the round table?' She was gabbling, her eyes blinking rapidly as she looked everywhere but at him. 'It's a cosier place to have coffee. Y'know, I'm thinking it would be great for Ida to have a café here. Maybe knock through to the vacant shop next door so that customers—'

She went to pick up the coffee cup again, but he closed his hand around her wrist to stop her. He wouldn't give her an excuse to evade him. Her hand stilled under his. 'Tell me. Now.'

Her eyes flickered up to meet his and then back down. When she spoke, her words came out in a rush. 'Kate told me the whole town is watching to see if I hurt you.'

In his relief, he cursed. 'Is that all?' He let go her wrist.

'What do you mean, *is that all*?' Hands on hips, she glared at him with the ferocity of a fluffed-up kitten. 'Don't you patronise me, Ben Morgan. Kate really freaked me out.'

He used both hands to push down in a gesture of calm. 'Kate exaggerates. Kate and the old-school people who were here before Dolphin Bay became a hotspot for escapees from the city. They all mind each other's business.'

Sandy's chin tilted upwards. 'And your business in particular, if Kate's to be believed.'

He shook his head. 'It's no big deal.'

'Are you telling me that's part and parcel of living in a small town?'

He picked up his coffee. Drank a few mouthfuls to give

him time to think. It was just as he had predicted. *Ben's old girlfriend is back.* He could practically hear the hot news humming through cyberspace. 'Yeah. Better get used to it.'

'I don't know if I can.' Her voice rose to a higher pitch. 'I'm used to the don't-give-a-damn attitude of the city.'

Ben thought back to how the town had pulled together for him after the fire. How it had become so stifling he'd had to get away. He'd thrown himself into high-risk money-making ventures because he'd had nothing to lose when he'd already lost everything. They'd paid off in spades. And he'd come back. Dolphin Bay would always be home. No matter that sad memories haunted him at every turn.

But why should that hothouse concern for him bother Sandy?

Her arms were crossed defensively against her chest. Was she using her fear of the townfolk's gossip to mask some deeper reluctance? Some concern she had about him?

He chose his words carefully. 'I can see that. But you're only here for four more days. We're not thinking beyond that, right? Why worry about what they think?'

'I just do,' she said, in a very small voice.

He put down his coffee, put his finger under her chin and tilted it upwards so she was forced to meet his gaze. 'What else did Kate say?'

'It wasn't Kate. There were some other women. Customers. They...they were talking about...about Jodi.'

Pain knifed through him at the sound of Jodi's name. People tended to avoid saying it in front of him.

His feelings must have shown on his face, because Sandy looked stricken.

'Ben, I'm so sorry...'

She went to twist away from him, but he stopped her.

'I should tell you about Jodi.'

The words would be wrenched from him, but he had to tell Sandy about his wife. There should be no secrets between them. Not if they were to enjoy the four days they had together.

'Ben. No. You don't have to—'

He gently put his hand over her mouth to silence her and she nodded.

He dropped his hand. 'I loved Jodi. Don't ever think otherwise. She was a good wife and a wonderful mother.'

'Of course.' Sandy's eyes were warm with compassion— and a touch of wariness.

'I'd known her all my life. But I didn't date her until I'd finished university and was working in Melbourne.'

Sandy's brows rose. 'University? You said—'

'You wouldn't catch me in a classroom again?'

'That's right. You said it more than once. I remember because I was looking forward to going to uni.'

'You can thank your father for my business degree.'

She frowned. 'My father? I—'

'He used to look at me as if I were something scraped off the bottom of his shoe. Left me in no doubt that I wasn't worthy of his daughter.' Ben would have liked to apply some apt swear words to his memories of Dr Randall Adams, but Sandy might not appreciate that.

Sandy protested. 'Surely he didn't say that to you? I can't believe he—'

'He didn't have to say it. I saw his sneer.'

Her mouth twisted. 'No wonder I never got your letters.'

Teen testosterone had made him want to flatten the guy. 'But he had a point. To be worthy of his daughter I needed to get off my surfboard and make something of myself. I had deferred places at universities in both Sydney and Melbourne to choose from.'

'You never said...'

'At the time I had no intention of taking either. I just wanted to surf every good break at Big Ray Beach and work for my dad when I needed money to travel to other surf beaches. That summer... I guess it made me grow up.'

He'd been determined to prove Dr Adams wrong. And broadening his horizons had been the right choice, even if made for the wrong reasons. And now fate had brought Sandy back to him. Now they met as equals in every way.

'You could have been studying at the same uni as me,' Sandy said slowly. She pulled a face that looked sad rather than funny. 'I won't say *if only* again.'

They both fell silent. But Ben refused to give in to musing about what might have been. He had tortured himself enough.

Sandy cleared her throat. 'What happened after you finished uni?'

'I was offered a job in a big stockbroking firm in Melbourne. Got an apartment and stayed down there.'

'But you came home for holidays? And…and met up with Jodi again?'

He could tell Sandy was finding the conversation awkward. She twisted the fabric of her skirt between the fingers of her right hand without seeming to be aware she was doing it.

'I had an accident in the surf. Got hit in the face with the fin of my board.' His hand went to the scar on his lip. 'Jodi was the nurse who looked after me at the hospital.'

And it had started from there. A relaxed, no-strings relationship with a sweet, kind-hearted girl that had resulted in an unplanned pregnancy.

He'd said there were to be no secrets from Sandy, but Liam's unexpected conception was something he didn't want to share with her. Not yet. Maybe never.

'Jodi moved down to Melbourne with me after we got married.'

'What…what brought you both back to Dolphin Bay?'

'I'm not a city guy. I'd had it with Melbourne. The insane work hours, the crowds, the traffic. Mum and Dad were tired of running the guesthouse. Jodi wanted to be with family when she had the baby.'

He gritted his teeth, trying not to let himself be over-whelmed by emotion when he thought of his baby son. The son he'd loved so fiercely from the moment he'd been placed in his arms as a newborn and yet hadn't been able to protect.

'I could trade shares from here. Start business projects here.'

There was another pause. Sandy twisted the edge of her skirt even tighter. 'Those ladies… They…they said Jodi's parents wouldn't be happy with me coming onto the scene.'

Ben clenched his hands into fists. Who *were* these busy-body troublemakers? If he found out he'd tell them to damn well butt out of his business.

He shook his head. 'Not true. Jodi's mum and dad are good people. They want me to…to have someone in my life again.'

Sandy's eyes widened. 'You know that for sure?'

'Yes. They've told me not to let the…the tragedy ruin my life. That…that it's not what Jodi would have wanted.'

'And you believe that? About Jodi?'

He nodded. His words were constricted in his throat. 'The night Liam was born she told me that if anything happened to her—she was a nurse and knew there could be complications in childbirth—she didn't want me to be on my own. She…she made me promise I would find someone else…'

'Oh, Ben.'

Sandy laid her hand on his arm. He realised she was close to tears. When she spoke again her voice was so choked he had to strain to hear her.

'How can I live up to such a wonderful woman?'

In a few shaky steps she made her way around the counter and stood with her back to him. She picked up a book from the display and put it back in exactly the same place.

'Sandy, it isn't a competition.'

Her voice was scarcely a murmur. 'There would always

be a third person in our relationship. I don't know that I could deal with that...'

'Sandy, didn't you hear what I said? Jodi would *want* me to take this chance to spend time with you.'

She turned to face him, the counter now a barrier between them. Her eyes, shadowed again, searched his face. 'Jodi sounds like...like an angel.'

Ben forced himself to smile through the pain. 'She'd laugh to hear you say that. Jodi *was* special, and I loved her. But she was just a human being, like the rest of us, with her own strengths and weaknesses.'

'Ben, I'm no angel either. Don't expect me to be. I'm quick to make judgements, grumpy when I'm hungry or tired—and don't dare to cross me at my time of the month. Oh, and there's the toilet roll thing.'

Despite the angst of talking about Jodi, Sandy made him smile. Just as she'd done when she was eighteen. 'You can let me deal with that.'

She pushed the hair away from her forehead in a gesture of weariness. 'I...I don't know that I've thought this through very well.'

'What do you mean?' he asked.

Fear knifed him again.

He'd had five major turning points in his life. One when he'd decided to go to university. The second when he'd married Jodi. The third when Liam was born. Fourth, the fire. And the fifth when he'd looked up from that wave this morning and seen Sandy standing on the shore next to his dog, as if she were waiting for him to come home to her.

Since he'd kissed her he'd thought of nothing but Sandy. Of the impact she'd made in less than twenty-four hours on his safe, guarded, ultimately sterile life.

He hadn't wanted her here. But her arrival in town had forced him to take stock. And what he saw was a bleak, lonely future—a half-life—if he continued to walk the solitary path he had mapped for himself. He had grieved. A part of him would always grieve. But grief that didn't heal could twist and turn and fester into something near madness—if he let it.

He would *not* allow Sandy to back away from him now. She'd offered four days and he was going to take them.

She took a deep breath. 'The you-and-me thing. What if it doesn't work out and I…and I hurt you again? You've endured so much. I couldn't bear it if I caused you more pain.'

'Leave that to me. It's a gamble I'll take.'

Sandy was his best bet for change. The ongoing power of his attraction to her improved the odds. Her warmth, her vivacity, made him feel as though the seized-up machinery that was his heart was slowly grinding back to life.

She gave him hope.

Maybe that was her real magic—a magic that had nothing to do with shop-bought fairy glitter.

There were four more days until she had to leave for Melbourne. He didn't know what he brought to the table for *her* in terms of a relationship. But he'd be a fool not to grab the second chance she'd offered him. No matter the cost if he lost her again.

'Are you still worried about the townsfolk? They're nothing to be scared of.'

She set her shoulders, tossed back her head. 'Scared? Who said I'm scared?' Her mouth quirked into the beginnings of a smile. 'Maybe…maybe I *am* a little scared.'

Scared of him? Was that the real problem? Was she frightened he would rush her into something before she was ready?

He ached to make love to Sandy. Four days might not be enough to get to that stage. But he could wait if that was what she needed. Even though the want, the sheer physical ache to possess her, was killing him.

'No need to be. I'm here to fight battles for you. Never forget that.'

At last her smile reached her eyes. 'You're sure about that?'

She looked so cute he wanted to kiss the tip of her nose.

He stepped around the counter towards her at the same time she moved towards him. He took both her hands in his and pulled her to him. This time she didn't resist. Her face was very close. That warm vanilla scent of hers was already so familiar.

'As sure as I am about taking that second chance we've been offered. Let's give it everything we've got in the next four days. Turn back the clock.'

She stared at him. He couldn't blame her for being surprised at his turnaround. The shadow behind her eyes was not completely gone. Had she told him everything that was worrying her?

'Are you serious?' she choked out.

'Very.'

She reached up her hand to stroke the side of his cheek. As if checking he was real. When it came, her smile was tender and her eyes were warm. 'I'm so happy to hear you say that. It's just that...' She paused

'What?' he asked.

'All these expectations on us. It...it's daunting. And what will we tell people?'

'Nothing. Let them figure it out for themselves.' He gripped her hands. 'This is just about you and me. It's always just been you and me.'

'And we—'

'Enough with the talking,' he growled, and he silenced her with a kiss.

A kiss to seal their bargain. A kiss to tell her what words could not.

But the kiss rapidly escalated to something hot and hungry and urgent. She matched his urgency with lips, teeth, tongue. He let go her hands so he could pull her tight. Her curves shaped to him as though they were made to fit and she wound her arms around his neck to pull him closer. The strap of her yellow dress slid off her shoulder. He wanted to slide the dress right off her.

He broke away from the kiss, his breath hard and ragged. 'We're out of here. To get some privacy.'

'Wh…what about the shop?' Her own ragged breathing made her barely coherent.

'How many books have you sold today?'

'Just…just a few.'

'Yeah. Not many customers. Too many gossips.' He stroked the bare warm skin on her shoulder, exalted in her shiver of response.

'They did seem to spend more time lurking around corners and looking at me than browsing,' she admitted.

Her hands slid through his hair with an unconscious sensuality that made him shudder with want.

'You shut down the computer. I'll set the alarm.'

'But Ida…'

'Don't worry about Ida.' He could easily make up to his aunt for any drop in sales figures.

Sandy started to say something. He silenced her with another kiss. She moaned a throaty little sound that made him all the more determined to get her out of here and to somewhere private, where he could kiss her without an audience.

The old-fashioned doorbell on the top of the shop door jangled loudly.

Sandy froze in his arms. Then she pulled away from him, cheeks flushed, eyes unfocused. Her quiet groan of frustration echoed his. She pressed a quick, hard kiss on his mouth and looked up wordlessly at him.

To anyone coming into the store they would look as guilty as the pair of teenagers they'd once been. He rolled his eyes. Sandy started to shake with repressed giggles.

He kept his arm firmly around her as they turned to face the two middle-aged women who had entered the shop. Both friends of his mother.

Two sets of eyebrows had risen practically to their hairlines.

News of kiss number two for the day would be rapidly telegraphed through the town.

And he didn't give a damn.

'Sorry, ladies,' he said, in a voice that put paid to any argument. 'This shop is closed.'

CHAPTER TEN

DESTINATION? SOMEWHERE THEY could have privacy. Purpose? To talk more freely about what had happened to each other in the twelve years since she'd left Dolphin Bay. And Sandy didn't give a flying fig that the two bemused ladies Ben had ousted from Bay Books stood hands on hips and watched as she and Ben hastened away from the shop.

Even just metres down the street she fell out of step with Ben and had to skip to catch up. He turned to wait for her, suppressed laughter still dancing around his mouth, and extended his hand for her to take.

Sandy hesitated for only a second before she slid her fingers through his. Linked hands would make quite a statement to the good folk of Dolphin Bay. Anticipation and excitement throbbed through her as he tightened his warm, strong grip and pulled her closer. She smiled up at him, her breath catching in her throat at his answering smile.

When she'd very first held hands with Ben the simple act had been a big deal for her. Most of her schoolfriends had already had sex with their boyfriends by the age of eighteen. Not her. She'd never met a boy she'd wanted to do more with than kiss. When she'd met Ben she'd still been debating the significance of hands held with just palms locked or, way sexier, with fingers entwined.

And Ben?

Back then he'd had no scars.

'Where are we going?' she asked, surprised when her voice came out edged with nervousness.

'My place,' he said. His voice didn't sound nervous in the slightest.

Did he live at the hotel? That would make sense. Maybe in an apartment as luxurious as the room where she was staying.

'Do you remember my family's old boathouse?' he asked as he led her down the steps in front of the hotel.

'Of course I do,' she said, and she felt herself colour. Thirty years old and blushing at the memory of that ramshackle old boathouse. Dear heaven, she hoped he didn't notice.

On the sand outside the boathouse, in the shelter of Ben's father's beached dinghies, she and Ben had progressed from first base to not-ready-to-progress-further-than-third.

She glanced quickly up at Ben. Oh, yes, he remembered too. The expression in those deep blue eyes made that loud and clear.

She blushed a shade pinker and shivered at the memory of all that thwarted teen sexuality—and at the thought of how it might feel to finally do something about it if she and Ben got to that stage this time around.

'I live in the boathouse,' he said.

'You *live* there?' She didn't know what else to say that would not come out sounding ill-mannered.

Instead, she followed Ben across the sand in silence, wondering why a successful businessman would choose to live in something that was no more than a shack.

But the structure that sat a short distance to the right of the hotel bore little resemblance to the down-at-heel structure of her memory. Like so much of Dolphin Bay, it had changed beyond recognition.

'Wow! I'm impressed,' she said.

Ben's remodelled boathouse home looked like something that could star on a postcard. Supported by piers on the edge of the bay, its dock led out into the water. Timber-panelled walls were weathered to a silvery grey in perfect harmony with the corrugated iron of the peaked roof. Window trim and carriage lamps had been picked out in a deep dusky blue. Big tubs of purple hydrangeas in glazed blue pots sat either side of the door.

Ben leaned down to pluck a dead leaf from one of the plants without even seeming to realise he did it. She wouldn't have taken him for a gardener—but then she knew so very little of what interests he might have developed in the years since they'd last been together at this rich-in-memories part of the beach.

'The boathouse was the only part of the guesthouse to survive the fire,' Ben said. He pushed open the glossy blue door. 'Jesse lived here before he went away. I had it remod-elled as guest accommodation, but liked it so much I kept it for myself.'

'I can see why,' she said. 'I envy you.'

A large ceramic dog bowl filled with water, hand-painted with the words 'Hobo Drinks Here', sat just outside the door. She remembered the look of devotion in the dog's big eyes and Ben's obvious love for him.

'Where's your adorable dog?' she asked, stepping through the door he held open for her, fully expecting the retriever to give Ben a boisterous greeting.

'Mum dog-sits him the days I can't take him to work with me,' he said. 'Seems she always has a houseful of strays. He fits right in.'

Sandy was about to say something about his mother, but the words were stopped by her second, 'Wow!' as Ben stepped aside and she got her first glimpse of the interior of the boathouse.

She only had a moment to take in a large open-plan space, bleached timber and shades of white, floor-to-ceiling windows facing the water at the living room end and a vast wooden bed at the other.

The thought that it would be a fabulous location for an advertising shoot barely had time to register in her mind, because the door slammed shut behind them and she was in Ben's arms.

Ben didn't want to give a tour of the boathouse. He didn't want to talk about the architectural work Jesse had done on the old building. He just wanted, at last, to have Sandy to himself.

For a long, still moment he held her close, his arms wrapped tightly around her. He closed his eyes, breathed in the vanilla scent of her hair, scarcely able to believe it was real and she was here with him. He could feel the warm sigh of her breath on his neck, hear the thud-thud-thud of her heartbeat. Then he kissed her. He kissed the curve of her throat. He kissed the delicate hollow beneath her ear. He pressed small, hungry kisses along the line of her jaw. Then he kissed her on the mouth.

Without hesitation Sandy kissed him right back. She tasted of coffee and chocolate and her own familiar sweetness. As she wound her arms around his neck, met his tongue with hers, she made that sexy little murmur deep in her throat that he remembered from a long time ago. It drove him nearly crazy with want.

Secure in the privacy of the boathouse, he kissed her long enough for them to catch right up on the way they'd explored kissing each other all those years ago. Until kissing no longer seemed enough.

The straps of her yellow dress gave little resistance as he slid them down her smooth shoulders. She shrugged to make it easier for him. Without the support of the straps, the top of her dress fell open. He could see the edge of her bra, the swell of her breasts, the tightness of her nipples. He kissed down her neck and across the roundness of her breasts, until she gasped and her hands curled tightly into his shoulders.

He couldn't get enough of her.

But with an intense effort he forced himself to pull back. 'Do you want me to stop?'

'No,' she said immediately. 'Not yet. I couldn't bear it if you stopped.'

In reply, he scooped her up into his arms. Her eyes widened with surprise and excitement. Her arms tightened around his neck and she snuggled her cheek against his shoulder.

She laughed as he marched her towards the bedroom end of the boathouse. 'Even more muscles than when you were nineteen,' she murmured in exaggerated admiration, her voice husky with desire.

She was still laughing as he laid her on the bed—his big, lonely bed. Her dress was rucked up around her slender tanned thighs, giving him a tantalising glimpse of red panties. She kicked off her shoes into the air, laughed again as they fell to the wooden floor with two soft thuds. Then she held out her arms to urge him to join her. Warm, vibrant Sandy, just as he remembered her. Only more womanly, more confident, more seductive.

He kicked off his own shoes and lay down next to her. He leaned over her as she lay back against the pillows, her face flushed, her eyes wide.

'I never thought I'd see you back here.' His voice was hoarse with need for her.

She kissed him. 'Do you remember the sand outside this place? How scratchy it was?' she asked. 'How we'd sneak off there whenever we could get away from everyone.'

'How could I forget?' he replied. Ever since she'd walked into the hotel and back into his life he'd thought of little else.

'This is so much more comfortable,' she said, with on-purpose seduction in her smile. She pulled him down to her to kiss him again. 'And private,' she murmured against his mouth.

Her kiss was urgent, hungry, and he responded in kind.

Outside on that sand as teenagers they'd fooled around as though they had all the time in the world. Now they had a clock ticking on their reunion. And they were playing grown-up games.

Within minutes he'd rid her of her dress and her bra. He explored the lush new fullness of her breasts. Kissed and teased her nipples.

He lifted his head and she made a murmur of protest. His voice was ragged. 'You sure you're ready for this?'

Sandy's eyes were huge. 'I should say no. I should say we need to spend more time together first, that we can't rush into anything we might regret.' Her voice broke. 'But I can't say no. I want you too much. Have always wanted you... Don't stop, Ben. Please don't stop.'

What she'd said about not rushing made sense. This was going faster than he could have anticipated. He should be the sensible one. Should stop it. But he was beyond thinking sensibly when it came to Sandy. *He only had four days with her.*

She kissed him. He kissed her back and was done for. The last restraints gone. He stroked down the curve of her belly, felt her tremble at his touch. Then her panties were gone and he explored there too.

'Not fair. I want to get you naked as well,' she murmured as she started to divest him of his clothes.

She kissed a hot trail across his chest as she slid off his shirt, stroked right down his arms. Her fingers weren't quite steady as she fumbled with the zipper on his shorts. It made the act of pulling them over his hips a series of tantalising caresses along his butt and thighs that made his body harden so much it ached.

Then they were naked together.

Sandy's heart was doing the flipping over thing so rapidly she felt dizzy. Or maybe the dizziness was from the desire that throbbed through her, that made her press her body close to Ben. Close. Closer. *Not close enough.*

Did that urgent whimper come from her as Ben teased her taut nipples with his tongue? As he stroked her belly and below until she bucked against his hand with need? She gasped for breath as ripples of pleasure pulsed everywhere he touched. Revelled in the intensity of the intimacy they were sharing.

This was further than they'd gone the last time they'd been on this beach together. Now she wanted more. Much more. He was as ready for her as she was for him. She shifted her hips to accommodate him, to welcome him—at last.

Then she stilled at the same time as he did. Spoke at the same time as he did.

'Protection.'

'Birth control.'

He groaned, pressed a hard, urgent kiss against her mouth, then swung himself off the bed.

Sandy felt bereft of his warmth and presence. The bed seemed very big and empty without him. *Hurry, hurry, hurry back!* She wriggled on the quilt in an ecstasy of anticipation, pressed her thighs together hard. Twelve years she'd waited, and she didn't want to wait a second longer.

But she contained her impatience enough to watch in sensual appreciation as Ben, buck naked, strode without a trace of self-consciousness towards the tall dresser at the other side of the bed. He was magnificent, her surf god, in just his skin. Broad shoulders tapering to the tight defined muscles of his back; firm, strong buttocks, pale against the tan of the rest of him; long, muscular legs. A wave of pure longing for him swept through her and she gripped her hands tight by her sides.

He reached the dresser, pulled out the top drawer.

Yes! Get the protection and get back here. Pronto!

But he hesitated—that taut, magnificent body was suddenly very still. Then he reached for a small framed photo that stood on the top of the dresser. It was too far away for Sandy to make out the details, just that there was a woman. Ben picked it up and slid it into the drawer, face downwards.

Sandy caught her breath.

Jodi. The photo must be of Jodi.

Ben didn't want her to see it. Didn't want Jodi seeing her naked on his bed.

And that was okay. Of course it was.

She had absolutely no reason to be upset by his action. He'd told her his late wife had loved him so unselfishly that she didn't want him to be alone. Sandy couldn't allow herself even a twinge of jealousy that Jodi had been the perfect wife.

But the desire that had been simmering though her suddenly went right off the boil. Despite the warmth of the day, she shivered. She pulled herself up on her elbows, looked around for something to cover her nakedness. She found his shirt, clutched it against her. It was still warm from his body heat.

Ben's gaze caught hers in a long, silent connection. Sandy's throat tightened. He knew she'd seen. But he didn't say anything. She knew he wouldn't. Knew she couldn't ask—in spite of his earlier frankness.

She realised with a painful stab of recognition that Ben had gone so far away, in such a different direction from the youth they'd shared, that she didn't know him at all any more. For all they'd shared over the last twenty-four hours, today's Ben had been forged by loss and grief beyond her comprehension.

She'd loved Ben back then, with the fierce intensity of first love. But now? How could she love him when she didn't know him any more? Wasn't this just physical attraction she was feeling? She had never had sex without love. The fact was, though, she was the one who had encouraged this encounter. How could she back down now?

And yet his look of excited yet respectful anticipation made her swell with emotion. Did she love him again already? Was that what the heart-flipping thing was all about? Had her heart just taken up where it had left off twelve years ago? What if these four days were all she would ever have of him?

Desire warmed her again. She wanted him. She would take the chance.

She smiled as Ben impatiently pulled open the drawer. But the smile froze as he continued to dig through the contents. He swore. Slammed the door shut. Looked through another drawer. Then another. He threw out his hands in a gesture to indicate emptiness.

'None. No protection. You got any?' His voice was a burr of frustration and anger and something that could have been despair.

'No. I…uh…don't carry it with me.'

She'd had no use for protection for a long time. Seemed as if Ben was in the same boat.

He strode back and sat on the bed next to her. He smoothed back a lock of hair that had drifted across her cheek in a caress that was both gentle and sensual.

'I want you so much. But I won't risk getting you pregnant.'

An unplanned pregnancy wasn't on her agenda either. No way would she suggest taking that risk, much as she yearned for him. 'I'm not on the pill. S…sorry.'

'Why should you apologise?' He groaned. 'I should have—'

'Could we…could we go buy some?' As soon as the words were out of her mouth she knew that was a ridiculous idea. Ben acknowledged it with a grim smile. No doubt some busybody citizen of Dolphin Bay would be behind the counter at the pharmacy and only too eager to broadcast the news that Ben and his old girlfriend were in need of contraceptives.

'Okay…bad idea.' She didn't know what else she could say.

Ben's handsome face was contorted with frustration, his voice underscored with anguish. 'Sandy. You have to know I won't be a father again. Won't have another child. Not after what happened to my little boy. Can't risk that loss…that pain.'

Oh, Ben. Her heart felt as if it was tearing in sorrow for him, for the losses she couldn't even begin to imagine.

'I…I understand,' she stuttered. But did she? Could she ever comprehend the agony he felt at losing his child? 'D… do you want to talk about it?'

He shifted his body further from her. But more than a physical distance loomed between them. He took a deep, shuddering breath.

'You have a right to know why I feel this way.'

'Of course,' she murmured.

'When my mother knew Liam was on the way she told me that I wouldn't know what love was until I held my first child in my arms. I scoffed at her. I thought I knew what it was to love.'

'Lizzie said something similar after Amy was born.'

Ben swallowed hard. It must be agony for him to relive his memories.

'A father's love—it was so unexpected. So overwhelming. My mother was right. I would have done anything for my son.'

'Of course you would have,' she murmured, feeling helpless. She didn't know what to say—a thirty-year-old single whose only experience of loving a child was her niece.

'Changing nappies. Getting up at all hours of the night the minute I heard a whimper. Rocking him in my arms for hours to soothe him when he was teething. I did all that. But…but I couldn't save his life.'

Survivor's guilt. Post-traumatic stress. Labels she thought might apply—but what did she know about how to help him?

'Ben, you're carrying a big burden. Did you have coun-
selling to help you come to terms with your loss?'

As soon as the question left her mouth she knew it was
a mistake. Ben so obviously *hadn't* come to terms with it.

His eyes were as bleak as a storm-tossed sea. 'I had coun-
selling. But nothing can change the fact I couldn't save my
baby son. End of story. On the day I buried him I vowed I
would never have another child.'

'Because...because you think you don't deserve another
child?'

'That too. But I couldn't bear the agony of loss again.'

She knew it wasn't the time to say that new life could
bring new hope. That there was the possibility of loss any
time you put your heart on the line. But how could she pos-
sibly understand what he'd gone through? Could she blame
him for never wanting to risk finding himself in that un-
imaginably dark place again?

'Ben, I'm so sad for you.' She took his scarred, damaged hand in hers and squeezed it, wanting him to know
how much she felt for him but was unable to express. He
put his arms around her and pulled her tight. She nestled
her face just below his shoulder, against the warm, solid
muscle of his chest.

But she was sad for herself, too.

She thought back to her birthday goals. *Get married and
have lots of kids. Three kids—two girls and a boy.*

It was as if Ben had read her mind. 'Remember how we
used to talk about having kids? When were barely more
than kids ourselves?'

'Yes,' she said. She swallowed hard against the lump of
disappointment that threatened to choke her. She'd always
seen being a mother in her future. Had never contemplated
any other option.

He pulled back from her and she was forced to meet
his gaze.

'So me not wanting kids could be a deal-breaker?'

She had to clear her throat before she answered, trying not to let him guess how shaken she was. 'Perhaps. For something long-term. But we're only talking four days, aren't we? It doesn't matter for...for a fling.'

'I guess not. But I wanted to make sure you knew where I stood.'

At the age of thirty she couldn't afford to waste time on any relationship—no matter how brief—that didn't have the possibility of children. Knowing that parenthood wasn't an option for Ben should make her pack up and leave Dolphin Bay right now. But she didn't have to think further than four days—and nothing could stop her from having this time with Ben. Come what may.

'I'm sorry, Sandy,' said Ben. 'This wasn't the way I thought things would pan out today.'

'It doesn't matter. I...I've lost the mood,' she confessed.

Suddenly she felt self-conscious being naked. With a murmur about being cold she disengaged herself from his arms. Fumbled around on the bed and found her dress. Pulled it over her head without bothering about wasting minutes with her bra. Wiggled into her panties. Found his clothes and handed them to him.

She felt very alone when he turned his back to her and dressed in awkward silence.

She sat on the edge of the bed and wondered how everything could have gone so wrong. 'Sunny Sandy', Ben had used to call her. But it was hard to see the glass-half-full side of finding out that he didn't ever want to have another child. And then there was that photo. How ready was he *really* to move on to another woman?

Ben wanted to pound the wall with his fists to vent his frustration and anger. He wanted to swear and curse. To fight his way through raging surf might help, too.

But he could do none of that. Sandy looked so woebegone sitting there, biting on her lip, her arms crossed defensively across her beautiful breasts. He had to control himself. Do anything in his power to reignite her smile.

His revelation that he didn't want more children had knocked the sunshine out of her. He appreciated how kind she'd been, how understanding, but dismay had shown on her face. But he'd had to put his cards on the table about a future with no children. He couldn't mislead her on such an important issue. Not that they were talking beyond these four days.

He reached out, took both her hands and pulled her to her feet.

'Sandy, I'm sorry—' he started.

'Don't say it again,' she said with a tremulous smile, and put her finger to his mouth. 'I'm sure we'll laugh about it one day.'

He snorted his disbelief. He would never see the humour in what had happened. Or had not happened.

'So what now?' she asked. 'Do I go back to the book-shop?'

He tightened his grip on her hands. 'No way. It's shut for the day. You're staying with me. We'll have lunch, then tonight I want to take you to a dinner dance.'

Her eyebrows rose. 'A dinner dance? In Dolphin Bay?'

She was such a city girl. She had no idea of how much the town had grown. How big his role as a business leader had become.

'The Chamber of Commerce annual awards night is being held at the hotel. As president, I'm presenting the awards. I'd like you to come.'

'As…as your date?'

'As my date.'

Her smile lit the golden sparks in her eyes in the way he remembered. 'I'd like that. This could be fun.'

'The speeches? Not so much. But there'll be a band and dancing afterwards.'

'Do you remember—?' she started.

'The dance?'

'I couldn't believe it when you asked me to dance with you.'

'I wasn't sure you'd say yes. You were the most beautiful girl there.'

She leaned up and kissed him on the mouth. 'Thank you for saying that.'

'You'll be the most beautiful girl there tonight.'

That earned him another kiss.

'Will I know anyone?'

'My parents. My brother, Jesse—he's back home for a couple days. Kate…'

Sandy's face tightened at the sound of Kate's name.

'Kate has a big mouth, but she also has a big heart,' he said.

'She can be confrontational.'

'Don't judge her too harshly. She means well.' He didn't want Sandy to feel alienated during her time in Dolphin Bay. That was one of the reasons he'd asked her to be his date for tonight, to go public with him. Encouraging a friendship with Kate was another.

'I'm sure she does. It's just that…'

'Yes?'

'Nothing,' she said, with an impish twist to her mouth.

He wasn't in the mood to argue with a female 'nothing'. 'C'mon. I'll make us some lunch.'

He kept her hand in his as he led her towards the kitchen.

'I didn't know you could cook,' she said.

She didn't know a lot about him. Some things she might never know. But his cooking prowess—or lack of it—was no secret.

'Basic guy-type stuff. Mostly I eat at the hotel. We could order room service if you want.'

'No. I like the idea of you cooking for me.'

She started to say something else but stopped herself.

He wondered if her ex had ever cooked for her. He sounded like a selfish creep, so that was probably a no.

'What's on the menu, chef?' she asked.

'Take your pick. Toasted cheese sandwich or...' he paused for dramatic emphasis '...toasted cheese sandwich.'

'With ketchup? And Snickers for dessert? I have some in my handbag.'

'Done,' he said as he headed towards the fridge.

Without realising it, he started to whistle. He stopped himself. Why would he want to whistle when he was furious at himself for the disaster in the bedroom and fresh with the memories of his loss?

'That's a sound I haven't heard for a long time,' Sandy said as she settled herself on one of the bar stools that lined the kitchen counter.

'It's rusty from disuse,' he said.

'No, it isn't. I like it. Don't stop. Please.'

Her eyes were warm with concern and understanding. Her yellow dress flashed bright in the cool, neutral tones of the kitchen. Her brown hair glinted golden in the sunshine that filtered through the porthole windows. Sandy. Here in his home. The only woman he had brought here apart from his mother and the maids from the hotel who kept it clean.

He picked up the tune from where he had left off and started to whistle again.

CHAPTER ELEVEN

SANDY WAS ONLY too aware that every detail of her appearance would be scrutinised by the other guests at the Chamber of Commerce dinner dance. Every nuance of her interaction with Ben would be fuel for the gossipmongers of Dolphin Bay.

In one way it amused her. In another it scared her witless.

In spite of Ben's reassurances Kate's warning still disconcerted her. All the people who would be there tonight knew Ben. Had known Jodi. Had even—and her heart twisted painfully at the thought—known his baby son. She wouldn't be human if that didn't worry her.

She wished she and Ben could spend the entire time they had together alone in his boathouse home. Just him and her, and no one else to poke their noses into the one step forward and two steps back of their reunion. But it seemed it would be played out on the open stage of Ben's tight-knit community.

Thank heaven she'd packed a take-her-anywhere outfit for Melbourne. She checked her image in the mirror of her hotel room with a mega-critical eye. Dress? Red, strapless, short but not too short. Jewellery? A simple yet striking gold pendant and a blatantly fake ruby-studded gold cuff from one of her fashion accessory clients. Shoes? Red, sparkling, towering heels. She thought she would pass muster.

The look in Ben's eyes when he came to her room to pick her up told her she'd got it right.

For a moment he stood speechless—a fact that pleased her inordinately. He cleared his throat. 'You look amazing,' he said.

Amazing was too inadequate a word to describe how Ben looked in a tuxedo. The immaculately tailored black suit emphasised his height and the breadth of his shoulders, and set off the brilliant blue of his eyes. There was little trace of the teen surfer in the urbane adult who stood before her in the doorway to her room, but she didn't mourn that. The crinkles around his eyes when he smiled, the cropped darker hair, only added to his appeal. It struck her that if she met the grown-up Ben now, for the first time, as a total stranger, she'd be wildly attracted to him.

For a moment she was tempted to wind her arms around his neck and lure him into her room with whispered words of seduction. She thought of the birth control she had discovered tucked into a corner of her suitcase, accompanied by a saucy note from her sister, Lizzie: *In case you get lucky in Melbourne.*

But Ben had official duties to perform. She couldn't make him late.

'You look amazing yourself,' she said. She narrowed her eyes in a mock-appraising way. 'Kinda like a surf god crossed with a tycoon god.'

He rolled his eyes at her words but smiled. 'If you say so.'

Her stratospheric heels brought her to kissing distance from his face. She kissed him lightly on the cheek, but he moved his face so her lips connected with his mouth. She nearly swooned at the rush of desire that hit her. As she felt his tongue slip familiarly into her mouth she calculated how much time they had before they were due at the dinner dance. Ten minutes. Not enough time for what she needed from Ben if things were going to get physical again.

Besides, she wasn't so sure that was the way to go when

their time together was so short. She didn't want to leave Dolphin Bay with a pulverised heart.

With a deep sigh of regret, she pulled away.

'C'mon, haven't you got awards to present?' she said.

She slipped her arm through his and they headed towards the elevator.

The first person Sandy saw when she walked with Ben into the hotel conference room where the dinner dance was being held was his mother. She clutched Ben's arm, shocked at the feeling of being cast back in time.

Maura Morgan had been wearing jeans and a T-shirt the last time she'd seen her; now she was wearing an elegant brocade dress. She was handsome, rather than beautiful, and she'd hardly changed in the intervening years. Her hair held a few more strands of grey, her figure was a tad more generous, but her smile was the same warm, welcoming smile that had made Sandy's stay at the guesthouse all those years ago so happy. And her voice still held that hint of a lyrical Irish accent that was a legacy of her girlhood in Dublin.

'Eh, Sandy, it's grand to see you. Who would have thought we'd see you here after all these years?' The older woman swept her into a warm hug.

'It's wonderful to see you again.' It was all Sandy could think of to say. But she meant every word. That summer, so long ago, there had been a wire of tension between her parents that at times had come close to snapping. Maura had been kind to her, and covered for her with her father when she'd snuck out to meet Ben.

Maura stepped back, with her hands still on Sandy's shoulders. 'Look at you, all grown up and even lovelier than when you were a girl—and friends with Ben again.' Her face stilled. 'Fate works in amazing ways.'

'It sure does,' Sandy agreed, reluctant to talk more deeply with Ben's mother. Not wanting to bring up the tragedies that had occurred since her last visit. She didn't know what

Ben had told Maura about her reasons for staying in Dolphin Bay. The reignited feelings between her and Ben were so fragile—still just little sparks—she wanted to hug them close.

Maura released her. 'Your mum and dad…?'

Sandy shrugged. 'Divorced.'

Maura shook her head slowly. 'Why does that not surprise me? And your sister?'

'Lizzie's still my best friend. She has a little girl, Amy, who's five years old and a real cutie.'

As soon as she mentioned Amy, Sandy wished she hadn't. Ben's son Liam had been Maura's only grandchild. But Maura's smile didn't dim. 'It's lovely to hear that,' she said. 'And do you—?'

Ben interrupted. 'Mum, I've sat you and Dad at my table so you'll get a chance to talk to Sandy during the evening.

Maura laughed. 'So quit the interrogation? I hadn't yet asked Sandy if she has room in her heart for a homeless puppy.'

Ben groaned, but Sandy could hear the smile in his protest.

'A puppy? I'd love one,' she said without hesitation. 'That is if…' Her voice trailed away. *Get dog of own once settled in Melbourne.* Could she really commit to a dog when her future had become so uncertain? Until she knew exactly how she felt about Ben at the end of the four days?

Maura patted her hand. 'I won't hold you to the puppy until we've talked some more.'

The genuine warmth in her voice did a lot to reassure Sandy that Maura did not appear to have any objection to her reunion with Ben.

She felt she could face the rest of the evening with a degree less dread.

Sandy outshone any other woman in the room, Ben thought as he watched her charm the bank manager and his wife.

It wasn't just the red dress, or the way the light caught her glittery shoes just like that darn fairy dust. It had more to do with the vivacity of her smile, the way her eyes gleamed with genuine interest at the details of the couple's daughter's high school results. He knew she was nervous, but no one would guess it.

It was a big, public step to bring her tonight—and he was glad he'd made it. It felt good to have her by his side. Instead of ill-disguised sorrow or embarrassed pity, he saw approval in the eyes of his family and friends. It was a big step forward.

But for the first time since he'd been elected president of the chamber Ben resented his duties. He didn't want to make polite chit-chat with the guests. He didn't want to get up there on stage and make a speech about the business community's achievements. Or announce the awards. He wanted to spend every second of the time he had left with Sandy—alone with her. They had less than four days—three days now—of catching up to do. If that included being behind closed doors, slowly divesting Sandy of that red dress and making love to her all night long, that was good too.

'We must catch up for coffee some time,' the banker's wife gushed in farewell to Sandy as Ben took Sandy's elbow to steer her away towards his table. He wanted her seated and introduced to everyone else at the table before he had to take his place on stage for the awards presentation.

'I'd like that,' Sandy called over her shoulder to the banker's wife as Ben led her away.

'Would you?' he asked in an undertone.

'Of course. She seems like a nice lady. But not any time soon.' She edged closer so she could murmur into his ear. 'We've only got a few days together. I want to spend every second of my spare time with you.'

'I'll hold you to that,' he said.

It felt unexpectedly good, being part of a couple again—even if only temporarily. He'd been on his own for so long.

Maybe too long. But his guilt and regret still gnawed at him, punishing him, stopping him from getting close to anyone.

And now Sandy was back with him in Dolphin Bay.

The president's table was at the front of the room. His parents were already seated around it, along with Kate, his brother, Jesse, and two of the awards finalists—both women.

If his father remembered how disparaging he had been all those years ago about the sincerity of a city girl's feelings towards his son, he didn't show it. In his gruff way he made Sandy welcome.

Jesse couldn't hide the admiration in his eyes as he rose from his seat to greet Sandy. 'I would have recognised you straight away,' his brother said as he kissed her on the cheek.

Ben introduced Sandy to the awards finalists, then settled her into the seat between him and Kate. 'I have to finalise the order of proceedings. I'll be back in five minutes—in time for the appetiser,' he said.

He wanted to kiss Sandy. Claim her as more than a friend in front of all eyes. But it wasn't the right time. Instead, he brushed his hand over her bare shoulder in parting before he headed backstage. Only Kate's big grin made him realise the simple gesture was more a sign of possession than a friendly kiss on Sandy's cheek would ever have been.

Sandy heaved a quiet sigh of relief as she sank into her chair. The worst of the ordeal was behind her. From the moment she'd entered the room she'd been aware of the undercurrent of interest in her presence beside Ben. Her mouth ached from smiling. From formulating answers in reply to questions about how long she intended to be in town. Even though Ben had smoothed the way, she felt she was being judged on every word she spoke. She reached gratefully for her glass of white wine.

Ben's empty seat was to her left, between her and Kate. Tall, dark-haired Jesse—every bit as handsome as in her memories of him—sat on the other side of her, engaged in conversation with his mother.

Kate sidled close enough to whisper to Sandy. 'Note that Ben didn't sit me next to Jesse. Probably worried I'd fling myself on his brother, wrestle him to the ground and have my way with him under the table.'

Sandy nearly choked on her drink. 'Really?'

'Nah. Just kidding. I actually asked him not to put me near Jesse.' Kate's green eyes clouded. 'It's hard to make small-talk with the guy I've wanted all my life when he sees me as more sister than woman.'

'Can't he see how gorgeous you are?' Sandy asked. In an emerald silk dress that clung to her curves and flattered the auburn of her hair, Kate looked anything but the girl next door.

Kate pulled a self-deprecating face. 'Thanks. But it doesn't matter what I wear. To Jesse I'll always just be good old Kate, his childhood pal.'

'You never dated him?'

'We kissed when I was thirteen and he was fourteen. I never stopped wanting him after that.'

'And Jesse?'

Kate shrugged. 'He was a shy kid, and I guess I was a convenient experiment. It never happened again. Though I must have relived it a million times.'

'He certainly doesn't look shy now.'

Jesse's full attention was beamed on the attractive blonde award finalist.

'Yep. He's quite the man of the world these days, and quite the flirt.' Kate kept her gaze on Jesse for a moment too long before returning it to Sandy.

Sandy's heart went out to Kate. 'That must be so tough for you. Ben told me Jesse's only visiting for a few days.'

'Yes. Jesse leads a construction team that builds low-cost housing in areas that have been destroyed by natural disasters. Think India, Africa, New Orleans. He only ever comes here between assignments.'

Sandy glanced again at Jesse. 'Good looks *and* a kind heart. No wonder you're hooked on him.'

'Kind hearts run in the Morgan family—as I think you well know.'

Was Kate about to give her another lecture about Ben? If so, she wasn't in the mood to hear it. 'Kate, I—'

Kate laughed and threw her hands up in a gesture of self-defence. 'I'm staying right out of the you-and-Ben thing. I've been warned.'

'Warned? By Ben?'

'Of course by Ben. You're important to him. Ben protects the people he cares about.'

Sandy loved the feeling Kate's words gave her. But, again, she sensed she might be getting out of her depth. Three more days in Dolphin Bay. That was all she was talking about after this evening. Deep in her heart, though, she knew there was a chance it could end up as so much more than that. She didn't know whether to be excited or terrified at the prospect.

After the starter course Ben took his place on stage. To Sandy, he looked imposing and every inch the powerful executive as he took the microphone to give a brief review of the year's past business activities. From the applause and occasional catcall from the audience it was apparent Ben was still very much the town's favourite son.

As he made a particularly pertinent point about the growth in revenue tourism had brought to Dolphin Bay Sandy thought she would burst with pride at his achievements, and at the way he had overcome such tragedy to get to this place. She wanted to get up from her seat and cheer. She caught his mother Maura's eye and saw the same pride and joy reflected in her face.

Maura acknowledged the thread of emotion that united

them with a smile and a brief nod, before turning back to face the stage and applaud the end of Ben's speech.

Sandy smiled back—a wobbly, not very successful smile. *Maura knew.* She bit her lip and shredded the edge of her dolphin-printed serviette without really realising she was doing so.

Could she kid herself any further that all she wanted from Ben was a fling? Could she deny that if she didn't protect her heart she might fall right back in love? And then where would she be, if Ben decided four days of her was enough?

CHAPTER TWELVE

BUT SANDY'S HEART was singing as she danced with Ben. He danced as he'd danced with her that first time twelve years ago, and it seemed as if the years in between had never happened. Although they kept a respectable distance apart their bodies were in tune, hips swaying in unison with each other, feet moving to the same beat.

Most of the people in the room had also got up to dance once the formalities of the evening were done, but Sandy was scarcely aware of them. She couldn't keep her eyes off Ben or stop herself from 'accidentally' touching him at any opportunity—shoulders brushing, hips bumping, her hand skimming his as they moved their bodies in time to the music of a surprisingly good local band. And, in spite of the other guests' ill-concealed interest in the fact they were dancing together, Ben did nothing to move away.

She longed to be alone with him. He had rhythm, he had energy, he had power in that big, well-built body—and she ached to have it all directed to *her*. Upstairs in her bedroom.

When the band changed to slow dancing music, she was done for. As Ben pulled her into his arms and fitted his body close to her she wound her arms around her neck and sighed. 'How much longer do we have to endure this torture? If I have to explain to one more person than I'm just here for a few more days, I'll scream.'

'Same. The strain of all this focus on us is too much.'

'How much longer do we have to stay?'

He nuzzled into her neck, murmured low and husky. 'See those doors that open up to the balcony?'

She looked across the room. 'Yes.'

'We're going to dance our way over there and out on to the balcony, as if we're going for some fresh air—'

'Won't everyone think we've gone to make out?'

'Who cares?' He pulled her tighter. 'That way we don't have to announce our escape by exiting through the main doors.'

'What about your duties?'

'I'm done with duty.'

'So now you're all mine for the rest of the evening?' she murmured, with a provocative tilt of her head.

His eyes darkened to a deeper shade of blue and his grip tightened on her back. 'From the balcony we'll take the door to the empty conference room next door and then to the foyer.'

'And then?' Her voice caught in her throat.

'That's up to you.'

Her heart started doing the flippy thing so fast she felt dizzy. She pulled his head even closer to hers, brushed her lips across his cheek. 'Let's go,' she murmured.

He steered her through the crowd, exchanging quick greetings with the people they brushed past, but not halting for a moment longer than necessary. Sandy nodded, smiled, made polite responses, held on to his hand and followed his lead.

They sidled along the balcony, then burst into the empty conference room next door, laughing like truant schoolkids. Ben shut the door behind him and braced it in mock defence with an exultant whoop of triumph.

Sandy felt high on the same exhilaration she'd felt as a teenager, when Ben and she had successfully snuck away from their parents. She opened her mouth to share that thought with him, but before she could form the words to congratulate him on their clever escape he kissed her.

His kiss was hard and hungry, free of doubt or second thoughts. She kissed him back, matching his ardour. Then broke the kiss.

She took a few deep breaths to steady her thoughts. 'Ben, I'm concerned we're moving too fast. What do you think?'

Ben glanced at his watch. 'This day is nearly over. That leaves us three days. I want you, Sandy. I've always wanted you.'

'But what if we regret it? What if you—?' She was so aware of how big a deal it was for him to be with her. And the heartbreak she risked by falling for him again. She feared once she made love with him she would never want to leave him.

'I'll regret it more if we don't take this chance to be together. On our terms. No one else's.'

'Me too,' she said. No matter what happened after these three remaining days, she never wanted to feel again the regret that had haunted her all those years ago.

Please, let this be our time at last.

'My room or yours?' she said, putting up her face to be kissed again.

Ben couldn't bear to let go of Sandy even for a second. Still kissing her, he walked her through the door, out of the conference room and into the corridor. Still kissing her, he punched the elevator's 'up' button.

As soon as the doors closed behind them he nudged her up against the wall and captured her wrists above her head with one of his so much bigger hands. The walls were mirrored and everywhere he looked he saw Sandy in that sexy red dress, her hair tousled, her face flushed, her lips swollen from his kisses. Beautiful Sandy, who had brought hope back into his life.

The raising of her arms brought her breasts high out

of her strapless dress to tease him. In the confines of the elevator the warm vanilla female scent of her acted like a mainline hit of aphrodisiac. He could make love to her there and then.

But, as it always had been with Sandy, this was about so much more than sex. This step they were about to take was as much about intimacy and trust and a possible move towards a future beyond the next three days. The responsibility was awesome.

It was up to him to make it memorable. He'd waited so long for her and he wanted their first time to be slow and thorough, not a heated rush that might leave her behind.

He trailed kisses down her throat to the swell of her breasts. She gasped and he tightened his grip on her hands. She started to say something but he kissed her silent. Then the elevator reached her floor.

Still kissing her, he guided Sandy out of the elevator and towards her room. He fished his master keycard out of his pocket, used it, then shouldered the door open. They stumbled into the room and he kicked the door shut behind them.

Sandy had imagined a sensual, take-their-time progression through the bases for her first-time lovemaking with Ben. But she couldn't wait for all that. It felt as if the entire day had been one long foreplay session. Every sense was clamouring for Ben. *Now*. Her legs were so shaky she could hardly stand.

She pulled away from the kiss, reached up and cradled his chin in her hands, thrilled at the passion and want in his eyes that echoed hers. Her breathing was so hard she had to gulp in air so her voice would make sense.

'Ben. Stop.'

Immediately, gentleman that he was, he made to pull away from her. Urgently she stilled him.

'Not stop. I mean go. Heck, that's not what I mean. I mean stop delaying. I swear, Ben, I can't wait any longer.'

She whimpered. Yes, she whimpered—something she'd never thought she'd do for a man. 'Please.'

His eyes gleamed at the green light she'd given him. 'If you knew how difficult it's been to hold back...' he groaned.

'Oh, I have a good idea what it's been like,' she said, her heart pounding, her spirit exulting. 'I feel like I've been waiting for this—for you—all my life.'

She kicked off her shiny shoes, not caring where they landed. Ben yanked down the zipper of her dress. She tugged at his tuxedo jacket and fumbled with the buttons on his shirt. Before she knew it she stood in just the scantiest red lace thong and Ben was in nothing at all—his body strong and powerful and aroused, his eyes ablaze with need for her.

Beautiful wasn't a word she'd usually use to describe a man. But all her copywriting skills deserted her as she sought to find another word.

He was her once-in-a-lifetime love and she knew, no matter what happened tomorrow or the day after or the day after that, that tonight she would be irrevocably changed. As she took a step towards him she froze, overwhelmed—even a little frightened—of what this night might unleash. Then desire for this man took over again. Desire first ignited twelve long years ago. Desire thwarted. Desire reignited. Desire aching to be fulfilled.

Ben swept her into his arms and walked her towards the bed. Soon she could think of nothing but him and the urgent rhythm of the intimate dance they shared.

Ben didn't know what time it was when he woke up. There was just enough moonlight filtering through the gaps in the curtains for him to watch Sandy as she slept. He leaned on his elbow and took in her beauty.

She lay sprawled on her back, her right arm crooked above her head, the sheet tucked around her waist. Her hair was all mussed on the pillow. He was getting used to seeing it short, though he wished it was still long. In repose, her face had lost the tension that haunted her eyes. A smile danced at the corners of her mouth. She didn't look much older than the girl he'd thought he'd never see again.

It didn't seem real that she was here beside him. Magic? Coincidence? Fate? Whatever—being with Sandy made him realise he had been living a stunted half-life that might ultimately have destroyed him.

How could he let her go in three days' time?

But if he asked Sandy to stay he had to be sure it would be to stay for ever.

With just one finger he traced the line of her cheekbones, her nose, her mouth.

She stirred, as he'd hoped she would. Her eyelids fluttered open and her gaze focused on him. His heart leapt as recognition dawned in her eyes. She smiled the slow, contented smile of a satisfied woman and stretched languorously.

'Fancy waking up to you in my bed,' she murmured. She took his hand and kissed first each finger in turn and then his palm with featherlight touches over the scars he hated so much. She placed his hand on her breast and covered it with her own.

'You were *so* worth waiting twelve years for,' she whispered.

'Yes.' He couldn't find any more words. Just kissed her on her forehead, on her nose, finally on her mouth.

Want for her stirred again. He circled her nipple with his thumb and felt it harden. She moaned that sweet moan of pleasure. She returned his kiss. Softly. Tenderly. Then she turned her body to his.

Afterwards she lay snuggled into him, her head nestled on his chest, their legs entwined. The sweet vanilla scent of her filled his senses. He held her to him as tightly as he could without hurting her. He didn't want to let her go.

Did she feel the same way about what had just happened—a connection that had been so much more than physical?

Did she know she had ripped down a huge part of the barricade that had protected him against feeling anything for anyone?

Hoarsely, he whispered her name.

The tenor of her breathing changed and he realised she was falling back to sleep. Had she heard him?

'Ben…' she murmured as her voice trailed away.

As Sandy drifted back into sleep, satiated not just with sexual satisfaction but with joy, she realised a profound truth: she'd never got it right with anyone but Ben. Not just the physical—which had been indescribably wonderful—but the whole deal.

Right back when she was eighteen she'd thought she'd found the man for her—but those close to her, those who had thought they knew what was best for her, had dissuaded her.

She tightened her grip on his hand and smiled.

Her heart had got it right the first time.

CHAPTER THIRTEEN

'So, is the sex with my nephew good?'

Sandy nearly fell off the chair near Aunt Ida's hospital bed, too flummoxed even to think about a reply.

Ida laughed. 'Not a question you expect a little old lady to ask?'

'Uh…not really,' Sandy managed to splutter as hot colour flooded her cheeks. She'd come to talk about the Bay Books business, not her private life with Ben.

Ida shifted her shoulders and resettled herself on the pillows, a flash of pain tightening her face. Sandy ached to help her, but Ben's great-aunt was fiercely independent.

'You don't actually have to answer me,' said Ida. 'But great sex is so important to a healthy relationship. If you don't have those fireworks now, forget having a happy future together.'

Sandy realised she had blushed more times since she'd been back in Dolphin Bay than she had in her entire life.

'I… Uh… We…' How the heck did Ida know what had happened with Ben last night? How did she know there'd been fireworks aplenty?

Ida chuckled. 'I'll take that as a yes, then. Any fool can see the chemistry between you two. Good. No matter what the world dishes up to you, you'll always have that wonderful intimacy to keep your love strong. It was like that for me and Mike.'

'Oh?' Sandy literally did not know where to look. To talk about sex with someone of her grandmother's age was a new and unnerving experience.

'I suppose you know about my scandalous past?'

'I heard that you—'

'But I guess you don't want to hear about that.'

The expression in Ida's eyes made it clear that Ida wanted very much to tell her story. And Sandy was curious to hear it. There hadn't been much talking about relationships in her family's strait-laced household. No wonder she'd been so naïve at the age of eighteen, when she'd met Ben.

Sandy settled herself back in her chair. 'Did you really run away with a sailor, like Ben says?'

'Indeed I did. Mike was sailing up the coast. We clicked instantly. I went back to his boat with him and—'

Sandy found herself gripping the fabric of her skirt where it bunched over her knees. She wanted to hear the story but she didn't—she *really* didn't—want to hear the intimate details.

'I never left. I quit my job. Threw my hat in with Mike. We got married on an island in Fiji.'

One part of Sandy thought it romantic, another thought it foolhardy.

'Even though you hardly knew him?' *But how well did she actually know Ben? Enough to risk her heart the way she'd done last night?*

'I knew enough that I wanted to spend every waking and sleeping moment with him. I was thirty-five; he was five years older. We didn't have time to waste.'

Was that message aimed at her and Ben? The way she felt right now Sandy hated being parted from him even for a minute. But there were issues still unresolved.

'What about…what about children? Did you regret not having kids?'

'Not for a moment. We couldn't have had the life we had with kids. Mike was enough for me.'

Could Ben be enough for her? Right now her heart sang with the message that he was all she wanted. But what about in years to come? If things worked out with Ben, could she give up her dreams of a family?

Ida continued. 'And I don't have time to waste now. Once I'm over this injury I want to go back to the places I visited with Mike. It might be my last chance.'

Sandy put up a hand in protest. 'Surely not. You—'

'Still have years ahead of me? Who knows? But what I *do* know is I need to sell Bay Books—and I want you to buy it from me.'

Again, Sandy was too flabbergasted to reply to the old lady. Just made an incoherent gasp.

'You told me you want to run your own business,' said Ida. 'And I'm talking a good price for stock, fittings and goodwill.'

'Yes… But…'

But why not?

Candles came a poor second to books. And she already had so many ideas for improving Bay Books. Hadn't she thought, in the back of her mind, that if there were a chance she might stay in Dolphin Bay she would need to earn her living?

'Why the "but"?' Ida asked.

'The "but" is Ben,' said Sandy. 'We're not looking beyond these next few days right now. I have to take it slowly with him. I'm interested in your proposition. But I can't commit to anything until I know if there might be anything more with Ben.'

Ida's eyes were warm with understanding. 'I know what Ben's been through. I also know he needs to look to the future. I'm hoping it's with you.'

'Thank you,' said Sandy, touched by the older lady's faith in her.

'I'll keep my offer on the table. But I'll be selling—if not to you, to someone else.'

'Can we keep this between us?' Sandy asked. 'I'd rather not mention it to Ben just yet. I don't want him to think I'm putting any pressure on him.'

'Of course,' said Ida.

Sandy felt guilty, putting a 'Back in One Hour' sign on the door of Bay Books—but meeting Ben for lunch was more important.

Ida's words echoed through her head. *She didn't have time to waste.*

She made her way to the boathouse to find the door open and Ben unpacking gourmet sandwiches from the hotel café and loading cold drinks into the refrigerator.

Again, he was whistling, and she smiled at the carefree sound. He hadn't realised she was there and she was struck by the domesticity of the moment. Did she want this with Ben? Everyday routine as well as heart-stopping passion? Much, much more than a few days together?

The answer was in his eyes when he looked up and saw she was there. *Yes. Yes. Yes.*

Yes to sharing everything.

Everything but the rearing of kids.

He put down the bottle he was holding, she dropped her handbag, and they met in the middle of the room. Ben held her close. She stood in his arms, exulting in the warm strength of him, the thudding of his heart, the way he smelled of the sea.

'I'm glad you're here,' he said.

'Me too,' was the only reply she could manage.

Her heart started a series of pirouettes—demanding its message be heard.

She loved him.

Emotion, overwhelming and powerful, surged through her. So did gratitude for whatever power had steered her back to him.

But could wounded, wary Ben love her back in the way she needed?

He kissed her—a brief, tender kiss of welcome—then pulled away.

'How did it go with Ida at the hospital?'

When she told him about Ida's questioning about their love-life he laughed, loud and uproariously.

'The old girl is outrageous,' he said, with more than a hint of pride. 'So what did you say to her?'

'I was so embarrassed I didn't know where to look.'

He pulled her close again. His voice was deep and husky and suggestive. 'What *would* you have told her?'

She twined her arms around his neck. 'I think you know last night was the most amazing experience of my life.' She had trouble keeping her voice steady. 'Why didn't I say yes all those years ago? Why, why, *why* didn't I fight harder for you?'

'Water under the bridge, remember?'

'Yes, but—'

'It mightn't have been such an amazing experience when I was nineteen.'

'Not true. You were the best kisser. Still are.'

'Always happy to oblige,' he said.

She smiled. 'Last night…the dinner dance…it was fun, wasn't it?'

'You were a big hit.'

'Was I? I'm still not quite sure how to handle the town-folk. In particular the way they compare me to Jodi.' *And I'm not sure how, if we have a future, I'll handle being second in your life.*

'You're still worrying about that?' He took her hand and led her to the bedroom. 'There's something I want to show you.'

'And I'm quite happy to see it,' she quipped. 'We can eat lunch afterwards.'

He laughed. 'That's not what I meant. But we can do that too.'

He went to the dresser. He opened the top drawer and pulled out the framed photo he had put there yesterday—the yesterday that seemed a hundred years ago. She braced herself, not at all sure she could cope with seeing Jodi and Ben together in happy times. She prayed the baby wouldn't be in the photo. One day she would have to go there. But not now. Not when this was all too raw and new.

Ben held the photo so she couldn't see what it was. 'It concerned me when you said you were worried about coming second with me. About being in the shadow of the memory of another woman. It's ironic that Jodi felt the same way about you.'

Sandy frowned. 'What do you mean?'

He handed her the photo. Astounded, she looked from it to him and back again. 'But it's of me. Of you. Of *us*.'

The simple wooden frame held a faded snap of her very young self and Ben with their arms around each other. She—super-slim—was wearing a tiny pink floral-patterned bikini; her hair was wet and tangled with salt and fell almost to her waist. She was looking straight at the camera with a confident, happy smile. Ben's surfer hair was long and sun-streaked and he was wearing blue Hawaiian print board shorts. He wasn't looking at the camera but rather down at her, with an expression of pride and possession heartrendingly poignant on a teenager.

She had to clear her throat before she spoke. 'Where did you get this from?'

'From you. Don't you remember?'

Slowly the memory returned to her. 'Lizzie took this photo. We had to get the film developed at the chemist in those days. I bought the frame from the old general store. And I gave it to you to…to remember me by.' She'd had a copy, too. Had shoved it in the back of an old photo album that was heaven knew where now.

'Jodi found it at the bottom of a drawer in my room just before we got married. She brought it to me and said we needed to talk.'

'I…I thought you would have thrown it out.'

'She thought so too. She asked me was I still carrying a torch for you.'

'Wh…what did you say?'

'I said I'd cared for you once but was now totally committed to her.'

Sandy swallowed hard against a kick of that unwarranted jealousy. 'You…you were getting married. Wouldn't she *know* that?'

'We were getting married because she was pregnant with Liam.'

Sandy let out a gasp of surprise. 'I…I didn't know that.'

'Of course you didn't. But she was sensitive about it. Wanted me to reassure her that I wasn't marrying her just because I "had to".'

'Poor Jodi.' Her heart went out to the lovely girl who had cared so much for Ben, and she wished she had more than vague memories of her.

'So, you see, as far as Jodi was concerned you were the "third person", as you put it, in our marriage.'

'I…I don't really know what to say. If…if you were married I wouldn't come anywhere near you.'

'I know that. You know that. And I'm sure Jodi knew that. But no matter how much I reassured her that we would have got married anyway, just maybe not so soon, she had that little nagging doubt that she was my second choice.'

'And yet you…you didn't throw out the photo.' She was still holding the frame in her hands, her fingers tightly curled around the edge.

'No. I went to put it in the bin, to prove my point, but Jodi stopped me. Said it was unrealistic to expect we wouldn't each come into the marriage with a past. She just wanted to make sure you stayed in the past.'

'And here I am...in...in the future.'

'I hadn't thought about this photo in years. Then, after that morning on the beach with you and Hobo, I dug it out from a box in the storeroom at the hotel.'

'And put it on display?'

Ben took the photo frame from her hands and placed it back on top of the dresser. 'Where it will stay,' he said.

'So...so why did you hide it from me yesterday?'

'I thought you'd think it was strange that I'd kept it. It was too soon.'

'But it's not too soon now?'

'We've come a long way since yesterday.'

'Yes,' she said. She made a self-conscious effort to laugh. But it came out as something more strangled. 'Who knows where we'll get to in the next three days?'

It was a rhetorical question she wished she hadn't uttered as soon as she'd said it. But Ben just nodded.

He picked up the photo frame and then put it back down again. 'If you're okay with it, I'll keep it here.'

'Of course,' she said, speaking through a lump of emotion in her throat. 'And I don't expect you to keep photos of Jodi buried in a drawer while I'm around.'

But, please, no photos of Liam on display. No way could she deal with that while she was dealing with the thought that if it worked out with Ben she would see the demise of her dream of having her own kids.

'She was a big part of my life. I'm glad you don't want to deny that.'

'Of course I recognise that. Like...like she did about me.'

She looked again at the long-ago photo and wondered how Jodi had felt when she'd seen it. How sensible Jodi had been not to deny Ben his past. She had to do the same. But there was still that nagging doubt.

'I still can't help but wonder if I can compete with the memory of someone so important to you.'

He cupped her chin with his big scarred hands. 'As I said

before, it's not a competition. You're so different. She was the safe harbour, calm waters. You're the breaking waves, the white-water excitement.'

'Both calm waters and breaking waves can be good,' she said, understanding what he meant and feeling a release from her fears. She hoped she, too, could at times become a safe harbour for him.

If she were to carry the wave analogy to its conclusion, Jason had been the dumper wave that had started off fast and exciting and then crashed her, choking and half drowning, onto the hard, gritty sand.

But what she felt for Ben defied all categorisation. He was both safe harbour and wild wave, and everything else she wanted, in one extraordinary man. And she longed to be everything to him.

But she couldn't tell him that. Not yet. Not until the three days were over.

'How long until you have to be back at the shop?' Ben asked.

'How long do we need?' she murmured as she slid her arms around his waist and kissed him.

CHAPTER FOURTEEN

SANDY TURNED THE 'Back in One Hour' sign—it had stretched to one and a half hours—so it read 'Open' and dashed into the shop. She spent a few minutes fixing her hair and make-up so the next contingent of too-interested ladies who came in wouldn't immediately guess how she'd spent her lunch hour. Wouldn't *that* make the Dolphin Bay grapevine hum…?

But customers were few—maybe she wasn't such a novelty any more. Or maybe, because it was such a hot day, people would rather be on the beach. She lifted her hair from her neck to cool it. It was warm in here today, despite her fiddling with the air-conditioning controls.

In the lull, after a lady had been seeking the latest celebrity chef cookbook and a man had wanted a history of the Dolphin Bay fishing fleet, she pulled out her fairy notebook. The glitter shimmered onto the countertop. It was time to revisit her thirtieth birthday resolutions.

She read them through again, with her Hotel Harbourside pen poised to make amendments.

1. Get as far away from Sydney as possible while remaining in realms of civilisation and within reach of a good latte.

Tick.

Dolphin Bay was four hours away from Sydney, and Ben's hotel café did excellent coffee. But her stay depended on a rekindled relationship of uncertain duration.

2. Find new job where can be own boss.

Tick.

The possibility of owning Bay Books exceeded the 'new job' expectations. She scribbled, *Add gift section to book-shop—enquire if can be sub-franchisee for candles.*

But, again, the possible job depended entirely on her relationship with Ben. She wouldn't hang around in Dolphin Bay if they kissed goodbye for good on Wednesday.

She hesitated when she came to resolution number three. As opposed to the flippy thing, her heart gave a painful lurch.

3. Find kind, interesting man with no hang-ups who loves me the way I am and who wants to get married and have three kids, two girls and a boy.

She'd found the guy—though he came with hang-ups aplenty—and maybe he was the guy on whom she'd subconsciously modelled the brief. But as for the rest of it....

Could she be happy with just two out of three resolutions fulfilled? How big a compromise was she prepared to make?

Now her heart actually ached, and she had to swallow down hard on a sigh. Children had always been on the agenda for her—in fact she'd never imagined a life that didn't include having babies. Then her mother's oft-repeated words came to mind: *'You can't have everything you want in life, Alexandra.'*

She put down her pen, then picked it up again. Channelled 'Sunny Sandy'. Two out of three was definitely a cup more than half full. Slowly, with a wavering line of ink, she scored through the words relating to kids, then wrote: *If stay in DB, ask Maura about puppy.* She crossed out the word 'puppy' and wrote *puppies*.

Unable to bear any further thoughts about shelving her dreams of children, she slammed the fairy notebook shut.

As she did so the doorbell jangled. She looked up to see a very small person manfully pushing the door open.

'Amy! *Sweetpea!*'

Sandy flew around the counter and rushed to meet her niece, then looked up to see her sister, Lizzie, behind her. 'And Lizzie! I can't believe it.'

Sandy greeted Lizzie with a kiss, then swept Amy up into her arms and hugged her tight. Eyes closed at the bliss of having her precious niece so close, she inhaled her sweet little-girl scent of strawberry shampoo and fresh apple.

'I miss you, bub,' she said, kissing Amy's smooth, perfect cheek.

'Miss you too, Auntie Ex.'

Her niece was the only person who called her that—when she was tiny Amy hadn't been able to manage 'Alexandra' and it had morphed into 'Ex', a nickname that had stayed.

'But you're squashing me.'

'Oh, sorry—of course I am.' Sandy carefully put her niece down and smoothed the fabric of Amy's dress.

Amy looked around her with wide eyes. 'Where are the books for children?' she asked.

'They're right over here, sweetpea. Are your hands clean?'

Amy displayed a pair of perfectly clean little hands. 'Yes.'

'Then you can take books and look at them. There's a comfy purple beanbag in the corner.'

Amy settled herself with a picture book about a crocodile. Sandy had trouble keeping her eyes off her little niece. Had she grown in just the few days since they'd said goodbye in Sydney? Amy had been a special part of her life since she'd been born and she loved being an aunt. She'd looked forward to having a little girl just like her one day.

Her breath caught in her throat. *If she stayed with Ben no one would ever call her Mummy.*

'Nice place,' said Lizzie, looking around her. 'But what the heck are you doing here? You're meant to be on your way to Melbourne.'

'I could ask the same about you. Though it's such a nice surprise to see you.'

'Amy had a pupil-free day at school. I decided to shoot down here and see what my big sis was up to!'

'I texted you.'

'Just a few words to say you were spending some time in Dolphin Bay. Dolphin Bay! Why *this* end-of-nowhere dump? Though I have to say the place has smartened itself up. And Amy loves the dolphin rubbish bins.'

'I took the scenic route down the coast. It was lunchtime when I saw the turn-off, and—'

Lizzie put up her hand to halt her. 'I suspected it, but now I get it. This is about Ben Morgan, isn't it? What else would the attraction be here? And don't even *think* about lying, because you're blushing.'

'I have caught up with Ben. Yes.'

Lizzie took a step closer. 'You've done a lot more than "caught up" with Ben, haven't you?'

Sandy rolled her eyes skyward and laughed. Then she filled her sister in on what had happened since she'd driven her Beetle down the main street of Dolphin Bay. Including Ida's offer to sell her Bay Books, but excluding Ben's decision not to have any more children.

'So, are you going to stay here with Ben?' Lizzie asked.

Sandy shrugged. 'We're testing the waters of what it might be like. But I feel the same way about him as I did back then.'

Lizzie stayed silent for a long moment before she spoke

again. 'You're not just getting all sentimental about the past because of what happened with Jason?'

Sandy shook her head. 'Absolutely not. It's nothing to do with that. Just about me and Ben.'

Just mentioning their names together made her heart flip.

'I remember what it was like between you. Man, you were crazy about each other.'

Sandy clutched her sister's arm. Lizzie had to believe that what she'd rediscovered with Ben was the real deal. 'It's still there, Lizzie, that feeling between us. We took up where we left off. I'm so happy to have found him again. Even if these few days are all we have. And I don't give a toss about Jason.'

'I'm thrilled for you—truly I am. I always liked Ben. And I love this shop. It would be cool to own it. Way better than candles.' Lizzie shifted from foot to foot. 'But now I've brought up the J word I have to tell you something. You're going to hear it sooner or later, and I'd rather you heard it from me.'

Sandy frowned. 'Is it about the wedding?' She hadn't given it another thought.

'More about the bump under What's-Her-Name's wedding gown.'

Sandy had to hold on to the edge of the closest bookshelf. 'You mean—?'

'They're not admitting to it. But the wedding guests are betting there'll be a J-Junior coming along in about five months' time.'

Sandy felt the blood drain from her face. Not that she gave a flying fig for That-Jerk-Jason. But envy of his new bride shook her. Not envy of her having Jason's baby. The thought of anyone other than Ben touching her repulsed her. But envy because *she* would never be the one with a proudly displayed bump, would never bear Ben's child.

'Are you okay, Sandy?'

Sandy took a deep breath, felt the colour rush back into her face. 'Of course I'm okay. It's a bit of a shock, that's all.'

Lizzie hugged her. 'Maybe you'll be next, if you end up with Ben. You're thirty now—you won't want to leave it too long.'

'Of course not,' said Sandy, her voice trailing away.

Lizzie was just the first to say it. If, in some hypothetical future, she and Ben decided to stay together it would start. First it would be, *So when are you two tying the knot?* followed by, *Are you putting on weight or have you got something to tell us?*

Would she would be able to endure her friends' pregnancy excitement, birth stories, christenings, first-day-at-school sob-stories? All the while knowing she could never share them?

She understood Ben's stance against having another child. Was aware of the terrible place it came from. But she couldn't help but wonder if to start a relationship with Ben predicated on it being a relationship without children would mean a doomed relationship. It might be okay to start with, but as the years went by might she come to blame him? To resent him?

'You sure you're okay?' asked Lizzie. 'You look flushed.'

'Really, I'm fine.' Sandy fanned her face with both hands. 'It's hot. I suspect this rattly old air-conditioner is on its last legs.'

'You could put in a new one if you bought the business.'

'I guess…' she said, filled with sudden new doubt.

Holding Amy in her arms, hearing about Jason's bride's bump, had shaken her confidence in a long-term relationship with Ben that didn't include starting a family.

She changed the subject. 'What are you guys planning on doing? Can you stay tonight?'

'That depends on you. I promised Amy I'd take her to see the white lions at Mogo Zoo. Then we could come back here, have dinner with you and Ben, stay the night and go home tomorrow.'

'That would be amazing. Let's book you into Ben's gorgeous hotel.'

When had her thoughts changed from Hotel Hideous to 'Ben's gorgeous hotel'?

She didn't feel guilty about putting the 'Back in Ten Minutes' sign up on the bookshop door—Ida had quite a collection of signs, covering all contingencies. It was hot and stuffy inside Bay Books and she was beginning to feel claustrophobic.

And she wanted to see Ben again, to be reassured that loving him would be enough.

Ben was stunned to see Sandy coming towards Reception with a little girl. The child was clutching one of Bay Books' brown paper bags with one hand and holding on tight to Sandy's hand with the other. All the while she kept up a steady stream of childish chatter and Sandy looked down to reply, her face tender and her eyes warm with love.

That newly tuned engine of his heart spluttered and stalled at the sight. It looked natural and right to see Sandy hand in hand with a child. The little girl might be her daughter.

Anguish tore through him. Liam would have been around the same age if he'd lived. *He could not go there.* Getting past what would have been Liam's first birthday had seen him alone in his room with a bottle of bourbon. The other anniversaries had been only marginally better.

Sandy caught sight of him and greeted him with a big smile. Was he imagining that it didn't reach her eyes? He forced himself to smile back, to act as though the sight of her with a child had not affected him.

He pulled her into a big hug. His need to keep their relationship private from the gossiping eyes of Dolphin Bay was in the past. He'd been warmed and gratified by the good wishes he'd been given since the night of the Chamber of Commerce dance. He hadn't realised just how concerned his family and friends had been about him.

'This is my niece, Amy,' Sandy said. 'Amy, this is my friend Ben.'

Ben hunkered down to Amy's height. 'Hi, Amy. Welcome to Dolphin Bay.'

'I like dolphins,' Amy said. 'They smile. I like crocodiles too. I've got a new crocodile book.' She thrust the brown paper bag towards him.

'That's good,' Ben said awkwardly. He was out of practice with children. Hadn't been able to deal with them since he'd lost Liam.

Sandy rescued him from further stilted conversation. 'Do you remember my sister, Lizzie?' she asked, indicating the tall blonde woman who had joined them.

'Of course I remember you, Lizzie,' he said as he shook hands. Though, truth be told, back then he'd been so caught up with Sandy he'd scarcely noticed Lizzie, attractive though she was.

'Who would have thought I'd see you two together again after all these years?' said Lizzie.

'Yes,' he said.

He looked down at Sandy and she smiled up at him.

'Can we book Lizzie and Amy into a room with a water view?' she asked.

We. She'd said 'we'. And he wasn't freaked out by it as much as he'd thought he would be. In fact he kind of liked it.

He put his arm around her and held her close. She clutched onto him with a ferocity that both pleased and worried him. There was that shadow again around her eyes. *What gave?*

He booked Lizzie and Amy into the room adjoining Sandy's, talking over their protests when he told them that the room was on the house.

'Dinner tonight at the hotel?' he asked, including Lizzie and Amy in the invitation.

Sandy nodded. 'Yes, please—for all of us. Though it will have to be early because of Amy's bedtime.'

'I'm good with that.'

The sooner Lizzie and Amy were settled in their room, the sooner he could be alone with Sandy. Their time together was ticking down.

Lizzie glanced at her watch. 'We have to get to the zoo.' She took Amy's book and packed it in her bag. 'C'mon, Amy, quick-sticks.'

Amy indicated for Sandy to pick her up and Sandy obliged. She embraced Sandy in a fierce hug.

'I'll bring you a white lion, Auntie Ex,' she said.

Auntie Ex? Ben was about to ask for an explanation of the name when Amy leaned over from her position in Sandy's arms and put her arms up to be hugged by him.

'Bye-bye, Ben,' she said. 'Do you want a white lion, too?'

Ben froze. He hadn't held a child since he'd last held Liam. But Amy's little hands were resting on his shoulders, her face close to his. For a moment it was the three of them. A man. A woman. A child.

He panicked. Had to force himself not to shake. He looked to Sandy over the little girl's blonde head. Connected with her eyes, both sad and compassionate.

He cleared his throat and managed to pat the little girl gently on the back. 'A white lion would be great—thanks, Amy.'

'A girl one or a boy one?' Amy asked.

Ben choked out the words. 'A...a boy one, please.'

'Okay,' she said, and wiggled for Sandy to put her down. Amy ran over to her mother.

'How are you going to get the white lions back here, Amy?' asked Sandy.

'In the back of the car, of course, silly,' Amy replied.

The adults laughed, which broke the tension. But Ben was still shaken by the emotion that had overtaken him when he'd stood, frozen, in that group hug with Sandy and Amy. And he couldn't help but notice how Sandy's eyes never left her delightful little niece. There was more than being a doting aunt in her gaze.

'Okay, guys, I have to get back to the bookshop,' Sandy said. She hugged Amy and Lizzie. Then turned to him and hugged him. 'I'm going to stay back for a little while after I shut up shop and flick through Ida's files. I'll see you for dinner.'

He tightened his arms around her. Something was bothering her—and that bothered him. 'Don't be too long,' he said, wanting to urge her to stay.

Lizzie and Amy headed for their car. Ben watched Sandy as she walked through the door. Her steps were too slow, her head bowed. She seemed suddenly alone, her orange dress a flash of colour in the monochrome decor of the reception area.

Was she thinking about how much she'd miss Lizzie and Amy if she settled in Dolphin Bay?

He suspected it was more than that.

Sandy had accepted his reasons for not wanting to risk having another child. But he'd seen raw longing in her eyes when she'd been with Amy.

When she was eighteen she'd chattered on that she wanted three kids. He'd thought two was enough—but he hadn't argued about wanting to be a parent. Fatherhood had been on his future agenda, too.

The ever-present pain knifed deeper. Being father to Liam had been everything he'd wanted and more. He'd loved every minute of his son's babyhood.

He took in a deep, shuddering breath. By denying Sandy her chance to be a mother he could lose her. If not now, then later.

It might make her wave goodbye and leave for Melbourne

on Wednesday, never to return to Dolphin Bay. Or, if she decided to stay with him, she might come to resent him. Blame him for the ache in her heart that only a baby could soothe.

Could he let that happen?

CHAPTER FIFTEEN

THE NEXT AFTERNOON Sandy trudged towards the hospital entrance. Fed up with the muggy atmosphere in Bay Books, and the rattling, useless air-conditioner, she'd shut up shop on the dot of five o'clock. To heck with going through more of Ida's files. She'd talk to Ida in person.

Whether or not she'd be able to have a sensible business conversation was debatable. She was too churned up with anxiety about the reality that a long-term relationship with Ben meant giving up her dream of having children. She tried summoning the techniques Ben had taught her to overcome her fear of monster waves but without any luck.

Her anxiety was like a dark shadow, diminishing the brilliance of her rediscovered love for Ben. Even memories of their heavenly lovemaking the night before, the joy of waking again in his arms, was not enough.

It felt like that long-ago summer day when she had been snorkelling with Ben at Big Ray Beach, out in the calm waters of the headland. It had been a perfect day, the sun shimmering through the water to the white sand beneath them, illuminating shoals of brightly coloured little fish darting in and out of the rocks. She and Ben had dived to follow some particularly cute orange and white clown fish.

Then suddenly everything had gone dark. Terrified, she'd gripped Ben's arm. He'd pointed upwards and she'd seen one of the big black manta rays that had given its name to the beach swim directly above them. She'd panicked, thinking she didn't have enough air to swim around it and up to the surface. But the ray had cruised along surprisingly quickly and she and Ben had been in sunshine again. They'd burst through to the top, spluttering and laughing and hugging each other.

Right now she felt the way she had when the light had been suddenly cut off.

She couldn't ignore Ben's stricken reaction when Amy had reached out to him yesterday. Her niece was discerning when it came to the adults she liked. She'd obviously picked Ben as a good guy and homed in like a heat-seeking missile. But all it had done was bring back painful memories for Ben.

If Sandy had held on to any remnant of hope that Ben might change his mind about having a child she'd lost it when she'd seen the fear and panic in his eyes.

And it hadn't got any better during dinner. She'd seen what an enormous effort it had been for Ben to take part in Amy's childish conversation. Amy, bless her, hadn't noticed. Her little niece had been too pleased she'd managed to get a toy girl white lion for her Auntie Ex and a boy one for Ben.

It must be so painful for Ben to endure—every child he encountered a reminder to him of what he had lost.

But it was painful for her, too, to know that Amy would be the only child she would ever have to love if she and Ben became a long-term couple.

Could she really do this? Put all her hopes of a family aside?

Would she be doomed to spend the next ten years or so hoping Ben might change his mind? Counting down the fertile years she had left? Becoming embittered and resentful?

She loved Ben; she didn't want to grow to hate him.

If she had any thought that her relationship with Ben might founder over the children issue should she think seriously of breaking it off now, to save them both future pain?

Her heart shrivelled to a hard, painful knot at the thought of leaving him.

She couldn't mention her fears to Lizzie—now back home in Sydney. Lizzie would tell her to run, not walk, away from Dolphin Bay. Her sister had often said giving birth to Amy was the best thing that had ever happened to her. She wouldn't want Sandy to miss out on motherhood.

Ben's decision not to have more children really could be a deal-breaker. Tomorrow was Wednesday and their future beyond tonight had become the elephant in the room. No. Not just an elephant but a giant-sized woolly mammoth.

As she neared the big glass doors of the hospital entrance she knew she had to tell Ida to take her out of the Bay Books equation. She couldn't consider her offer while she had any doubt at all about staying in Dolphin Bay.

But almost as soon as she was inside the hospital doors she was waylaid by the bank manager's wife, a hospital administrator, who wanted to chat.

By the time she got to Ida's bedside it was to find Ben's aunt in a highly agitated state.

'Why haven't you answered your mobile? There's smoke pouring out of Bay Books. Ben's there, investigating.'

It was nothing Ben could put his finger on, but he could swear Sandy had distanced herself from him last night. Especially through that awkward dinner. At any time he'd expected outspoken Lizzie to demand to know what his intentions were towards Sandy. And Sandy's obvious deep love for Amy had made him question again the fairness of depriving her of her own children.

But tomorrow was Wednesday. He *had* to talk with Sandy about her expectations—and his—if they were to go beyond these four awesome days.

She wasn't picking up her mobile. Seeing her would be better. He headed to Bay Books.

Ben smelled the smoke before he saw it—pungent, acrid,

burning the back of his throat. Sweat broke out on his forehead, dampened his shirt to his back. His legs felt like lead
weights. Terror seized his gut.

Sandy. Was she in there?

He was plunged back into the nightmare of the guesthouse fire. The flames. The doorknob searing the flesh of
his hands. His voice raw from screaming Jodi's name.

His heart thudded so hard it made him breathless. He
forced his paralysed legs to run down the laneway at the
side of the shop, around to the back entrance. Dark grey
smoke billowed out through a broken pane in the back
window.

The wooden carvings. The books. So much fuel for the
fire. A potential inferno.

Sandy could be sprawled on the floor. Injured. Asphyxi-
ated. He had to go in. Find her.

Save her.

He shrugged off his jacket, used it to cover his face, leaving only a slit for his eyes. He pushed in his key to the back
door and shoved. The door gave. He plunged into the smoke.

'Sandy!' he screamed until his voice was hoarse.

No response.

Straight away he saw the source of the smoke. The old
air-conditioning unit on the wall that Ida had refused to let
him replace. Smouldering, distorted by heat, but as yet with
no visible flames.

The smoke appeared to be contained in the small back
area.

But no Sandy.

Heart in his mouth, he shouldered open the door that led
through into the shop. No smoke or flames.

No Sandy there either.

All the old pain he'd thought he'd got under control
gripped him so hard he doubled over. What if it had been a
different story and Sandy had died? By opening up to Sandy
he'd exposed himself again to the agony of loss.

He fought against the thought that made him wish Sandy had never driven so blithely back into Dolphin Bay. Making him question the safe half-life that had protected him for so long.

Like prison gates clanging shut, the old barriers against pain and loss and anguish slammed back into place. He felt numb, drained.

How could he have thought he could deal with loving another woman?

A high-pitched pop song ringtone rang out, startling him. It was so out of place in this place of near disaster. He grabbed Sandy's mobile phone from next to the register and shoved it in his pocket without answering it. Why the *hell* didn't she have it with her?

He headed back to the smouldering air-conditioning unit, grabbed the fire extinguisher canister from the nearby wall bracket and sprayed fire retardant all over it.

Then he staggered out into the car park behind the shop.

He coughed and spluttered and gulped in huge breaths of fresh air.

And then Sandy was there, her face anguished and wet with tears.

'Ben. Thank heaven. *Ben.*'

Sandy never wanted to experience again the torment of the last ten minutes. All sorts of hideous scenarios had played over and over in her head.

She scarcely remembered how she'd got from the hospital to Bay Books, her heart pounding with terror, to find horrible black smoke and Ben inside the shop.

But Ben was safe.

His face was drawn and stark and smeared with soot. His clothes were filthy and he stank of acrid smoke. But she didn't care. She flung herself into his arms. Pressed herself to his big, solid, blessedly alive body. Rejoiced in the pounding of his heart, the reassuring rise and fall of his chest as he gulped in clean air.

'You're okay…' That was all she could choke out.

He held her so tightly she thought he would bruise her ribs.

'It wasn't as bad as it looked. There's just smoke damage out the back. It didn't reach the books.'

He coughed. Dear heaven, had the smoke burned his throat?

Relief that he was alive morphed into anger that he'd put himself in such danger. She pulled back and pounded on his chest with her fists. 'Why did you go in there? Why take the risk? Ida must have insurance. All that wood, all that paper… If it had ignited you could have been killed.' Her voice hiccupped and she dissolved into tears again.

He caught her wrists with his damaged hands. 'Because I thought you were in there.'

She stilled. 'Me?'

'You weren't answering your phone. I was worried.'

The implication of his words slammed into her like the kind of fast, hard wave that knocked you down, leaving you to tumble over and over in the surf. His wife and son had been trapped inside a fire-ravaged building. What cruel fate had forced him to face such a scenario again? Suffer the fear that someone he cared for was inside?

She sniffed back her tears so she was able to speak. 'I'd gone to visit Ida. To talk…to talk business with her.' *And to mull over what a future without kids might mean.* 'I'm so sorry. It was my fault you—'

'It was my choice to go in there. I had to.'

His grip on her hands was so tight it hurt.

'All I could think about was how it would be if I lost you.'

He let go her hands and stepped back.

Something was wrong with this scenario. His eyes, bluer than ever in the dark, smoke-dirtied frame of his face, were tense and unreadable. He fisted his hands by his sides.

She felt her stomach sink low with trepidation. 'But you didn't lose me, Ben. I'm here. I'm fine.'

'But what if you hadn't been? What if—?'

She fought to control the tremor in her voice. 'I thought we'd decided not to play the "what-if?" game.'

Beads of sweat stood out on his forehead. 'It was a shock.'

She heard the distant wail of a fire engine and was aware of people gathering at a distance from the shop.

Ben waved and called over to them. 'Nothing to worry about. Just smoke—no fire.'

He wiped his hand over his face in a gesture of weariness and resignation that tore at her. A dark smear of soot swept right across his cheek.

'Sandy, I need to let the fire department know they're not needed. Then go get cleaned up.'

'I'll come with you,' she said immediately.

This could be their last evening together.

He hesitated for just a second too long. 'Why don't you go back to the hotel and I'll meet you there?' he said.

One step forward and two steps back? Try ten steps forward and a hundred steps back.

'Sure,' she said, forcing the fear out of her voice.

He went to drop a kiss on her cheek but she averted it so the kiss landed on her mouth. She wound her arms around his neck, clung to him, willing him with her kiss to know how much she cared for him. How much she wanted it to work out.

'Woo-hoo! Why don't you guys get a room?'

The call—friendly, well-meant—came from one of the onlookers. She laughed, but Ben glared. She dropped her arms; he turned away.

So she *wasn't* imagining the change in him.

She forced her voice to sound Sunny-Sandy-positive. 'Okay. So I'll see you back at the hotel.'

She headed back towards Hotel Harbourside, disorientated by a haunting sense of dread.

Ben hated the confusion and hurt on Sandy's face. Hated that he was the cause of it. But he felt paralysed by the fear of losing her. He needed time to think without her distracting presence.

Thanks to this special woman he'd come a long way in the last few days. But what came next? Sandy deserved commitment. Certainty. But there were big issues to consider. Most of all the make-or-break question of children. He'd been used to managing only his own life. Now Sandy was here. And she'd want answers.

Answers he wasn't sure he could give right now.

CHAPTER SIXTEEN

Sandy was just about to turn in to the hotel entrance when she stopped. It wasn't exactly anger towards Ben that made her pause. More annoyance that she was letting herself tip-toe around vital issues she and Ben needed to sort out if they were to have any hope of a future together.

Ben needed to be treated with care and consideration for what he'd been through. But she had to consider her own needs, too. Decision time was looming. If she was to go to Melbourne and interview for the candle shop franchise she had to leave here by the latest tomorrow morning.

She turned right back around and headed down the steps to the beach.

The heat was still oppressive, the sand still warm. At this time of year it wouldn't get dark until nearly nine.

Before the sun set she needed answers.

She found Ben sitting on the wooden dock that led out from the boathouse into the waters of the bay. His broad shoulders were hunched as he looked out towards the break-water.

Without a word she sat down beside him. Took his hand in hers. In response, he squeezed it tight. They sat in silence. Her. Ben. And that darn woolly mammoth neither of them seemed capable of addressing.

Beyond the breakwater a large cargo ship traversed the horizon. Inside the harbour walls people were rowing dinghies to shore from where their boats were anchored. A large seagull landed on the end pier and water slapped against the supporting posts of the dock.

She took a deep breath. 'Ida wants to sell me Bay Books.'

'Is that what you want?' His gaze was intent, the set of his mouth serious.

She met his gaze with equal intensity. 'I want to run my own business. I think I could make the bookshop work even better than it already does. But you're the only reason for me to stay in Dolphin Bay.'

'An important decision like that should be made on its own merits.'

'The bookshop proposition's main merit is that it allows me to stay here with you.' *Time to vanquish that mammoth.* 'We have to talk about where we go from here.'

His voice matched the bleakness of his face. 'I don't know that I can give you what you want.'

'I want you, Ben. Surely you know that.'

'I want you too. More than you can imagine. If it wasn't for…for other considerations I'd ask you to stay. Tell you to phone that candle guy and cancel your interview in Melbourne. But…but it's not that straightforward.'

'What other considerations?' she asked, though she was pretty sure she knew the answer.

He cleared his throat. 'I saw how you were with Amy.'

'You mean how I dote on her?'

He nodded. 'You were meant to be a mother, Sandy. Even when you were eighteen you wanted to have kids.'

'Two girls and a boy,' she whispered, the phrase now a desolate echo.

'I can't endure loss like that again. Today brought it all back.'

She wanted to shake him. Ben was smart, educated, an astute businessman. Why did he continue to run away from life? From love.

'I appreciate your loss. The pain you've gone through. But haven't you punished yourself enough for what happened?'

He made an inarticulate response and she knew she had hurt him. But this had been bottled up for too long.'

'Can't you see that any pleasure involves possible pain? Any gain possible risk. Are you *never* going to risk having your heart broken again?'

His face was ashen under his tan. 'It's too soon.'

'Do you think you'll ever change your mind about children?'

She held her breath in anticipation of his answer.

'Since you've been back I've thought about it. But four days isn't long enough for me to backtrack on something so important.'

Deep down she knew he was only giving voice to what she already knew. She wanted Ben. She wanted children. But she couldn't have both.

Slowly she exhaled her breath in a huge sigh. 'I can take that as a no then. But, Ben, you're only thirty-one. Too young to be shutting down your life.'

His jaw set in a stubborn line. 'It wouldn't be fair for me to promise something I can't deliver.'

'I…I understand.' But she didn't. Not really.

She shifted. The hard boards of the dock were getting uncomfortable.

'And I appreciate your honesty.'

His gaze was shrewd. 'But it's not good enough for you?'

She shook her head. 'No. It's not.'

Now she felt the floodgates were open. 'It was compromise all the way with Jason. I wanted marriage and kids. He said he had to get used to the idea. I moved in with him when I didn't want to live together without being married. Fine for other people. Too insecure for me. But I went along with him, put my own needs on hold.' Her attempt at laughter came out sharp-edged and brittle. 'Now I hear he's not only married, but his wife is pregnant.'

'That…that must have been a shock.'

'I can't go there again, Ben. Can't stay here waiting for heaven knows how long for you to get the courage to put the past behind you and commit to a future with me.'

Ben looked down at where the water slapped against the posts. She followed his gaze to see a translucent jellyfish floating by to disappear under the dock, its ethereal form as insubstantial as her dreams of a life with Ben.

'I'm sorry,' he said.

She didn't know whether he was apologising for Jason or because he couldn't give her the reassurances she wanted.

'I…I won't make all the compromises again, Ben,' she said brokenly. 'No matter how much I love you.'

She slapped her hand to her mouth.

The 'L' word.

She hadn't meant to say it. It had just slipped out.

Say it, Ben. Tell me you love me. Let me at least take that away with me.

But he didn't.

Maybe he couldn't.

And that told her everything.

'I'm sorry,' he said again, his voice as husky as she'd ever heard it. 'I can't be what you want me to be.'

If he told her she could do better than him she'd scream so loud they'd hear it all the way to New Zealand.

Instead he pulled her to him, held her tight against his powerful chest. It was the place she most wanted to be in the world. But she'd learned that compromise which was all one way wouldn't make either of them happy.

'I'm sorry too,' she murmured, fighting tears. 'But I'm not sorry I took that turn-off to Dolphin Bay. Not sorry we had our four-day fling.'

He pulled her to her feet. 'It's not over. We still have this evening. Tonight.'

She shook her head. 'It's perfect the way it is. I don't want to ruin the memories. I...I couldn't deal with counting down the hours to the last time we'll see each other.'

With fingers that trembled she traced down his cheek to the line of his jaw, trying to memorise every detail of his face. She realised she didn't have any photos to remember him by. Recalled there'd been a photographer at the dinner dance. She would check the website and download one. But not until she could look at his image and smile rather than weep.

'Sandy—' he started.

But she silenced him with a kiss—short, sweet, final.

'If you say you're sorry one more time I'll burst into tears and make a spectacle of myself. I'm going back to my room now. I've got phone calls to make. E-mails to send. Packing to do.'

A nerve flickered near the corner of his mouth. 'I'll call by later to...to say goodbye.'

'Sure,' she said, fighting to keep her voice under control. 'But I'm saying my goodbye now. No regrets. No what-ifs. Just gratitude for what we had together.'

She kissed him again. And wondered why he didn't hear the sound of her heart breaking.

Ben couldn't bear to watch Sandy walk away. He turned and made his way to the boathouse. Every step was an effort, as if he were fighting his way through a rip.

His house seemed empty and desolate—the home of a solitary widower. There was a glass next to the sink with Sandy's lipstick on the rim, but no other trace of her. He stripped off his smoke-stained clothes, pulled on his board shorts and headed for Big Ray Beach.

He battled the surf as if it were a foe, not the friend it had always been to him. He let the waves pound him, pummel him, punish him for not being able to break away from his self-imposed exile. The waves reared up over him, as if harnessing his anger at the cruel twist of fate that had brought Sandy back into his life but hadn't given him the strength to take the second chance she had offered him.

Finally, exhausted, he made his way back to the boat-house.

For one wild moment he let himself imagine what it would be like to come back to the house to find Sandy there. Her bright smile, her welcoming arms, her loving presence.

But the house was bare and sterile, his footsteps loud and lonely on the floorboards. That empty glass on the draining board seemed to mock him. He picked up the photo of him and Sandy on the beach that long-ago summer. All their dreams and hopes had stretched out ahead of them—untainted by betrayal and pain and loss.

He put down the photo with its faded image of first love. He'd lost her then. And he'd been so damned frightened of losing her at some undefined time in the future he'd lost her now.

He slammed his fist down so hard on the dresser that the framed photo flew off the top. He rescued it from shattering on the floor only just in time.

What a damn fool he was.

He'd allowed the fears of the past to choke all hope for the future.

Sandy had offered him a second chance. And he'd blown it.

Sandy. Warm, vibrant, generous Sandy. With her don't-let-anything-get-you-down attitude.

That special magic she'd brought into his life had nothing to do with the glitter she trailed around with her. Sandy's magic was hope, it was joy, but most of all it was love.

Love he'd thought he didn't deserve. With bitterness and self-loathing he'd punished himself too harshly. And by not forgiving himself he'd punished Sandy, too.

The final rusted-over part of him shifted like the seismic movement of tectonic plates deep below the floor of the ocean. It hurt. But not as much as it would hurt to lose Sandy for good.

He had to claim that love—tell her how much she meant to him. Show her he'd found the courage and the purpose to move forward instead of tripping himself up by looking back.

He showered and changed and headed for the hotel.

Practising in his head what he'd say to her, he rode the elevator to Sandy's room. Knocked on the door. Once. Twice. But no reply.

'Sandy?' he called.

He fished out the master key from his wallet and opened the door.

She was gone.

The suitcase with all her stuff spilling out of it was missing. Her bedlinen had been pulled down to the end of the bed. There was just a trace of her vanilla scent lingering in the air. And on the desk a trail of that darn glitter, glinting in the coppery light of the setting sun.

In the midst of the glitter was a page torn out from the fairy notebook she always carried in her bag. It was folded in two and had his name scrawled on the outside.

His gut tightened to an agonising knot. With unsteady hands he unfolded the note.

Ben—thank you for the best four days of my life. I'm so glad I took a chance with you. No regrets. No 'what ifs'. Sandy xx.'

He fumbled for his mobile. To beg her to come back. But her number went straight to voicemail. Of course it did. She wouldn't want to talk to him.

He stood rooted to the ground as the implications of it all hit him.

He'd lost her.

Then he gave himself a mental shaking.

He could find her again.

It would take at least ten hours for her to drive to Melbourne. More if she took the coastal road. It wasn't worth pursuing her by car.

In the morning he'd drive to Sydney, then catch a plane to Melbourne.

He'd seek her out.

And hope like hell that she'd listen to what he had to say.

Sandy had abandoned her plan to mosey down the coastal road to Melbourne. Instead she cut across the Clyde Mountain and drove to Canberra, where she could connect to the more straightforward route of the Hume Highway.

She didn't trust herself to drive safely in the dark after the emotional ups and downs of the day. A motel stop in Canberra, then a full day's driving on Thursday would get her to Melbourne in time to check in to her favourite hotel and be ready to wow the candle people on Friday morning.

She would need to seriously psyche herself up to sound enthusiastic about a retail mall candle shop when she'd fallen in love with a quaint bookshop on a beautiful harbour.

Her hands gripped tight on the steering wheel.

Who was she kidding?

It was her misery at leaving Ben that she'd have to overcome if she was going to impress the franchise owners.

She'd cried all the way from Dolphin Bay. Likely she'd cry all the way from Canberra to Melbourne. Surely she would have run out of tears by the time she faced the interview panel?

She pulled into the motel.

Ben would have read her note by now. Maybe it had been cowardly to leave it. But she could not have endured facing him again, knowing she couldn't have him.

No regrets. No regrets. No regrets.

Ben was her once-in-a-lifetime love. But love couldn't thrive in a state of inertia.

She'd got over Ben before. She'd get over him again.

Soon her sojourn in Dolphin Bay would fade into the realm of happy memories. She had to keep on telling herself that.

And pray she'd begin to believe it.

CHAPTER SEVENTEEN

BEN REMEMBERED SANDY telling him about her favourite hotel in the inner-city Southbank district of Melbourne— all marble, chandeliers and antiques. He'd teased her that it sounded too girly for words. She'd countered that she liked it so much better than his preferred stark shades of grey.

He'd taken a punt that that was where she would be staying. A call to Reception had confirmed it. He walked from his ultra-contemporary hotel at the other end of the promenade that ran along the banks of the Yarra River. He'd wait all day at her hotel to see her if he had to.

It was a grey, rainy morning in Melbourne, mitigated by the brilliant colours of a myriad umbrellas. Ben watched a hapless duck struggling to swim across the wide, fast-flowing brown waters of the Yarra.

Was his mission doomed to such a struggle?

He found the hotel and settled in one of the comfortable velvet chairs in the reception area. He didn't have to wait for long. He sensed Sandy was there before he glanced up.

He was shocked at how different she looked. She wore a sleek black suit with a tight skirt that finished above her knees and high-heeled black shoes. A laptop in a designer bag was slung across her shoulder. Her hair was sleek, her mouth glossy with red lipstick.

She looked sexy as hell and every inch the successful businesswoman.

Sandy the city girl.

It jolted him to realise how much he'd be asking her to give up. Now she was back in her own world would she want to settle for running a small-town bookshop in Dolphin Bay?

She must have felt his gaze on her, and stopped mid-stride as he rose from the chair. He was gratified that her first reaction was a joyous smile. But then she schooled her face into something more neutral.

For a moment that seemed to stretch out for ever they stood facing each other in the elegant surrounds of the hotel. He had to get it right this time. There wouldn't be another chance.

Sandy's breath caught.

Ben.

Unbelievably handsome and boldly confident in a superbly cut charcoal-grey suit. Her surf god in the city. She had trouble finding her voice.

'What are you doing here?' she finally managed to choke out.

He stepped closer. 'I've come to tell you how much I love you. How I always loved the memory of you.'

Ben. This troubled, scarred man she adored. He had come all the way to Melbourne to tell her he loved her, smack in the middle of a hotel lobby.

She kept her voice low. 'I love you too. But it doesn't change the reasons why I left Dolphin Bay.'

'You gave me the kick in the butt I needed. I'm done with living with past scars. I want a future. With you.'

He looked around. Became aware they were attracting discreet interest.

'Can we talk?'

'My room,' she said.

They had the elevator to themselves and she ached to kiss him, to hold him. That would only complicate things, but for the first time she allowed herself a glimmer of hope for a future with Ben.

Ben was grateful for the privacy of Sandy's hotel room. He took both her hands in his. Pulled her close. Looked deep into her eyes. 'More than anything I want a life with you.'

'Me too, Ben.'

'That life would be empty without a child. *Our* child.'

He watched her face as the emotions flashed over it. She looked more troubled than triumphant.

'Oh, Ben, you don't have to say that. I don't want you to force yourself to do something so important as having children because you think it's what *I* want. That…that won't work.'

The fear he'd been living with for five years had been conquered by her brave action in walking away from him.

'It's for your sake, yes. But it's also for my own.' He took a deep breath. 'I want to be a dad again some day.'

The loss of Liam had been tragic. All potential for that little life gone in a terrible, pointless fire. But no matter how much he blamed himself, he knew deep in his gut he had not been responsible for those out-of-control flames. No one could have predicted how the wind had changed. No one could have saved Jodi and his son.

'I know you were a brilliant father in the little time you were granted with Liam. Everyone told me that.'

'I did my best.'

The four words echoed with sudden truth.

He deserved a second chance. Another son. A daughter. A baby who would grow into a child, like Amy, and then a teenager like he and Sandy had been when they met. It would not diminish the love he'd felt for Jodi and Liam.

'I want a family again, Sandy, and I want it with you. We'll be good parents.'

Exulting, he kissed her—a long, deep kiss. But there was more he needed to talk about before he could take her back home with him. He broke the kiss, but couldn't bear to release her hands from his.

'How did your interview go?' he asked.

'The Melbourne store is mine if I want it.' She was notably lacking in enthusiasm.

'*Do* you want it? Because if your answer is yes I'll move to Melbourne.'

Her eyes widened. 'You'd do that?'

'If it's what it takes to keep you,' he said.

She shook her head. 'Of course I don't want it. I want to buy Bay Books from Ida and knock through into the space next door to make a bookshop/café. I want to have author talks. Cooking demonstrations. A children's storyteller.'

The words bubbled out of her—and they were everything he wanted to hear.

'I want to ask Ida to order matching carvings for the café from her Balinese woodcarver.'

'That can be arranged. I own the café. The lease is yours.' He ran his finger down her cheek to the corner of her mouth. 'Will you come back to Dolphin Bay with me?'

Sandy was reeling from Ben's revelations. But he hadn't mentioned marriage—and she wanted to be married before she had children.

She'd feared he was too damaged to love again—and look what had happened. What was to stop her proposing?

'Yes,' she said. 'I want to come back to Dolphin Bay. Be with you. But I—'

He silenced her with a finger over her mouth. 'One more thing.'

'Yes?' she said.

'Life is short. There's no time to waste. We could date some more. Live together. But I'd rather we made it permanent. Marry me?'

In spite of all his pain and angst and loss he'd come through it strong enough to love again. To commit.

But she didn't kid herself that Ben's demons were completely vanquished. He'd still need a whole lot of love, support and understanding. As his wife, she could give it to him by the bucketload. Ben still had scars—and she'd help him to heal.

'Yes, I'll marry you. Yes, yes and *yes*.'

He picked her up and whirled her around until she was dizzy.

They were laughing and trying to talk at the same time, interspersing words with quick, urgent kisses.

'I don't want a big white wedding,' she said.

'I thought on the beach?'

'Oh, yes! In bare feet. With Amy as a flower girl. And Hobo with a big bow around his neck.'

Her fairy notebook would be filling up rapidly with lists.

'We can live in the boathouse.'

'I'd love that.'

'Build a big, new house for when we have kids.'

Maybe it was because her emotions had been pulled every which way, but tears welled in her eyes again. Ben had come so far. And they had so far to go together.

She blinked them away, but her voice was wobbly when she got the words out. 'That sounds like everything I've ever dreamed of...'

She thought back to her goals, written in pink.

Tick. Tick. Tick.

* * * * *

Was this a good idea?

Tess wondered if she really should extend this impromptu date with another drink. It was Monday and she needed to be at work early. But, even though Graham had a kid and felt not so much her normal type, she had this crazy, weird connection with him. She couldn't *not* stay.

And it had been a long time since she had no-strings-attached fun with a hot guy.

When their round of drinks arrived, Graham clinked his glass against hers. "I'm glad you stayed. Feels as though we're dancing around—"

"Hooking up?"

He gave her a serious look. "Is this what we're doing? Hooking up?"

Heck, she didn't know. But this night with Graham felt right. It felt like something more than just fun. It felt like magic. Like Graham was her perfect match. "Maybe."

Moving slowly he lightly brushed her lips with his. Her pulse sped at the first touch, and she leaned in for more. She knew with absolute clarity that she didn't want just one night with Graham.

HIS FOREVER GIRL

BY
LIZ TALLEY

MILLS &
BOON®

Published in Great Britain 2014
by Mills & Boon, an imprint of Harlequin (UK) Limited,
Eton House, 18-24 Paradise Road, Richmond, Surrey, TW9 1SR

© 2014 Amy R. Talley

ISBN: 978 0 263 91260 9

23-0214

Harlequin (UK) Limited's policy is to use papers that are natural, renewable and recyclable products and made from wood grown in sustainable forests. The logging and manufacturing processes conform to the legal environmental regulations of the country of origin.

Printed and bound in Spain
by Blackprint CPI, Barcelona

A 2009 Golden Heart Award finalist in Regency romance, **Liz Talley** has since found a home writing sassy Southern stories. In her current books, she's visiting one of her favorite cities—New Orleans. Liz lives in north Louisiana with her hero, two beautiful boys and a large number of animals. She enjoys laundry, paying bills and creating masterful dinners for her family. She also lies in her biography to make herself look like the perfect housewife. What she really likes is new shoes, lemon-drop martinis and fishing off the pier at her camp. You can visit her at www.liztalleybooks.com to learn more about the lies she tells herself, and about her upcoming books.

Special thanks to the Elsensohns at Mardi Gras
Decorators for sharing the business aspects
of Mardi Gras.

This book is dedicated to my nieces and nephews—
Audrey, Ava, Sam, Davey, Mikayla, Byron,
Christian and Devvin. I don't always see you,
but I carry you in my heart.

CHAPTER ONE

TESS ULLO SLID ONTO a stool and knocked her knuckles against the weathered bar. "The usual, Ron. Stat."

The bartender with ripped biceps and a sweet smile sauntered over. "That kind a day, hon?"

"God, yes." Taking Granny B to the doctor and running all the errands the older woman had piled up on her list wasn't for the faint of heart. Tess's Italian grandmother wasn't of the sweet variety—more like the salty-with-a-side-of-vinegar kind. For seven hours, Tess had "helped" her grandmother find a bath mat the perfect shade of periwinkle. All that running around came after hearing Granny B tell the technician doing the mammogram about her sex life with Tess's long-departed grandfather. Tess would never look at the picture of the stern-faced man dressed in his Navy uniform in quite the same way. *Scarred* wasn't even the word for what she felt. "Took Granny B out today."

"Yikes. I'll make it a double," Ron said with a twinkle in his eye.

Tess gave a wave to Petra Ostrav who worked in the paint department at Tess's family company. The diminutive woman sat close to her lover, Paola, a beautiful Chilean dancer who headlined at a top-notch gentleman's club. Otherwise there were not many patrons on this late Monday afternoon. Maybe it was the weather—misty rain fell outside the open plantation windows of the bar located not far from the French Quarter in the Marigny district. Or maybe the small crowd was because it was Lent and the devout were being, well, devout.

Two-Legged Pete's was a regular joint for the employees of Frank Ullo Float Builders—owned and operated by Tess's father—so she usually knew someone when she dropped by. Of course, she'd been a more frequent patron at Pete's recently since Mardi Gras was over and she'd stopped seeing her on-again-off-again boyfriend, Nick. She'd caught him with Merri Wynn right after Christmas. Nick had defended himself by claiming they weren't exclusive, but Tess didn't care. Still felt like a slap after they'd spent the previous weekend talking about a possible future together.

Her phone buzzed and she slid it from her purse. The text was from Gigi Vastola, her best friend.

Can't get away from the office. Sorry, babe.

Damn it.

Tess had wanted some girl time with her bestie, but she understood. Gigi worked with a law firm on Canal Street, climbing the ladder toward partnership, which meant her friend often got trapped after hours preparing cases. No biggie. They'd catch up later. Tess would have one drink then maybe head to spinning class…or home to watch *The Bachelor*.

The door opened and Tess caught the movement out of the corner of her eye. She cocked her head and looked—like everyone else in Two-Legged Pete's—at the man in a raincoat shouldering his way in. A navy suit and a conservative tie showed beneath the black trench. He sported a fresh haircut and had a jaw of granite.

Nice.

But very out of place for a casual joint like Pete's.

Tess snuck a peek at her middle-of-the-week jeans and

long-sleeved sweater. Although the sweater had a pinprick dot of bleach on the hem, the bright green made her eyes look deeper. And she'd worn her UGG boots so she didn't look totally sloppy.

Jeez. Why was she taking stock of herself? Because a good-looking dude walked in? Or maybe it was because Granny B had pointed out she needed to do something with her hair and wear more flattering shoes.

She glanced at the table of women who looked like bank tellers. Every woman stared at the guy, too. One woman tucked a curl behind her ear, and another wiped the mascara shadow from under her eyes.

Even Ron sucked in his gut.

The stranger nodded at the bartender, who in turn gave him a quite charming smile. The man slid onto a stool three down from Tess as Ron flew toward him like a magnet toward a metal pole.

"Hello, there," Ron said, showing his dimples.

Good Lord.

"Hey," the man said, reaching into the open coat for what she presumed was a wallet. "I'll take a J.B. and Coke, easy on the ice."

Ron lifted an eyebrow. "J.B., huh? My kind of man."

Tess snorted. She couldn't help it. She hadn't seen that kind of bad flirting since Gigi got drunk and tried a top-ten list of bad pickup lines on every man at the Columns on Valentine's Day. Okay, that was only a month ago, but still Ron not only took the cake…he'd already licked the spoon.

Typical Ron.

"Hush," her friend said, slinging an arm her way, but not daring to take his eyes off tall, dark and hewn-from-granite.

Tess giggled. Yes, she actually giggled.

Damn it.

The man looked over at her and smiled.

Oh, hell, no. She'd pull out dimples, too…if she had any to use. She smiled as if they all shared one big joke.

"Ron's a consummate flirt," she said, jabbing a finger at her bartender bud. "You'll fall prey if you stand too close."

"Oh, please. You stand closer than anyone, *mon amie*. You love my flirting." Ron grabbed a bottle of the amber liquid from the back shelf and held a glass to the light.

The stranger laughed and the sound tickled Tess's stomach.

Whoa, girl. Down.

"True," she said, pulling her own drink toward her. Ron made her gin gimlet just as she liked it—simple syrup, muddled cucumber, tarragon and Hendrick's. Delish. "When it comes to flirting, you're the don."

"Ron the Don? Sounds like a wrestler." The stranger quirked an eyebrow. He turned toward her allowing his gaze to travel lightly over her. A shiver ran through her. Dear Bessie, he had the prettiest blue eyes that would exactly match the bathroom rug her Granny B had spent eons searching for. Good humor twinkled in the periwinkle depths, and Tess felt more than the warmth of the gin in her girl parts.

Dang, he looked good enough to sop up a biscuit with, and Tess didn't even eat biscuits. Carbs were the enemy, after all, but this man made her want to change her mind.

"What brings you to Pete's? We don't get much tourist traffic," Ron asked, pouring a generous amount of whiskey into the tumbler then topping it with soda.

"Job interview. Someone at the company mentioned this place when I said I wanted a local pub." The man pulled the drink to him, sipped and nodded in satisfaction.

"Really?" Ron said, swiping at the bar with a towel and sliding a surprised look at Tess, keeping her in the conversation. "Good to know we're getting recommendations around here."

The stranger made a sound in the back of his throat that sounded like an agreement, and Tess sipped her drink, trying not to out-and-out stare at the hotness mere feet from her. She had to be ovulating because her hormones had shifted into overdrive and clamored for her to put on some lipstick and sidle closer.

She ignored her hormones because they made bad decisions. In fact, last time they'd led her to a strange bed, overly polite note and a cold cup of coffee the morning after. Tess had stopped letting her girl parts dictate her love life.

The man glanced at the TV that was broadcasting something with racing dirt bikes. "Any way I can talk you into turning to the Rangers game? Wanna check the score."

Ron looked like someone had farted. "Hockey?"

"Nah, baseball. Preseason."

Despite her declaration to keep her distance, Tess slid onto the next stool. "Feliz is pitching. They're checking out his arm after rehab."

The man smiled at her.

God, his smile was good.

No, not good. Sexy. And not just sexy but up-against-a-wall-naked sexy. Tess was certain she'd seen such a smile only twice…and the aftereffects had resulted in its moniker. Though up-against-the-wall-naked sex wasn't as hot as it sounded. Required a lot of balance.

"Ugh, baseball?" Ron groaned but lifted the remote. "The only thing good about baseball is the way the players look in those tight pants."

"I'll concede that point," Tess said, dragging her purse over, telling herself she moved closer to the man only because it gave her a better view of the TV.

"That's what all the ladies say," the stranger said. So was that a message to Ron? Or to her? "And, uh, I guess some guys."

Ron found the right station. Texas was up 5–2 in the third inning. The Rangers' designated hitter was at the plate, swinging and missing at low and inside.

"Shamburg's gonna throw that pitch at him all night," Tess said.

"A lady who knows baseball." The man looked pleased at the revelation. But, really, there were lots of girls who liked baseball. Okay, maybe not *lots*. But others.

"I'm not obsessed but I watch."

Ron nodded. "Yeah, she keeps stats."

The stranger raised an eyebrow. "Really?"

"I like the Astros best," she said, tugging a notebook out of her purse. "I've gotten into a habit of studying batting averages and making predictions. My brother was a bookie during his college years and paid me to help him. Old habits die hard…and now I like the whole challenge of dissecting the game."

"Bookie? Does he still—"

"Nah, he's a priest."

The man's laughter made her stomach twitch. He looked even better laughing and the bar lights caught the rain droplets in his dark hair. Her hand rose to wipe them away, but she caught herself in time and instead lifted the pen, jotting down the starting pitcher and his ERA.

"I'm Graham." Hotness extended a hand.

"Tess." She tucked the pen and pad into her purse and took his hand. It was damp but warm. "Nice to meet you."

Now that they'd introduced themselves she definitely wanted to keep the conversation flowing, but couldn't come up with a topic. Maybe more baseball?

"Hey, there. I'm Angela," a woman drawled from behind Tess.

Graham spun on his stool. "Oh, hi."

The woman who'd earlier tucked her hair and put on

lip gloss stood behind them with a gleam in her eye. Like a predator.

Graham pulled at his tie.

"Would you like to join me and my friends? We're celebrating a promotion, and we've ordered stuffed mushrooms and smoked oysters." Angela gave Graham a come-hither gaze that made Tess shift on her stool. Jeez, the woman was good.

Graham looked ambushed and his eyebrows lowered a fraction. Tess could almost hear the wheels creaking, turning, churning, trying to figure out how to respond to the overt invite.

"Well, I'll take some of those stuffed mushrooms," Tess joked.

Angela shot her "the look"—the one that said something needed to be stuffed, and it wasn't the mushrooms.

Graham looked like a man who had swallowed a lemon. Okay, maybe not that uncomfortable or sour, but Tess could tell he didn't want to go with Angela and couldn't say so without being rude.

Aw…he was a sweet guy. Tess should help him.

"Actually Graham and I have been catching up," Tess said.

A few seconds tripped by and finally her handsome stranger nodded. "Yeah, it's crazy and such a coincidence, but Tess was my blind date to Sadie Hawkins back in '97."

Tess rolled her eyes. She had been eleven years old in '97, but she wouldn't correct him. If Graham said they went to Sadie Hawkins together, they went to Sadie's together. "Small world, huh? All because he asked Ron to turn to the Rangers' game."

Graham gave Angela a small regretful shrug and then gave his attention to Tess. "You know, stuffed mushrooms would be good before we go to dinner."

Dinner?

Well, all righty then.

"Perfect," Tess said, with a sunny smile.

Angela stood there for a moment, looking unconvinced. Graham turned back to her. "Thanks for the offer, Angela, but I don't want to crash your girls' night out. Go celebrate, and I'll send a round of drinks for you and your friends."

Angela gave a shrug and fake smile. "That's sweet of you."

"The least I can do after that nice invite."

"Send the waitress. She's been on break for fifteen minutes and we're empty," she said to Ron before sashaying to her friends.

"You're the nice guy my mom's been begging me to find," Tess cracked, admiring the way Graham's dark hair brushed the collar of his white dress shirt. The tugging at his throat had loosened the striped power tie and he'd unbuttoned the top button showing gorgeous tanned skin at his throat. His five o'clock shadow gave him a rakish air. "But you don't have to feel obliged to take me to dinner."

"Of course I don't. But come to think of it, you do remind me of Ainsley Braddock, my Sadie's date."

Huh. What did that mean? He wasn't taking her to dinner?

Disappointment stung her. Which was crazy. She didn't know this man from Adam. Which she always thought a stupid saying because she didn't know Adam. Okay, she had a cousin named Adam, but—

"I would love to take you to dinner. That is, if you're free."

Tess nodded, wondering if it was a mistake to look so eager. Her stomach growled and she decided dinner was dinner. And if it were with a handsome stranger, she'd have news to share with Gigi when she called her later. There was something appealing about being spontaneous, something exciting about having dinner with Graham of the power tie and wing tips. "A friend was supposed to meet me after work but couldn't get off. I haven't eaten yet so…that sounds fun."

Graham lifted his glass and clinked it against the one she held in her hand. "Then it's a date."

They both drank and Ron shook his head. "How do you do it? Any time I go to a bar, I go home with a tab and that's it."

Tess laughed. "Joanne would be pissed if you came home with anything other than a bar tab."

"Pregnant women are such downers. She used to be fun," Ron grumbled.

A perplexed expression gathered on Graham's face.

Tess helped him out. "Ron isn't gay. He's just an indiscriminate flirt. Always chasing that tip."

Ron lifted a shoulder. "I never said I was gay."

"You implied it," Graham said.

"No, you made an assumption based on my comment regarding men in baseball pants." Ron's eyes danced with laughter. He loved flipping stereotypes.

"Ron has a twisted sense of humor," Tess said, finishing off her gimlet. The crisp taste and slight buzz made her feel invincible. Or maybe that was due to the fact she'd picked up a hot guy in a bar. Okay, only for dinner, but even so, she felt better about her crap day with Granny B who had ended it by declaring Tess would never see a single piece of jewelry in her will. "Do you want to order stuffed mushrooms? If so, we better put in an order. Daryl's slow."

"Hey, good food requires patience," Ron said.

Graham centered his attention on her. "Let's roll. I'm hungry for more than an appetizer."

"Meow," Ron purred, before moseying toward a customer at the other end of the bar.

Tess's cheeks blistered even though she knew it was a joke.

Graham's gaze slid over her, lingering particularly on her mouth. Tess licked her lips before she could catch herself—and he definitely noted the movement. "I'm not familiar with the Marigny area so I don't know any restaurants close by."

"I'm not dressed overly nice, so we better stick to casual." Tess glanced outside. "Looks like the rain is gone and the stars are out. Why don't we walk toward the Quarter? It's not far and you know there's something there to tickle the fancy."

Tess hopped off the stool, tossing a ten and five on the bar to cover her drink and give Ron a decent tip. Joanne had only a month to go until she delivered their first child, and money was tight for the couple.

"I'll defer to the local." Graham withdrew a credit card and drummed his fingers on the bar while Ron slid the card through the machine. Then he stood, lifting an attaché case. "Let me lock this in my rental and we'll head out."

"Have fun, you two," Ron called holding up his bar towel and giving it a wave.

And so Tess walked out of Two-Legged Pete's with a good-looking man and the expectation for good food, good wine…and maybe something more.

Or maybe she wanted it to be more than what it was.

Either way, it was better than watching *The Bachelor*.

CHAPTER TWO

GRAHAM NAQUIN POPPED the trunk of the Chevy Malibu and placed his briefcase inside, slamming the lid with finality.

So…he'd picked up a random chick in a bar.

Outside his current comfort zone in a huge way. In fact, it was something he'd vowed not to do for a while. His focus was on getting his crap together.

In the past couple of months, he'd abandoned the impulsive, carefree Graham, electing to play everything safe. Hadn't worked all that well for him so far, but he liked thinking he was a man who considered every decision thoroughly before moving forward. But tonight he hadn't even tried to apply the brakes. Nope. He'd tossed out that white lie about Sadie Hawkins and backed it up with re-extending the offer for dinner.

He almost felt like himself again…like lady luck winked at him and dealt him a winning hand. Like things were going his way finally.

Smiling at Tess, trying like hell to convince himself an impulsive dinner date was a good idea, he waved an arm in the direction of the French Quarter. "Lead on."

In the damp air, Tess's beach-streaked hair had curled around cheeks scattered with freckles. Her eyes were the color of wet moss, and not much about her implied overt sexiness. More like friendly puppy or kid sister.

Okay. Not exactly friendly puppy. Or sister.

Tess also had full lips and a stubborn chin. Her perfectly-proportioned breasts were nicely outlined in her sweater and her caboose was tight. She wore those weird brown boots all the teenagers wore and jeans that looked comfy and trendy at the same time. She smelled like apples—sort of fresh and fruity. She had an all-American vibe, but there lay a promise in the sway of her hips, a hint of mystery in her smile. Tess reminded him of that one Christmas he'd found a forgotten present beneath the tree.

She'd sucked him in, stretched him outside his intentions…and damned if he wasn't intrigued by the connection between them. It felt like something he'd never felt before. Or maybe he was on a high from nailing his interview.

"Wish I were dressed nicer so we could go somewhere swanky," she said as they fell in step on the deserted sidewalk.

"I see how you roll," he said, laughing when her eyes widened.

"No, I'll totally pay for my own dinner. It's just you're dressed nice and if it's been a while since you've been to New Orleans…"

"I come to New Orleans often enough…just not since November. Besides, New Orleans is a city where even the cheap eats are good." Graham looked back toward the edge of the Marigny District, spotting the huge warehouse he'd toured that afternoon in the distance. Something warm and right settled in his gut at the thought of returning to his first love. The sound of tugboats blowing their horns on the Mississippi echoed the certainty in his soul.

"So a job interview brings you to the Big Easy?" Tess asked. The puddles along the worn streets tossed back reflections of the buildings. Occasionally someone rode by on a bike or a cab passed as the rhythm of the city re-established itself after the early spring rain. The squeal of brakes, the rev of engines and the occasional shout of laughter accompanied the music spilling into the streets.

The earthy smell of New Orleans which had once been like bacon and eggs to him filled his nose.

"Yeah, I worked for NASA for six years, but with all the federal cuts, my project was canned. Since I have to relocate, I wanted to come home. Something called me."

"That's almost romantic," she said.

"Except it was an actual phone call," he said, with a wry smile. No one had ever accused him of being romantic.

Her laughter tightened something within him. He glanced at her profile. Her nose tilted up, button cute. He liked that. Cute. Like he could drop kisses on it all night. Then and there, he revised his earlier impression. There *was* something sexy about Tess.

"Did you get the job?"

"Not yet, but I have a good shot because I have experience in the field. Years ago I started a company doing what this guy does, plus I got my MBA on top of my engineering degree. But who knows? Felt like the interview went well and the guy's pressed to find someone soon."

"Good for you," she said, tossing him a smile. "Where do you live now?"

"Houston."

"So you'll be transferring here?"

He nodded. "I have some job leads in Houston, but my family lives here. Well, my brother lives on the Northshore, but that's essentially here. You originally a New Orleans's girl?"

"Born and raised. Can't you hear the accent?"

Each region of the Crescent City had its own dialect. "Not from the Westbank or New Orleans East. Uptown?"

"Close enough. My parents still live in Old Metairie."

"I went to Jesuit. You?"

"Country Day." Whoa, swanky, yet Tess didn't give off that vibe.

"Class of '93."

Tess whipped her head around. Obviously the woman excelled in math. "Then why did you tell Angela you took me to Sadie Hawkins in '97?"

He laughed. "Because you didn't look old enough to have gone in 1993."

"So you thought you looked young enough for 1997?" She laughed again. Her laugh was low and raspy. Another thing he liked about her.

"Touché," he conceded as they turned on Decatur Street, skirting the edge of the eclectic, high-rent neighborhood. "So where shall we eat?"

"You have a favorite?"

"I have lots of favorites." And he did. Galatoire's. Dickie Brennan's. Elizabeth's. Irene's. GW Fins. And on and on and on. "Somewhere with a good po'boy? Haven't had good Nawlins bread in forever."

"Central Grocery is closed but we can try Maspero."

"Let's go for it."

She turned her head again and he wondered if she thought he'd meant on some level other than dinner. Maybe he did mean it that way. Things had been so stressful lately with being out of work, depleting his savings and dealing with Monique's demands he'd pulled out of the dating scene months ago. He hadn't been to dinner with a woman in a while…not counting his brother's girlfriend the night before.

What would it hurt?

Tess had nice curves, a good sense of humor and kept baseball stats. Not to mention she'd agreed to go to dinner with a stranger. Many would think her actions dangerous, and maybe to an extent they were, but something about her spontaneity and her self-assurance struck admiration in him. He liked a woman who knew what she wanted, who didn't shrink from the fray, but waded in bold and in control of herself.

She reminded him of his ex-girlfriend Monique in that way—decisive and thoroughly modern. But that's where the comparison ended. Tess had a sweetness and honesty Monique lacked. He patted his breast pocket where he usually put his phone. Thinking of Monique reminded him of their daughter—he needed to call Emily before nine o'clock.

As they got closer to Maspero which sat across from Jackson Brewery, almost on the corner of infamous Jackson Square, the crowds thickened. Tourism reigned supreme in New Orleans. Here and there tourists gawked at street performers while others swigged beers in foam cups and eyed the open storefronts selling offensive T-shirts and Mardi Gras beads.

When they arrived at the restaurant, they found a short line. Graham gave the hostess his name and then motioned to the bar with a raise of his eyebrows.

"Yeah. Abita Amber," Tess shouted, a warm smile curving her mouth.

That smile made him forget all his troubles. He needed to recapture his previous mood. He'd nailed the interview—he'd read that much in the old man's face. Graham had been in the zone, dressed to impress with the knowledge to back up his proposals. Everything in New Orleans was falling in place. Including getting his social life on track.

Stop overthinking and walk toward good things in life, Graham.

He paid and went outside, handing the icy beer to Tess, clinking the bottle with his. "To new beginnings."

"And to your new job."

"I'll drink to that," he said, lifting the bottle to his lips. In that instant he felt something swell in him he hadn't felt in so long, not since he'd left New Orleans six years ago. Maybe it was joy. Or freedom. Or both. He wasn't sure which it was, but he embraced the warmth, that feeling of possibility. All that lay withered inside him revived, swelling to life with sweetness.

After cashing out his 401K last month so Emily could continue going to the Montessori school she'd been attending for the past two years, he needed to feel good about something. To chase hope of a better future and pin it down.

Ten minutes later his name was called and they slid into wooden chairs at a table facing the floor-to-ceiling doors looking out on Toulouse Street. Passersby strolled, collars up against the wind sweeping in with the cool front. A slight draft wafted in but it wasn't enough to keep them from picking up the menu.

"I already know I'm blowing my diet on a shrimp po'boy," Tess said licking her lips, a move that heated his blood.

What would she taste like?

Apples?

Or something spicier perhaps?

"And maybe some gumbo, too. Suddenly I'm starving." She looked up at him.

Yeah. Him, too.

He cleared his throat and tried to tame his desire for her. This wasn't a date…or maybe it was. He wasn't sure what they were doing.

"You don't have to buy my dinner," Tess said, with a little shake of her head. "This isn't really a date."

"It's not?" he asked.

"I don't think so. Maybe it is." She gave a wry twist of her lips. "In all honestly, I don't know why I said I'd go to dinner with you. You're a total stranger."

"It's not that different than meeting someone from a dating website if you think about it. In fact, it's almost like an old-fashioned date. Two people meet, they're attracted to one another, and then they—"

"You're attracted to me?" she asked. A faint pink bloomed in her cheeks and the refreshingly honest question made him like her even more. And he already had a healthy like for her. "Yeah, that sounded sort of middle-schoolish. Been hanging out with my nephews too much."

"Actually I thought it was understood I'm attracted to you. Otherwise I'd be sharing stuffed mushrooms and wings with Angela and the girls."

"Well, good to know. I'm pretty hungry but I'd hate to think this was a mercy date."

"Far from it," he said, unable to contain the desire he had for her.

His salacious gaze didn't put her off. In fact she smiled wider before turning to the waitress.

After they ordered po'boys and a cup of gumbo, a comfortable silence descended. He took the time to study her. Her eyes weren't really the color of moss so much as the color of a magnolia leaf: rich, fertile green. The freckles weren't overly pronounced, merely sprinkled across her rounded cheekbones. She had delicate eyebrows and small earlobes from which winked simple solitaire diamonds.

Tess cleared her throat. "So if this is a *date,* you should tell me more about yourself. I know you went to Jesuit, grew up here and worked for NASA, but what about your… hobbies?"

"Hobbies?"

Tess made a face. "That lame, huh? Guess I have issues with uncomfortable silence."

"Felt like a comfortable silence to me."

"Really? Hmm…" She smiled, opening a package of crackers from the bowl on the table. "Sorry. Should have taken Angela up on the appetizers. I'm starving."

He'd been eyeing the crackers himself, so he mimicked

her. "Me, too, but I didn't want to look like I had no self-control."

"No sense in standing on ceremony. As my nephews say, *YOLO*."

He crooked an eyebrow.

"You Only Live Once," she clarified.

Perfect reason to ignore the flicker of logic edging in on his good time with Tess. YOLO. He liked that. "Okay, a little about me. I read the newspaper every morning, don't have a Facebook account, like dogs over cats, have a seven-year-old daughter and I'm a Scorpio."

"You have a daughter?"

"Somehow I knew that would stand out to you. Yeah, Emily. She's beautiful, smart and can tie her own shoes. Big accomplishment. She lives here in New Orleans with her mother and I don't see her often. Another reason I want to move back."

"Wow, a kid, huh?"

"Deal breaker for you?"

"No, I've just never dated a guy with a kid. Not that we're dating. This is a special circumstance. Or something."

"Or something. But we're going with it, right?"

"Definitely. I'm having fun."

The waitress arrived with their gumbo, and with unspoken agreement they dug in. The gumbo was decent and minutes later both cups were empty.

Graham pushed his bowl to the side. "So tell me about you."

"Nothing special. Graduated from Carnegie-Mellon in industrial art design, work for my dad's company and live in a loft in the Warehouse district. I ride a bike to work most days and I do the *New York Times* crossword puzzle every Sunday even if it takes me until lunch. I don't have children, pets or a lactose intolerance. Big Italian family, no ties to mafia, though my brother likes to infer it."

"The priest?"

"No, the surgeon."

"Accomplished family," he murmured.

"Exactly what my father expects. I'm the baby of the family and the only girl. I have three older brothers who excel at their careers, but I'm the only one who followed in my father's footsteps."

"*Three* older brothers?" He feigned loosening his collar.

She laughed as the waitress set huge po'boys in front of them. "You don't have to worry. They're all my size and busy with families. I see them only at Sunday dinner. Now Granny B, she's the one you should worry about. She once accosted the mailman for being cheeky."

"Cheeky?"

"Yeah, had something to do with Publishers Clearing House and apparently he didn't take Granny B seriously. The woman is a menace."

"But you love her," he said as she crossed herself and then dug into her meal.

"That's required, too," Tess joked, but the warmness in her eyes said differently.

He picked up the sandwich and took a bite. "Oh, mmm."

"Yeah," she agreed wiping cocktail sauce from the corner of her mouth. "I forgot how damn good these are."

Graham couldn't stop thinking about how good it felt to be home…to be with this cool chick. He really liked her casual openness along with the mystery. Tess was like a box his grandfather once had. On the outside simple, smooth lines but once the key turned, the inside held carvings of exquisite beauty.

And he really wanted to open her.

And do bad things to her.

The waitress delivered the check and they both reached for it.

Tess grabbed the small purse she'd hung on the back of the chair. "Let's split, okay?"

"I like to think of myself as a gentleman," he said, reaching for his wallet.

"How are you not a gentleman? Really, I feel more comfortable splitting the check."

"But next time I pay and we do this for real," he said, surprising himself with the offer. But why not? He'd get her number and when he next came to New Orleans—whether it was in a moving truck or merely to visit his family—he'd call her.

"Deal. Next time we dine, I'll wear an LBD and heels."

No clue what LBD was and his face must have given it away.

"Little black dress," she said.

"In the words of Ron, *meow*," he joked.

They smiled at each other, possibility hovering over them.

"Want to have a drink at the Carousel Bar?" she asked. "It's not far."

He thought about his rental car and wondered how safe it was. He'd thankfully purchased rental insurance—this was New Orleans, car theft capital of the South, after all. Then he looked at Tess's lips. She'd swiped them with lip gloss and he caught a whiff of strawberry or something similar. Yeah, he wouldn't mind dessert. "Sure. I'm not ready to go back to my hotel room."

Hotel room. That sort of sat between them.

This time Tess's smile held a secret…and a challenge. "So don't go back. Come with me instead."

CHAPTER THREE

TESS LOOPED HER PURSE STRAP over her shoulder and wondered if it was a good idea to extend the impromptu date. As the person in charge of scheduling the Mardi Gras float rotations, she had a 9:00 a.m. meeting with the art director of Bacchus regarding the 2016 theme. Plus she had to start on the proposal she'd promised Miles Barrow, the captain of Oedipus, too. But, even though Graham had a kid and felt not so much her normal type, she had this crazy, weird connection with him. She couldn't not go. "Let's roll."

They strolled out the door and down Decatur until they reached the street that would take them to the Monteleone Hotel and the infamous bar slowly spinning like a carousel. Through the windows she could see they weren't busy. Monday night wasn't ideal for partying in the Quarter, but New Orleans never felt deserted. The city still moved around them, lights flashing and the streetcar making a run down Canal.

They slid onto stools and ordered cocktails.

"I love this place," she said, turning to him and trying to decide whether she wanted to take him home. It had been a long time since she had no-strings-attached fun with a hot guy.

"Yeah," he commented with a self-deprecating smile. "I'm glad we extended the date. Feels as though we're dancing around—"

"Hooking up?" She smiled, taking a sip of the drink sat before her.

"Is that's what the young kids call it?" His gaze lowered to her lips.

"Oh, please. You're gorgeous and single—don't even pretend you don't take a girl home now and again."

"Me?" He grinned, with a shake of his head. "I'm just a lowly computer-geek-turned-engineer. My idea of a hot night is *Dr. Who* and a pint of Ben and Jerry's."

"Geek?" She snorted, taking in his perfectly tailored suit and frat-boy tie. "Even if you qualified, don't pretend you haven't been thinking about getting into my jeans."

He jerked his gaze to hers. "Into your jeans? I've been thinking about how to get you out of your jeans."

She mocked a shocked expression.

Graham's eyes widened as if he might have gone too far. "I didn't mean to imply—"

Tess laughed before pressing one finger to his lips. "Please imply. I've been pretty much contemplating the same thing. You without that jacket, tie and no doubt plaid boxers."

"I'm wearing boxer briefs," he drawled, his eyes dipping again to her mouth.

"Goodie," she purred with a flirty smile. "I'm not used to hooking up with a guy when I'm this sober."

She hoped like hell he didn't think she was so capricious she'd screw any man who bought her a drink. She wasn't. She expected at least two drinks. Laughing at herself and the sudden case of nerves, she picked up her martini and took a gulp.

"Is this what we're doing? Hooking up?"

Tess glanced over at him. She didn't want to seem too eager. Heck, she still wasn't sure if hooking up with Graham was a good idea. It had only been at Christmas she'd dumped Nick. Maybe she needed to give herself some time…or maybe she needed to have a nice little rebound fling.

Or maybe this was neither of those two things. Maybe this was something more than just fun. Felt that way. Felt like magic. Felt like Graham was her perfect match. "Maybe."

Graham watched her, his Nordic eyes sliding down and dipping briefly at her neckline. "I've wanted you since you told me Feliz was pitching for the Rangers tonight. I think we'd be fantastic together."

Tess leaned toward him. "Wanna find out?"

His lips looked soft. She'd never thought such a thing about a man before, but at that moment she wanted to feel them on hers. Why not see if the tension between them was as electric as she suspected? Why waste time wondering what they could know in seconds?

Graham set down his drink and leaned close to her, pushing an errant strand of hair from the corner of her mouth. "You talking a little chemistry experiment?"

Her breath quickened and her eyes dropped to his mouth. "No sense in taking this any further if we're not... compatible."

Lightly he brushed her lips with his and she caught his taste. Yeasty and warm with beer. Her pulse sped at the first touch, and she leaned in for more.

But Graham was a tease.

He dotted little kisses along her jaw, making her stomach flutter with excitement.

"Oh," she breathed, the warmth spreading as he moved steadily back toward her mouth.

But then he decided to stop teasing and covered her mouth with his, sliding a hand around her neck to clasp the back of her head, tilting her so he could gain better access.

Like rain on the parched earth, Tess welcomed the onslaught of desire. She opened her mouth, only slightly, her tongue flitting out to taste him, evocative and flirty, but Graham tasted rich as expensive wine or fine chocolate. Addictive.

He responded to her invitation and hot desire slammed into her like a midnight train eating up track when his fingers stroked the nape of her neck and his tongue stroked hers.

Tess didn't want to stop, but she did.

Because if she didn't stop now, she might not be able to. Because if she didn't stop now, she might straddle him right there on a stool in the Carousel Bar.

Wouldn't be the first time, but nothing had ever come of any guy she'd hooked up with randomly…and for some reason she didn't want Graham to go down as a guy she'd never meet again. She wanted to wear a little black dress and killer heels she didn't need but had to have because they made her legs look long and lean. She wanted moonlight and champagne…or at least a really good pinot grigio. She didn't want just a one-night stand with Graham.

And that surprised her.

Pulling back, she whispered, "I think I got my answer. You?"

"Oh, yeah. I'm definitely going to need your number." He touched a finger to her nose in a move that should have been corny but was anything but.

"So you want to walk me home?" Her voice was thick… almost seductive, so she cleared her throat.

"Some water," the bartender said, setting down two icy glasses in front of them. "So I ain't gotta call the fire department."

She picked up the glass and toasted the bartender who winked at her before moving on to a guy waving a twenty on the other side.

"He has a point. We can't do that again without charging people admission," Graham said, looking as if the kiss had shaken him down to his wing tips. His smiled at her and picked up his water, a tinge of awe in those blue eyes.

And like a hit of smack, he made her suddenly crave more of him. She wanted to inhale him, taste every square inch and lose herself in something primal and good and irresponsible.

Maybe meeting Graham at Two Legs was a moment-in-time thing. What if there would never be a black dress, nice dinner and moonlight? What if Graham didn't get the job? Never walked back into her world again?

Would she regret the missed chance to immerse herself in him?

Yeah, she would. So...

"When are you leaving?" she asked.

He gulped down the ice water, his strong throat moving as he swallowed. She wanted to kiss him there. Where the pulse beat in his neck, right above the loosened tie. "To-morrow morning."

Indecision.

She hated when she felt this way. Hot and fast? Or slow and...?

"You want another drink?" he asked, nodding toward her half-finished pomegranate martini.

"Not really."

"Oh," he said, sounding disappointed. Grabbing the hand she'd tucked in her lap, he cradled it. Stroking her inner wrist, he contemplated his empty glass. She could tell he didn't want the evening to end...and neither did she.

"Pay for the drinks, Graham," she said.

Hooking an eyebrow, Graham turned to her.

"Unless you don't want me to see you in those boxer briefs?"

Like magic, his wallet appeared. Tossing enough cash to cover the drinks and tip on the bar, he pulled her to her feet. "You sure?"

Tess slid her hand up his lapel, cupping his jaw and dropping a light kiss on his lips. "We're not going to overthink this."

He pulled her toward the door. "Cab?"

"My place isn't far. Let's walk."

"Or run." He spun her into his arms, pressing her against the rough brick, not caring a homeless man slept in the alcove a few yards away.

Tess tugged his head down, her mouth eagerly meeting his. This time she wasn't stingy with opening her mouth and it inflamed her even more. He pressed himself against her, sliding his hands down to her hips in order to pull her against his erection. Warmth turned to frenzied fire.

"Oh," she breathed, her hands knotting in his short wavy hair. "Maybe we better hurry."

He smiled against her.

"Yeah, y'all should," the old bum squawked. "Unless you want a little company."

"No, thanks," Graham called, wrapping an arm around Tess and pulling a five out of his pocket and dropping it in the man's tipped-up hat. "Something for you, sir."

"Not as good as what you're about to get, brother," the man cracked.

"True," Graham called out over his shoulder, not slowing up as they crossed Canal Street. Several blocks later she pulled her keys from her purse, struggling to keep her hands from shaking. Right before she pushed through the front entrance of the building, Graham caught her elbow. "You sure?"

She looked up, surprised he'd try to stop now. "You trying to talk me out of having hot, uncontrollable, slightly dirty sex with you?"

He swallowed, his teeth flashing in the darkness. "That's what's on the menu?"

"It'll be better than the stuffed mushrooms you turned down. I promise." She held the door open with no regret.

"I like your confidence."

GRAHAM ROLLED OVER and glanced at Tess asleep in the moonlight. Long lashes lay against her upper cheeks. The smattering of freckles were more pronounced against her luminous skin. Wild locks of dark gold mixed with light brown caught in the light. She looked so innocent.

And not so much like the hellcat who had pinned him down, taken control and brought him the most excruciatingly pleasurable orgasm he'd ever experienced.

And it wasn't just the skill Tess possessed in bed, it was the passion she plied it with. She'd taken his breath away as she made love to him with both reckless abandon and deliberate focus. Her girl-next-door vibe hid a consummate lover.

Thank God he'd invited her to dinner.

She'd fit him perfectly. The projections and reliefs of her body meeting his in such a way he'd felt like a jigsaw puzzle finally completed. Sounded hokey, but he felt that way. He'd never met someone like Tess—a woman he'd had an immediate connection with. Walking into her world felt like a fate thing.

"Mmm," she groaned snuggling against his body, her lovely breasts brushing his chest as she wound an arm around his lower stomach. "That was *soooo* good."

"Beyond good," he said, pushing a hank of hair from her face.

She opened those gorgeous eyes and blinked sleepily up at him. "I fell asleep. Sorry."

"Why?" he whispered, sliding a hand down to cup her bottom. She arched against him, sliding a leg over his, fitting herself to him and giving him better access.

"I don't want to sleep tonight. I want to make love all night. That was an appetizer. Remember?"

"Right." He pulled her atop him, sighing as she allowed her legs to fall to either side of his hips. With her breasts plumped against his chest and her smiling eyes studying him, he almost believed he could fall in love with a woman in less than twenty-four hours.

Lifting his hips, he teased her with his stirring erection. "Ah, Tess, you might kill me tonight."

"Then we'll die happy." She lowered her mouth to his, dropping tiny kisses against his lips. "I don't want morning to come. Let me have these hours."

He cupped her ass and moved her against him. He wanted to be inside her again. But not yet. Not until he tasted every inch of her. Not until he made her shudder and arch against him. Not until she screamed his name, grabbed the sheets and lost every ounce of sanity she possessed.

He might be a geeky engineer, but he was a determined geeky engineer who prided himself on his attention to detail…and he was about to get it so right with Tess.

Flipping her, he pulled himself back, staring at her in the faint light before dropping his head and tugging her nipple into his mouth. He glanced up as she sighed and closed her eyes. Minutes later after making her writhe beneath him, he slid down her soft belly. "Your appetizer was good, baby."

Her only response was a moan. Graham ducked his head and rained kisses around her belly button. "But I'm hungry for dessert."

"Oh, sweet—" Tess arched against him as he slid lower.

"You taste so good," he murmured, his hands lifting her hips.

Tess's hands slid to his hair, fisting in the depths. "Graham."

He sighed as he lowered his head and dropped kisses

along her hip bone. "I'm so glad I walked into that bar and saw you. It's like getting the sweetest of gifts, Tess."

"Oh, Graham," she begged, wiggling her hips. "Please—"

And so he gave her what she wanted.

BY THE TIME Tess slid from her bed, she'd managed a good hour or two of sleep and that was it. She'd be toast for her meeting, but she had no regrets.

All night, she and Graham had laughed, dreamed and made love on those new sheets, and it had been the most wonderful night of her life.

Seriously.

She'd had lovers—ever since she'd let Justin Hogue go all the way with her the night of her senior prom—but she'd never had one like Graham. She couldn't believe how good they'd been together. Everything he did felt ten times more incredible than with any other guy. Tess had hit the jackpot with the unlikeliest of guys, and it felt a little surreal…and maybe a little scary. Sex had never been so mind-blowing before.

She glanced at the suit folded on the funky polka-dot chair that matched her apple-green duvet and smiled. Buttoned-up, wing-tip boy. Who'd have thought?

Joy bubbled inside her as she walked naked into the bathroom and turned the knobs in the shower. Waiting for the water to heat, she glanced back and found Graham still asleep, sprawled on his stomach, the sheet barely covering his splendid backside.

She stepped into the marbled shower stall and sighed as the hot water coursed down her body. Minutes later she felt two arms slip around her.

"Got room for me?" he murmured in her ear, causing goose bumps to shiver down her length.

She turned, wrapping her arms around his neck and

grinning at him as he brought her body against his. "Always."

"You'll change your tune when I use all your hot water."

"I have a tankless hot water heater. I don't run out." She rocked her hips against his.

"Oh, my naughty Tess. We could have some fun in here, huh?"

Wiggling her eyebrows, Tess turned and handed him the loofah. "Do my back?"

"As long as I can also do your front."

Tess sighed and the shower that normally took her ten minutes stretched into twenty-five.

Finally, wrapped in a fluffy robe, Tess stood cradling a steaming mug of coffee in her kitchen. Graham walked in, towel tucked around his waist.

"When do you leave?" she asked, pulling a carton of eggs from the depths of her mostly empty fridge. If she had some onion and spinach, she could make an omelet. But, alas, only a few cartons of yogurt and a pint of creamer.

"As soon as I take a cab back to my car."

"Don't bother with a cab. Since I have a meeting with a client today, I'm not taking my bike. I can drop you off."

He smiled and something in her chest grew warm. "Damn, I thought I would ride on your handle bars, but I guess since I have to wear my suit…"

"Handle bars? I totally have a basket you could sit in," she joked.

"Hope it's still there."

"The suit or the car?" she said, grabbing a pan from the dish rack.

"Both," he said, sliding his arms around her and dropping a kiss on her ear. "Is it going to sound totally crazy to say this was the best night I've had in forever?"

She leaned back into him. "No. I feel like we've known

each other for longer than a day. It's strange, but I'm loving it."

"Yeah, I'm loving it, too. This feels right. I can't wait to come back to New Orleans. I can't wait to take you out in that black dress and then bring you back here and take it off."

Tess set the eggs and pan on the stove and turned in his arms, lifting on her toes so she could kiss him. "I can't wait for you to come back, either."

Kissing her thoroughly, Graham smiled at her, his blue eyes full with something deeper than she expected. "I'm going to get the job, and then we're going to celebrate. This is a fate thing. I can feel it in my bones."

"You think so?" Tess searched his eyes, afraid they were going too fast. After all, though she knew every inch of his body, she didn't know much else about him. There was no room for talk of something serious, right? Just because they'd fit together so well, just because he'd made her heart gallop, her body sing and her soul shine brighter, didn't mean they were moving toward the *L* word.

No. Tess couldn't allow herself to go over the cliff after one night with a man. That was movie crap. Not real life.

But when she looked at Graham, she could almost believe in love at first sight.

"I know so," he said, kissing her again, taking away any doubts she had about a guy walking into a bar and tying a girl up in ribbons of fate.

Tess pulled herself away and jogged to the bar between the kitchen and living area. Picking up her phone, she handed it to him. "Here. Put your info into my phone. Where's yours? I'll put in mine."

They tapped the info into each other's phones. He handed Tess her phone and she set it on the bar and directed him to the table. "I'm not the greatest of chefs but

I can manage eggs and toast. Then I have to run. I need to go by my office before my meeting at nine o'clock."

"That's fine. I need to get going, too. I'm stopping by Emily's school and I need to hit Houston before rush hour. And you never told me where you work. Is it—"

The harsh shriek of the teakettle going off interrupted him. Tess turned around and snatched it off the burner, accidently touching the hot kettle to her wrist.

"Ow!" She set the kettle on another burner and ran some cold water over her arm. Total klutz…or maybe she was nervous about talking about taking whatever this was to another level…or maybe she was scared it was all too good to be true.

"Let me get ice," he said, scrambling to the freezer.

Thirty minutes and two pieces of burnt toast later, Tess stood outside her apartment dressed in her best go-to-meeting business dress that happened to match the deep pink burn on her wrist. Graham wore his suit, tie stuffed in pocket, shirt open at the neck. His tousled dark hair made him look exactly what he was—a businessman who'd gotten lucky…and not much sleep.

To Tess he looked terrific.

They kissed, a slow, sweet kiss laden with goodbye and tinged with possibility.

"I'll call you soon," he said.

"Good," she said, running a hand along his jaw. "I'll be waiting."

CHAPTER FOUR

A month later

FRANK ULLO SHOVED the lab report from his oncologist's office into the top drawer and spun his chair toward the bulletin boards. Pinned up were various sketches of Mardi Gras floats dated from 1967 to present. Elaborate plans cobbled together into breathtaking beauty. His life's work sprawled across a wall—a reminder of what he'd built and sustained…and what he was about to hand over to the man sitting on the other side of his desk.

Doubt fluttered in his gut before he centered himself. He had to keep emotion out of this decision. Had to remember what he did now was for the best…even if it was a bit chickenshit of him.

Then he touched the photo on his desk as he often did. A tap for luck. In the silver frame smiled three dark-headed teenaged boys and a fierce little girl who snarled at the camera. Frank cherished this particular picture of his other life's work: his children. Each boy stared back at him, intelligent, smirking with their father's Italian temperament. Their chins jutted out with their mother's Irish stubbornness.

And centered in the middle was Therese, his Tess.

His hellion with dark blond hair and eyes blazing a path to the heart. A difficult child, Tess challenged everyone around her as much as she blessed them with her warmth. The girl never took no for an answer and wrapped her older brothers around her proverbial pinky. Tess was never a princess...more like a bruiser in soccer cleats with a crooked hair bow and bandages on her knees. Tess—his sunshine girl with an unceasing passion for all she did.

And he felt very, very sure she would hate his guts for what he was about to do.

He tapped the photo again, making sure it faced him. Then picking up the phone, he dialed Billie. "Hey, ring Therese. I need to talk to her."

Billie gave him her usual monotone. "Whatever you want, Boss."

Frank pressed his hands against the ink blotter and looked across his desk at Graham Naquin, the man he'd hired to become the next chief executive officer of Frank Ullo Float Builders. "This ain't gonna be easy. My vice president of operations don't know about this."

Graham folded his hands across his stomach and squared his chin. He was maybe too handsome for this job, too slick and together. Doubt nickered at Frank, but he squashed it.

"It's never easy for employees to accept change," Graham said. "My coming on board will take some adjustment but I'm determined this will work. I'm a good fit."

"You are. But this employee's a little different because she's my daughter."

Mr. Spit and Polish actually grew green around the gills. "Your daughter—who is the VP of Operations—doesn't know you're hiring me to run the company? Don't you think you should have told her before you hired me?"

Frank didn't like to be questioned, but Graham wasn't altogether wrong in his comment. "Yeah, but I got my reasons. She ain't ready to run a company. I'm not saying she's deadweight or anything. She's good at her job, but she don't have the head for making tough decisions. And let's face it, we still live in a man's world."

Graham's eyes widened and he got kinda choky-looking. Briefly Frank wondered, yet again, if he'd missed the boat on the whole equality thing.

"I'm not sure I feel comfortable with this situation, Frank. You should have been up front about her earlier. I'd rather not start the job with animosity in the workplace. Transparency is always best in business dealings."

Frank shrugged. He couldn't just say "I have cancer and I'm trying to protect my daughter." But that was his main reason. Wasn't like he wanted to hand over the reins of his company to anyone, but in a few days he'd have a stent placed in his ducts to alleviate the jaundice he'd been suffering. Then he'd start weekly chemo treatments to help shrink the tumor and prevent further metastasizing, and that would make him feel like shit. He'd have to rest and stay away from people who could make him sick. The least he could do for his employees and family was to leave the company in capable hands…and Graham Naquin seemed almost too good to be true.

The kid had graduated in mechanical engineering and then started a float company with two others—Upstart thrived and was currently the biggest thorn in Frank's side. Graham could take Frank's company on his broad shoulders and free him from the day-to-day minutiae. And hopefully, the energetic engineer holding a new MBA could revitalize a business mired in its own success.

Frank didn't want to place that burden on his Tess. She already thought she could handle more than she actually could. "I wasn't trying to dupe you, if that's what you're implying. Things are delicate, you see."

"I think there is a lot you're not telling me, Frank, and that worries me. If there is something I need to be aware of, you need to be forthcoming about it. Don't set me up for failure, especially with your family."

"The only one of my children who works here is

Therese, and she's a good girl even if she is headstrong. She's young, you know? But family is more important to her than ruffled feathers. Give her a day or two and she'll see she's not prepared to deal with the business end of this company. Her head's in her art, designing the floats and dazzling the krewes. We all have our talents, right?"

Graham pressed his hands down his thighs, smoothing his trousers, and then refolded them in his lap. Nervous for a man who exuded extreme capability. But Frank would give him being a little nervous. Frank had known this would be hard.

A knock sounded at his office door and Tess stuck her head in. "Hey, you wanted to see me?"

"Come on in, honey," Frank said, motioning her into the room. She wore her customary jeans and T-shirt and a flash of guilt struck at not making the meeting more official, at not giving Tess a chance to get her professional game face on. Another mistake he'd weather.

Graham's eyebrows drew together and he spun around as Tess stepped inside. Frank saw his body go rigid. "Tess?"

Tess's eyes widened and her mouth gaped for a second. "Graham?"

For several seconds they stared at one another in shock.

"Wait, you know each other?" Frank hadn't considered Tess might know the young man he'd chosen to run their family business. Graham had lived in Houston for the past six years, but since the man had grown up in New Orleans, it wasn't impossible. But this seemed more than casual.

Tess ignored his question and closed the door before advancing toward his desk, her gaze crackling. "What are you doing in my father's office?"

Graham stood. "You're Therese?"

"I prefer Tess." She crossed her arms and shot a look from her father to Graham. "Yeah. So back to the original question—what are you doing here? I assumed you didn't—" And then her mouth snapped shut as something altogether different flitted through her gaze. In that moment, Frank realized however his daughter knew Graham, it hadn't ended well. Which meant this situation wasn't going to be slightly uncomfortable. Nope, it was atomic-wedgie uncomfortable.

"I—" Graham made another choked face and shook his head. "You never told me your last name. You put, uh, Two-Legged Tess in my phone."

"Thought it was cute and memorable. Big fail, huh?" she said, voice like poison darts. Even Frank wanted to duck.

He cleared his throat. "Two-legged Tess? What the hell are you two talking about?"

Graham sat like he'd been hit by bad news. "I met your daughter at the bar you recommended to me after the interview. Two-Legged Pete's."

"Wait a sec, *you* told him about Pete's?" Tess asked, her eyes narrowing as something in her head started clicking. Her voice faded as she murmured, "At a job interview."

Her head whipped around, her arms dropped, fists at her sides as she faced the new CEO. "You had a job interview with my dad. A job interview for what?"

Graham sank in the leather chair. Or was it cowered? "Christ, this is crazy. How are you Frank Ullo's daughter?"

"Why are you interviewing for a position I don't know about?"

Both of them directed their gaze toward Frank.

"Okay, okay. Tess, have a seat," he said, gesturing to the chair beside Graham.

"I think I'll stand." She crossed her arms, her chin jutting out. "I don't want to sit for what you're about to tell me because obviously I'm the last to know about what's going down at our *family* company."

"This is exactly the reason I had to make this decision."

Her eyes glittered like icy, cold emeralds that reminded him of his wife Maggie's when she was pissed. "What decision?"

"If you'd sit, I'd tell you. But as usual you're acting like your mother," Frank said, annoyed a simple announcement and introduction could get bogged down in drama before he'd said his piece. But what had he expected from Tess? *Reasonable* wasn't her middle name.

"If it means that much to you, fine." Tess sat. "So what's the deal, Dad?"

"The deal is a change that's been forthcoming here."

"Really?" she said at a near growl. Graham averted his gaze to the sketches on the wall.

"You know I've been talking about retirement in the past several weeks. Now's the time. I wanna pull back and enjoy life with your mother before I cash in my ticket."

Tess said nothing…just stared at him. Frank nearly shifted in his chair, but refrained because he was a man, damn it. He didn't shrink under the disdain of any woman…much less his youngest child who hadn't even reached age thirty yet. Hell, she was still a kid.

"And?" she asked.

"I hired a headhunting company to look for someone who could—"

"You hired a headhunting company?" Tess arched one eyebrow. Frank felt the steam coming off her. She had never been laid-back, but she had a good temperament on most days. Everyone at Ullo liked her. She got what she wanted, but it was because she always leaned on people rather than pushed them. Honeyed words and all that. Still, when crossed, her Irish-Italian temper simmered out of control.

"That's what I said, Therese. These guys go out and find—"

"I *know* what they do. You should have inferred my question to mean *why* not *who*."

Frank had to think about that because he hadn't had a fancy liberal arts education—he'd been raised on the streets and got his business smarts from what had always worked for him. "I hired a headhunter because I can't leave the company with no one to look after it. You need help and your brothers have their own careers."

Tess slapped her hands together. "Perfect. I see where this is going now. You want a *man* to run the company instead of trusting your own flesh and blood. You're just that egotistical and misogynist."

"I don't know those words, but if you think this is because of what you ain't got between your legs, you're wrong." Leave it to Tess to think this was about gender. Okay, maybe ten percent of his reasoning had to do with her being a woman. He wanted Tess to find love, settle down, have some babies—something hard to do running a company like Frank Ullo. But mostly this was about protecting her. She couldn't shoulder the entire burden of this place alone.

Tess had amazing talent and a keen intellect, but she possessed very little business acumen. For the past seven years, ever since she'd graduated and come to work for him, they'd done wonderful things together. Tess had found better materials for their floats, and her clever design work had krewes lining up, willing to pay big bucks for Ullo to design their floats. Frank had handled the business end and thus far it had worked like a well-oiled engine. He didn't see any reason to change things. She had to understand that. "This is about doing what's best for our company."

"How can you say that?" she asked in a small voice. It was as if the anger had dissipated, leaving a shaken shell in its place. Somehow this was worse. Anger he could handle. Hurt? Not so much.

"This ain't personal, baby," he said, leaning forward, keenly aware the PET scan report he'd received from the doctor a week ago sat in the drawer beneath the blotter. It pulsed into his psyche, reminding him how little time he had to settle things...how little time he had to insure his family stayed healthy, wealthy and stable.

"Wrong. It's extremely personal." Tess stared at the family crest ring he'd given her for her college graduation. "More than you even know."

Graham had very wisely stayed out of the fray, but now he looked at Frank, something wavering in his eyes. Briefly, Frank wondered what he didn't know about Graham Naquin...and what the man had meant to his daughter.

"I shouldn't be here for this conversation, Frank," Graham said.

"Of course you should. You're going to be working with Tess. Better to clear the air and get us all on firm ground."

"No, he's right. This is between you and me," Tess said, her voice low. "This is about you not trusting me."

Frank shook his head. "You're being dramatic, Tess. This is—"

"No. You hid this from me because you knew what would happen. Don't act as if you didn't know I'd be upset. You created the drama, Frank."

Frank snapped his fingers. "Don't call me Frank. And this does concern Graham. He'll be working with you."

"As what?"

Frank shrugged, almost too scared to say the words. "Technically, he'll be the chief executive officer. Your job will remain the same. He'll need you to help him—"

"No." Tess slammed her hand on his desk. "I don't accept this."

Frank narrowed his eyes. "You don't have a say."

"The hell I don't. I've worked here all my life. In case you've forgotten, my last name is Ullo. You're skipping over me, your daughter, to hire someone else. I don't accept that."

"This is *my* company. Not yours."

Tess reeled back as if he'd slapped her.

Graham shifted in his chair. "I'm stepping outside."

"Yes, go." Tess jabbed a finger at the door.

Graham ignored her and looked at him. In his eyes, Frank saw frustration and something else that looked like regret. "I'll take a walk and return in half an hour."

"Take a walk off the pier, why don't you?" Tess said, before turning a frosty gaze to her father. No more defeated Tess. This was his pissed-off sunshine girl who had scored the winning goal in the state soccer finals. She didn't know the words *give up*.

Graham didn't take the bait. He merely shook his head and walked out.

The door snicked closed and Tess put her hands over her face. "Why are you doing this, Dad? I've been working so hard to earn… I thought you wanted me in this company. I thought it was understood that I would take over when you retired."

"There are things you don't understand, honey," he said, softening his tone.

"So why didn't you come to me and discuss the issues you had? Instead of doing that, you went behind my back. In fact, you interviewed him on the day I took Granny B to the doctor so you could hide it. I suppose you swore Billie to silence, too?"

"Billie doesn't know everything that goes on in this company."

"Ha." Tess sank back into the chair. "Well, the solution to all this is simple—tell Graham you were wrong. Tell him thanks, but no thanks. I'm totally prepared to run Frank Ullo Float Builders, and you can do a step-down retirement over the next several months. This is what I've been preparing for over the past seven years—an Ullo running *our* company. I'm going to pretend like you didn't say the company belongs to you."

"But it does."

"Technically, but it's ours. Our family's."

"I'm not firing Graham. He signed the contracts this morning."

Her gaze went feral. "What I say doesn't matter?"

Frank closed his eyes. *Knowing* that telling Tess would be hard was way different from actually doing it. He hadn't told his children about his pancreatic cancer diagnosis, except for his son Joseph who'd been his consult during the whole process. Frank still wanted to talk to Maggie about how to handle telling them. Hell, he still hadn't come to terms with the thought of not making it to next Christmas.

But he wouldn't use his illness to make Tess relent. He knew he wasn't the best father in the world, but he'd never resorted to manipulation with his children. He ignored the small voice that said he'd tricked Tess to get his way in the first place. "You matter to me more than you know, but in this instance I will stand firm. You're not ready to run the company. Plain and simple."

"But why? If you knew you were going to retire this soon, you should have brought me in and prepared me. You should have taught me what you do. None of this makes sense. You were always so proud I followed in your footsteps. I just thought…" Tess covered her face again with her hands.

For a few moments neither of them said anything.

"I'm not staying if you hire him." Tess dropped her hands, her gaze resolute.

"So you'll quit?" Frank had never even contemplated the possibility his daughter would leave if he didn't give her the wheel. "Like a child taking her toys and going home, huh?"

"No. I'm not being unreasonable in leaving a place where I have little respect."

"You know that's not true."

"Doesn't feel like it, Dad." Tess swallowed hard. "I refuse to remain where there is no future for me."

"Tess, there's always a place for you here. This is your home, your family."

"No. This isn't how family feels. Instead it feels like I don't matter at all. Feels like you gave me some shell of a job to keep me in New Orleans, to keep me under your control."

Now Frank felt as if he'd been slapped. "You love what you do."

"Yeah, I do. I love this company, but I'm not staying while you wrap it in a bow and give it to some jerk a headhunter found for you. Really, Dad? It's like a frickin' nightmare, that's what this is." She rose. "But that's the way it's going to be. As you pointed out, this is your company and you can do what you want with it, but you might as well have disowned me."

"Don't be unreasonable, Tess."

"Call it what you want, but I don't work here any longer."

"Tess," he said her name like a prayer. Never had he wanted to hurt her. Why couldn't she see that?

Because she didn't know his reasons. She didn't know he had one foot in the grave and the other in quicksand.

"Consider this my notice. I'll finish out the day and gather my stuff."

"Don't do this. You're in the middle of designing for Bacchus and we've got props in bay that need your direction. What about the meetings you have this week? What about our customers?"

Tess shook her head. "Dave will see the designs through, and you now have Graham to figure out the rest."

Like a soldier, his daughter squared her shoulders and marched to the door.

"Tess, don't do this. Everything will be the same as yesterday. I promise. Graham is a good man."

She paused, her hand on the doorknob. "You're wrong, Dad. It'll never be the same again because you don't trust me. Good luck with Graham. In my experience he's not so much a man of his word."

She gave him a sad, sad smile. And then she walked out.

CHAPTER FIVE

TESS STALKED OUT of her father's office feeling like she'd entered a boxing ring with a world champion. One punch and she was out. Her mind couldn't wrap around what had happened moments ago.

How had her Tuesday gone so wrong?

It had started well with new bodywash in her shower, a good coffee from Cuppa Joe's and the sun on her shoulders as she biked through the awakening French Quarter. Fog had burned off the river by the time she'd reached the warehouse, and every line on her sketches that morning had been true. It had been a banner morning that had turned to hell in the blink of an eye.

Graham Naquin.

Bastard. Usurper.

The irony of the man she'd thought her forever guy being the person taking the helm of Ullo was like someone shoving a spoonful of crap into her mouth and expecting her to say "mmm." But this was one spoonful she wasn't going to swallow.

How dare her old man hire him? *Him*. The very person who had almost broken her heart. Okay. *Had* broken her heart. Which sounded strange since she'd known him for such a brief time, yet for a while it had felt every bit as real as what her parents had.

She'd eaten a lot of ice cream trying to get over the false start with Graham. In fact, she'd wolfed down a half gallon in twenty-four hours. That's how much cream and sugar she'd needed to soothe the hurt of rejection.

And now this. She would have to run to California to work off what was likely about to be spooned down in mourning of the thing she loved most about each day—her job.

Dear God, she was no longer employed at Ullo.

As Tess pushed through the metal door into the stairwell, her knees gave way. Sinking against the cold cement steps, she struggled for a breath.

This wasn't happening.

No way.

She was an Ullo. She'd grown up skipping through the phantom floats hulking like huge freighters bobbing at a wharf. Tess had worked summers perfecting sculpting foam, schlepping papier-mâché onto props and wiring fiber optics. She'd taken extensive art lessons, chosen a major in industrial art and ignored the tryouts for the Junior U.S. Soccer team…all so she could work for her family's business. All because she wanted to be the one child who pleased their father by caring more for Frank Ullo Float Builders than for herself. She'd sacrificed so she could do what was right, what would be best for their family business.

And it had been for nothing.

Unshed tears gathered in her throat. She wanted to cry, wanted to lie down right in the dusty stairwell and sob until she ran dry. But she wouldn't give the world the satisfaction of knowing her disappointment. Of the betrayal.

Her father didn't think she was good enough.

"Damn it," she whispered into the air around her.

"Tess." The door opened with a whoosh, nearly nailing her in the shoulder. Billie's head popped into the stairwell.

"Hey," Tess managed to say, hoping like hell the tears in her eyes weren't noticeable.

"What in the name of Sam Hill is going on?" Billie asked, darting a look at the inner recess of her office. "Your father said you quit."

"I did."

"Why?" Billie looked like someone had run over her cat.

"Ask my father."

"Don't you think I did? He buttoned up his lip like a preacher in a whorehouse. Said you no longer wanted to work here and to send a note to Accounting so you could collect your last check. Sister, what's going on?"

"Nothing you need to worry about, Billie. This is between my father and me."

"It has to do with that good-looking guy Frank hired, doesn't it? I knew something was going on when your dad got all secretive, wanting me to show him how to use the fax machine and getting all those calls from Texas."

Tess pulled herself from where she slumped. "Yeah, you're about to be working for that good-looking guy." The words hung in her throat. She didn't want to think about Graham Naquin. She'd spent far too much time thinking about the son of a bitch already. She'd just stopped longing for him. Or mostly stopped moping around waiting for his call.

"Huh?"

"Dad's retiring. Might as well be the first to tell you."

"Retiring? No. He hasn't even made a peep about—"

"Well, he is. Soon."

"I had no idea." Billie's face crinkled as she soaked in the ramifications. "So Frank basically hired this guy over you? His own daughter?"

"You're a sharp cookie." Tess gave Billie a half smile that hurt like hell to deliver.

"Smart cookie. Not sharp," Billie muttered, sadness etched on her face. "I can't believe this, Tess. I'm sure he has a good reason. Something's wrong. I've had this weird feeling. He's been saying strange things, and I wondered what was up. But this?"

"Not a good enough reason. I don't know what's going on, but I'm not about to watch him give Frank Ullo to some asshole."

"He seemed okay to me. Together, polite, nice ass."

"Yeah, well, he's an ass all right. Good luck," Tess said, giving Billie a quick squeeze. Billie had been with her father for forty years so Tess couldn't fathom the woman not knowing about Graham Naquin, the interview and Frank's plans. That her father had kept them from his most trusted assistant boggled the mind. "I'll see you around, 'kay?"

"How? You won't be here. What am I going to do without my Tess? Who's going to make chocolate-oatmeal cookies and post pics of delicious man candy in the ladies' room? How are we going to function without you?" Billie wouldn't let go.

"Just like you did before I worked here."

"Don't do it, honey. It's your pride standing in the way. Pride's a tricky thing." Billie pulled back and looked at her with eyes the color of chocolate chips. She had always reminded Tess of the teapot in *Beauty and the Beast*—if it had a wry sense of humor, a dirty mouth and a way with advice. Billie always seemed to know what to do—but not this time.

This time Tess wouldn't be cajoled into accepting her father's decision. She was many things, but she wasn't a blinking jackass. Her father had gotten his point across with bloody accuracy. He had no faith in Tess, therefore Tess had her back against the wall. It was either give in and hate herself, or quit, get a new job…and gather together the remains of who she was.

"I have to do this, Billie. I'm good. I have to prove that. Not only to Dad, but to myself. I don't need Frank Ullo. Frank Ullo needs me."

"Of course we need you. You know that. Don't go, Tess. Work through this. Change is always hard, but when you come through on the other side, you see it's for the best."

"Hiring someone else is not for the best, Billie. Change or no change. Dad chose a stranger over me, and I got the message loud and clear."

Billie shook her head. "Oh, honey."

Tess jogged down the stairs, heading toward her desk which sat with several others in a sectioned-off area of the warehouse. Tess liked to be near the action—the place where the ideas on paper became full-fledged art ready to roll down the parade route carrying the krewes and the thousands of throws revelers begged for. She'd loved the nook she'd carved out, and though the warehouse often grew noisy, she enjoyed feeling like a cog in the machinery that created magic for millions of people during the four-week Mardi Gras season. She focused better in an area she could move around, a place where she could see her visions carried out.

"Hey, Tess," Dave Wegmann said, spinning in his chair, scratching his balding head. "Reeves Benson called about the Hera bid and wants you to call him back. Thought I'd sneak down here and take a peek at what Petra did with the globe."

"He left a message with you?" Tess asked, trying like hell to pretend today was any other day. No way would she break down in front of Dave. He'd been here for as long as she remembered, first as a sculptor, then he'd moved to painting. After two back surgeries, he'd taken design courses and started working as the art director. Tess had learned all she knew about float building at Dave's knee, and when she'd come to the company, they'd split the load of design, meeting regularly to schedule work and solidify the vision for each krewe's contracted floats.

"Your phone kept ringing and it was driving me crazy.

I'm also looking for the specs on the Cleopatra sea crea-
ture. Upstart's trying to schmooze Cary Presley with some
crazy hydra with motorized heads, so this float's gotta
be stellar."

Any other time and Tess would agree, but she could
hardly speak, much less bolster Dave on the Cleopatra
bid. She sank into the squeaky chair beside the one Dave
sat in and looked at the files and sketches scattering the
surface of her desk.

Where to even start?

"Tess? You okay? You look weird."

"Yeah."

Dave shook his head and hunkered down, his fingers
moving deftly over the face of the calculator, his eyes
screwed up in concentration. "Okay, I found the file. Just…
wanna…see…if…this…matches."

She probably needed to get a box to put her stuff in. She
had funny pictures tacked up on the corkboard beside the
huge filing cabinets that held all the past year's designs
and sketches. Those designs would be systematically replaced over the course of the next few months with new
designs for 2015, paying special attention to the repur-
posing of all the props. At Ullo they reused every part of
the float, even joking about trading out toilet seats yearly.
They begged, bartered and stole from last year's floats to
create the awesomeness of Mardi Gras 2014 for the various krewes around New Orleans and the outlying areas.
A flurry of meetings nearly a month ago before this year's
parades had finished rolling had cemented projects for the
upcoming season and those of 2016.

Tess picked up the bumblebee with the crazy boppy an-
tennae Jules Roland, the head sculptor, had given her on
her birthday. Tess the busy bee.

The clip of hard soles on the concrete floor interrupted
her thoughts. Then she saw the wing tips.

"Tess?"

She looked up, meeting Graham's blue eyes. Damn, they were pretty eyes. Too bad he was a creep.

"What?"

He swallowed and she watched the powerful muscles in his throat convulse. She'd kissed that sweet spot at the base of his neck. He'd smelled so good—sort of citrusy and clean—and he'd tasted salty and warm. Very solid. Very sexy.

"We need to talk."

Dave looked up, tucking his pencil behind his ear. He raised bushy eyebrows. "What's going on? Who's this guy?"

Tess glanced over at her friend and mentor. "You'll understand soon enough, Dave. But don't worry. I've got this."

She stood. "I don't have much to say to you, Mr. Naquin, but what I do have will be better said in private." Ice hung in her words…. Exactly what she intended. Part of her boiled over with anger, hurt and disappointment. The other part felt frigid and empty.

Graham had caused that particular arctic front when he'd never called…and then hadn't been man enough to return the call she'd made two weeks ago.

Total asshole.

She stalked toward the exit, wishing she hadn't worn jeans and sneakers. High heels tapping on the floor would have been much more dramatic. Pushing the bar that would lead to the smokers' lounge high above the rough waters of the Mississippi, Tess inhaled not smoke, but the brackish, fetid air of the river. No one sat on the porch, but she didn't want to be interrupted, so she quickly took the worn steps down to the deck several feet below, now glad she'd worn her tennis shoes.

Reaching the smaller landing holding an ancient pic-

nic table and two chained deck chairs, she spun around.
"You bastard."

Graham stopped by the last step, shifting his gaze toward a tugboat pushing a colossal rusted barge. "I deserve that."

"Yeah, you do."

"I didn't call you."

His words were a day late and a dollar short. Didn't matter anymore. She'd decided twenty minutes ago when she'd seen him sitting in her father's office as the heir apparent she was way over the infatuation that had dominated her thoughts and body for weeks after he left her loft. That ship had sailed. Bye-bye.

"You think this is about you not calling?"

"It was rude."

"It *was* pretty rude. But what did you think I wanted? Commitment? You were a fun screw, that's it. So, no, this isn't about you not calling."

Something in his eyes wavered and she could tell he hadn't expected such a casual dismissal. "A fun screw, huh?"

"For you, too, I imagine. If it were anything more you would have called me, right?" She lifted an eyebrow, feeling the righteousness in her anger.

"About that. See, there were some things going on...." He looked away, hiding from her, but she didn't care. She meant what she said—what she felt—Graham meant nothing to her on that level. He was a used-to-be.

But on a professional level...

"What I have to say to you has nothing to do with that night a month ago. That's over. This is the here and now, and you are the bastard who slinked into my company and stole my job."

"Now, wait a minute." He held up a hand. His was a nice hand—manicured nails, strong blunt fingers, wide palm.

Very capable hands that had stroked her, loved her and made her believe in something that wasn't real. "I didn't slink into anything. In fact, your father never even mentioned you. I had no idea until today that he had a daughter who worked in the company."

Knife wound. Tess clasped her chest before she could think better of betraying her emotions.

Her father hadn't even mentioned her?

"What do you want me to say? Did he mention Dave? Or how about Petra? Jules? Red Jack? Bennie B? Or Scooter O'Neil?"

"No, he went over the departments, but never said he had a daughter who headed up operations. You know I didn't sneak in here trying to steal anything from you. You can be pissed, but you have to be fair."

Jabbing a finger at him, Tess said, "I don't have to be anything. Don't tell me what to do."

Graham slid his hands into his pockets, making his shoulders beneath the poplin dress shirt look amazingly broad. Yeah, she hurt, but she hadn't failed to notice his masculine charms, which pissed her off all over again. "Fine."

For a few seconds they stood, defensive and wary.

Tess sighed. "What do you expect me to say?"

"Nothing. I don't know. It's a hard situation, but right now I don't feel I can take the job." He looked almost like a dog trying to nose the bone her way after he'd already gnawed off the fattest parts.

"Oh, please. Who passes up a job like this?" she said, trying not to hiss at him.

God, please tell me he's not that stupid. Please tell me this isn't some capricious acceptance of a job. She couldn't handle it if he treated it like it was no big deal.

Graham shrugged. "Everything's pretty much ruined.

I can't be your father's pawn in a game I don't even understand."

"Pawn?"

"Well, something's up. Otherwise you would have been in on this from the beginning, right? I don't know why your father has done what he's done, but I'm wading in uncharted waters without a compass."

Tess didn't want to admit he was partly right, didn't want to forget the asshole status she'd assigned him. None of his admissions fixed anything in the world falling apart around her.

"I'm not going to lie. I need this job—it's the best thing that's ever happened to me—but I never slinked in. I never took anything from you. I'm not saying I'm blameless or you shouldn't be angry, but don't paint me as what I'm not. I was a jerk to you, but I did nothing wrong in regard to this job."

"A jerk I can deal with. This? Not so much," she said, turning her head toward the far bank of Algiers Point. She didn't want him to see the cracks in her. Didn't want him to know how much his callous disregard almost a month ago had dinged her pride, had made her wonder why she wasn't good enough for a guy to want as more than just a good time.

Why buy the cow… Her mother's voice echoed inside her head.

Maybe that was Tess's problem—she wanted to be in love, craved the touch of a man who would love her back, so much she plunged in without checking the depth.

In Graham's case the water had been about six inches deep.

Splat.

Graham moved closer, his steps sounding sympathetic, even though Tess knew that was impossible. "Don't," she said, flinging out a hand.

"What?"

"Don't come near me."

He stopped, resting his hands on his hips. "Look, it will be easier for everyone if I dissolve the contract and move on. It's the least I can do in this situation."

Tess snorted. "The least you can do? Whatever. Spare me your sympathy."

"It's not sympathy. I'm trying to do the right thing."

"Well, don't. I'm not working here. My father obviously doesn't value me enough to think I can handle our family business. I won't waste your time with how that makes me feel. He's not giving the job to me so I could give a rat's ass who takes it."

Graham searched her face with shuttered eyes of arctic blue. "I can break the contract."

"No, you can't. My father gets what he wants, and he's never played well when it comes to business. If you quit, he'll sue you, wrap you up in red tape and hire someone else."

Graham swallowed again. Hard. "Surely once I tell him our relationship—"

"Why? We don't have a relationship. It was sex. Meaningless sex. Let's not make it what it isn't. Besides, why would he care? He's a misogynist Italian who could have run the mafia but decided he'd rather screw people legally. Don't let his Hush Puppies shoes fool you. Frank Ullo's a shark."

Graham seemed to think about this. "I still don't feel right though. Doesn't feel good to me."

So now he feels bad? He should have felt bad two weeks ago when she put her heart on the line and called him, when she told him she'd never felt this way about anyone and asked him to call her. That's when he should have been honorable and at least given her the decency of a call.

But she didn't say that. Instead she shrugged. "Too bad.

You're the new boss. Might as well start thinking about who you are and how you want to be perceived by everyone here. He's not going to let you go easily. He doesn't care about 'feelings.'"

Graham shook his head and she could feel his frustration. Welcome to the club, buddy.

"How can I take your job?"

"It wasn't my job. My dad made his point—this is *his* company. Not mine. I suppose your first order of business will be to hire my replacement." Tess stared toward the door. Like a wave heading her way, she could feel the emotion inside her building. She didn't want to stay here any longer with a man who had rejected her as a woman. The man who had taken what she thought to be hers.... A man she still felt an ungodly attraction to even as her world unwound. Tess could pull off the ice-princess routine for only so long.... She was coming undone, and she'd be damned if she did it in front of anyone. Much less him. "See ya around."

She tried to slide quickly by him, but he reached out. "Wait, Tess."

"Please don't touch me," she begged, her voice almost at a whisper. She really couldn't stand the tenderness in his touch. He felt sorry for her. That was all. And something about that hurt more than if he'd been the ruthless son of a bitch she'd wanted to paint him as.

"What can I do to make this right?" he asked, his voice plaintive and so freaking sincere.

"You can't. Only I can make this right by moving on and proving I can be more than daddy's little girl. The best you can do is to take care of this company. There are a lot of good people here and they deserve better than a half-assed job by their new boss."

She wrenched her arm from his grasp and climbed the

steps that would lead her to a place she loved…a place where she no longer belonged.

Quitting had been her choice and it had been one she had to make. Her assumptions had gotten her nothing but wounded pride, but she knew she wasn't part of this business merely because her name was Ullo. She was good at her job. She'd brought in new accounts and the floats she oversaw were detailed and cost-effective. She hadn't done well because her father owned the company…she'd done well because she'd pushed herself to live up to his name.

And now she would take her experience and foresight to a new company. She would show the world—and her father—just how good she was.

"Tess?" Graham's voice carried on the river breeze.

He stood etched hard against the muddy waters and soft emerging spring green of the brush along the riverbank.

"I'm sorry."

Tess lifted her chin. "At least someone is."

CHAPTER SIX

GRAHAM TWISTED THE KEY in the door of the apartment he'd rented two weeks ago and pushed inside.

What a crappy day.

The dim room was hardly welcoming with an old leather couch that had a rip in the arm, a big-screen TV perched on a less than sturdy table and a single flowered armchair donated by his brother's girlfriend. The place looked pathetic, but it would have to do until he could afford some new stuff. Currently, he had bills due and wanted to take Emily camping at the beginning of summer.

The contract he'd signed had given him a nice salary, a large enough expense account and a car. Soon, he'd be back to where he once was, replenishing his meager savings and funding the retirement fund he'd depleted. The severance package NASA had given him had helped buffer the loss he'd taken on the sale of his condo. Damn housing market had tanked and he'd been upside down on the gated executive condo he'd bought five years ago. He'd been relatively smart with his money, thank God, but it still hadn't been enough to weather all the notes and student loans he'd collected over the years. Growing up poor made a man want things and Graham had been no exception—something he regretted when he'd looked at where he'd spent his money.

But this was to be his new start. Landing the Ullo job had been like gravy on the grandest of Thanksgiving dinners. Running a successful multi-million-dollar Mardi

Gras company would take him back to his roots, allow him to use his skill set in a way NASA never had. While the mechanical engineer in him loved the technical aspects of cutting-edge innovation, the artist in him had mourned the loss of pushing past the boundaries creatively.

But now his success tasted like last night's dinner coming back up.

Tess.

When she'd walked into Frank's office, a myriad of emotions had galloped across him, starting with delight and ending in bitter regret.

She was right. He was a bastard.

He reached for the remote, tuned the TV to *Sports Center* merely so he could hear another human voice and then he went to the kitchen to find last night's leftover takeout.

His phone jittered on the bar.

Emily.

His heart brightened.

"Hey, sweetheart," he said.

"Daddy!" she cried, a smile in her voice.

"What are you doing?"

"I had homework today," she said excitedly.

"Wow, you're already doing homework in second grade?"

"Dad," she said, using a teenage voice. "Of course. Most kids don't like homework, but I do."

"That's because you're a smarty pants."

She giggled, and he tucked that laughter into his soul. He'd screwed up a lot of things in life, but Emily had been the one perfect example of how an emotionally infantile man could grow into something better than his own father. Graham had made being a good father a vow.... Another reason he'd been adamant about returning to New Orleans. "I can't wait to come to your house. There's a pool there, right?"

"Yep, and a tennis court."

"I don't know how to play tennis," she said, her voice a little breathless. He could hear the rattle of cabinets in the background.

"Maybe you can take lessons? That would be fun, right?"

"Maybe," she said, chewing something. "I'm not good at sports stuff."

"You don't have to be good. It will be fun just to be out in the sun, moving around." Graham had noticed Emily had started putting on some unhealthy weight. Monique had laughed it off, talking about Christmas cookies and king cake, but Graham suspected Emily was left too often to her own devices after school, snacking and sitting in front of the TV glued to the Disney channel. Being here would give him a better handle on her health…a better handle on building a stronger relationship with his daughter. "Where's your mom?"

"She's with Josh. They're in a meeting or something. I'm in her office. I did my homework and now I'm eating a snack and watching *Saved by the Bell*."

Saved by the Bell?

"It's an old show. Mom said she watched it when she was little. Isn't that funny?"

"Yeah, princess, it is. Look, I'm going to pick you up on Thursday, okay?"

"Cool," she said, her attention waning, most likely caught by the campy sitcom. He thought he heard the sound of Screech's voice.

"Tell your mom to call me later, okay?"

"Mmm-hmm."

"Emily? What did I just say?"

"Uh—" She paused. "I don't remember."

"Tell your mother to call me."

"Oh, right. Bye, Daddy," Emily said, still distracted, but

Graham would take it. He loved every minute of hearing her breathless little girl voice. Something about her innocence buffered the guilt floating inside him...made his day not so crappy if only for a few minutes.

God, he wanted to do better by her.

And he would.

"Bye, pumpkin," he said before pressing the end button. Tossing the phone on the counter, he sighed and wiped a hand over his face. He had to get his shit together. That's what a good father did.

He had to be there physically for Emily, picking her up from after school care, spending weekends proving he wasn't the same as his old man. He wouldn't chase sparkly things or shirk his duty to his child. Emily was the reason Graham couldn't bow out of Ullo.

It had been so long since he'd felt confident about who he was. He'd gotten a taste of it that night exactly a month ago when he'd met Tess. That night, he'd been the man he'd once been—the man who had not only dreamed but made things happen. The man who hadn't failed with Monique, who had never been laid off, who had never paid a bill late, who had never taken medicine to pull himself out of depression. That magical night had given him a piece of himself back, cracking open the door to a new tomorrow.

But then he'd slammed it closed out of fear. Out of embarrassment of who he'd become. Yeah, it was a stupid reason to toss a chance for happiness with Tess away, but something inside him had balked about coming to her with so little to offer.

Panic had grabbed him by the throat. No matter how well he'd presented himself in his pressed suit and expensive shoes, buying drinks like he had a bankroll in his pocket, he'd known he'd been a facade of the man he'd once been.

All he could think about was his father with frayed cuffs

and a shitty-ass excuse for why he couldn't afford to pay school fees. He'd looked in his bathroom mirror and seen the man who'd failed so often, who'd cared so little he'd rather take his life than get a job beneath him and show his sons how real success worked. The fear of turning into that man ate at him and convinced him to wait to call Tess until he was in a better place.

"Shit," he said to no one...because no one was there. Story of his life. "Ah, you're pathetic. You effed up with Tess. Game over."

His words echoed in the apartment and as he looked at the Chinese takeout box in his hand, he felt anger wash over him. So he lived in shitty circumstances now, and he'd blown any chance he had with a woman who had made him feel the way he hadn't felt in years—whole.

But it was a new day. A new beginning. He had a job, a challenge and a daughter who needed him. No time for feeling sorry for himself.

He was Graham Naquin—over-educated, nearer to forty than thirty and possessing all his teeth.

He was in it to win it.

The world was his oyster.

He would kick ass and take names.

Because he refused to be the man who'd raised him. He might have been down, but he wasn't out.

Graham Naquin was a fighter.

TESS SIPPED THE lukewarm café au lait and studied Gigi who glowered like a jail warden.

"Draw unemployment," she said, her red eyebrows drawn together.

"No. I don't want unemployment. I'm getting another job." Tess stared at her computer, trying to figure how best to position the experience she had. It was damn hard writing a resume with a single company as your only employer.

"Where?" Gigi pushed her tight red curls off her face and sucked on the straw of her iced tea. Gigi hated coffee but loved Cuppa Joe's with its bright red couches and black lacquered tables. Soft '80s rock flowed through the speakers and modern art displayed at irregular angles decked the walls. It had a cool, comfy vibe, so they met here as regularly for Wi-Fi and coffee as they did at Two-Legged Pete's for drinks with more kick.

"Not sure. I love design work and haven't been able to do as much of it for the past few years because I've been working with clients. Maybe I'll freelance."

Gigi snapped her fingers. "Didn't your father say this dude started a Mardi Gras float company way back when?"

"No, Graham told me the company he interviewed for was something he'd done before.... Wait, uh, maybe he did say he started a company, but I haven't a clue which one. There are a lot of smaller ones."

"Give me that," Gigi said, tugging Tess's laptop toward her. "Let's see what we can find on him."

Tess scooted her chair closer, wondering why she hadn't already done that. She often used social media to scan the guys she dated, but Graham had said he wasn't on Facebook.

Gigi typed away like a flame-tipped woodpecker on crack as Tess sipped her coffee and looked around at the world still turning even though hers had crashed that afternoon. How could people still laugh, still make jokes, still flirt across the room? Didn't her sadness permeate their happy, shiny faces?

"Bingo!" Gigi crowed, sitting back with a smile. "You're never going to believe this one."

Tess tipped the computer so she could see the screen. "Holy crap. Upstart?"

"Yeah, that's crazy, huh?"

Tess reeled with the news. Upstart, run by the effervescent Monique Dryden, had grown to become Frank Ullo's staunchest competition…and Graham Naquin had been one of the founders?

Gigi started reading. "Monique Dryden started Upstart Floatmakers in 2003 with her partners Graham Naquin and Josh Laborde when the three post-grad students, on a whim, created a sci-fi float for the Krewe of Vader, a satirical sci-fi fantasy krewe started by Jimmie Ray Dietzel. The three friends' collaboration led to a passionate venture—" Gigi wiggled her eyebrows "—which united a film student, an engineer and an art history graduate in like purpose. Building their floats using high-tech materials, cutting-edge light displays and fuel-efficient design has vaulted the 'Little Engine That Could' into the big leagues in float design."

Gigi stopped reading out loud and skimmed the article, her lips moving as fast as her blue eyes. "Wow, he sold his interest in the company and moved to Houston to work for NASA."

Tess looked away. She didn't want to know any more. Something about Graham having a relationship with Monique Dryden made the coffee curdle in her stomach. She'd met Monique many times at fundraisers and the occasional Mardi Gras ball and had found the vivacious brunette to be smart and gorgeous. She'd always made Tess feel a giantess next to her dark, diminutive beauty.

"All this is pretty interesting…almost coincidental," Gigi said. "You sure he didn't know who you were? This smells funny."

"He didn't. I never gave him my last name, and obviously my father didn't care to mention his daughter Tess frequents Two-Legged Pete's and takes home random hot guys. Graham didn't have any more of a clue than I did. I'm certain about that. Besides, how would it have benefited him? My dad didn't tell me what was going on."

Gigi stared out the window at the world moving by in the late afternoon light. "Know what you should do?"

"I'm scared to ask," Tess joked, trying to forget she was devastated, trying to find what little humor she had left after cleaning out her desk and passing her key to Billie.

"You should talk to Monique Dryden about a job. Bet she would love to sink her teeth into you." Gigi gave a sharky lawyer grin.

Tess made a face. "That would be...I don't know...too weird. Plus, it's doubtful she has an opening."

"Don't know until you ask, do you? And how awesome would that be? You'd totally teach your dad and Mr. Fancy Pants Naquin a lesson."

"But it's—" Tess rooted around for the right word "—treason. I'll stick with trying freelance design or something. I can't work at a rival company."

"Why not? It's a job. Your father screwed you, and Graham Naquin literally screwed you. Don't play the victim. Turn the tables on them."

Gigi didn't understand family the way Tess did. Her best friend's parents had split in a bitter, contested divorce rendering their only daughter a bone to be fought over. Finally after winning joint custody, Gigi's father moved to California and pretty much forgot about the daughter "he loved beyond himself." The whole messy affair had left Gigi cynical.

"I'm not you, Gigi. Ullo is part of my family and I can't hurt my family."

Gigi just stared at her for a good ten seconds. Censure, and maybe disappointment that Tess wasn't jumping to get revenge on her father and Graham, clearly visible on her face.

Seriously, how could Tess work for the company that had given Frank Ullo the most competition over the past two years? Sounded too in-your-face for Tess's taste.

Then again, Gigi wasn't totally off base. Working for Upstart would be a great way to prove to her father he'd made a colossal mistake, and Tess could prove to herself she could make it in this business without her father's name. Would it really be so evil?

The hurt, bitter part of her said *no*. And the tied-to-her-family, devoted part of her screamed *yes*.

But loyalty to family went both ways, didn't it?

Her father hadn't felt compelled to keep it all in the family…so why should she?

Self-doubt gathered inside Tess. What if everything she thought she'd been was a lie? What if she wasn't as good at designing floats or hustling krewes as she assumed she was? What if everyone else had pulled Tess's weight, winking at each other over the boss's daughter's incompetence? What if she sucked?

Tess glanced at the computer. Hell, she couldn't even write a resume. What was the difference between freelancing float designs and anchoring a desk at another company? Not much.

"Maybe it wouldn't hurt to drop by Upstart with a re-sume…if I can get the stupid thing finished," Tess said, gulping the last of her coffee, wishing she didn't even have to think about resumes, family loyalty or the fact she forgot to grab her favorite water bottle out of the company fridge. She couldn't think past the hurt…and Gigi wasn't helping by planting the seeds of rebellion within her.

Gigi smiled, obviously pleased Tess considered her diabolical plan for revenge. Blood in the water excited her, made her hungry rather than faint. "Bold, ballsy and very Tess-like."

"What?"

Gigi shrugged. "We're friends for a reason. You might smile and laugh more than I do, but we both have an innate need for justice, for righting wrong and bringing balance to the world. And we do what it takes."

Is that what taking a job with another Mardi Gras float builder would be? Righting a wrong? Didn't feel that way, but Tess did want to prove everything she'd done as an executive in her father's company wasn't because she was an Ullo but rather because she was good at it. She trampled the self-doubt and thought about how satisfactory it would be to work for the company Graham had abandoned. There was something deliciously wicked about turning that screw…a sort of flagrant "suck it, big boy."

"You're right. I'm ballsy and I right wrongs. I should have a cape."

Gigi laughed. "Get a green one. Matches your eyes."

Tess rolled those green eyes. "Besides, a job is a job, and right now I need one. So I better get this resume finished so I can pound the pavement tomorrow. Hmm…never had to do that before. I'm liking the challenge of having to really earn my way. Is that crazy?"

"No. It's normal. There are very few people who have a job waiting on them when they graduate from college." Gigi shoved her glass aside and rummaged through her purse. "Hurry and finish. I want to get to The Columns for happy hour. I need a date for a company party and I want to hit up the after business crowd before they go home to their Labradors."

"Or wives."

Gigi pulled a lipstick from her purse and made a face.

The last thing Tess wanted to do was go to a bar, even as nice as The Columns was. She wanted to go home, eat some comfort food, watch *Seinfeld* re-runs and sulk about the shit sandwich life had handed her. No, not life. Her father and, to a degree, Graham. Okay, in fairness, Graham had only hurt her feelings when he hadn't called like he said he would…and being awarded her job didn't help matters. But, hey, she was Gigi's wingman just like Gigi was for her. Maybe after an hour she could leave. "Fine, but I have to go by FedEx first. No more free copies for me."

Gigi gave a humorless laugh. "Like the rest of us."

"Whatever," Tess said, wondering why her friend saw her as different merely because she'd worked for her family. Did that make her privileged? Lazy? Entitled? She had never thought so because she'd worked hard, but maybe the world thought her life had been too easy. And maybe it had been. Maybe being truly on her own would be good for her.

But her heart told her differently.

She'd loved who she was three days ago. Well, except for Graham's knock to her ego. But even that she'd gotten over. Mostly. Her life had been gravy…and now it was soured wine.

"Put on lip gloss and brush your hair. Don't forget you're available, too. Wouldn't hurt to find a little something-something to take your mind off tall, dark and deceitful."

"My mind was never on him," Tess lied.

Gigi gave her *that look,* the one that plowed through the bullshit. "You actually used the line 'I found *the* one' after that night with Graham Naquin. He was on your mind."

"I had forgotten about him until today." She lied again because it was easier that way.

"Whatever you say, hunny bunny. He's a job stealer anyway."

"Technically he didn't steal my job. According to Papa Dearest it was never mine to begin with."

"So you say. Still, it's time to find someone who will make you feel better."

A man instead of ice cream? It *would* be better for her thighs, although she didn't want a man at present. Better to stay home and get her shit together…but there was that whole loyalty thing.

Tess shooed Gigi away. "Go fix your makeup or something. I can't think while you're nipping at me. I need to put the finishing touches on this resume before I can go out with you."

Gigi huffed, but did as suggested, flouncing away, sliding a smile at a cute guy in a Brooks Brothers suit and pink tie. Tess refocused on her resume, wishing it looked a little fuller. But she was who she was.

And who was that?

She'd thought she knew. She'd been beloved daughter, tolerated sister, good friend and devoted VP of operations in the family company…but now?

Tess felt like she'd been dropped into a maze. Every turn presented a barrier. No job. No man. Anger at her father…and Graham. Self-doubt. She'd never had such barriers that required her to backtrack or climb over hurdles to reach her goal.

But Tess knew something about herself—she may have lived a charmed life, but she wasn't going to lie down and flop about, bemoaning her state. She'd find a new job even if it meant going to the competition. Nothing wrong with a modern woman taking control of her life, leaving conventions behind.

And maybe she'd even get a new man…or not.

All she did know was that Graham needed to be a memory, and Frank Ullo needed to learn his daughter wasn't a doormat.

Plugging the flash drive into the computer, Tess downloaded her resume and renewed her determination to prove to the world she could kick ass and take names.

Tess Ullo was a fighter.

CHAPTER SEVEN

GRAHAM PULLED UP to the curb in front of the house in which he'd once lived. Looked the same. Felt different.

The Orleans brick with the intentional plaster smears and the beige stucco had once seemed so modern, so very much "them." But now it looked pretty much like what it was—a new townhouse in a decent area of Metairie, crowded in like the others. Pansies lined the sidewalk. Graham only knew they were pansies because he'd planted the same flowers in that spot years ago. He wondered if Josh planted them now.

The door opened and Emily flew outside, dark pigtails flying, smile as wide as sunshine.

"Daddy!" she screamed, her sneakers slapping against the sidewalk.

Graham scooped her up, squeezing tight. Two chubby arms curled around him. "Hey, pumpkin. Jeez, you've grown a foot since I last saw you."

Emily tilted her head and grinned, one tooth missing. "I've been taking vitamins."

"Oh? That's the reason?" He gave his daughter one last squeeze and lifted his head to see Monique approaching. "Hey."

She gave him a cool smile…as always. "Hey. As you can see she's beyond ready for dinner with Daddy Graham."

Daddy Graham?

"Yeah," Emily said, waving a five-dollar bill. "Daddy

Josh gave me some money for the arcade. I'm gonna play skee ball."

"Daddy Josh?"

Monique brushed manicured fingernails across an imaginary horizon. "That's what Em calls Josh. Easier that way."

"Really?" Graham said, eyeing his former fiancée, wondering whether this new term had come from ease or a vindictive way to twist a fork in Graham. Monique enjoyed creating drama. It's what made her brilliant as an artist... and nearly impossible for Graham to live with.

She lifted a shoulder and gave him a half smile. "For Emily."

"What's wrong?" Emily asked, her forehead crinkling as she glanced at him. Her brown eyes looked worried even as her rounded cheeks were flushed with excitement.

"Nothing, sweetheart," Graham said, giving Monique the "we'll talk about this later" look. "Let's get going."

"I don't have to sit in a booster anymore," Emily said, eyeing the sedan Ullo had delivered to him that morning. "I'm big now."

Emily had grown in the past four months. She'd always been such a tiny girl with brown velvet hair and fluffy fairy skirts. As a mature seven-year-old, she wore a T-shirt with silvery looking stuff on it and trendy teenager-looking jeans. Her sneakers had sequins on them, and the hair bow was noticeably absent. A small glittery purse hung at her side.

But he had no idea if she needed a booster seat or not—another mark against him as a father. He'd never thought to check that kind of stuff. Monique had always handed him the car seat or the diaper bag or the medicine. He didn't even know the pediatrician's name anymore.

This was why he'd had to come back to New Orleans. This was why he'd had to ignore the ignoble feeling within him when he'd found out about Tess yesterday and make himself indispensable to Frank Ullo and his company.

"So you're the new Frank Ullo, huh? Never even crossed my mind something like this could happen," Monique said, eyeing the Toyota Avalon before lifting her gaze to him. "Highly ironic you're working for my competition. It's almost Machiavellian."

"It wasn't intentional," he said, opening the rear door. Emily climbed in, looking around the leather interior, poking at buttons. "I told you as much when we talked last month. It's a perfect opportunity for me, doing something I'm good at. It puts me back in New Orleans. Back in Emily's life as her father. Her only father."

Monique narrowed her dark eyes. "Feels like you're punishing me. Upstart was yours, too, at one time, and you're making this personal when it's not. You'll take food from the mouth of your child, merely so you can look good."

"You really believe everything is about you, don't you, Monique?" The dislike he had for Monique would forever overshadow the passion they'd shared. She always held a piece of herself back, setting barriers she protected with a crushing disregard for others. She was a faucet, hot or cold, but never both together.

Her gaze was frosty…but wasn't it always now? "Tell yourself that, Graham, but anyone can see the writing on the wall."

"This isn't revenge, Monique. It's about a job. Not allegiance. In case you didn't get the memo, I need this… and I can't return to Upstart, now can I?"

Her bitter laugh was answer enough.

"Exactly." He closed the door and faced his ex. Monique didn't step back as he crowded her slightly. No, not Monique. Small, delicate with dark arched eyebrows, a bowed mouth and wavy hair, Monique was a fiery ballbuster. Even as Graham despised her for what she'd done to him, he admired her ability to stand her ground...all five feet one inch of it. "This isn't war, so don't don the armor."

"I'll do whatever I wish to do, Graham."

"Of course you will, but I'm asking, for all of our sakes, don't make this personal. There is plenty of business for both Ullo and Upstart."

"You didn't used to feel that way," she murmured, an almost savage look in her eye. "You hated Frank Ullo. You hated that he controlled the market and squashed smaller businesses trying to take a piece of the pie. That's changed now because he signs your paycheck?"

"Upstart is no longer in the position it once was. Frank Ullo isn't, either. You know that." He wanted to get out of there before he and Monique started shrieking at each other on the street. Dealing with her had become more and more contentious in the past two months...ever since she learned he intended to come home to New Orleans. Monique liked having control and the agreement they had over Emily would change.

Josh walked out wearing a pair of dark jeans and a weirdly patterned shirt with a hot pink tab collar. Tall, lanky with a soul patch on his chin, Graham's former best friend had a wicked sense of humor, a badass restored Harley and a shitty sense of loyalty to a friendship started back at Jesuit. He'd been too weak to resist Monique... probably still was.

"Hey, Monique, we gotta jet," he called, not even meeting Graham's gaze.

Irritation flashed in Monique's eyes. "We'll go when I'm ready, Josh."

Emily knocked against the window, pressing her button nose against the glass smudging it. Graham smiled and nodded, dangling the keys.

"We're going to head out, Monique. Text me when

you're through with your fundraiser and I'll bring Emily back. I'm guessing it won't be too late since it's a school night?" Graham started around the front of the car.

"I'm not finished talking about this, Graham," Monique said, smoothing the lines of a dress that was too short, but still looked incredible on her. Monique's beauty had never been in question. Even as slight as the woman was, her essence screamed "lush" and "sensual." It was her heart he questioned. As determined as she was to create an empire she could control, she had one fatal flaw—her ego. Often Monique valued her own worth above the truth. This inability to see the writing on the wall was the main reason Graham didn't fight for Upstart. Well, that and the fact Monique and Josh had started sneaking around sleeping together.

"Well, I'm finished discussing this. Everything will work better if you shut down whatever you're working up inside yourself about me running Frank Ullo. I'm not competing with you. I'm trying to take care of Emily."

"You could have done that with another company. You could have done that from Houston."

"But I didn't want to," he said, before sliding into the car. "Don't forget to text me."

Shutting the door, he shut out the dissonance Monique always created in his life, and instead focused his attention on the only reason he'd done Monique and Josh a favor tonight—the bouncing, wonderful Emily. "Ready to roll, squirt?"

"Can we go to the pet store and see the kitties?" she asked, ignoring his question.

Graham pulled away from the curb, unable to resist glancing at Monique who stared angrily after them. He wished he didn't get satisfaction in needling her. He'd have to be very careful to keep the fragile peace between them for his daughter's sake. Wouldn't be easy because Monique had never been easygoing or amiable to anyone's opinion but her own. Once he'd teased her, calling her his little general, but now that moniker wasn't teasing. "Fasten your seatbelt, Em," he said, slowing and pulling to the curb.

"I want a kitty, but mommy says 'absolutely no.'" Emily clicked her belt into place, and though the child looked big enough for the seat, Graham made a mental note to check the laws regarding child safety and cars.

"Well, pets are a big commitment, Emily," Graham said, pulling out and winding his way toward Veterans Avenue so he could take Emily to dinner and the arcade.

"I'm old enough. I can pour out its food, get it water and take care of it when it's scared."

"What about poop? You think you can scoop out a litter box? What about the vet? Pets cost money."

"I have some money. Grandy Pete gave me ten dollars last week for dusting his room and brushing Pumpkin, his big ol' cat."

Grandy Pete was Monique's irascible grandfather. Graham couldn't imagine the older man caring for a cat much less a little girl—the man had spent much of his life on the bayou, shucking oysters and shrimping. He now lived in an apartment behind a convent in the Lower Garden District, a place between Upstart headquarters and Monique's digs in Metairie. Graham had helped him find the place and move in, something that had proven easy since the eighty-year-old man had exactly two trunks of clothing, a guitar and a memory foam pillow. Colorful only halfway described Pete. "It will take more than ten dollars, Em. But we'll talk to Mom about the possibility of a pet."

"I can keep Muffin at your house," she said, brown eyes peeping over the gray leather seat.

"Muffin? Oh, no. I see your game here, missy." He laughed, deciding it felt good. The past few days had been tense, and he needed the lightness his daughter gave him. "And sit back in your seat."

"Please," she wheedled, sinking back as instructed. "She can keep you company when I'm not there."

"I don't need company." *At least not that of a cat.*

"Yeah, you do. You need a kitty."

"Wrong."

Emily crossed her arms and gave him a look that was all her mother. "I knew you'd say no. Just like Mommy."

Something inside him moved. He wished it hadn't. He wished he didn't have such guilt where Emily was concerned, but he'd missed so much in moving to Houston and going to work for NASA. At the time it had felt best for all concerned—best for him, certainly—but he'd left the raising of his daughter to Monique, being Daddy only in the summers and on a rare holiday. "How about a truce?"

"What's that?"

"It means you walk my way, and I'll walk yours. We'll meet in the middle."

Emily made a face. "We're in the car."

"It's a metaphor."

"Huh?"

He laughed. "Never mind. I have an idea. There used to be a place by a supermarket that sold fish. How about an aquarium for your room at my townhouse? Do you like fish?"

"Not as much as kitties," she said.

"We'll start with fish and see how you do then we'll work up to something fluffy with claws."

"Like Nemo?"

Turning off busy Veteran's Highway into the parking lot housing a specialty aquarium store, Graham decided an aquarium was something he could handle. Not sure how much company fish would be, but he needed things to fill up space in his near-empty apartment. And maybe he could find an actual person one day, too. He'd wanted to move forward in his life, and that meant not spending his nights alone.

Tess's face popped into his thoughts making him feel both guilty and lustful at the same time—a hard to accomplish feat but Graham obviously had that particular talent.

He should have called. But what would that have changed? Might have made it worse instead of better when he'd discovered who she was...when she'd discovered who he was and for what job he'd interviewed.

Too late to worry about it.

Fate had handed him his cards and he could play only what was in hand.

"I want three fish," Emily said, unfastening her belt as soon as he shifted the car into Park.

"Let's get four," he said.

"Cool," his daughter said, bouncing on the backseat, reminding him the present was where he dwelled. No time for past mistakes—over Tess, Monique or his failure as a father—to haunt him.

He had fish to buy.

FRANK ULLO WATCHED his wife as she rolled out the pasta, hands moving deftly as they'd done many times before, knowing the right texture, careful not to add too much oil or too much flour. Making perfection as she did each Sunday.

"I love to watch you make the cannoli," he said, sliding slowly toward her, mindful of the dressing on his side. The stint placement hadn't been bad, but he was still tired and tender. Wrapping an arm around her waist, he laid his head on her shoulder.

Maggie's deep sigh seeped into him much like the sadness that had permeated their life over the past two months. It had all started with the jaundice and stomach pain. Frank had thought it was an ulcer, but the medicine his internist prescribed hadn't touched it. It was then he'd contacted a headhunter. Somehow he'd known the prognosis wasn't good. He'd known he needed help. Not an easy thing for a man like him.

"You never watched me make cannoli before," she said, her hands never ceasing as she rolled the edges between her fingers and thumb, but she tilted her head so it rested upon his.

"Meh, I never stopped to see things before. Knowing death has caught hold of you by the neck changes what you see in life."

"Shush, Frank, don't say things like that. I hate when you talk about dying. You're not dying. We're fighting this."

He didn't have the words to protest. Maggie had set her foot down, defying the reaper to touch him. She was a tough opponent. Old Grim didn't realize what he was up against.

"The kids will be here in half an hour. Frank, Jr. is never late." Frank looked around the place his wife felt most comfortable in. Maggie had returned the emerald earrings he'd given her for their thirtieth wedding anniversary, taking the money to an appliance center and custom ordering the huge Viking range. He'd laughed because he could never convince his Maggie she was worthy of jewels...not when she'd rather be barefoot and making his grandmother's red sauce. Maggie may be as Irish as the Blarney Stone, but she cooked like she was a fifth-generation Italian.

"Tess is coming," Maggie murmured, picking up the sharp knife and cutting the dough.

"It's Easter," he said with a shrug. "Family is family."

"She's angry and hurt, and rightly so."

Frank stepped away, picking up the flour and sealing

it into the large storage container, helping Maggie where he could. But he had no words to say regarding Tess. His youngest had been difficult from the moment she'd entered the world, screaming and impossible to console. As wonderful as Tess was, nothing was easy with her. From her being allergic to disposable diapers, formula and gluten to her choosiness over schools, clothes and hair bows, Tess overwhelmed any space she occupied.

"You have to talk to her, Frank. You have to make her go back to work for the company."

He shook his head. "No. I'm not doing that, Maggie. Tess molds everyone to her, arranging her life so it fits her needs, her demands. She hasn't had much set against her and I think it would be a mistake to fix this for her. She needs to understand my side of this. She needs to see I'm not doing this capriciously or with any intention other than doing what is best for the company."

"She's your daughter." Maggie turned and prodded him with her gaze. They'd had this same conversation over and over in the past week, but Frank wasn't easily moved. On this he would stand firm.

He knew to some degree he'd failed Tess. His only girl, his last baby, she'd gotten all the petting and doting he'd held back from his boys. Whatever Tess wanted, Frank made sure she got. He'd been so proud when she'd declared she'd follow in his footsteps, even as he worried about her ability to handle a business like Frank Ullo. Tess thought she could handle everything thrown at her. Thing was, life hadn't thrown much at her. She'd lived a golden existence, and as Frank thought about his company and his daughter, he could see his child had never been tested in any way.

Tess needed to learn more than what he could give her. She had to be challenged, had to live outside of the bubble she'd been so safely ensconced within.

Maybe he was wrong. Maybe he was playing God, testing his daughter much like God had tested Job.

But he knew his Tess. She would not only survive, she would thrive.

"Yes, she is my daughter, and so I know she will make her way."

"Make her way? Frank, she's a hard worker and loves the company. Sure, she's young, but you should have made her the CEO and hired this fellow to work for her."

"I know what the company needs, Maggie. Trust me on this—it's the right thing. The rubber is meeting the road and time will tell us where we go. You understand?"

His wife of forty-five years shook her head. "You're a stubborn goat."

"Like my daughter…and my sons."

"I don't see this as you do, but I will trust you. I have always trusted you. But tread softly, Frankie. These are strange times for us."

He sighed. "Times I don't wish on my enemy, but this is what we're left with, Maggie."

"Are you going to tell them about the cancer today? Tell them about the operation this past week?"

"It's the wrong time. People want to feel joy at Easter."

"It's always the wrong time," Maggie said, turning to the bowl containing the mascarpone cheese, stirring with a furrow between her lovely green eyes. Maggie meant business when she cooked for the family. "But you don't have much more time. Next week you'll start the chemotherapy. We've already hidden all the tests, and I don't know how we managed that as nosy as this family is."

"Easy to do when your kids are busy living." Frank looked out the window at his shady backyard. Everything bloomed—the huge azaleas clustered around the sprawling live oak anchoring the landscape. A beautiful waterscape tumbled water over the stones mined from a quarry in

Arkansas. Birds darted through the canopy and the world looked soft and beautiful…as if something as ugly as cancer couldn't exist.

And it made Frank angry.

Why had this happened to him? Why now? At the end of his life when things should be simple…when he deserved to sink into his recliner and put his feet up?

He'd worked so hard his whole life, pouring blood, sweat and tears into creating something worthwhile, something good. He'd come from humble beginnings, born the year after the U.S. entered World War II, his father dying that same year in the Pacific. He'd been raised by a working single mother who married a man who drank hard and hit harder. Eventually, Frank dropped out of high school and went to work sweeping a warehouse owned by a celebrated early float maker. Soon after he put down his broom and learned how to build the floats rolling for some of the earliest parades like Comus and then Rex.

Years later after a stint in the army, Frank returned and bought a warehouse with his savings and a loan from Maggie's father. He'd started Frank Ullo Float Builders, and because he loved what he did, it had grown into the international business it was today. Finally, he'd been thinking about taking it easy, traveling to Italy for the summer, duck-hunting with his sons and watching his grandkids play soccer every Saturday morning.

Irony bit a man in the ass sometimes.

A sound at the door told him his reverie must end.

"Papa Frank?" Max bellowed, feet slapping the wood floors as the five-year-old headed for the kitchen.

Frank spun as Maggie wiped her hands on her apron. "Sugar, I told you about running in the house."

Their grandson skidded to a halt in front of his grandmother who smiled through her fussing. "Sorry, Gee, but look what the Easter Bunny put in my basket." He waved a lacrosse stick in the air.

"Jeez, Max. Put that down before you break something," Frank Jr. said, entering the kitchen, snatching the stick from his youngest son's grasp and dropping a brusque kiss on his father's cheek then turning to Maggie. "Happy Easter, parents."

Maggie started the hugging and kissing as Max's older brothers poured in, looking for snacks before dinner. Finally Frank Jr.'s wife, Laurie, stumbled in with a casserole dish and a tired smile.

Frank watched this part of his family, soaking in every detail, brushing away any annoyance he'd normally feel at the boys tussling over the remote or snitching too much chocolate from the candy dish. Then Joseph arrived with his quiet wife and even quieter twin girls. Michael showed up with a bottle of Cabernet and an Easter lily for his mother. And finally, Tess rushed in to good-natured ribbing from her older brothers about being late as usual.

Frank's mother, Bella, plodded in behind his daughter, sharp-eyed and grumpy about being late to dinner.

"She shows up ten minutes late. Ten minutes I had to listen to Ira Messamer complain about his damned gout. I didn't know a man could whine so much about swollen feet."

Tess, dressed in trim pants and a cotton shirt that hugged her figure, rolled her eyes. "I told you I had to stop for rolls. You said it was okay."

"A little late, you said," Bella, otherwise known as Granny B, muttered. "Not a whole ten minutes."

Tess looked at Maggie with a tight smile. "Next time see if Frankie can pick up Granny B. Please."

Granny B shot a look at Tess. "Mind your manners, missy. I'm not too old to take you over my knee."

"Yeah, you are," Tess said.

Frank almost laughed, except his mother would swat at him, so he kept his mouth shut. Tess glanced at him, but quickly averted her eyes. The frostiness told him all he needed to know about where he stood with his daughter. Far away. Perhaps even across the ocean.

"I get no respect, especially from her," Granny B said, jabbing a finger at Tess, even as something in her dark eyes sparked with admiration. Granny B thought the sun rose and set with her Tess…not that she'd ever let on. Tough as a cornstalk and soft as a brick, Isabella Ullo hadn't stayed long with a man who hit her or her son. She'd left Mick MacDougall two years after she'd married him, going to work at the Bon Sucre hotel, catering to the elite of society. She'd stayed for forty years before moving to a small retirement community in the Garden District.

Tess snorted. "You're being difficult, Granny B, because you can. Ten minutes isn't late."

"Have you ever met Ira Messamer?" Granny B cracked lifting the lid on the sauce, smelling it critically. "Too much garlic, Maggie."

"You know she can't have garlic, Mom," Tess said with an evil gleam in her eye, "for the same reason I have to carry around a silver stake and have her at the home before sunset."

"Hah," Granny B said, "I wouldn't suck your blood if you paid me in cash. Probably half vodka anyway."

The women all laughed, and Frank sank into the moment—typical teasing Sunday banter between the women in his family. How many more of these would he have? He wasn't sure. The doctors had been blunt—his cancer would move fast. The chemo he'd start next week would only slow the inevitable—there was a sliver of a chance he'd survive longer than six months.

So he sat in the middle of his family stocking up the images in his mind, piling them into a suitcase in his memory, carefully arranging them so when the pain came, the sickness overwhelmed, he could unlock the sound of Max's laughter, the curve of Maggie's cheek, the way Joseph tried to count Tess's freckles. Tears filled his eyes and he quickly turned his head, refusing to sully even one second of this day.

He'd tell them about his cancer another day—a day that wasn't about resurrection and new beginnings.

No, he wanted today full of sunshine…full of love.

And it might happen even if he'd invited Graham Naquin for coffee and dessert.

CHAPTER EIGHT

TESS SAT AT THE TABLE with her family and tried to pretend this Easter Sunday was like every other one that had gone before—full of deviled eggs, impromptu egg hunts and at least one chocolate bunny ear. She was pretty good at talking a niece or nephew into sharing.

But it wasn't the same.

Anger and betrayal made her mother's sauce taste of ashes. Hurt laced even the green-bean casserole bland Beth had thrown together...if such a thing were even possible. Not Beth's being bland—which she probably couldn't help, being married to Joseph—but the whole green-bean casserole tasting like tears.

Same old smiles, same old jokes, same old china filled with food Tess's mother and sisters-in-law had slaved over. She should be enjoying the home-cooked meal rather than picking at the jicama-and-shrimp salad and poking at the ziti.

The frustration over what her father had done had stitched itself inside her and refused to be undone. Not that Tess wanted it undone. In one way she liked what the soreness gave her—a hunger she'd never had before, a need to prove herself. Even admitting she craved the challenge, however, Tess couldn't erase the deep hurt at her father not believing in her. His failure to hand her the keys had knocked a hole in her she couldn't see filling anytime soon.

"Cat got your tongue, Tess?" Michael asked, his dark eyes studying her over the frames of his glasses. Father

Michael Ullo read people who didn't want to be read—a talent he put to use often. In this case Tess knew her mother had told him what had happened. Michael knew why she was quieter than normal, but for some reason wouldn't let her get away with it.

"Just enjoying Mom's cooking as usual," she said, chasing a noodle around her plate with her fork.

Michael took another sip of wine. "Yeah, I see. Ravenous, aren't you?"

Tess tossed him the "shut the hell up" look. As usual, Michael ignored her. God forgive her, but Father Michael could be super annoying.

"Might as well get everything out in the air before dessert, Therese," Frankie, Jr. said, taking a butter knife away from Max before he could saw a flower from the arrangement her mother had put together. "Kid table next year."

"Me or Max?" Tess cracked.

"Both?" Frankie deadpanned.

"Let it drop before you ruin today, Frankie," Tess said, watching her brothers exchange looks. They'd always treated her like their child rather than their sister. Tess had been the ultimate surprise to her aging mother and father, throwing off the whole balance of the family when she'd arrived nine years after Michael, the youngest brother.

"We can't have every Sunday like this," Joseph complained, giving Beth a knowing look. As a neurosurgeon, Joseph usually took a backseat to his brazen older brother who chewed up district attorneys every week as a highly sought-after defense attorney. Michael always held his own—the white collar did wonders for respect in their Irish-Italian Catholic family.

Tess glared at her brothers, pissed they'd waited until everyone was held hostage by her mother's red sauce to bring up the rift between her and her father. "We're going to do this now?"

Frankie Jr. shrugged. "We're all here."

Tess's father cleared his throat and everyone stopped fidgeting and slurping their tea. "We ain't doing nothing to destroy this day, boys. Leave your sister alone. What happened between me and her is business, not of concern to the family."

Tess lowered her head. She wasn't sure if it was because she was so angry at his words or relieved she wouldn't have to slug it out over Easter dinner. Lifting her head, she stared defiantly at a cream-colored camellia in the flower arrangement.

"Feels like it's more than business, Dad," Joseph said, tossing down his napkin. "It's damned uncomfortable is what it is."

"Well, it's not your concern. Tess is my daughter. I'm her father. Nothing changes that." Frank set down his fork. He hadn't eaten much, either, which was very unlike him.

Granny B's sharp eyes took in all that went on at the table. "What's he talking about? Of course she's his daughter. Stubborn enough, isn't she?"

Maggie inhaled and blew out a sigh. "Everyone looks ready for dessert. Who wants cannoli?"

Tess ignored her mother, jerking her gaze to meet her father's. "He's right. Nothing changes that." Tossing her napkin down, she scooped up her plate and headed toward the kitchen.

Maggie followed, picking up the empty roll basket. Tess knew her mother hated conflict at the table, but could do nothing. Her stupid brothers were responsible for the discomfort.

The older nephews and twin nieces sat at the kids' table in the kitchen and all turned wearing guilty expressions, when she and Maggie entered the kitchen.

Maggie took one look at the uncovered plate of cannoli

sitting on the granite counter and jabbed a finger at Conner. "I told you to stay out of the dessert."

Conner wiped the cheese from the corner of his mouth. "I love you, Gee."

"Flattery will get you another cannoli," Maggie said, rolling her eyes, but softening. The woman was a sucker for her grandchildren. "Sorry, Tess. I told Joseph not to say anything. You know how he hates everything wrinkled."

"Well, too damn bad," Tess said, scraping her plate into the trash. Joseph's twin girls, Margaret Ann and Meghan, gasped. "Sorry, girls."

Conner and Holden grinned, obviously enjoying the strong language—a family argument couldn't compare to middle school where naughty language wasn't so much colorful as the norm. Tess wasn't so old she didn't remember how an eighth grader rolled.

"He's trying to smooth out wrinkles in a world that's not his. He chose to be a doctor. Frankie chose to be a lawyer. And maybe God chose Michael, I don't know, but none of them are involved in the company outside of hanging out in our float stand during parades or showing up at an occasional ball, so they aren't involved in this."

"They're members of this family, and that is enough."

Tess set the plate in the sink and winced as it clattered against a soaking pot. "Dad said this isn't about the family."

"You and I both know differently." Her mother shot a frown at Holden, who wiped his mouth with the back of his hand. "Napkin, Holden."

Holden and Conner rose in silent communication, grabbed a few cannoli and headed out to the yard.

"This isn't the time or the place, Mom," Tess said, tossing her hair over her shoulder, eyeing the two girls watching them with rapt attention.

"You're just like him. That's the problem."

Tess opened her mouth to deny her mother's declaration, but the doorbell rang.

Maggie made a face. "Who could that be?"

Tess shrugged. The family was there, so had to be a neighbor or a friend dropping by.

"Girls, help Auntie Tess with the dessert. I'll see who's here and find out who wants coffee and cannoli." Maggie tucked her fading auburn hair behind her ears and headed toward the foyer.

Margaret Ann and Meghan cleared the table before coming to stand beside the stove. Tess located the serving spoon and uncovered the other plate of cannoli, eying the chocolate and pistachio coating. Her appetite hid behind the cold wall between her and her father, but surely she could summon enough enthusiasm to have her mother's Easter cannoli?

She'd just started serving when she heard his voice.

His voice.

Graham Naquin.

The spoon clattered to the tiled floor. "Shit."

Margaret Ann blinked at her.

"Yeah, I know, Margaret Ann. It's a bad word, but, baby, trust me. It fits the situation."

"Oh," her niece said, glancing at her sister whose eyes were wider than normal.

Not like Tess could explain that the guy she'd fallen at least a one-fourth in love with, had amazing sex with and lost a job to had shown up at her family's Easter dinner. Using the obscenity was mild compared to what she wanted to do, which was barge into the dining room and call him a no-good bastard. But this wasn't a soap opera, so she picked up the spoon and tossed it in the sink.

"Why?" This from Meghan.

"Huh?" Tess swiped at the tile floor with a paper towel, removing the crumbs.

"The reason you said *shit*," Meghan persisted.

"Shh!" Tess said, slapping a hand over Meghan's mouth and looking around for Beth. "Don't repeat that word. Ever."

Margaret Ann wrinkled her brow. "So why does it fit the situation?"

"Have you ever had a best friend who you thought was super cool, but then she kicked dirt in your face and went off to play with someone else?"

Meghan peeled Tess's hand from her mouth. "Kay-Kay didn't kick dirt but she did dump my bubbles out."

"Well, that's what this is like. Kind of." Tess eyed the hall leading to the dining room and tried to decipher the hum of conversation coming from there. She couldn't hear exactly what was being said, but the vibe seemed congenial.

Pinching her cheeks and rubbing her bare lips together, Tess tossed her hair and scooped up two plates of cannoli. "Later, gators."

"We wanna see the mean girl," Meghan said.

"It's not a girl," Tess whispered, wishing she could hold a finger up to her lips and shush the chatty eight-year-olds. "It's a man."

"Ohh," Margaret Ann said, her eyes growing wide. She gave an excited smile to her sister. "It's a boy...which is kind of gross and kind of interesting."

"Shh," Tess said again before throwing back her shoulders and sashaying into the dining room.... At least she thought it was a sashay. She'd never taken dance. Interfered with soccer.

Everyone turned and stared. Imaginary crickets chirped.

"I have cannoli," she trilled with a fake smile plastered on her face.

"Us, too," one of the twins said.

Tess set a plate in front of Michael and then one in her

own place. Sinking into her chair, she refused to look at the man standing beside her father. Refused. Picking up a fork she cut into the crisp pastry with the sinful filling. "Mmm…this is fabulous, Mom."

Michael stared at his plate and tossed Tess a questioning look. She could feel the guilt emanating off her family. Why did they feel guilty? Wasn't their fault her father had invited the enemy into the fold.

"Thank you, honey," Maggie said, shifting eyes to her husband then to Tess. Getting no help, she rose. "And who else would like some dessert?"

A few murmured responses met her mother's inquiry. Then silence fell again, hard and loud.

After several stretched minutes, Frankie Jr. cleared his throat. "So, Graham, would you care for some coffee?"

Frankie Jr. What a nice boy. So mannerly for a shark. So hospitable toward the man who had screwed his sister then not bothered to call her like he'd said he would. So welcoming to the man who would take over the family business. Did Frankie even know he extended the hand of politeness to the wolf who would eat them?

"No, thanks," Graham said. Everyone's attention was on him. But not Tess's. She was busy pretending Graham wasn't intruding on her family Easter dinner.

Why in the hell was he here anyway? Why on God's green earth had her father invited him to a family meal? If she didn't know her father better, she'd think it was designed to rub her nose in the mess he'd made of their relationship. But while her father was many things, he wasn't a total bastard. No way he invited Graham to needle her. He had other reasons.

Silence sat among them. Even Joseph, impeccable surgeon able to withstand excruciating ten-hour surgeries with a steady hand, squirmed in his chair.

Finally Beth smiled. "So, Graham. Frank told us you have a daughter who is close to our girls' age."

Not a question but an invitation.

"Emily. She's seven and with her mother today. I'm actually on my way over to her house to take Em her Easter basket. Frank asked me to stop by and meet his wife. I had no idea the entire family would be here. I hate to interrupt. Sorry."

His words were softly spoken, like an apology meant for Tess. But instead of soothing her, they made her angry. She didn't need his damn pity. If her father wanted Graham here for their family get-together and if he wanted Graham to take over their family business, fine. Tess had no say. If she had, she wouldn't be stabbing her cannoli, trying not to launch herself on the floor and pitch a temper tantrum the way Max had at the last family dinner.

Self-control—hadn't she told Graham it wasn't her strong suit? So he'd been forewarned if she launched herself at him and clawed his eyes out.

Her anger must have crackled because Michael picked up the knife nearest her hand and moved it. Tess glared at him and he shrugged.

"So you're the fellow who stole Tess's job?" Granny B piped up, tackling the cannoli one of the twins had set in front of her.

Tess shot Granny B a fierce look designed to zip lips, but, of course, Granny B didn't give a flying fig whom she offended. Never had.

"No, ma'am. I didn't steal anything," Graham said, nodding his thanks at Joseph who had so thoughtfully brought him a chair.

"Frank gave you control of his business, control of the empire he built from a scrap of nothing into something that paid for this house, my house and a trip to Italy last year. He trusts you. He gave you what he'd give a son."

"But not a daughter," Tess said before she could stop herself. Setting down her fork, she glanced at her father. He looked miserable. Good. And ironically, Graham sat to his right, also looking miserable. Doubly good.

"Tess," her father breathed, shaking his head. "Let's not do this now. I invited Graham over for coffee and dessert last week, before our kerfuffle. This is not the time or place."

"Kerfuffle? Right," she said. "You ready to go, Granny B?"

"Nope," the older woman said, picking up a piece of cannoli and popping it into her mouth. "This is like watching *The Young and the Restless*...only better."

"Mother." Frank cast a cautionary glance to his mother.

"Frank," she replied in the same voice, pursing her lips, a vicious gleam in her eyes. "You set this in motion. Did you think your daughter would let it slide? She's a good girl, but she's an Ullo."

Tess pushed away from the table. She couldn't do this anymore. "Mikey, take Granny B home for me, 'kay?"

For a priest, Michael knew enough about a woman not to make a fuss when she meant business. He nodded and went back to his dessert as if it were more important than saving sinners.

Tess didn't bother saying goodbye. She walked toward the living room where she'd left her purse, her sandaled feet soft on the carpet—yet another time when she could have used the angry staccato of heels to drive her point home. Damn it.

Scooping up her clutch, she headed for the door. She shouldn't have come. Should have faked a stomachache. The pain was too raw, the betrayal too recent for her to put on a smiling face and play happy family. But she'd wanted to be with her brothers and mother. Not her father—she'd planned to pretend he wasn't there, but that hadn't worked. Not when Graham had showed up looking fresh, handsome and ready to be the golden boy he obviously was.

"Tess?"

Stopping on the wide porch, she spun toward Graham who stood framed in the open doorway of her parents' home. "Don't, Graham."

"Tess, please. I didn't know you'd be here. Truly."

"Doesn't matter," she said turning toward the driveway crowded with a BMW, a Mercedes and Michael's priest mobile, aka a black Caddy. Her small Prius looked out of place…a true representation of who she was among her talented, over-accomplished brothers. Tess: quirky, trendy and socially conscious. But not successful and stable enough. Is that what her father saw when he looked at her?

No substance? Not smart enough to rise to the top? No penis?

She'd never thought so before, but now she didn't have a clue how anyone saw her. Hell, she wasn't sure how she saw herself.

Walking quickly toward her car, Tess caught sight of Graham's ride sitting at the curb. A little salt rubbed in her wound.

Reaching her car, she pulled open the door, but Graham's hand slammed it closed. "Damn it, Tess. Stop. Please."

"Move, Graham."

"No," he said, shaking his head, his blue eyes intense, apologetic and riled all at the same time. He wore a polo shirt and a well-worn pair of jeans. The blue stripes in the shirt made his eyes look brighter and his shoulders broader. Tess wished she hadn't noticed. And the scent of his cologne tickled her nose, making her long to inhale and savor his unique smell. Instead she concentrated on a scar on his forearm.

"I didn't come here for this."

"So why did you come?"

"Your father asked me to dinner, wanted me to meet your mother. I refused the family meal, but told him I'd stop by for dessert."

Tess snorted.

"Do you think I would come if I knew you were here?" he asked.

She arched an eyebrow. "It's Easter, Graham. Where did you think I'd be?"

"I don't know, but I'm not stupid. I'm not trying to cause you pain."

"You're not that important to me. You could be anyone who took over Ullo. You don't matter to me. My anger is directed at my father."

"And me."

Tess tugged on the handle, but Graham still held the door shut. "Fine. I'm pissed at you. You're a bastard, not just because you happen to be the person my father hired over me, but because you aren't a man of your word."

Graham sighed and with his other hand he brushed back the dark hair falling into his eyes. "I really liked you, Tess."

"I could tell. Enough to screw but not enough to—"

"You're wrong."

"Don't think so. You never proved any differently, and I got the message." Tess looked pointedly at Graham's hand flat against the window. "If you wouldn't mind taking your hand away, I really want to get the hell out of here. I'm tired of thinking about you, that night and…everything. So move."

"Tess." His voice was raw, full of emotion.

Her heart ached. But only for a second. "There's no need for any more words. You've apologized…. I just can't accept that apology right now. Things are too shitty. Or maybe I'm too immature to be the bigger person. I don't know, but I do know I want to leave. Now."

"I wish things were different," he said, lifting his gaze to hers. In his eyes she saw the regret and it gave her a flicker of understanding. "I wasn't ready to offer someone a relationship. I wish you understood that it wasn't you, it was—"

"Me? Yeah, I've heard that one. Might have even used it a time or two myself. Truth is you didn't want me enough to fight through all that stuff." She hardened herself against the self-pity that thought inspired. "What happened was a one-time thing—just another one-night stand with some guy in a moment of weakness."

"No, it wasn't," he said, pulling his hand away. "You can tell yourself that. I can tell myself that. But we both know it wasn't."

"Yeah?" she asked, pulling open the car door. "But here's the question. If this—" she swished her hand back and forth between them "—wasn't sitting between us, would you ever have called?"

He stood silently for several seconds. "Yes. I had every intention of calling you, and I would have been prepared to grovel at your feet for forgiveness for my bad behavior."

Inside Tess the tangle of emotion that had been knotting for the last several hours rolled over, crushing even her anger for a moment. She wanted to believe him. Wanted to push aside the wall between them for a moment, so they could go back to being just a girl and just a guy who had found a piece of magic on a rain-dampened night. But—

"Too late," she said softly sliding into her car and starting the engine. For some reason tears pricked her eyes and her throat tightened with emotion.

Pulling the door shut, she buckled up, put the car in Reverse and eased out, peering over the other parked cars on the shady street.

She no longer had the luxury of looking backward.
Only forward.
There were new paths to blaze and new men to love.
If only she could believe her own decree.

CHAPTER NINE

STANDING IN THE Ullos' driveway, Graham watched Tess drive away.

She hated him.

Fine.

She didn't forgive him and she likely never would.

Fine.

What more could he do?

Quit. The inner voice sounded like an echo, like something whispered to a character in a movie, carried on a breeze in the misty gloom of evening.

But this wasn't a movie and the sun bearing down on his shoulders reminded him where he stood. In the glaring now.

Trudging toward the Ullo home, solid stone and stucco with massive columns and a message of "Somebody with power lives here," Graham decided he had to move forward. Though quitting would send Tess a message, it would put him in the poorhouse. Living paycheck to paycheck reminded him he didn't have the luxury of playing the martyr. No amount of self-sacrifice would appease Tess. She would need time to temper her opinion of him and even that might not be enough.

He'd hurt her.

Not just by taking the job Frank offered, but by not calling. Taking the job had merely pissed her off. Anger on top of hurt was never a good look on a woman...and he couldn't blame her.

Shaking his head, he closed his eyes before entering the discomfort he'd left a moment ago. He'd tried to convince himself what he'd shared with Tess that night was run-of-the-mill. Seemed a rational thing to do. Treat it like every other one-night stand he'd ever had. Tess was a random hookup—a nice one—but nothing ever amounted to anything with hookups. He'd even convinced himself she wouldn't care whether he called her back or not. But he'd fooled himself. It was easier than facing the truth.

Graham was on a short trip to becoming his father, a man who'd had so much potential but had thrown away his dream over pride. He'd left New Orleans, spent too much and lived too recklessly, all to soothe his ego…and had paid the price when he'd opened his wallet and found it empty.

Tess didn't date losers like Graham. She deserved better. So he hadn't called her.

Doubt whirled in him and the bitter feeling of failure pecked at his psyche. Sadly, he'd grown accustomed to feeling that way over the last few months, and it would be hard to repair things between him and the only person who'd made him forget his failures for one night.

It was, as Tess said, too late.

"Hey," the door opened and the priest stood there. Michael. "Is Tess gone?"

"Yeah," Graham said, trying to clear his throat of the knot sitting within.

Michael narrowed eyes that looked just like his father's. "Something more is going on here."

Graham shook his head but didn't argue. He didn't particularly like the idea of being struck by lightning or having a piano dropped on his head for lying to a priest.

"Yeah, I know Tess, and I can see right through this thing. You knew her before you took her job?"

"Look," Graham said, aggravation rising to replace the sadness in his gut. "I didn't take anyone's job…except maybe your father's. I had nothing to do with what happened between Tess and Frank."

"You had a little to do with it, but I'm not talking about that. I'm talking about something else. I know Tess."

"So you've said," Graham muttered, jerking his head toward the entrance of the house. "Shall we?"

"What?"

"Go back inside? I need to make my exit and thank your mother for the, ah, coffee."

"You never drank it," Michael said dryly.

Graham gave him a flat stare, somewhat liking the man despite his acerbic and prying comments.

"I'm watching you," Michael said, doing that double-finger jab at his eyes and then turning them to jab at Graham.

"Better mind my p's and q's then." Graham didn't try to keep the sarcasm from his voice.

"You better. The big guy is on my side."

Graham snorted. "God?"

"No, Eddie 'the shark' Russo. He's about 6'4" and cracks skulls for a living. Friend from my bookie days." Michael smiled, but Graham wasn't sure if the man was kidding or not. Where was the pious man of the cloth? Michael almost looked like a shark himself. Guess when it came to protecting little sisters from jerks like himself all bets were off.

"Right," Graham said, slipping by the man who came to his nose in height but didn't budge from his original stance. Entering the house, Graham headed directly for the dining room.

Everyone's head swiveled toward him when he reentered the dining room...except for the old bird with the naughty gleam in her faded eyes. She was digging into her dessert with a relish reserved for those under the age of ten and over the age of eighty.

"I'm sorry," he said, not sure he offered the apology for the whole craptastic debacle or for following Tess without asking their pardon.

Frank stood with a wince. "Actually I'm the one who should apologize. Making this change in my business has cast a pall on my family. Unintended, but there it is all the same. Things have been difficult lately." Shooting an inscrutable glance at his wife, Frank gestured to the chair Graham had abandoned earlier.

"Understood, and I apologize for my role in this difficult process. I had looked forward to meeting you, Mrs. Ullo, but I feel it would be better if I go ahead and take my leave."

"Oh, don't do that," Mrs. Ullo said, trying on a smile. Something around her mouth trembled, making Graham wonder if there was more to Frank's words than what had been revealed. "Call me Maggie. And please, have a little coffee. Maybe a cannoli?"

"I thank you, but no. I want to spend some extra time with my daughter today, and Monique's not patient."

"I find it odd you had a relationship with Monique Dryden," Joseph said, setting his napkin beside his plate. "But Dad told us it's one of the main reasons why he hired you."

"Because of Monique?" Graham cast a searching look toward Frank.

"Not because you share a child and not because I'm trying to take a jab at her. She's a talented woman if not a thorn in my paw. Monique's smart."

"That I can't deny. She was always the brains behind the operation. I was merely the brawn who stumbled into her world and became enraptured with Mardi Gras and building the floats. For a while it was enough."

Everyone at the table, the five-year-old included, watched him as if he'd dug up a rock, revealing what was beneath…and that was what his relationship with Monique had turned into—something crawly and dark. Something he didn't like exposing to the light of day.

"So I'll say goodbye. I wish you all a Happy Easter," Graham said, wanting desperately to do much as Tess had—get the hell out of there.

A chorus of byes met his ears as he turned toward the exit. Frank joined him on his walk to the front door. Michael had disappeared and the heavy wood door stood cracked open, allowing daylight to slash inside the darkness.

"Look, Graham. I'm sorry about Tess. Her reaction, or rather her actions, have nothing to do with you. Wouldn't matter who I had hired, the result would be the same. She's young and doesn't understand the ways of a man or the ways of the world."

"Perhaps she doesn't understand because you haven't told her why you hired me," Graham said, his voice falling like raindrops on a flat rock.

For a moment Frank stared at him. "You don't know me or my daughter."

"Perhaps not, but from the beginning you've mishandled this. You knew she thought she would be the next CEO of Frank Ullo, but you still proceeded to hire an outsider. That makes me wonder about your reasons."

"Wonder away. I did what I thought best for the company and Tess," Frank said, his heavy eyebrows drawn together. "If that's mishandling, then so be it."

"Just my opinion, but I daresay it's one your family shares." Graham paused for a moment, trying to find the words he needed to drive his point home. "Look, this job is my dream job—I can admit that. But I took it with the expectation you and I would work together for a few months, and then once I earned your full confidence, I could take the helm. My goal was clear—bring Frank Ullo back into focus with new technology and cutting-edge design. But I can't do that if our relationship demands I measure my every word. I won't always agree with you, and this matter is a personal one, but it's also a situation that spills over. Your mishandling of Tess affects your employees and affects how they see me and deal with me."

"My employees understand. Trust me."

Graham sighed. "I've been there for four days and you're wrong. They know you're Frank Ullo, but their loyalty is to the company and Tess was part of that. Do you know how many times this week I've heard 'Tess handles that' or 'Tess knows where the info on that account is'?"

"She's worked there since she got out of college. It's going to be hard to not have her, but we'll manage. Change is hard, right? Never was going to be easy to do this." Frank pulled open the door. Laughter filled the air and Graham caught sight of a teen running with a lacrosse stick and two girls about Emily's age chasing him. He recognized one as the girl who had brought in the cannoli with Tess. Squeals and shrieks followed as a small boy chased the girls with a water gun. Frank watched with a hungry look on his face.

At that moment, something reverberated within Graham. And he knew, absolutely knew, what had been going on for the last month. A careful study of Frank's face—the circles under his eyes, the sallowness of his skin, was all it took to get a clearer picture.

"Are you sick, Frank?"

The older man jerked back as if he'd been punched in the chest. His skin turned ashen. "What makes you ask?"

"I don't know. Something."

Frank glanced around as if making sure no one had overheard Graham's question. "Let's talk later."

Graham nodded, understanding Frank hadn't told his family about his condition.

A sweet longing to lift Emily into his arms and inhale her sweetness, the pure innocence of a seven-year-old untainted by the difficulty of living as an adult in a bitter world slammed into Graham. "Sure, but until then, no matter what your answer to my question is, I suggest you go to Tess and try to heal the hurt inside her. It's not hard to say 'I'm sorry.'"

Frank's mouth set into an unyielding line. "I haven't done anything wrong. I'm a businessman, something Tess forgets. This isn't about loving your child. It's about doing what is best for everyone concerned."

Graham stepped outside. "Just think about it, Frank. Life's too short, you know?"

Again, Frank's face lost its color and Graham knew things were bad for the man. When he put everything together—the rush to hire him, the hiding of the decision from Tess and the haunted look on the man's face—he could see the writing on the wall. Frank Ullo was a very sick and scared man.

"Goodbye, Graham. Thank you for coming," Frank said, once again grabbing the reins and becoming the man who didn't bend.

Graham made his way to the car Frank had sent him, eyeing the big Easter basket sitting on the back floorboard beneath the new booster seat he'd bought for Emily. He hoped the bunny hadn't melted and that his daughter would consent to riding in the seat she still needed, according to the state laws he'd looked up a few days ago.

Daughters were indeed hard to manage, swerving around feelings, tip-toeing around their dreams, hot-stepping out of arguments a father couldn't win, but Graham wouldn't trade his Emily for a billion dollars.

And he knew Frank felt the same.

Graham just wished things were different between himself and Tess, wished he could have a second shot with her. Even now, as hard as it was between them, he wanted her. Wanted to trace the curve of her stubborn jaw, kiss the corner of her delicious mouth and gather all her sweet, hot wonderfulness against him.

But Graham had learned long ago he didn't always get what he wanted, so he would shelve the desire for Tess and try and focus on what he'd come to New Orleans to do—be a better father to his daughter and kick ass as the CEO at Frank Ullo.

Those things he could do.

He hoped.

TESS EYED HER REFLECTION critically in the bathroom mirror. She'd twisted her hair into a messy knot—a look *Cosmo* said was professional but also revealed her playful side. Swiping a creamy nude lipstick across her lips and clasping a cool Norman cross necklace she'd bought during the French Quarter Festival around her neck, Tess blew herself a kiss and left the bathroom.

Her first job interview and her stomach had filled with jumpy frogs.

After leaving her parents' house, she'd dropped by Cuppa Joe's for a frappé and checked her messages. To her surprise, she had two: one from Joe Rizollo who ran Mardi Gras Creations and one from Monique Dryden. Against a small niggle of doubt she'd smothered with the justification she'd been screwed by her father and Graham, Tess had followed through and sent her resume to Upstart and a few other of her father's competitors. She'd half hoped no one would call so she didn't have to step across to the other side. But when the bitterness edged in on her, when the hurt of Graham not calling and then taking over what she'd loved for so long surfaced, she didn't feel so bad about interviewing for a position at Upstart.

She carefully placed the files of her best past designs inside the attaché case her mother had given her when she'd graduated from college. Fortuitously she'd re-created many of the designs with software because many of the hard copies were filed at the Ullo warehouse. Dave wouldn't mind forwarding some to her, but she hadn't wanted to ask.

Half an hour later she pushed through the door of Upstart Float Design and Rental with the crowing rooster emblem centered in the glass. A man with a loud silk shirt and cargo pants sat kicked back at the desk. He snapped to attention when Tess approached.

"Hey, you must be the Ullo chick," he said with a shy smile.

Ullo chick?

"Yes, I'm Tess Ullo," she said with a businesslike nod.

"Yeah, I actually met you once at one of the balls. Endymion? I don't remember. Anyway, Monique's on a call right now. Negotiation's her deal. Have a seat over there. Can I grab you a coffee? Water?"

Tess walked over to the small reception area and sat in one of the folding chairs, pressing her hands over her navy pencil skirt. "No, thank you."

"Oh, I'm Josh, by the way. I'm Monique's partner and husband." He gave her another smile. Josh's face looked lean and hungry, like a stray dog. He had an earring that dangled, a soul patch on his chin and wore a newsboy tweed hat to complement his New Orleans artist look.

She might be biased but if Monique was stupid enough to trade Graham in for this guy, she might not want to work for the woman. Josh wasn't unattractive by any means, but Graham made Josh look like the Shaggy to his buff Fred.

Some girls liked a Shaggy, but Mr. Uptight Naquin who performed magic with his mouth and had a butt she could bounce quarters off was definitely more Tess's type. To each her own.

The office door opened and Monique swept into the reception area like a queen greeting her subject.

"Ah, Tess Ullo. You actually showed up," she said in a melodious voice.

Monique wore a tight pair of leggings beneath a bright sweater that dropped to midthigh. Her dark wavy hair brushed thin shoulders revealed by the wide boatneck. Her flawless skin was enhanced by subtle makeup and large diamonds winking in her ears. Blood-red polish tipped her elegant fingers. She made Tess feel like an over-dressed heifer.

"Yes, and I appreciate your replying to my inquiry."

Monique gave a secret little smile. "You're Frank Ullo's daughter, and I'm thinking you're a pissed off Frank Ullo's daughter, so of course I'm interested, darling."

Tess raised her eyebrows, struggling to her feet in the serviceable pumps, wishing she hadn't dressed so formally. Fish out of water.

"Come on in. Josh, get us some coffees around the corner."

"Aye-aye, Captain," Josh joked with a salute.

In that instant Tess totally understood why Graham hadn't lasted with Monique. Tess waited to see if the woman would mutter "good boy" before following her into the office.

Seconds later Tess sank into the armchair situated in front of Monique's massive modern steel desk. Monique landed on her bright red office chair as gracefully as a butterfly and popped a pair of glasses on her nose. Extending her hand she blinked at Tess.

Tess stared at her.

"I'm waiting to see your designs," Monique said. She might as well have added "dumb ass."

"Oh, sorry," Tess said, opening the attaché and pulling out a folder before placing it in Monique's hand.

Monique waffled through the designs, her eyes narrowing, occasionally turning the paper this way or that. "These are good."

"Thank you," Tess murmured.

"But let me be honest," Monique said, tossing the copies onto her immaculate desk. "I'm not looking for an art designer so much as I'm looking for someone who can bring in new business. That's why I left you a message yesterday."

Tess didn't know what to say to that. She'd wanted to do design work only. Felt less Benedict Arnold.

Monique smiled. "You intrigue me. Even more than having considerable experience in the float decorating business, I like what you're doing—a little revenge, if I'm not mistaken. Your old man pissed you off by hiring Graham, and you want him to pay. I love that kind of emotion. It burns holes in things. It makes things happen. Know what I mean?"

"You're saying you want to hire me because one, I'm an Ullo, two, I'm pissed at my father and three, you love the idea of stealing from your ex-husband."

"Not my ex-husband. I was smart enough not to marry Graham. That would have been disastrous." Monique snorted and it was cute. When Tess snorted it wasn't cute. More like a sinus infection.

"But—"

"Yes, we have a child together. But that's all. Graham and I are water under a bridge with a fast current."

Tess relaxed a little. She didn't really know what to think about Monique. Part of her didn't like the relish showed at one-upping not only her competition but her ex-lover. Like a predator, Monique smelled blood on the trail. Yet part of Tess warmed to the same idea—she wanted to make her father pay for his mistake…and Graham, too. Nothing wrong with that, right?

Still, Monique put her on edge. There was something untamed about the woman and Tess knew she wasn't one to trust.

So who went to work for someone like Monique?

Someone reckless. Someone fueled by emotion and not thinking clearly. Someone who needed to prove herself.

Someone exactly like Tess.

"I can put you on as co-director of art and design and I will pay you well, but I want something in return."

Tess raised her eyebrows.

"Some of Frank Ullo's business."

Tess's gut heaved at the thought of tearing clients away from the company she'd helped build over the last few years. Her name was attached to that business. Tess couldn't take from the company that had given her so much. She set her feet on the floor, intending to leave, but then that same inner voice that had prodded her to contact Monique Dryden whispered to her now.

Didn't seem to matter to your father, did it? Daddy doesn't think you're vital to his business. He thinks Graham can do better. Prove him wrong, Tess. Tell her yes.

Tess tossed her hair, her confidence returning. "My plan was for design work—"

"If that is all you have to offer, I'm not interested," Monique said, crossing her arms. "I have a designer and I oversee all proposals. It would be overkill. But I'm willing to pay for your 'experience' with the krewes."

Tess stared at the hot pink stapler sitting on the desk, realizing Monique desired what Joe Rizzolo and every other company would desire—her ability to snag business. This wasn't about her talent. "Well, I have the keys to the kingdom. As point woman for the krewes we did business with, I have a list of contacts a mile long and a good relationship with each captain and art director."

"Which is why I'm happy to pay you handsomely," Monique said, her mouth stretching into a grin over white teeth. Passing Tess several papers, Monique sank back into her chair. "This is my offer along with contract terms."

So formal. Tess allowed her gaze to flicker over the salary which was more than fair. So final.

If she signed on with Upstart, she'd be betraying all she'd been. An Ullo working for the competition? Tess could hardly fathom the thought, but she needed a job. Her father might have covered tuition and helped finance her loft, but Tess paid her own way. She had two months' rent in her savings, but that was it. She needed a job sooner rather than later and once she signed on, her designs would convince Monique she was an asset in more than one way. "Can I have until Wednesday? I need to have my attorney review these."

"Of course, but no longer. Your service to Upstart is valuable right now. We have a month or so to pin down these krewes and set our contracts for 2016. I still need some floats rented for 2015."

Rising, Tess extended her hand. "I'll be in touch. Thank you for taking this meeting and for the offer."

Monique ignored Tess's hand and instead picked up the drawings, shoved them in a folder and handed them to Tess. "I know what you're thinking. I'm too ambitious. Maybe even bloodthirsty. Does that scare you?"

Tess shook her head.

Monique laughed. "It's okay. I *am* ambitious. I want to succeed. This business has been a good ol' boy network for too long. I bet you did a lot of your father's work, but the krewes wanted to deal with Daddy, didn't they?"

"Yeah, but that's the way it is down here."

"Maybe so, but I'm tired of being marginalized and I think we can do great things together, Tess. Take that anger at being thought of as less and channel it into something new and challenging. Come be a part of a company that refuses to be shoved aside because a woman runs it. Time to prove to the world that Tess Ullo can stand on her own two feet." Monique moved around the corner of her desk and glanced down at Tess's shoes.

Tess frowned. "Yeah, I know. I thought they looked like interview shoes."

Monique smiled, this time looking younger and not so apt to eat her young. "A little tame, but you can buy something fierce with your first paycheck. You'll need something fabulous to wear to schmooze with the clients. In the business world, a gal has to be willing to use every advantage she has."

"Even her legs?" Tess joked.

"Especially her legs," Monique said, assessing Tess again. "You're pretty, and with the right clothes and makeup, you'd be devastating."

"Thanks, I think," Tess said inching toward the door, shoving both the contract and the folder in her case. "I'll be in touch."

Josh bumbled in with a tray holding three cups of coffee.

"I'll be waiting for good news," Monique said, reaching out for her cup, nodding at Josh to give Tess hers.

Tess refused the cup and instead pushed out the door into the cloudy Monday. The day reflected her emotions—gray.

Or maybe not so gray. After all, she'd just gotten a job offer.

One she really didn't want.

But this is what she'd set into motion when she'd mailed her resume last week. She'd have to deal with it.

Her phone buzzed in her purse, and hope sprang inside her. Maybe it was her father calling to say this was all a bad nightmare. Or maybe it was Graham calling to say…what?

There was nothing left to say between them.

They were over before they'd even gotten out the gate. Okay, they'd gotten out the gate several pleasurable times, but the race had already been run. Both she and Graham were losers.

It was Gigi.

"Hey," Tess said into the phone.

"Come meet me for lunch. I got a scoop."

"On what?" Tess pressed the button on her key fob and unlocked her car.

"Your man, that's who."

Tess blew out a breath. "Gigi, I don't have a man."

"Nick has dumped Miss Slutfest and is out and about. He told Shari Grabel he missed you." Gigi made a low noise in her throat.

"Well, I don't miss him. If you like Nick so much, why don't you date him?"

"Maybe I will." Gigi laughed. "Is he good in bed?"

"Lord, Gigi," Tess complained, pulling her seatbelt on. "I'll meet you because I've got a scoop…and a contract for you to review."

"You got the job at Upstart?" Gigi crowed, before lowering her voice. "I would be happy to review that contract for you at a time of your convenience, Ms. Ullo."

Tess rolled her eyes. "See you in a few."

Tossing her phone on the seat, Tess pulled away from the Upstart office, nestled next to the den they'd built from an abandoned grain storehouse in the 9th Ward. Her life had been turned entirely upside down. But she might as well go to lunch with Gigi. She hoped wherever they went had ice cream. Suddenly, she felt like she needed a double scoop with chocolate sauce.

CHAPTER TEN

GRAHAM HAD SPENT all of Monday and Tuesday in meetings with the team at Ullo and in impromptu lunches or cocktails with board members and captains of various krewes. Tess's leaving had stunned the team at Ullo and many of the major players who wrote the checks for the krewes were nervous about a new person taking charge of one of the oldest float builders and decorators in the Crescent City. Graham had smiled so much his face hurt.

Frank had given him an empty office that had been used for storing files and supplies. His new assistant, Billie, had grabbed one of the full-time painters and had him clear out the boxes and bring in an unused large wood table and chair. The rest had been left to Graham, but much like his new apartment, the space remained Spartan.

He'd just sunk into his chair when a knock sounded at the door. "Come in."

Frank stormed in like he owned the place...which Graham supposed he technically did. "I'm going to kill her."

"Who?"

"Tess. She went to work for your old company."

"Wait! What? Tess is working for Upstart?" Something heavy dropped in his stomach. Tess had gone to work for Monique? "Why?"

"To punish me, of course." Frank leaned across the desk and knocked his knuckles against the calendar blotter that was still pristine. "To punish you."

"Shit."

"You can say that again."

"Shit."

Frank rubbed a weary hand over his face and stepped back. "Already got a call from Edward Mendez's office. Tess has her claws in him and has subbed a bid for outfitting and renting most of Pan's floats. She knows what we charge and she's going to undercut us. She's also friends with Edward's daughter-in-law. This ain't good. The Krewe of Pan is a big account."

Graham straightened. "We can deal with it. We have your reputation and I have inside knowledge of how Upstart works."

"We gotta take a meeting with Ed. Whatever he wants, he gets. Understand? We gotta make sure we keep the super krewes before even considering harvesting some of the smaller krewes around the metro area. We have the talent and workforce here. Gotta move and shake."

"What about you?"

Frank sighed and sank gingerly into the folding chair. His face fell as if he just grasped the ramifications of his former VP and daughter working for the competition. "I won't be here much."

Graham sighed before he could catch himself.

"I know. I had hoped to have Tess to ease you into this, to be your guide, but with things the way they are in my personal life…"

"Can you clarify for me?"

"I know you know something is wrong, and you're a perceptive man." Frank looked at the closed door, his thoughts obviously drifting away. Graham gave him space and sat quietly as the older man gathered his words. "Thing is, I have pancreatic cancer."

"Jesus," Graham breathed, reeling back so that his chair butted into the wall. He'd known something was up with

Frank's health, but pancreatic cancer was almost always a death sentence. "What is… How…"

How did you ask a man something like how long you got?

"Three to six months, depending on the success of the chemo. I actually start this week over at Oschner. It's gonna make me sick and I won't be able to do much other than puke my guts up for the next few weeks."

Graham had no words. How could he?

Frank stared down at his clasped hands. "Everything's pretty much screwed. This whole thing with Tess. I don't know what to do. I never thought she'd be this mad. Never thought she'd turn her back on family and quit the business."

"But you knew she'd be hurt," Graham noted.

"Sure. She's like her mother. She don't like when she has no say so I knew she'd be ticked, but I thought eventually she'd see things my way. This," he waved a hand in the air, "ain't a one-person job. You gotta have someone to be your right hand."

Graham wondered if he could make things easier for Frank. He couldn't. Nothing would be easy for this man. He faced dying and a daughter who was angry enough to take her talents and knowledge to the competition. "It will be okay."

Frank looked up. "No, it won't."

"So we will make it okay. You have a viable, reputable business that has always put forth outstanding product, and now you have me. Fate led us to one another. You can trust me. I, too, have contacts. And experience. We needed Tess, but we won't let that stand in our way."

Frank looked down at his hands, looking older than he had when Graham had first met him. For a few moments the man didn't speak. "My whole life I've always known what to do. Always. But I've lost a grip on this."

"The truth usually works, Frank. I'm assuming neither Tess nor your sons know about your illness?"

"Joe knows. He's the one who set me up with an oncologist, but he can't tell anyone on account of a confidentiality clause. He's upset I haven't told everyone yet, but I wanted to do it—"

"On your terms," Graham finished the statement for him.

"No, that's not what I was going to say. I didn't want to do it at Easter is all."

"You're facing a tough battle, Frank. Not here at Ullo—that's why you hired me. I'm going to take care of things here." Even as he spoke the words, he said a small prayer that it would be true. That he could rally the troops that had been lackluster at best, keep the accounts they had and give Frank some peace of mind. "But you've got to help yourself as you prepare to fight cancer. You need your team, and Maggie needs support and help. Tell your family and allow them to do what they need to do for you."

For a second Frank bristled and Graham prepared to argue, but then it was as if the air leaked out of him. "How do I tell them? How do I destroy all they've known about me?"

"I've only known you for a short time, Frank, but I sense your biggest flaw is your desire to handle every aspect of not only your life, but your kids'. You don't like to be weak, and I get that—it's in our makeup as men. But fact is, you're not merely man, but human. Which means you are vulnerable. Don't allow pride to stand in your way of admitting you were wrong or of asking for help."

Frank rolled Graham's words around in his mind—Graham could see the battle within the man who stepped down yesterday at the CEO, officially handing the reins of the company to Graham with little fanfare. All the employees had seemed confused...unsettled at the news their leader stepped down so casually.

Finally, Frank nodded. "You're a smart man."

"Not always. It's easier to see what someone else needs to do than to apply the same logic in one's own life. I've made a lot of mistakes, and I'll make a ton more. It's the human condition. We can't control the world around us, and at times, we can't control our own responses. I do a lot of backpedaling. In fact, I need to do some with your daughter myself."

Frank searched Graham's face for an answer to his admission, but Graham would give the man nothing more than the suggestion he'd also wronged Tess. Frank had matters to settle with Tess, and Graham had ones of his own. Both men had handled Tess badly.

Rising, Frank set his hands on his hips and squared himself like a puffer fish ready to fight. "I'll handle my life. You handle this company. I trust the man you are, Graham. Don't make me regret it."

Graham nodded, hoping like hell he could do all Frank needed him to do. It would start with procuring the contract with the Krewe of Pan. Time to schmooze and dazzle. Time to show the world he'd left behind he wasn't a one-trick pony. Applying his vast knowledge of materials and construction, Graham knew he could revolutionize Frank Ullo Float Builders. Graham was back doing what he'd loved, doing what he'd started before the wheels had fallen off at Upstart, before he and Monique became more enemies than lovers. The task before him was large, but not impossible. He needed time to win over his new employees. He needed time to heal Tess.

Problem was, time wasn't exactly something he could control any more than Frank could.

ALMOST TWO WEEKS after signing a contract at Upstart, Tess had the first twinge of doubt. Oh, hell. Who was she kidding? She'd felt close to vomiting when she'd signed the

Upstart contract and followed Monique to her new cubicle. Making the decision about joining arms with the competition hadn't been easy, but the more Tess lay in bed, beneath the sheets she and Graham had tangled themselves in, thinking about her father and how he'd created a path for her that she'd followed like a stupid cow, never looking to the left or right, only ahead to what she thought her destiny, the more pissed she'd grown…at her father and herself. She'd never allowed herself to consider any other world but her father's, and he'd never demanded much from her. To say Tess had been stretched and put through the paces was such an underwhelming statement it was almost a lie.

Going to work would piss off her father—and Graham—and that thought pleased Tess. Neither had valued her.

Of course, Gigi had been smart, insisting on a provisional three-month period to protect both Monique and Tess in case the job didn't work out, but Tess was thrilled by the blank slate spread before her. Here was a chance to make her mark in a whole different way.

The first few weeks hadn't been easy. Outside of avoiding her family like the plague, Tess had spent much of the time navigating the torrents of Monique's complex ego. Monique demanded she have the final say in each design and had changed a few of Tess's visions. Tess had bitten her tongue over a few, choosing to bend rather than break.

But the biggest challenge came when she faced Cecily Webb, the head of design for Upstart. The fifty-year-old artist, who'd been with Monique since Graham had left the business, resented Tess and obviously wasn't going to play fair, if her cold treatment was any evidence. Not to mention, the woman seemed to have hoodwinked the staff by giving counter directives on several float designs, making Tess look wishy-washy. Monique seemed to look on with amused tolerance, as if she thought it best for Tess to handle Cecily herself.

At Ullo Tess had had final say in design work…even when it came to her father. And she'd never had to deal with fellow employees who didn't love her.

"Hey, new girl." One of the papier-mâché guys who worked on a sculpture of a pig flying motioned her over.

"Yeah?" Tess asked, walking over to the man wearing overalls and a fedora—artists were wonderfully weird.

"You told Halle to make this part larger, but I think it distorts the face."

Tess studied the sculpture critically. "I think the larger body will have more punch. The face will be forward but this prop is on the back of the float, so the effect is in the wings and body. Let's do it that way."

The man frowned and studied the shape in front of him for a few seconds. "Cecily trusts my judgment."

"I trust the design. Nothing to do with you, Ben."

"Whatever you want."

Tess closed her eyes and sucked in a short breath. "I'm open to suggestions for the poster board props along the sides. What do you think?"

"Bacon?"

Okay, so Ben was a master of sarcasm. "Hmm…actually I like that idea. Let's go with bacon."

"Seriously?" He made a face, but after a few seconds he laughed. "It *would* be ironic."

"And I love ironic. Let me check with the captain before we go to too much trouble, but I think the effect will be almost iconic. Good call."

Ben smiled turning back to the large foam pigs torn down to basic concept.

Score one for the new girl.

She strolled over to where Upstart's head sculptor showed Monique the start of the huge image of the gov-

ernor that would be affixed to the float for the Krewe
D'Tat's royalty float. Never easy to win the trust of a group
of artists. By definition, artists had their own ideas about
what worked, and at a Mardi Gras float company they
were often free to interpret many props in their own way,
but Tess wanted this lead float for the satirical krewe to
be spot on. She'd promised Mark Curtis it would have the
proper "wow" factor the acerbic krewe demanded.

"Let's build the nose bigger," Monique said studying
the work-in-progress. "It needs over-emphasis to give the
right effect."

"I agree," Tess said with a nod, sweeping her hand over
the entire sculpture. "Makes it more comical...like the guy
on *Mad* Magazine."

Monique tossed her a smile. "Exactly."

Score two for the new girl.

Yesterday Monique had asked Tess to attend a meeting
with the Krewe of Cleopatra and they had contracted five
of the company's thirty rental floats. Tess had worked on
some designs for the company that would meet their theme
of "Take it to the Dance Floor" but also be versatile for
several other krewes that would be looking to rent. As of
yesterday, Monique hadn't altered the sketches.

Maybe Monique would trust Tess's visions soon...
rather than merely tugging her along for liquid lunches
with krewe fat cats.

"Mommy!" the shriek came from their left.

Graham's daughter. Tess had seen her once from afar
and hadn't engaged her yet, hoping she could forget every
aspect about the man.

Tess watched as a rounded little body collided with
Monique, causing her to stumble in the too-high-for-the-
warehouse stilettos.

"Emily," Monique admonished, trying to gain her
footing. Louie, the head sculptor who'd been passing by,

pressed a hand against the woman's back and kept her from falling.

"A spider!" the child cried, burying her head against her mother's thighs.

"A spider?" Monique asked, prying the little girl off her. "All this over a little spider? Emily, Momma is working, honey."

The little girl kept her eyes shut and refused to let go of her mother's leg. In fact, she re-strengthened her grip and held on for dear life. "It was really big and mean-looking. It had hair on its legs like a tarantula. I'm not going back in there."

"Emily, let go. I'm going to fall," Monique said, pushing against the little girl's shoulder.

"It's probably just a wood spider," Tess said, rather unhelpfully.

Emily's eyes opened and they were the exact bright blue of her father's. Damn.

"Who are you?" she asked.

Tess managed a smile, wishing the child didn't look so much like her father. "I'm Tess. I'm new here."

Loosening her hold, Emily tilted her head like an inquisitive puppy. "I like your watch."

"Thanks," Tess said, looking down at the Cookie Monster watch Gigi had bought her as a joke. Turns out, it was the watch she chose most often over the Rolex her father had given her last Christmas. "I'm a big fan of cookies."

"Me, too." The little girl smiled, finally unwinding from her mother's leg, seemingly forgetting about the child-eating spider in the next room.

Monique ignored them both, choosing to tap on her phone.

Graham's daughter wore her light brown hair in a ponytail with streaming green ribbons. Her cotton dress was wrinkled and she looked as if she'd been eating cheese puffs because her lips were ringed in orange. Her cheeks were adorably chubby as was her middle. She looked nothing like her sophisticated mother, and for a moment, Tess felt absolutely sorry for the poor baby, as if she could see Monique disliked this about her own daughter. Wasn't fair of Tess to allow this immediate thought to pop up, but there it was all the same.

"Mom, can I have some Girl Scout cookies? I can share with Tess."

Meanwhile Monique had turned to Louie. "Make those adjustments and I'll take a look before the mâché goes on."

"Mom?" Emily intoned in that whiny voice invoked by almost every child on the planet.

"Whatever you want, Emily. Just don't ruin your lunch. Your father will be angry." Monique moved toward another painting bay, the click of her heels accompanying her dismissal of her child.

Emily's expression dissolved into bitter disappointment. Tess felt her own heart flinch in response.

"Know what? I'm about to take a break and go to Magglio's for a slushie. You want to come with me?" Tess asked, having no such intention but feeling like she needed to do something more than stand there watching Emily hunger for a crumb of her mother's affection.

Emily's blue eyes lit. "Yes, please." Then she yelled across the wide aisle, "Mom, can I go?"

Monique tossed her inky hair over her shoulder and looked at Tess. "You're already taking a break?"

"Actually I've been working on sketches for Eddie all morning and I need something more than coffee. Saturdays were made for strawberry slushes, don't you think?"

"Yay." Emily clapped.

"Sure," Monique said before turning back to another painter to inquire about a shade of brown that didn't match on one part of a prop.

Tess motioned Emily toward the exit. The little girl skipped ahead, pushing the exit bar, struggling against the heavy steel door. Tess shoved it open, allowing sunshine to tumble inside the dusty building.

Outside, the world was in weekend mode…or maybe it merely felt that way. Tess usually didn't come in to work on the weekend, but Monique had demanded she drop by and show her the preliminary sketches for Edward Mendez's krewe. The woman salivated over the chance to earn some of the krewes' business. So Tess had tugged on old jeans and a too tight T-shirt because she hadn't had time to do laundry and hustled down to Upstart to show Monique her sketches.

Needless to say, Tess had spent the last two hours making the adjustments Monique wanted. Tess had liked them the way they were and her father never would have nickel-and-dimed her lines or colors, but she now accepted she wasn't in charge.

Monique was…and her controlling nature was very evident.

Something she'd run into when it came to the sketches for Oedipus. Tess had worked personally with krewe captain Miles Barrow for years, but Monique and Cecily had already completed designs for the floats. Tess all but insisted she be given the chance to design something for the krewe's silver anniversary, a kernel of an idea she'd been playing around with for months. Tess hoped a superior design might dazzle Monique enough to give her the account. Monique relented, telling Tess she could work on the Oedipus design on her own time, but she would decide which designs were subbed to Miles based on cost, ease and design.

"I like Coca-Cola slushes," Emily said, jarring Tess from her contemplation. The child looked up at Tess as they waited to cross the intersection. "You like strawberry best?"

"I'm a strawberry-mixed-with-Coca-Cola girl. I like peach, too."

"Yuck," Emily wrinkled her nose, sticking out her hand so Tess could lead her across the street.

"Well, I like it." Tess laughed, looking down at Graham's daughter. Emily wasn't a beautiful child, but Tess had a sneaking suspicion she'd grow into quite a looker. She had long legs, thick wavy hair and a sparkle of good humor in her eyes…and Graham had gifted her with the most beautiful eyes.

Minutes later after snitching a brownie made by Alva Magglio herself—a treat since Alva had contracted rheumatoid arthritis and shifted the baking over to her daughter-in-law who didn't have the touch—Tess and Emily made their way back to Upstart's den. Sitting outside in his shiny silver car was the man Tess had tried like the devil to forget…and failed, of course.

"Daddy!" Emily screamed, trying to run across the street without looking.

Tess grabbed her, yanking her back and causing Emily to drop her slushie. "Emily, you can't cross without looking."

"My slushie," the little girl groaned looking down at the mess on the edge of the street.

"I'll get you another, but it's more important you don't end up as roadkill."

"What's roadkill?"

Graham jogged over, scooped up the busted cup and narrowed his eyes at Emily. "Young lady, you are not to cross the street without an adult. You nearly got hit by that truck."

Lip edging out, Emily dropped her head. "Sorry."

Graham tossed the crushed cup in the garbage can outside Magglio's. He wore a pair of khaki shorts, a plain T-shirt and running shoes. Tess had never seen anything sexier on a man. Well, except his suit. Graham had looked hot in his buttoned up suit and power tie. And, well, he was smokin' without clothes. So maybe he looked sexy-level eight on a ten-point scale, but it was enough to do funny things to Tess's resolve to hate him.

Okay, not hate him. Maybe just an eight on her dislike scale. Or a seven.

"Hey," he said to Tess, his smile wary. "Why are you with Em?"

"Well, we *were* having a slushie." Tess held up her own cup.

"Mine got smushed. Can I have another?" Emily asked.

Graham reached down, scooping Emily up into a hug. "Gotta have my sugar first." Dropping a kiss on Emily's nose, he jerked his head back toward the corner store.

"Yay," Emily said, dropping her own kiss on Graham's nose.

Tess's heart expanded at the pure beauty of a daddy and his girl. And then when she thought about her own father, it split open. Tess had always been daddy's girl. What was she now that they had no words for each other? It had been almost three weeks since she'd quit Ullo, and a layer of ice had built between them. Still, she could see no way to go back to where she'd been.

"You know, I think I'll have one, too." Graham set Emily down.

"Well, I should get back," Tess said.

"No," Emily said, tugging on Tess's shirttail. "Stay with us. Daddy's nice. I promise. And we're going to the park today. I can swing myself."

"Really?" Tess offered her hand up for a high five.

Slapping her hand against Tess's, Emily spun toward the door of the store, pressing her nose against the glass.

Alva must have waved her in because she pushed through, nodding her head and laughing.

Tess and Graham were left alone on the corner.

"Gotta say I was surprised to hear you went to work for Monique. Came out of left field," Graham said, toeing a cigarette butt.

"Why? I needed a job and I know this business."

Graham's gaze rose to hers. "I get it."

"Do you?"

"Yeah," he said, not offering anything more on the subject.

"Are things going well?"

Tess didn't answer. Merely looked at him with a "what the hell do you think?" look.

"Yeah." Graham's eyes dropped slightly as he studied her lips, then they dropped even lower to where her breasts strained at her too tight T-shirt advertising Big Mouth Sam's Blues bar. The suggestive slogan "Open Wide" didn't help, either.

Her mind tripped toward the way she'd run her fingers under his T-shirt, the way she'd licked that little place at the base of his throat, the way he'd tasted, the way he'd felt moving inside her.

Sweet Bessie, Tess. Stop reliving those moments. You can't allow yourself to go there. You can't allow your resolve to fade.

"I gotta go," she said, spinning away, wanting to stretch the tight T-shirt away from her chest, not merely so he'd stop dropping his gaze to her breasts but because she needed to breathe.

"Wait," he said, his hand closing around her bicep. His touch was warm. *He* was warm and she wanted to wrap herself in him in spite of hurt that clung to her much like that T-shirt. "Don't go on account of me."

"I have to go on account of you. Don't you get it? I

can't—" She snapped her mouth closed and tried to pin down the reason she couldn't stay right where she was. Because he'd been a jerk? Because her father had chosen him over her? Because she didn't want to like him, didn't want to let go of her hurt? She wanted to nurse it, obsess over it like Gollum and his precious ring, because it felt like that was her right.

He dropped his hand. "How about we strike a truce?"

Tess started shaking her head.

"For Emily's sake?"

"I just met your daughter this morning. Presumptive to think I'd do anything for her sake."

"Then for me. For you. For being grown-up people in a bad situation."

She wanted to step away and tell him to go to hell. She wanted to lean against him and close her eyes. But she did neither. Instead Tess stood there and looked confused.

Maybe because she was confused.

She wanted to hate him...but she didn't.

"Fine," she said, stretching out a hand. "We'll agree to be polite to one another. That's all I got."

Graham looked at her hand. "Just polite? Seems cold."

"Really?" Tess said, dropping her hand. "What do you expect? We work for rival companies and our 'relationship' lasted for all of twelve hours."

"Thirteen," he said, reaching forward and picking up the hand she'd dropped.

Oh, she knew exactly how long they'd spent together that night nearly two months ago—thirteen hours, eight minutes. Something about his knowing, too, plinked a few heartstrings.

Graham studied her hand clasped between his. "I'm sorry, Tess. I don't know how much more I can say it to you. I guess I can't. I'll see you around." He released her hand and turned toward the store where Emily stood inside waving, a huge, loving smile on her face.

Tess waved back to the child and headed back to Upstart, her step heavy as her heart. She wanted the heaviness to leave. She wanted to be happy again.

But life wasn't always happy, was it? Life held as many tears and as much loneliness as it did hugs and belonging. Tess had just skidded into that other 50 percent for maybe the first time in her life…and it pretty much sucked.

Monique met her at the front door, carrying a pink duffel bag. "Where's Emily?"

"With her father. Her drink spilled and he went to get her another."

"Uh, he's been spoiling her."

"That's what daddies do," Tess said, sliding past the woman and reentering the warehouse.

"Tess?" Monique called, turning toward her. "I hope you're happy here. I'm glad you're here at Upstart."

Unexpected words delivered by a tough-as-nails woman. Tess still couldn't read Monique—they'd only spent two weeks together. Still, the words did what they were intended to do. "It's been hard for me, but I'm determined to carve my niche here."

"Good. We want you happy. Happy Tess means happy Upstart."

Tess wouldn't go as far to say "happy" but she nodded anyway. "I'm going to run by Edward Mendez's offices and drop off the corrected sketches, and hopefully I'll have my vision for Oedipus ready by Monday."

"Good. And don't forget we have drinks with the Rivera brothers on Monday afternoon. The Prometheus account isn't as big as the others, but they've been with me for several years. I want them to meet you."

Right. Dog-and-pony show. The Ullo name hard at work again. Well, at least Monique hadn't lied to her about her reasons for hiring her...or done anything behind her back like Tess's father had. If Tess hadn't been an Ullo and hadn't the connections she had with the krewes, she wouldn't be working for Monique right now.

Sometimes honesty sucked. Maybe she'd rather have smoke blown up her skirt and be told how great she was at designing floats. Or maybe she'd have to earn that designation.

Carving a niche wasn't as easy as Tess had hoped.

CHAPTER ELEVEN

FRANK ULLO LOOKED down the table at his family. It had been three weeks since Easter Sunday. Two and a half weeks since he started the experimental drugs that had ravaged his body. He'd lost nearly ten pounds and looked like something the dog had barfed up.

"Dad, you don't look good at all," Frankie Jr. said, not bothering to stop shoveling Maggie's lasagna into his mouth. His wife, Laurie, wasn't much of a cook, so every Sunday Frankie approached lunch like a man who'd spent twenty years in a third-world prison.

"Hush, now," Maggie said, sliding her eyes to Frank and giving him a small nod.

Frank looked down at where Tess sat studying the food on her plate. They hadn't spoken since she'd left that Easter day, and frankly, he was so angry at her for quitting Ullo and working for Upstart, he didn't want to talk to her… especially since he felt so damn weak and helpless. His daughter should be ashamed to even sit at the table, eating the food Frank Ullo bought.

Graham had said a lot of things about making peace with Tess, but Frank wasn't ready to do that just yet. Tess had purposely poked a stick at him…and the damn thing was sharp. He wasn't saying anything to her. He didn't care what anyone else thought.

Maggie kept staring at him. She wanted him to tell them all about why he looked like death. Something other than the

"I'm a bit under the weather" he'd been using with everyone he saw over the past week.

"Your father has something he wants to tell all of you," Maggie said, setting down her fork and giving him a final "get on with it" look.

"Let everyone finish their food, woman."

"Don't you 'woman' me, Frank Clyde Ullo," Maggie said, anger shooting from her eyes.

"Meh," Frank said, shoving his food to the side. His stomach rebelled and he rose. "Pardon me."

His family looked up at him, concern etched on their faces.

"What's going on with Pop?" Michael asked his mother.

Maggie shook her head as Frank left the table. He needed to make it to the lavatory so he could puke his guts out. No big deal, right? He hadn't been able to hold down anything but applesauce for the past few days. He hated applesauce now.

Minutes later, he emerged from the restroom, shaky on his feet, but determined to return to the table. He'd already spent much of his time in bed, and he wasn't giving up his Sunday lunch with his boys and Tess…even if she and he weren't talking.

"Pop?" Michael said, rising and coming to his aid. Taking his elbow, his youngest son steered him to his place at the head of the table. "You okay? Can I get you anything?"

Frank patted his son's arm as he sank into the chair. Such a good boy. Always had been. Ran a bit wild in school, but always so caring, nursing felled baby birds, teaching children how to play hopscotch and sitting for hours in the yard contemplating God's world. "I'm good."

Joseph raised his eyebrows, as if to encourage Frank to let the cat out of the bag. But this cat would scratch and create havoc in his family.

Maggie had tears in her eyes. His boys sat, eyebrows

gathered in concern. And his Tess still stared at her plate, taciturn, an unfeeling statue.

"What your momma wants me to say is that I got cancer and I'm dying," Frank blurted, slapping a hand on the table. "There, Maggie, I told them."

A collective sucking in of breaths met his ears.

"Oh, my God," Laurie cried, clasping a hand over her mouth and turning to her husband. Frankie Jr. sat still as dawn, his mouth open, his brown eyes growing angry. His oldest never liked surprises.

Joseph exhaled with a groan. "Dad…"

"What? Your mother wants you all to know. So there. Now you do."

"Frank," Maggie yelled, tossing her napkin on the table, her face crumpling even as her eyes blazed outrage. "What on God's green earth is wrong with you?"

"It's the truth. You been nipping at my heels like a dog wanting me to tell them," Frank said, trying for a nonchalant shrug even as he was wound as tight as a Swiss clock inside. It was out there for all to know—he was dying.

"Not like that," Maggie cried before heading at a fast clip toward the kitchen. Laurie and Beth came to the same unspoken conclusion, rose and followed.

Frankie Jr. leaned back in his chair. "Christ, Dad."

"Hey," Michael admonished, holding up a hand, his black cassock and white collar stark against his shocked face. His youngest son cast a worried look at Tess who still sat frozen in place. Her eyes were wide and because she'd refused to even glance his way, Frank hadn't a clue what she thought or felt. "Let's all take a deep breath and a moment to think before we speak."

The scrape of Tess's chair against the floor was the only response to Michael's plea. His daughter flew toward the living room, not bothering to utter a word.

"Well, that's getting to be a regular thing," Frank said,

his heart sinking at the sight of Tess running. He'd thought her being forced to talk to him a silver lining in his delivering such terrible news. The slam of the front door told him there was no silver lining. There were just stormy, pain-filled clouds hovering over all of them. Maybe Tess more than anyone else. The hurt between them prevented even an umbrella to shield her from the onslaught of the rain that would fall.

And it would fall. Joseph, the oncologist and Maggie could talk all they wanted of his beating this, but Frank knew his chances were slim to none. He'd ignored the symptoms for too long. He'd started feeling weird before Christmas and because Mardi Gras was breathing down his neck, he'd ignored it, telling himself he was just older, more stressed with the business he'd lost that year. But it wasn't age or stress. And his casual dismissal had repercussions.

"I can't believe this is how you told us." Frankie Jr. shoved his empty plate toward the crystal saltshakers Frank's mother had given Frank when he'd gotten married to Maggie. She'd said they'd been made in the old country as if that was the most special of things. The shakers worked and that's all that had mattered to Frank, but now he wondered if he'd missed too much in life, wondered if he'd been too dismissive of what mattered most. Took dying to appreciate living. "Very shitty, old man."

"What? There's a better way? You can't put lipstick on a pig. Ain't no good way," Frank said, his stomach cramping and his vision a bit spotty. He really wanted to lie down, but couldn't leave things this way.

"Joseph, you want to explain this? Then someone should go check on Tess." Frankie Jr. assumed the role of firstborn, his gaze not quite so angry as resolute. Frankie Jr. always met problems head-on. That particular trait made him a fine trial attorney and a fine older brother to his siblings.

Joseph launched into a complicated description of his stage of cancer (not good) and the experimental drugs (not guaranteed) as Frank listened in objectively. Easier to do so than to think about what was happening within his body… though feeling the effects of the cancer and drugs wasn't an option. Couldn't wish those away. Joseph finished explaining the diagnosis, the symptoms of the chemo and the likely outcome (neither good nor guaranteed) as Maggie came back and sat down, reaching for his hand. Tears still in her eyes, she nodded at him. Frank's heart swelled at the love in her eyes. God had blessed him his entire life. How could he complain when he'd been given so much?

"This is why you asked us to not bring the kids. This is why Granny B isn't here," Frankie Jr. said, his expression no longer shocked. Just sad.

"We thought it would be better for you to tell your children yourself. Obviously your father has no tact when it comes to relaying delicate information," Maggie said. "Your father will tell Granny Bella this evening. We're taking her leftovers and a napoleon from La Madeleine's. She's been bugging us for one, says they're better than Gambinos or the ones I make from scratch. Maybe that will help somehow."

Michael rolled his eyes and gave a harsh laugh. "That's *so* going to make telling her easier."

"Where's Tess?" Maggie asked, staring at the empty seat.

"She bolted," Michael said, rising from the table, craning his neck toward the living room. "I'll go see about her."

"No, give her a little time. Things have been hard on her lately." Frank knew his daughter. She needed time to process. Time to figure out how to react. Tess was much more complex than most thought. On the surface she'd always been quick to smile and quick to action, but beneath her positive exterior beat a discerning woman…a woman who needed time.

Michael hesitated. "What about her, Dad? I sort of humored you in hiring that Graham guy. He seems okay. Capable. But now we're talking about…"

His youngest left off, shifting his gaze to his brothers who occupied the right side of the table.

"We're not sure what the results will be," Joseph intoned.

"No, he's right," Frank said, waving a hand, fighting against the sheer exhaustion knocking at his door. He'd need to leave the table soon, but first he had to finish what he'd started. "Graham is part of this. I needed someone to run Ullo."

Michael lifted his eyebrows. "But not Tess."

"Not alone," Frank said, shaking his head. "I never meant for her to see it the way she did. I merely looked for someone to come in and do what I do so she could keep doing what she did. I wanted to find her a partner. Didn't want to stress her with the undue burden of running Ullo alone. Graham was to be the new me."

"Why didn't you tell her that from the beginning?" Frankie Jr. asked in a very lawyerly way.

"I don't need to be cross-examined. I just puked my guts up," Frank said, rising on shaking legs. "Tess needs to see things for herself. She's young and thinks she can handle everything tossed her way. She's arrogant and spoiled. I did her a disservice and I'm paying for it."

"Tess isn't wrong here, Dad," Michael insisted.

Frank held up a finger. "But she's not right, either. Leave her alone for a bit and let her find her way. She needs that right now. She needs to feel a bit of the bite life gives."

After a moment, Michael nodded, his dark eyes meeting Frank's. In that gaze, Frank saw his boy understood. Michael had a way of seeing into the future and getting the big picture.

"Okay, we'll give Tess space. But you have to think about things with her," Frankie Jr. said, rising to take

Frank's elbow and assist him from the room. "And you gotta fight, Dad. We're all here with you through this."

Frank patted his son's hand and then reached out and clasped Joseph's shoulder. "I got a son to pray for me, a son to heal me and a son to get my affairs in order in case the first two don't work. I'm set."

Passing by Michael, Frank reached out and roped the boy into him, kissing him on the head.

"What's Tess for?"

"Reminding me who I was and who I am."

With that, he slowly crawled toward the open door, hooking toward the stairs.

THE SOUND OF HER SOLES slapping the pavement was little comfort, but the rhythm gave Tess something to cling to.

Her father was dying.

Slap, slap, slap.

He'd known this when he hired Graham.

Slap, slap, slap.

He'd refused to apologize to her, knowing he was sick.

Slap…slap…slap.

Tess stopped and bent over, her lungs burning, her eyes aching from unshed tears. Sucking in breaths, she held on to her knees and tried to pretend like everything that had happened in her life within the past few months was a nightmare.

That's it.

Pinch yourself and wake up, princess. This isn't real.

"Ma'am?" The words came from behind her.

Tess shut her eyes.

"You okay?" A young female voice.

Tess stood up, placed her hands on her hips and tried to still her ragged breathing. She knew tears leaked from the corner of her eyes…or was it sweat? She looked over her shoulder to find a girl of about thirteen or fourteen studying her with concern. "I'm okay. Thanks."

"You sure? I mean…" The teen glanced down at what Tess wore.

Right. She had on jeans and a pair of ballet flats. Not exactly running gear. "Yeah."

Not like she'd planned for a run through Old Metairie. Kinda happened when a gal found out the father who she supposedly hated was dying. Guilt and grief had crashed down on her. All she could think to do was run. Out the door. Down the street. All the way to…Bonnabel Avenue?

"Thanks," she called out to the girl with a wave. Unusual for a teenager to check on someone like that.

Tess pushed the sweat-dampened hair from her face and sucked in the humid air as she turned back the way she had come. Around her the quaint, expensive neighborhood hummed with children laughing, the sound of a lawn mower and the swoosh of cars down Metairie Road, which was strung with businesses, some open, others not. She'd run a decent way for a chick in ballet flats.

The phone in her front pocket vibrated and she pulled it out.

Michael.

She wasn't ready to talk to her brother about her father. Too close to home and the sadness would sheet off of Michael—the man felt everything so deeply. Tess didn't want to feel anything at the moment. She wanted to hide. To avoid. To pretend. For at least fifteen minutes. Maybe an hour. Or maybe she could hide from the entire afternoon.

Pressing the button to bring up her contacts, she hit Gigi's number. Several rings and a voicemail later, she hung up. A ding sounded. Text message from Gigi.

Found a date to the wedding. I'm trying him on right now. Catch up with you tomorrow. This might take a while ;)

No Gigi.

Tess wondered if she should call Nick. He'd been calling lately. Probably because he was lonely. But Nick was a dead end. At one time she'd hoped they could end up as more than what they were, which was a sometimes convenience. No sense opening that can of worms.

The phone vibrated again. Michael was a persistent devil…for a priest.

"Hey," she said into the phone. "I'm not ready to deal with Dad and this shit, okay? I can't—"

"Tess?"

She pulled the phone from her ear, looked at it and then tugged it back again. "Graham?"

"Yeah."

"What—why are you calling me?" Tess asked as she looked both ways and crossed the street that led to her parents' house.

"I don't know. Well, I do. There are a couple of good reasons, I guess, but mostly I wanted to check on you."

He knew about her father…knew Frank would tell them today. "You know about Dad's cancer?"

Duh. Of course he knew. Graham was her father's new golden boy, his trusted right-hand man, and she was, yeah, just his daughter. Resentment burned in her gut before she batted it down. She couldn't handle any more negative feelings. She could barely deal with what was squeezing the breath out of her. So Graham knew her father was dying. Big deal. The important fact was *her father was dying*.

She stifled a sob, catching it with her hand.

"Actually I guessed something was wrong," Graham said with a sigh. "Last week when your father came in to tell me you went to work for Upstart, he finally told me the truth. Shocked me to realize if he weren't facing what he's facing, I wouldn't be here in New Orleans…or at least not at Ullo. And I would never have met you."

Tess swallowed at a different emotion burgeoning within the grief swelling within her gut. The only reason she and Graham had happened in the first place was because her father had gotten sick. Bittersweet emotion coasted on crippling regret.

"What do you want me to say?" she said, stopping, realizing she'd rather walk all the way home than go back to that dining room table and her mother's tears. She just couldn't do it. She wasn't strong enough. Not yet.

"Nothing," he said, his voice weary. "I just worried about you."

His words hit her between the eyes. Graham cared. She already knew this, even if his initial actions after they'd slept together proved differently. But in the light of the afternoon, his slight felt very, very small compared to learning her father was dying.

"What are you doing right now?" she asked.

"I'm driving back from Monique's. Emily spent the night with me last night. Headed toward the grocery."

"What area? What street?"

"Uh, West Esplanade and Transcontinental." He sounded confused.

So was she. "Can you come get me?"

A surprised pause. "Where are you?"

"On the corner of Old Metairie and Sycamore," she said, wondering what in the hell she was doing asking him to come get her. In her mind, hell, in everyone's mind, Graham was the enemy. She was supposed to hate him for what he'd done, not ask him to rescue her from the tidal wave of grief threatening to wash her away.

"I'm on my way," he said.

Clicking the phone off, Tess sank down on the curb and set her head against her knees. Her body ached to cry, to release all the bitterness she'd held within. She needed something. Maybe a cocktail. Or maybe she needed therapy. Could a shrink help her figure out her life? Inside,

Tess felt like a ripped sail on a forgotten boat, fluttering in the gale with no hope of repair.

In the past her family had always reeled her in and stitched her up, assuring her all would be right again. But her father couldn't fix this. Nor could her mother or brothers. No one could.

A car turned onto the street, slowing down. But it was a red convertible Mercedes with a thin blonde at the wheel. The over-sized sunglasses blocked the woman's eyes, but somehow Tess knew she looked concerned.

Tess raised her hand and waved.

The woman waved back and sped off.

And people thought some New Orleanians weren't friendly. Two strangers in the space of twenty minutes checking on her.

Eight minutes later Graham pulled up, rolling down the window. "Tess?"

She lifted her head and suppressed the sob rising within her. Why Graham? Why the man who'd stolen her dream? Why was he the one she wanted on the day she found out her daddy was dying?

Because he felt like someone to watch over her as much as he felt like someone who could move her forward. Any other lifetime, and Graham Naquin would be the perfect man.

But not in this life.... Graham could never be her Mr. Right because he'd already stepped into the shoes of Mr. Wrong.

"Hey," she said, reaching for the door. Climbing inside the cool exterior, she tried not to give in to the tears, but her heart didn't get the memo her brain sent out.

"Sorry, sorry," she choked on the sobs, wrapping her arms around herself, rocking slightly. "I don't know why—"

His hand on her back felt so good and it only made her

cry harder. The car moved, but only a swerve to the curb before he put it in Park.

"Tess," he said, his voice soothing like a velvet night skimming over her.

"I can't stop. I can't—"

"Hey," he said, sliding his hand up to push her hair back, "Just get it out. Just let it all out, Tess."

So she did. For a good five minutes she sobbed against the dashboard of the car her father had brought her one-time lover and present rival. The entire time she cried, Graham rubbed her back, comforting her.

Finally, Tess sat back, wiping her face with her hands.

"Here," Graham said, pulling a travel package of tissues from the compartment that separated their seats. "Use this."

Tess took the tissue and wiped her face, before grabbing another to blow her nose.

A few seconds ticked silently by. The world outside the car moved—a man on a lawn mower, an older lady walking a fluffy dog and squirrels scampering up and down the graceful oaks. All going about their business on a Sunday afternoon.

"I'm pathetic," Tess said finally, tearing her gaze from a bed of tulips dancing in the breeze to his. "I don't know why I called you."

His smile tipped the corners of his mouth. "How is it pathetic? Besides, I called you."

"Oh, yeah. But I shouldn't have asked you to come."

"Why?"

"Because."

He issued a soft laugh. "Things are weird between us, but that doesn't mean I don't care about you, Tess."

"I know," she said exhaling, looking back down at the tissue wadded in her hand.

"I'm very sorry about your father," he said.

Tess's heart squeezed and she pressed her fingers to her temples where a dull headache throbbed. "It feels surreal. All of this."

Graham draped his hands over the steering wheel and stared at the sunshine filtering through the leaves. For a long while he didn't speak, and somehow the stretch of quiet comforted her more than empty platitudes. Eventually he turned back toward her.

"You want to go somewhere?"

Tess nodded. "I can't go back yet. My thoughts are too mixed up, and I don't know what to say to my dad yet."

"He'll understand," Graham said, turning the key, bringing the car to life. Pulling away from the curb, he hooked a quick left and backed around so they were headed back toward Metairie Road. "Coffee?"

Tess shook her head. Her rolling gut couldn't handle the acrid brew or the shot of caffeine.

"Something stronger?"

"No."

Graham said nothing more. Merely drove toward New Orleans, bypassing the on-ramp and going under I-10, passing Delgado and the cemetery with the raised tombs sitting vigil over the city. As he drove, radio on a soft rock station, Tess tried to gather up her shredded pride and erect the defenses she'd put in place weeks ago. She didn't want to open the door to Graham again.

So why'd you ask him to come get you?

She didn't have the answer.

Turning off the boulevard, he looped around and entered City Park. Pulling into a parking lot, he shut off the engine. "Let's walk."

Without waiting for her answer, he climbed out and shut the door. Her door opened and Graham leaned in, extending his hand.

Tess looked at it. She didn't want to touch him. Didn't

want him to crawl inside the walls she'd so carefully put back into place.

"You don't want to walk?"

"I don't want to do anything. I don't want to feel anything. I don't—"

"Get out," he said, not unkindly, but with a firmness that told her he was used to stubborn women…or stubborn seven-year-old girls. "You need to process. You need to walk."

"I already walked." She looked up at him.

He arched one eyebrow, looking quite dashing in the bright afternoon light, wearing a pair of shorts and a long-sleeved T-shirt pushed up his forearms.

Tess sighed. "Fine."

He locked the car behind her and started down the nearest path. Around them kids shrieked, adults jogged and a group of twenty-somethings played Frisbee golf. Unlike the lush privacy of Audubon Park, City Park was more open, with a golf course, several playgrounds, tennis courts and even a small amusement park. And there were lots and lots of paths to pound while examining the ups and downs a gal's life took.

For a long time they walked, side by side, footfalls falling soft.

"How am I supposed to be angry at him?" Tess said finally.

"Good question."

"You're not much help, you know."

"I've pretty much screwed up every relationship in my life, Tess. I'm not here to give you advice."

She stopped. "What are you here for?"

He shrugged. "I'm not sure. To be your friend?"

"To be my friend?"

"We can be friends, can't we?"

"I don't know. For two people who don't really know

each other, we sure have a lot between us." She fell in step beside him again.

For several more minutes they walked without talking. Arriving at a small pond, Tess veered off the path and sank down onto a bench. Graham settled beside her and they both contemplated the water buzzing with dragonflies, lined with lanky irises.

"I feel empty. Numb," Tess said.

Graham sat down, clasped his hands and said nothing.

"You sort of suck as someone to talk to."

At that, he laughed. "I told you. No good with advice."

"Why didn't you call me?"

"I did call you. I'd been thinking about you all morning. The whole time I was with Emily, I kept thinking about how much I love her and want to protect her. And then I thought about Frank and you."

"I don't mean today. I meant after our night together."

"Oh, that," he said, staring down at his clasped hands. "It's hard to answer. I can say a lot of things about why I didn't, but I suppose I'm embarrassed by the real reason." He looked out at the pond and said nothing more.

"I shouldn't have asked. Don't know why I keep bringing it up. Guess it seems so unlike you. Jeez, the thing is I don't know you well enough to even say that," Tess said, shaking her head. "I've got way more important things to think about, don't I? A new job and my father dying. Yeah, my plate's sorta full right now."

"Come back to Ullo."

Tess stiffened. "What…what do you mean?"

"You need to be there. It's where you belong."

"You'll step down?"

Graham made a face. "I can't step down—I need the job." He glanced away from her, hiding from her any vulnerability.

"My father doesn't need me at Ullo. If he did, he would

have appointed me the CEO. He would have given me what I have worked so hard for. In case you didn't get the memo—I'm not wanted."

She might as well have added "and you didn't want me, either," but she had to let that hurt go, had to stop clinging to the sucking wound in her pride...to the idea she wasn't worth the effort. Why did she hold her fist so tight around Graham's rejection? Did she really think love had blossomed between them?

Stupid.

And now because she couldn't let the offense go, she came off as pathetic. This was now her issue, not his. He'd apologized.

Graham brushed his knee against hers, jarring her out of her reverie. "So much would be solved if you would just change your mind and come back."

"For you," she said quietly. "But not for me. Falling back into who I was, forgetting the total dismissal my father gave me, would be taking the easy way. But it wouldn't be the right way. Not for me."

"So you're going to teach the old man a lesson, huh? And in doing so, make my task harder? Hurt the company you loved?"

"I'm not being spiteful. I'm doing what is right for me.... My father manipulated me again today. He knew what his announcement would do to me, but he tossed that ace onto the table." She wondered if her father had used the cancer card to manipulate her. Otherwise, why hadn't he told her and her brothers when he'd been diagnosed? Why hadn't he told her before going to a headhunter and hiring someone to run the company? She didn't understand him any more than she understood the reason she sat beside Graham in the dying light of the day.

"So you're going to keep this wall between you. You're going to work for Monique…work on stealing the very accounts you helped bring to Ullo? That's your plan?"

"You make me sound like a bad person. I'm not. I'm just not giving in to my father's wishes. I'm not accepting his vision for my future. He wants me to fall in line and do what he expects, but I'm not going to do that. I'm devastated about the cancer, but that doesn't change anything."

She stood and stepped away. She didn't want to talk about her father anymore. No more allowing the love she felt for him to mold her intent. Nothing had changed her goal: to prove herself to everyone. To prove to herself she could make her own future without her father's name, without her father giving her all she had. This was business. Wasn't that what her father had said?

It's not personal….

But it felt that way.

"Tess," his voice followed her, pricking at her resolve. It was business between her and Graham, too. She shouldn't have asked him back into her world, shouldn't have showed weakness in front of him.

"We should head back to the car," she said, moving in the direction they'd trod minutes before, not bothering to look over her shoulder.

He spun her around. She jerked her arm away, but he didn't release his grasp. "Tess."

Armor in place she looked up at him, at the softness in his blue eyes. "What?"

"What's wrong with you?"

"You know what's wrong with me. The same thing that has been wrong with me since the day I walked into an ambush in my father's office. Life has been bitch-slapping me, serving me up shit sandwich after shit sandwich. I'm pretty full on what life's been giving me. Look, you were nice to come and get me, to play the knight on a white horse, but I shouldn't have asked it of you."

He dropped his hand. "So nothing between us has changed?"

"How can it? You're still you. I'm still me. And between us is a gap full of hurt, anger and betrayal. Nothing has changed."

Graham's mouth formed a line and gone was the softness he'd lent her when she'd needed it. "I'll take you back."

"I'd appreciate it."

GRAHAM LOOKED DOWN at Tess as she stood in front of him, chest heaving with emotion, green eyes resolute, and his heart ached.

He should take her home and be done with her. After all, she'd made everything so damn difficult in his life. Things were supposed to be good—he had a decent job and a steady paycheck. Emily had fallen back into the same easy relationship they'd shared that summer. Monique had taken the high road…for a little while at least. Life smelled like a summer rose.

Yet Tess was the thorn pricking him.

He thought about her constantly. The way her skin felt beneath his fingertips, the scent of her hair, the way she'd made love to him, fierce and tender at the same time. He wanted her desperately. Wanted to sink inside her, brand her, make her his.

But he was so far away from having Tess in his bed, he might as well be standing on the other side of the world.

And her leaving Ullo had made his workplace a living hell. Not only was he juggling more than what he'd signed on for, but the staff resented the hell out of him. The coffee Billie brought him was old, papers were misplaced and a cold shoulder would have been welcome compared to the icy reception he'd received. It was a wonder he didn't have frostbite.

Everything would be so good if Tess would come back. *Damn her stubborn pride.*

"Don't shut the door, Tess," he said, giving a last-ditch effort to bring her to him...even if it was begrudging.

"The door is already shut." Her delicious lips pressed into a line and she crossed her arms.

"No, it's not," he murmured, brushing her hair back from her face.

She batted his hand, even as something hummed between them. He felt the buzz of desire and knew she felt it, too. "I can't, Graham. Things are too complicated. We made our beds, and now we'll lie in them whether they're lumpy or not."

"Somehow I don't think lumps would bother me a bit as long as you were in that bed with me. I still think about you tangled in those soft sheets."

"That's all we can ever be—a memory," she said, her glance dropping to his mouth before shooting back up to his eyes. "We can't go backward."

"You can tell yourself all kinds of things, Tess, but convincing yourself you don't feel something and actually feeling something... Those are two different things, baby." He clasped her elbows and brought her to him.

Tess let him.

More than anything he wanted to kiss her, but after the afternoon she'd had, he knew it would be manipulating her emotions for his gain, so he merely wrapped his arms around her and held her with tender resolve.

Tess was angry and hurt, but she needed him. This he knew. For a few seconds she held herself stiff, refusing to relax, but suddenly, as if someone had cut an invisible string, she sagged against him, wrapping her arms around him, her face tucked against his chest.

For a full minute, he held her, dropping the occasional kiss atop her head, begging his body to remember this wasn't about sex. It was about proving to Tess there was a connection beyond their bodies.

She inhaled deeply and then exhaled.

"You do what you need to do, Tess, but remember this," he murmured, loosening his grasp and looking down at her. "We have something between us. It's not going to go away because either of us *want* it to."

Her green eyes, soft as the grass lining the path, lifted to his, and in that moment he saw the truth. Her lips were parted and he couldn't resist the invitation.

Lowering his head, he kissed her softly, tasting the sweetness briefly before stepping away. "I'll take you home now."

Wiping her lips, Tess straightened and turned from him. Like a soldier she marched forward, spine straight. Part of him withered, but another part deep inside knew her. Knew she'd thrown up defenses, protecting herself because she needed to survive the day.

In his bones, in his very gut, Graham knew he and Tess belonged together…or at least deserved the chance to see if they did.

But how?

It was the question he'd mulled over night after lonely night. He'd tried to tell himself he didn't want her. He'd convinced himself things were *too complicated*. But still his mind and heart nudged him away from being logical toward the one thing he'd always clung to—hope.

Where there's a will…

Tess disappeared around a curve before ducking back. "You know the way back, don't you?"

Graham smiled. "Put one foot in front of the other."

She made a face. "I'll meet you at the car." And then she spun and disappeared again.

Graham stood a second longer and started after her, the hope inside him uncurling and stretching in the small crack she'd opened in her resolve.

CHAPTER TWELVE

FRANK WATCHED AS the nurse slid the needle into the vein in his arm. A quick sting and it was over. A turn of a ring and the liquid started flowing into his body into his bloodstream.

Go forth and conquer, he silently beseeched the drug.

Leaning back in the hospital bed, Frank closed his eyes and wished for the umpteenth time that day that he was mulling over figures at the office, calling James to tell him to order more primer, arguing with Tess over using paper too expensive for the floats.

"Frank?" Maggie's voice worried him.

He cracked open an eye. "Still breathing."

"Stop making those jokes." Maggie, with her hair in a topknot and the cut of her jacket, looked as if she'd skidded back in time to when he'd first met her. 1962. Pretty as a magnolia, sitting on an iron bench in the Quarter, eating an ice cream with one of her coworkers from Henry's department store. She didn't look all that different to him now. The years had been kind to his Maggie.

"You tell Jack Baumgartner to keep his hands off your can, Mags. I've seen the way he looks at you."

"What?"

"He's always had his eye on you, and he'll move in before I'm cold in the ground."

"I can't believe you," she said, rising, crossing her arms and giving him her best evil Maggie glare. "As if I would

even consider going out with Jack Baumgartner. Maybe
Perry Underhill, but never Jack."

"Perry? Meh, he probably has herpes or something.
He's slept with half your bridge club." Frank eyed Maggie, trying to see if she was serious or not. He didn't like
Perry with his overly white smile, golfer's tan and cheap
shoes. The man acted as if he were the George Clooney
of the country club, swilling around the card room, plying
the ladies with vodka collinses and a thick layer of charm.

"Lydia Babin said he was totally clean. She made him
present her with a clean bill of health before she would
climb on for a ride," Maggie said, smooth as velvet...even
though a wicked smile hovered at her lips.

The nurse writing down crap on a little clipboard snick-
ered.

"Lydia slept with Perry? What? She hard up or something?"

Maggie laughed. "Well, yeah, she was married to a man
who raised crickets and sold them for bait for five years...
a man who had sex with her only twenty-four times. She's
so hard up she'd likely sleep with Jack Baumgartner, too."

"The woman only had sex twenty-four times?" the nurse
said, spinning around and looking horrified.

"She kept a journal," Maggie said gravely. "Very little
sex because her husband had erectile dysfunction. The
woman is due some fun."

Frank snorted as the nurse saluted. "Okay, Mr. Ullo, I'll
be back in a bit. Try to rest." She winked at him and shot
Maggie an encouraging smile. Nothing about chemo was
much fun, but the employees in the cancer center worked
hard to make the environment as welcoming as possible.

Silence descended like a cold blanket. Maggie looked
down at her nail, pushing at a cuticle, trying to pretend
everything was normal.

"You talk to Tess?" he asked.

"Yeah, she came back while you were asleep. Oddly enough Graham dropped her off. Couldn't get a word out of her about that, though."

"Graham?"

"You know, the man you hired over her."

"I didn't hire him over her. I hired him for her."

Maggie frowned. "That makes no sense and you know it. But I can't figure out how she came to be with him that afternoon. After your ill-timed announcement, she disappeared for hours. Her car stayed, so she had to have run into him or something."

Frank nodded, not quite understanding how his daughter had ended up with Graham, but understanding why. Something had happened between Graham and Tess—he'd seen that firsthand in his office. They'd both been shocked to see the other…and then there was guilt and anger. He wasn't the sharpest tool in the shed, but he could put one and one together to get a solution. Tess and Graham had something going on long before Frank had hired Graham. "I don't know why Graham brought her home. I don't even feel like I know Tess anymore."

Maggie harrumphed.

"What?"

"Who's to blame for that? You've handled things wrong at every turn, Frank. I tried to tell Tess you didn't mean to make her feel unappreciated, but she's like a damn billy goat. Won't be budged."

Frank said nothing. Part of him harbored deep anger at his daughter for being so irrational, for putting Frank Ullo Float Builders in jeopardy. But another part of him admired her courage and conviction. His daughter refused to be a victim, refused to take the easy way. She *was* his daughter. "She has that right."

"How can you say that? You're sick. Everything has changed, Frank. She's being intentionally stubborn."

"Only because she believes in herself. I like that about our girl."

"She's hurting. You're hurting. And both of you are too bullheaded to make it right. Doesn't make sense at a time like this to be so set against each other. You need her, and she needs to be there for you."

"It makes sense to me, Maggie. I know Tess loves me, but I also know she's had me wrapped around her little finger ever since she gave me that first gummy smile. I've given her the world—the best schools, a new car on her 16th birthday, a job after she finished that expensive college. We made our boys walk a tougher road than Tess."

Maggie frowned. "So you're trying to teach her to stand on her own two feet now?"

"It's not the best time, and I never intended it to be this way. But when I saw how she reacted to not being given control of the company, I knew I'd made a mistake in raising her. I'm not saying she ain't a good girl, Mags. But she's never been tested. Tess has leaped and now she must deal with where she's landed. We all have to deal with where she's landed."

His wife of forty-nine years shook her head. "I don't understand you."

He gave her his boyish crooked smile, the one he'd used to get in her pants all those years ago. "Yeah, you do. Deep down you know Tess needs space and some growing room."

"But you don't have much tim—" Maggie clamped her mouth closed and blinked away sudden tears.

"Come here," he said, motioning her to him.

She moved toward him, reaching out to clasp the fingers he wiggled her way. Her touch warmed him, comforting him, giving him strength the way it always had. "Oh, Frank, this is terrible."

He nodded because she was right—it was. Clasping her

hand, he tugged her to him, around the confounded machines. Maggie bent down and pressed her lips to his. "I love you, Maggie, my Irish lass."

Her fingers lightly caressed the side of his face, which was scruffy because he hadn't bothered to shave that morning. "I love you, too."

"Say it," he begged, grinning up at her.

"My Italian stallion." She laughed and his heart lightened.

"Hell, yeah." He gave a fist pump with his free hand. "I'll give you a ride, too, princess. Just as soon as I stop vomiting every hour."

She sighed and rested her forehead against his, smelling like spring and spearmint. She favored mint gum and expensive perfume, and she smelled like home.

"I'll take you up on it, Frank, but until then, I'll focus on your being sick meaning the medicine is doing its job."

Frank closed his eyes and prayed her words were true. Please let it be true.

TESS WATCHED AS Emily bounced on a scrap piece of metal, the thwump, thwump, thwump of the assault echoing in the large warehouse. The child was dressed in a pair of athletic shorts and a too small T-shirt that hugged her little tummy. Long red-and-black polka-dotted socks covered her legs and a pair of new cleats contributed to the incessant noise.

Monique was nowhere to be seen.

"Hey, Emily," Tess said, shouldering her new messenger bag containing the drawings she needed to tweak by hand that evening. It had been a long Tuesday of meetings with potential and long-standing Upstart clients—all after a Monday evening meeting with the captain of Prometheus and his partner. And two nights of crying over her father and the argument she'd had with her mother. All Tess wanted was an hour at the gym, a protein shake and the comfort of her bed. She didn't want to think. Didn't want to feel. Just wanted to pretend everything was peachy keen. But she wasn't going to ignore the chubby seven-year-old bouncing and thwunking her way along the tin.

Emily's face lit up. "Hey, Tess!"

"What are you doing out here? You could get hurt on that."

The child hopped off the scrap metal. "I'm waiting on Mom to take me to guess where?"

"Where?"

"Soccer! I'm going to play this summer. Isn't that so cool?"

"The coolest."

The clack of Monique's high heels drew both their attention. The woman advanced like a field general...if a field general wore Jimmy Choo shoes and Chanel. "Let's go, honey."

"I'm ready, Mom," Emily said, scrambling over to a pink gym bag and backpack that sat on a stack of wood. "I'm wearing my ladybug socks, see?"

Monique made a face. "Oh, baby, I'm sorry, but I don't have time to take you to soccer today. Mommy has a thing tonight. You can go tomorrow."

Emily's eyes widened. "No, practice is today. It's the first one. I have to go."

"Sorry, honey. I absolutely can't take you today. We can try and phone your father, but otherwise, I'm dropping you at Grandy Pete's and then I have to scoot over to Mr. B's Bistro for an important meeting." Monique shifted her attention to Tess. "It's with Miles Barrow. Nothing I need you for."

If Tess didn't know how much in love Miles was with his wife, she might think Monique was using some creative bargaining to get the captain of Oedipus's signature on the dotted line, using those assets she was so proud of.

Oedipus had always contracted with Ullo for the super krewe's float building needs, but Monique seemed to think next year would be different. Tess had been working on some really good stuff for the krewe, hoping Monique might present her designs over the ones she'd done herself.

But Monique could do what she wished—it was her company. The boss lady had already informed Tess she was expected at the krewe's annual May Madcaps and Cocktails social on Saturday night, so maybe Tess could get an answer from Monique by then.

Up until this point, Tess had done what Monique had asked for when she hired her—bring in new accounts. The men and women of the krewes had been impressed to find Upstart employing an Ullo, even as the question sat in each of their eyes as they pulled out their pens to sign on the dotted lines of the contracts pulled out at the ready.

Still, something felt shady about the "thing" Monique had that evening.

Emily stomped her foot, bringing Tess's attention back to the seven-year-old with a stormy face.

"Mom, I have to go. Have to. Dad signed me up and that's like a promise," Emily said.

"I didn't say you couldn't play. Just not today."

"It's supposed to be good for me. Dad said." Emily crossed her arms, face taking on an expression that teetered between mulish and distraught.

"Emily, I said no. Your father should have checked my schedule."

"He did. You said yes. Remember?" Emily persisted, edging closer, looking as if she neared fit-pitching stage. "So take me. You promised."

"Hush," Monique said, jabbing a finger at her daughter.

"I can take her," Tess said.

Crap. Why had she just volunteered? Jeeza Louisa. She needed to go to the gym and pound out her frustrations, run the pain of her father's diagnosis away, sweat out the longing for the kid's father. She hadn't been sleeping well. Stress ate away at her, souring her appetite, making her stomach ache. She'd lost a few pounds and had baggage under her eyes so big they needed luggage tags.

Emily tackled her with a hug. "Thank you, Tess. Thank you."

Tess gave the kid an awkward pat. "I know how much fun soccer is. It was my sport."

Monique cocked a perfect eyebrow at her. "You don't have to do this. Emily can go next time."

"No problem," Tess lied. Because taking a seven-year-old to soccer practice, no doubt across town, meant she'd likely be skipping the gym. "Where do I drop her off?"

"I'll have to look at the flyer her father gave me. He said he'd be there to register her or something like that, and he'll take her home."

Great. The last person she wanted to see. Actually he *was* a person she wanted to see and that was the problem. She didn't want to think about him, about the way she'd sobbed like a baby in front of him, about the way she'd so easily said, "Come rescue me." Made her feel weak.

But obviously when it came to Graham, she was weak.

"Okay, I'll make sure Graham is there before I go."

Monique nodded. "Good. Let me get you his number just in case."

"I have it," Tess said.

Monique lifted her gaze from her phone. "Why would you have Graham's number?"

Busted.

"Ah, I think my father gave me all his contact information when I left, you know, so if I needed access to anything I'd left behind..." Lamest excuse ever.

"I thought you weren't talking to your father," Monique said, sliding her phone back into her designer purse.

"It was in an email. My contacts synced up automatically." Tess tried to sound like it was no big deal. Like she'd never wrapped her legs around Graham and shattered against him during the best sex she'd had in forever.

"Oh, well, I'll see you tomorrow. Wish me luck," Monique said with a shrug before giving Emily the eagle eye. "Be good."

"I'm always good," Emily said with a grin that looked far from angelic. "Let's go, Tess."

"Good luck, Monique," Tess said, relieved the woman hadn't pressed the issue over Graham's phone number.

Emily grinned up at her with an excited gap-toothed smile. "I don't want to be late for my first practice. We're the Lake End Ladybugs. See my socks?"

"Cool," Tess said, allowing Emily to pull her toward the door. "Uh, do I need your car seat?"

"I don't sit in a car seat. I'm not a baby," Emily said, rolling her eyes.

Tess almost laughed. "Never thought you were, ladybug."

"Well, Dad makes me ride in a booster seat. He looked up rules on the internet and says I'm still not big enough to sit regular, but I'm in second grade. My dad just doesn't get it."

Or maybe he did. Something about Graham taking the time to look up rules regarding booster seats and signing his slightly overweight daughter up for soccer made Tess like him even more…something she didn't want to do. But there it was. Graham Naquin was a decent guy even if he'd stolen her place at Ullo and dropped her like a bad habit…for whatever unstated reason.

Wait. She was supposed to forget about that. Let it go.

Twenty minutes later, Tess pulled into the sports complex in Metairie. The afternoon had softened into evening and the emerging green field in front of her was a sea of activity.

"I wonder what field you're supposed to meet on," Tess remarked as Emily opened the car door. Emily's cleats were untied, so Tess sat the girl back on the backseat and bent to double-tie them.

"Daddy!" Emily screamed in her ear. Tess jerked up and conked her head on the top of the door frame.

"Ow," she said rubbing her head and turning toward Graham, who wore a pair of khaki pants and a mint-green broadcloth button-down. Tess tried to look like she hadn't just broken into a sweat merely looking at him.

"Hey, where's your mother?" Graham asked, scooping up the child who'd launched herself at him.

"She hadda go to a meeting. Like always," Emily said, grinning at her father. "Look at my socks. Mom got them for me."

Graham peered down at the child's legs. "Looks like a ladybug to me." He lifted his eyes to Tess and her heart sped.

Stupid heart.

"I'm just the chauffeur. Since you're here now, I'll go," Tess said pushing the car door closed.

"No," Emily yelled, wiggling out of Graham's arms. He dropped her to the ground and she bolted toward Tess, grabbing her hand. "You gotta watch me, Tess. You said you like soccer."

"But your dad is here," Tess said.

"Pleeeease." Emily made puppy dog eyes at Tess.

Damn it. Tess had never been able to resist puppy dog eyes. She sighed. "I'll watch for a little while."

"Yippee!" Emily whirled around like only a seven-year-old could do.

Graham eyed Tess. "How did you get suckered into this?"

Emily overheard and said, "Mom said I couldn't come, but then Tess said she'd take me. Tess plays soccer, too."

"I only play a few Saturdays a year. I sub," Tess muttered, hoping he didn't think she had volunteered merely so she could see him. She'd done this for Emily. Because it was crappy that her mother had chosen business over her daughter. Upstart seemed to be Monique's primary focus in life, and though Tess could attest to her father seeing business as important, he'd never put it over her or her brothers. He'd made almost all of her soccer games even during Mardi Gras season.

Graham gave her a smile that made her stomach flop over.

Stupid stomach.

She shrugged off her reaction to his charm. "So where are we heading? Uh, for soccer practice," Tess clarified.

Graham turned to study the fields. "The guy said it was the field in the back left."

Minutes later they stood in a gaggle of kids, a couple of moms and one older man struggling to balance on crutches. The man sat his clipboard on the collapsible bleachers and turned toward where they all stood. Emily stood close to Graham, looking uncertain.

"Hey, everyone. I'm Jim Thisbe and I'm the coach of the Lake End Ladybugs. As you can see, it's going to be a bit difficult for me to coach this season, but I'm hoping to have a few of you assist me. Anyone have any experience coaching soccer?" Jim eyed Graham, his eyebrows raised in a hopeful manner.

Graham gave a quick shake of his head. "Sorry, dude."

Emily pointed a finger at Tess. "She plays soccer."

Jim smiled at Tess. "Very good. Love having a female coach. Always a great role model for these young girls."

Little heads with swinging ponytails turned her way. Tess felt like the kid in school who got called on and didn't know the answer. "Uh, I'm not a parent. I'm a friend."

"That's okay," Jim said, with a panicked smile. He looked like he might latch on to her leg if she took off running. Of course, she'd have the advantage since he was gimped up. "Friends are just as good as parents."

Not really, but she was sure Jim was convinced of its truth. "You don't understand. I'm not really available." Tess gave him an apologetic smile.

"Oh." Jim looked at the other parents assembled. "Anyone else know how to play soccer? Anyone?"

Blank looks all around.

One woman held up a hand. "I have a cousin who played. I can ask him if he'll be willing to help."

Jim snapped his fingers. "Good. That will work."

"Are we going to play today?" one of the other girls asked, bouncing a pink-and-black soccer ball. "I got a new ball."

"Uh, sure," Jim said, unclipping forms from his clipboard while balancing on one foot. One of the mothers had pity on him and helped to pass out the paperwork. "If you will fill these out, make the check payable to the organization, and then I'll turn all the registrations in at one time to the league."

He then turned and blew his whistle. Tess sank onto the bleacher feeling both guilt and relief. Graham and the other parents set about filling out forms. Jim hobbled around and tried to instruct the kids. Good-natured? Check. Determined? Check. Good coach? Uh, not a chance.

Tess stood. The least she could do was teach him a couple of warm-up drills that would focus the frolicking kidlets and work on their eye-foot coordination.

"Hey, Jim," she called, approaching the area where the kids basically wrestled with each other in line. "I'll give you a little help today."

The man literally looked as if he would hug her. "Thank you…"

"Tess," she supplied for him, waving the kids over to form a circle around her. "I've played soccer for as long as I can remember, so I've got a lot of great warm-ups you can use."

Tess kicked off her ballet flats, the cool grass heavenly beneath her toes, and split the group into teams, showing them a simple relay drill that would keep them all busy.

Graham jogged over. "You got roped into bringing Emily. You shouldn't have to do this."

Tess gestured to Jim who had sunk onto the bleachers, gathering the paperwork. "He can't do this."

Graham looked over at Jim. "No, he can't, so you'll have to show me these drills and I'll sign on as the assistant coach. I can't have the team fall apart. I need Emily out here in the fresh air, running, kicking and participating in something besides Playhouse Disney."

Tess looked around at the other girls smiling and laughing as they worked the balls around the cones. She remembered that feeling of working together as a team, sweat rolling down her back, eyes on the goal at the end of the field. She'd always had good coaches—men and women who'd sacrificed their personal time to help kids learn the sport. Maybe this was an opportunity for her to give back…and spend more time with the new sexy assistant coach.

Strike that, moron. It's for the kids.

"Tell Jim I'll help out. It's the least I can do to insure these girls get to play and learn the sport the right way," Tess said before she could talk herself out of it.

"Really?" Graham looked over at her, his expression slightly guarded, slightly hopeful. Damn, the way that man looked at her made her shivery.

"Sure. I've never coached, but it can't be too hard."

An hour later, Tess wanted to eat those words. She'd never worked with a group of seven-year-olds, and it was, well, challenging. They squabbled, they dawdled, they tripped, they cried and they had to be soothed with overly kind words. But still, even with all those challenges, Tess enjoyed teaching the fundamentals to the girls. Coaching them felt like the right thing to do, especially when at the end of practice Emily wrapped her arms around Tess's legs and hugged her.

"Thank you, Tess. You're the bestest coach ever."

Tess patted the child's back. "I'm not sure about that, but you're welcome."

Emily looked up, her eyes bright, her chubby little cheeks flushed from the last running drill. "You'll come on Thursday won't you?"

Tess looked up and caught Graham's eye, and in that moment, Tess knew there was no other place she'd rather be on Thursday afternoon. Except maybe Disney World. She had a thing for the Mouse and the rock-n-roller coaster. Or maybe Tahiti. Those beaches looked heavenly. "Of course. I'm going to help Coach Jim this season."

"Yay!" Emily crowed.

Jim walked over and extended his hand, but since it caused him to lurch sideways, Tess waved it away. "Did I just hear right? Are you going to come back and help out?"

"I'll see you Thursday," she said with a smile. "You need help, and though I've never planned on being a soccer coach, the job found me."

Jim cracked a huge smile. The man was in his early fifties with thinning hair, a trim physique and a nice smile. "Best news I've heard in a while. I signed up to coach because Harv Turner, who runs the league, was short on coaches. That was before I hit an infamous New Orleans pothole on a recent bike ride and learned what it feels like to tear an ACL." He looked down at his booted foot and grimaced.

"Ouch," Tess said, looking down at the cast before glancing back up. "I'll try my best."

After getting the details on practice times and game schedules, Tess and Graham headed toward the parking lot. Emily skipped between them, smiling, rambling on about school and someone named Jillian who got in trouble for chewing gum and bringing in her iPhone. The intimacy of the moment struck Tess and she felt odd being a part of something that was very much "family" in nature, but at the same time, she liked being part of Graham and Emily.

Scary.

When they reached her car, Graham took her elbow and turned her to him. "Thank you, Tess."

The warmth of his hand on her arm, the way his gaze caressed her made her body warm. Unconsciously she leaned toward him. Or maybe she was conscious of wanting to be closer to him. "Uh, you're welcome. I wanted to do it for Emily."

The corner of his mouth twitched. "Just for Emily, huh?"

And for you. So I can be close to you if only for an hour.

But she didn't say that. The awareness pulsed between them—it always did. Tess wanted Graham. She needed to feel his arms around her again. She craved him with a "what the hell" abandonment the way she craved chocolate when she had PMS. Maybe one kiss?

And in his eyes she saw he wanted the same thing—his lips, her lips, hot, wet, fulfilling.

"Tess," he breathed, lifting his hand, reaching for her jaw.

"No," she said, finding her resolve and stepping back. "We can't."

"Why?"

"Because we're in a parking lot…with your daughter."

Graham shook his head. "Jesus, I think about you all the time. I'm starting to think you're a disease."

"Just what every woman wants to be called," Tess murmured, trying to pretend his words didn't swat at the resolve she'd shoved in front of raw desire seconds ago.

"You know what I mean," he said.

"We said all that needed to be said Sunday." *Way to remind him how much you needed him a few days ago.*

"I'm not giving up," he said, shifted his gaze over to where Emily balanced on a low bar in the jogging park workout area.

"It can't work. Things are too complicated—I can barely tread water right now, barely stay afloat. No way in hell can I fight against the waves for something we can never go back and capture." She closed her eyes briefly, trying to convince herself as much as Graham. "We're a missed opportunity. It's not going to work no matter how much we wish differently. I just—"

"Why? Because of Monique and Upstart? Because I didn't call? Or is it because your father thought I would be a good fit to run Ullo?"

She jerked because his words were a slap of reality.

"Actually, that's it exactly. There's too much between us." She scooted back, bumping into her car. "It's best we remain exactly what we are."

"Which is?"

"I can't even begin to put a name to it." She unlocked her car, gave Emily a wave and slid into her car. Like a frightened bunny, she scurried away from the want, the hunger—the fact she wanted her words to be a lie.

But they weren't.

Graham didn't make sense.

She caught sight of Emily holding his hand as they made their way toward his car, and her heart shattered into small pieces.

As she pulled out onto the highway, her phone rang. Caller ID showed it was her ex-boyfriend Nick.

Maybe that's what she needed—a distraction. Nick had always been her favorite distraction. Handsome, wealthy, spoiled and always ready for a good time, he was the perfect someone to occupy her time, to pull her away from all thoughts of Graham. Picking up the phone, she pressed the answer button. "What's up, Nicky?"

CHAPTER THIRTEEN

THE DAY AFTER soccer practice, Graham trudged into the office, cursing the key that always stuck in his office door. He flipped on the lights, glad he was the first one at the office. Somehow the stillness of the warehouse comforted him. In the small quiet of the morning he felt he could accomplish anything.

He surveyed his domain as he set down his briefcase. Finally all the old files had been removed and the office was in workable shape. Plans for the upcoming season, some drawn by Tess, others by Dave Wegmann, the designer, littered the table, ready for Graham to review and stamp with his seal of approval. He'd had to rely on skills he hadn't used in years to tweak a few plans, and that very day he had meetings scheduled with two krewe captains looking to rent at least twelve floats. Their themes had been turned in weeks ago, but the work had gone unfinished because Tess had left. Graham had divided them between him and Dave. Though Graham had never been talented creatively, he'd managed to get some ideas on paper for a series of Egyptian-themed floats.

He needed to hire somebody else in design, but had left the position open for several weeks more because he'd hoped Tess's anger would grow cold and she'd come back to Ullo and resume the work she'd left behind.

Damn stubborn woman.

A sound outside the door had him spinning in his chair. Dave peeked inside.

"Oh, hey. You're here early." The man was clasping a folder in hands that looked too large to wield a drafting pencil skillfully. Dave looked nervous.

"Have to get here early—we have a lot to do," Graham said, motioning him inside.

Dave grunted and came in, setting the folder on the worktable. "Here are the sketches for Caesar's Muse floats. I think it's going to work nicely. Maybe have to have the carpenters do some adjustments on the ship. Wasn't sure if it would come in under the height maximum. We gotta clear the Causeway Bridge."

Graham leafed through the drawings and specifications. "Looks good. Are we going to have room for the waves on the back of the float?"

Dave shrugged. "Dunno. Maybe."

Graham lifted his eyebrows. "Dunno?"

"Look, I wanted to talk to you anyhow. I've been thinking about making a change."

"A change?"

"Yeah, I've been here a long time, you know?"

Graham felt something sink in his stomach. He'd wanted to talk to Dave later today about stepping up to fill Tess's position and then maybe hiring a grad student from Delgado's art program to train as a designer. He had to do something to fill the gap Tess left, but the words coming out of Dave's mouth made him long for the Pepto-Bismol he had hidden in his drawer. "Don't tell me you're leaving?"

"Sorry. I have an offer from Toledano Bros. It's closer to my house and with Tess gone and Frank sick, I feel like it's a good time to leave."

"I'll give you Tess's job."

"You should have weeks ago," Dave said, crossing his arms and trying to look angry. The man didn't seem to have much ire in him, so it was akin to a toddler refusing a vegetable.

"I had hoped to talk Tess into coming back—that's the only reason I didn't ask you to step into her shoes."

"Yeah, well." Dave shrugged and looked away. "I've been here forever, but I ain't good with change and I ain't good working with them asshole krewe captains, so I really don't want Tess's old job. Figure if everyone else is changing things, it's a good time to make this one for myself. Here's my letter."

Graham sighed, wishing he could slam his fist on the desk instead. "There's no way I can talk you into staying? Ullo needs you. I need you."

"I'm sorry, Mr. Naquin. I've made my mind up." The large man stepped back, ducking his head. "I'll stay for the next two weeks, give you time to find someone else."

Mild panic knocked at the door to Graham's soul. Sliding into the CEO's position at a stable, reputable company was supposed to be easy. But Frank Ullo Float Builders was no longer stable. Mere weeks into the job and everything had started unraveling at an alarming rate. "What about Frank?"

Dave stopped in flight. "That's who I feel the worst about, Mr. Naquin. Frank's been like a father to me."

"Then why abandon him when he's down?"

The man's head shot up. "I'm not—"

"Yeah, you are. This company is in transition and we need stability. We need men like you." He stopped short of begging, but thought if he had to drop to his knees, he might.

"I already told Mack I'd come over to Toledano. Rita wants me to work there, too. Gas is high as a cat's back and I ain't exactly getting younger."

"Just through this season. With a raise. And then we can see how you feel."

Dave cast his eyes toward the table with all the plans spread out, labeled by krewe and float number. Several seconds ticked by as the man grappled with the offer…with thoughts of doing what was right for the company he'd help build into prominence. "I suppose I owe Frank that much."

Graham stopped a huge sigh of relief. He didn't want Dave to know how scared he was to lose him. Or maybe he did. Appealing to Dave's sense of decency worked. "Thank you, Dave. I appreciate that on Frank's behalf. It will be a comfort to him during this hard time."

Dave nodded. "Okay, I gotta go call Rita. She's going to be pissed, but maybe the raise will help. How much will I get?"

"Whatever Tess made."

"I was already making what Tess made. Her old man didn't give her more just because she was his daughter."

"Okay, I'll look at the numbers. This was off-the-cuff, man. Honestly, I'm going to have to look at—"

"In good time, Mr. Naquin," Dave said, a slight smile around his mouth. "Maybe you need to call a meeting. You know, announce Frank's illness officially and tell everyone you need help. They don't know you, but they love Frank, and nothing makes a person feel like helping out more than knowing they're needed."

Graham paused in sifting through the images and looked up at Dave. "First, please call me Graham. And second, thank you. Not just for staying, but for realizing I need help. You're right. I need to stop trying to spin plates and build a team."

Dave nodded. "No one knows you yet. Everyone's on pins and needles, scared about stuff, about Frank, about Tess, about losing business. But we'll all feel better if you are more accessible. This ain't about being a CEO or a COO or whatever you're calling it. It's about leading a team. You can't lead what you don't know. That's what made Frank and Tess good. They knew us, loved us. That's what works in this business."

"You're absolutely right. Guess I've had my head up my ass." Graham walked over to Dave and extended his hand. "You came in to quit, but you just may have ended up saving Frank Ullo Float Builders. Thank you, Dave."

The man took his hand. "This is gonna sound nuts, but I actually feel relieved. I really didn't want to leave—just wanted to feel like I was valued. How about we have pizza at that meeting? And you might want to invite some of the seasonal people, too. Let everyone in on your plan for continuing Frank Ullo's success."

A plan? He'd had one, but problems had started flying at him. He'd wanted to meet with each head—carpenters, sculptors and painters—to talk about new materials, better construction, efficiency. Keeping up with Tess and Upstart had started wearing on him. But Dave was right. Before he could go out and reconquer the Mardi Gras world, he had get his foundation secure. That meant getting the employees of Frank Ullo on board with a vision. He needed them to feel good about where and who they worked for.

"Pizza sounds perfect," Graham said, eyeing the high metal desk sitting just inside the office area. Billie wasn't here yet, but he'd take Dave's approach—tell the woman how much he needed her. How much Frank needed her.

Maybe hearing an appeal for help would soften the woman.... Maybe he'd get fresh coffee without having to make it himself.

As that thought hit him, Billie walked into the office area, carrying a box of Krispy Kreme Donuts and a frown. "Frickin' traffic is absurd. I nearly got sideswiped by some idiot on the bridge."

"Morning, Buttercup," Dave crowed.

Billie gave him the finger. Dave's laugh echoed in the lobby.

Maybe it wasn't such a good idea to talk to Billie right now. Her mood wasn't bad...it was putrid.

But then she smiled, obviously enjoying the ragging she gave Dave. Then she zeroed in on Graham and her expression changed.

"Good morning, Billie," he said.

"What's good about it?" she asked, her expression dead serious.

"You're alive and have donuts?"

She stared at him for a few seconds. "Okay, there's that."

"When you have a second, I want to talk to you about having a staff meeting for everyone here at Ullo."

She raised her eyebrows. "You want to call a meeting in the warehouse?"

"I think we need one, don't you?" Graham said, shooting a glance to Dave who nodded his agreement.

"About Frank?" Billie asked setting down the donuts and switching on her computer.

"And Tess and the situation we're facing in securing the same business we've had for the past few decades. We need everyone to channel their energies and offer up solutions. Basically, we need to have a come-to-Jesus meeting."

Billie looked thoughtful. "Okay. I can shoot a memo to all the departments to make it official, but the easiest way will be to call all the heads of the departments. When you want it?"

"Sooner rather than later," Dave interrupted.

"I thought you were quitting?" Billie asked Dave.

"Graham talked me out of it."

She turned to Graham. "Really? This guy talked you out of going to Toledano?"

Graham smiled. "I do have talents."

"I never thought you didn't."

"Well, I'm not sure it was talent. I'm pretty sure a grown man near to tears helped bring him around. I fell just short of hitting my knees and begging."

Dave laughed. "It wasn't that bad."

"Thankfully, I didn't have to do either of those things, but I was prepared. I need you, Dave." And then he looked at Billie. "I need you, too. I've been trying so hard to hold things together, to give everyone the impression I have everything under control."

Billie straightened. "Well, then. I think we need that meeting and we need some pizza for lunch. Those guys will do anything if you set a pie in front of them."

Graham smiled. "Dave said the same thing. Order whatever pizza you want and set it for tomorrow. We've got to get back on track. For Frank's sake."

Billie lifted her coffee mug. "For Frank's sake."

Dave nodded. "Damn straight."

FRANK LOOKED AT THE PHONE as if it were defective before setting it back on his bedside table.

He felt like shit. The doctors hadn't lied when they said the cancer-killing meds surging through his bloodstream would rob him of his energy. No, not just his energy, but his flippin' manhood. He'd tried to put on a game face for Maggie, but he knew she knew. It was a game they played. A game all married couples played.

"Did you get in touch with her?" Maggie asked, entering their bedroom with a cup of tea. She'd gone to a health food store and come back with all kinds of disgusting tasting teas and several packages of nasty gum that were supposed to beat back the nausea.

"She don't answer," he said, making a face at the steaming cup that smelled like the backside of a troll…or what he imagined a troll's backside to smell like. "She ain't ready to talk to me yet."

"Tess is stubborn. Like Bella."

Frank sighed. When he'd tenderly taken his mother's hand and revealed his diagnosis, she'd uttered words he'd never heard her use before…right before telling him to get the hell out of her house. Then she'd called him a liar and accused him of playing with her emotions. She'd even thrown a bottle of menthol rub at him.

Frank hadn't known how to handle the diminutive woman who'd called him a selfish son-of-a-bitch, and he damned sure wasn't going to point out her insult actually doubled back on her. He'd merely picked up the—thankfully plastic—bottle of menthol rub, set it on the chest Bella had imported from the old country and shut the door softly behind him.

The heavy wood didn't block out the sound of his mother crying.

God, there was no way a man could prepare himself for hearing his mother sob her heart out, especially when it was something he'd never heard before. Not even during those hard years of covering her bruised face with pancake makeup and losing a baby at the hands of the bastard Frank had never called father had Bella lost control of her emotions.

Maggie rubbed his shoulder, drawing his thoughts back to Tess and the reason she wouldn't respond to his call. "Time is all she needs."

"Who? Mom or Tess?"

"Both of them?"

"My mother is in her nineties, Mags. And there is that time thing."

Maggie arched an eyebrow but didn't say what they were both thinking. Time wasn't exactly overflowing from his pockets.

"Well, I've had about all I can stand of her stubbornness—Tess not Bella—and if our daughter doesn't call you before Sunday, she and I are going to have a little heart-to-heart."

"Don't, Maggie. Let her alone. She'll come around."

"Yeah, she will, even if I have to plant my foot on her

rump." Maggie held out the tea. "Now have a bit of this to help with the ickies."

"I don't want it, Mags."

"Come on, Frank. You'll feel better."

"Have you tasted that crap?" he asked, pushing the cup back toward her.

"No," Maggie said, trying again to get the cup in his hands. "I don't need it, but you do. It will help you feel less nauseous so you can eat. You need to eat something, sweetheart."

"I tell you what. I'll drink it if you will."

Maggie stared down at him, frowning for several seconds. Setting the cup down on the bedside table, she huffed, "Fine. Be right back."

Frank smiled as she stalked toward the door, her fanny swaying, her brownish-red hair bouncing at her shoulders. If he didn't feel like barfing up the dry toast he'd struggled to get down earlier, he'd pull her into bed and remind her what she did to him every time she entered... and exited...a room.

Minutes later she returned with another steaming cup in hand. "I have mine, so let's have tea, my fine gentleman."

"Bah, you know I ain't no gentleman. That's why you married me."

Maggie smiled as she lifted the tea to her lips. "So I'm not into stuffy old boring by-the-book guys. You got me pegged."

And then she took a sip.

Before spitting it right back into her cup.

"Dear God, that's terrible," she said, coughing and setting the cup beside his on the bedside table.

Frank laughed and opened the drawer beneath the two cups. "In that case, can I interest you in a piece of chewing gum?"

Maggie laughed and that was all he needed to feel better. In fact, he should suggest it to the doc the next time he went in for the chemo—Maggie's laughter in a bottle.

Cures whatever ails you.

Now if he could just get his daughter to talk to him… and get his mother to realize he wasn't a liar.

TESS JOGGED TOWARD the sideline of the soccer field, the whistle from her refereeing days slapping a rhythm against her sternum. They'd wrapped up practice early…not because they'd accomplished much, but because the attention span of a seven-year-old resembled that of a dog. She might as well have yelled "Squirrel!" every five seconds.

"Okay, Ladybugs, huddle up," she shouted, beckoning the frolicking seven-year-olds toward where she stood. They tumbled over one another, giant bows bobbing as they skidded to a halt around her.

"We're so good we're going to beat everyone," one little girl said with a fist pump.

"Yeah, the other teams are gonna eat our dust," another one said.

"Yay!" Emily squealed, hopping around, making all the other little girls do the same thing. They looked like popcorn on acid.

Tess blew the whistle. "Okay, settle down. We still have work to do before we can take on any challengers. And, first thing first, we have to work on a team cheer."

Ten blinking eyes met her gaze.

"We gotta have a cheer?" one asked.

"Well, sure. It's how we show unity. The other teams will know exactly who they are playing when we do our Ladybug cheer. So I'm giving you a homework assignment," Tess said with a smile.

"Awww," several groaned.

"Well, this is a fun homework assignment," Tess conceded, putting her arms around the nearest girls and drawing them into a huddle. "I want all of you to go home and work on a fun little chant. Something about being red, black and not afraid of anyone."

"Are ladybugs mean?" Emily asked, her expression growing concerned.

"Of course not, but they're tough just like we are. Can everyone do that?"

Heads nodded, bows bobbed and smiles met hers.

"You're the best coach ever," one girl said. Tess thought her name was Piper. She needed to go over the roster and put names with faces.

"And you're the best team," Tess said, deciding she'd missed her calling. Who cared about Mardi Gras floats when there was kids' soccer to coach? "Now everyone put your hand in. I'm going to count to three, and then we're all going to yell 'ladybugs,' okay?"

More head bobbing.

"1-2-3—"

"Ladybugs!" they all screamed.

The team broke and scampered toward their parents sitting in the collapsible stands, and Tess walked to where Graham stood cleaning up the paper cups around the cooler he'd brought.

"Good practice," he said looking up. He wore athletic shorts and a T-shirt that skimmed his toned stomach. He was totally drool-worthy, but Tess pretended he had a wart on his nose and hair growing out of his ears. No noticing his thighs with the sprinkling of hair. No ogling the smooth tanned nape of his neck. No thinking about licking those abs.

Nope.

Not at all.

"Yes, they did better today."

"You're really good with them," he said, squinting against the sun. "I'm glad you volunteered to help."

A warmth blossomed inside her. She shrugged it off. "I'm not the best, but I'm better than poor Jim."

The both turned and looked at Jim who waved at them from the top of the bleachers. He had his leg propped up and looked relaxed in his new job of team manager.

"Seriously, Tess, thanks for doing this."

"Surprisingly, I like it."

Emily came galloping over. "Guess what?"

"What?" Both she and Graham said in unison.

"Kathryn is inviting me to her birthday party. We're going to ride ponies!"

"Cool," Tess said, offering the child a high five.

Out of the corner of her eye, Tess spotted Monique charging across the field in her wrap dress and metallic strappy sandals. Her oversize sunglasses covered most of her face, but she smiled at Emily as she approached them.

"Mom!" Emily shouted, kicking it into high gear to reach her mother. Monique caught Emily's shoulders before she bulldozed her over. "You came to practice...but it's already over. You shoulda seen me. I kicked the ball good today. I'm pretty awesome at this soccer stuff."

"Good, sweetie," Monique said, heading toward where Tess stood with Graham. Tess couldn't see her boss's eyes, but she had the feeling they carefully studied her and Graham, weighing, measuring...perhaps even suspecting. Especially after Tess admitted having his cell phone number. "Tess, what are you doing here, and why are you wearing a whistle? Are you coaching the team?"

"I told you I volunteered to help Jim. I brought Emily to practice, remember?" Hmm...what was Monique's game? Or maybe she had ADD and hadn't really listened when Tess had told her.

"Oh, of course," Monique said, propping her glasses on her head and glancing at Graham. It wasn't a possessive glance though it was familiar. "And you're helping, too?"

Graham nodded. "Jim needed it."

Monique looked over at Jim before shifting her attention back on her ex. "I'm sure it's nice for Emily to have her father so involved in her everyday life. Finally."

Monique's words should have been complimentary, but they sounded anything but. A sudden wave of dislike flooded Tess. The woman liked making Graham feel guilty for the years he'd been in Houston, and that seemed such a petty thing to do in front of their daughter. In front of Tess.

"Yeah," he said, smiling at his daughter, who came and nestled herself against his side. He wound an arm about her shoulders, squeezing her to him. "I'm happy to help the Lake End Ladybugs get ready to win the championship."

Emily giggled.

"You shouldn't get her hopes up," Monique said.

"Why not shoot for the stars? Right, Em?" Graham patted his daughter's back and gave Monique a sharp look.

"Yeah, you should have seen us practice. We're good," Emily said, nodding at Tess. Tess smiled back, affirming the girl, though she wasn't so sure they could win a game, much less the championship.

"Time to go, Emily. Tell your father bye. Tess, too," Monique said, suspicion tight around her mouth. Maybe she didn't suspect a physical thing with Graham as much as she suspected he might try to mine tidbits about Upstart. Tess hadn't thought how it might look from a business standpoint to be coaching soccer with Graham…Upstart's rival.

Jeez. They were a Maury Povich show waiting to happen.

Emily gave each of them a hug and even jogged over to Jim and bestowed one on him. Seemed like Graham was right—a little fresh air and exercise brought out the best in his daughter.

Seconds later, Tess stood with Graham, watching Emily

and Monique stride ahead of Jim who hobbled behind them toward the parking lot.

Graham lifted the cooler off the bleacher and tucked it under his arm, looping the plastic garbage bag over his arm. "Sorry about Monique. She's good at popping bubbles. I'm trying to get her to look at the bright side with Emily, let the kid dream a little."

"You don't have to apologize for Monique," Tess said, picking up her clipboard, falling into step beside him.

He cocked his head. "You're right. I'm sure you've learned quickly who she is."

Yeah, she had. Tess respected Monique's drive and business smarts, but she would have likely never been friends with the woman. There was something hard about Monique, something that told Tess when push came to shove she couldn't rely on her boss to have her back. Very different from the way she'd felt at Ullo. Of course, maybe that's because her daddy was her boss and she'd always known she was safe. She didn't want to talk about Monique with Graham, so she changed the subject. "Are you going to the Oedipus thing tomorrow night?"

He slid blue eyes over to hers. "Of course. They're one of our biggest accounts."

Tess lifted her eyebrows. "Oh, you sure about that?"

"As sure as it gets."

"Mmm," came Tess's response.

Graham stopped. "You love this, don't you?"

"What?" she asked turning around. "I'm making conversation. It's what friends do."

"No, you're protecting yourself by playing a little game between Ullo and Upstart. Keeps you from feeling anything, keeps you from wanting me."

"Why, you egotistical—" Tess whipped her head around to find him grinning at her. "I'm not playing games, Graham, merely giving you a heads-up in regards to Miles.

Monique had drinks with him Tuesday night—that's why I brought Emily to soccer. So don't accuse me of games when I'm being more than nice to warn you."

"And why would you do that?" His face grew serious.

"Huh?"

"Warn me?"

Tess stopped midstride. She spun toward him, mouth open. But…she didn't know what to say. Why was she warning him? She had no business saying anything about Upstart's plans for Oedipus, or the fact Monique had pulled out all the stops to tear the lucrative account from the hands of the new Ullo CEO. Was he right? Was she needling him to keep herself from falling prey to the attraction between them, or did she subconsciously want to help the company she'd loved for so long? Or maybe she felt like she should rub his nose in Upstart's success, proving she was loyal to Monique. Her actions and emotions mystified her. It was as if she were in a house of mirrors, her image stretched and distorted at every turn.

Graham studied her, his expression not what she was accustomed to. No soft blue eyes full of sympathy or alight with passion. Instead he looked intrigued. It was a good look on him—made him intense and somehow even more desirable. This man who had hurt her now stood ready to protect her father and the company he'd built with sweat and tears. It should have pissed her off, but instead, something inside stilled at the thought.

"Just wanted you to know what you're up against," she muttered, moving toward her Prius, wanting to escape Graham examining her every motive.

"I thought at first this was about inserting something between us so you didn't jump my bones and have your wicked way with me in the parking lot," Graham said, trailing behind her, seemingly unwilling to let the conversation die.

She wrinkled her nose. "As if."

"But that's not it. You can't help it, can you?"

"Help what?" She faced him, chin up. No way she backed down, even if she longed to get in her car and escape…just the way she had two nights ago. Sticking her head in the sand had become a strategy. Ask her father. She couldn't seem to dial the number and return his two phone calls. Not like she hadn't tried. She just didn't know what to say to him yet.

She needed time, but that had been her excuse all along. Time. Maybe it would run out before she was ready.

"You left your heart at Ullo."

No shit, Sherlock. Of course she had left her heart at Ullo, but that didn't mean she hadn't tried to move on. She'd spent the past weeks since she'd signed the contract with Monique putting her all into designing brilliant floats for Upstart. She had stuff that was going to blow Miles Barrow's mind for the Oedipus floats…if Monique submitted it. Anger and hurt tied to her pride were good motivators and she'd created some of her best work over the past few weeks.

And it should have been for the company that carries your name.

At that thought, anger flooded her. He didn't have to be so smug, questioning her loyalty to her new job…even if it was partly true. "My allegiance is to the person writing my paycheck. When Upstart does well, I do well. Tomorrow night I'll prove to Miles and Oedipus that Upstart can and will build their floats in 2016. And they will be the most stunning, beautiful and cost-effective floats in the history of parading."

"So you think Upstart will replace Ullo as their go-to floatmaker?" Graham said, his eyes flashing beneath the parking lot light blinking on. No more smiles. Game on.

"Every dog has its day. Upstart has been whittling away

Ullo's business for the past two years. I've already brought in the captain of Thor, and Stacy Reynolds just gave us all of the floats for Rhea. We're almost too busy...but not for Oedipus, of course. That parade would be icing on the very large cake we'll be serving." Tess turned and unlocked her car, the beep-beep punctuating her declaration.

And then Graham smiled at her. Not the sexy smile he'd used that beautiful night under the stars, or the sad one he'd given her in the park last Sunday. No, this one was sharky and slightly amused. Like he toyed with her. "Well, do your damnedest, sweetheart."

She bristled. "Oh, you can bet I will."

His smile got larger. "And why don't you warn your boss—tell Monique she'll stay a small potato. I don't care if she went down on Miles under the table at Brigstons, she's not getting that account."

"You sexist pig," Tess growled, disappointment flooding her at his presumption of how Monique...or any woman did business. "You think women earn business by getting on their knees? We don't have to give sexual favors to get accounts. Our work speaks for itself. How dare you imply such a thing?"

His expression shuttered. "That's not what I meant and you know it."

"You used the words."

"Don't slant the intent. I wasn't implying Monique offered sexual favors for Oedipus's business. My point was no matter how good the offer from Upstart, you aren't getting the account. Period. I'll do whatever it takes, but the long-standing agreement between Ullo and Oedipus will stand. I'll bet my job on it."

Tess lifted her eyebrows. "We'll see. And it might literally be your job on the line. You forget how well I know my father. He won't suffer you to lose Miles's business.

Paired with the other losses…" She trailed off with a shrug, feeling a little ugly, but a lot powerful.

But she didn't want to see Ullo lose business, even if she herself was making moves toward accomplishing just that. Why did Graham *and* Ullo have to lose in order for Tess to win?

"I'll see you tomorrow night, Tess," Graham said, his tone detached. A pang of regret flickered inside her at his coldness. This was what she wanted, right? They were on the opposite sides of a river with no bridge in sight. It was Ullo versus Upstart. Graham versus Tess. With no real winners.

She nodded and lowered herself into her car. "Yeah, I'll see you."

Graham walked away and Tess told herself she was glad. But she wasn't. Her heart hurt for what had been between them…and what would never be again.

The other side, a place where hope lay, felt very far away.

CHAPTER FOURTEEN

TESS WALKED INTO the Oedipus May Madcap Mixer with Nick on her arm...or rather she was on Nick's arm. Either way, she'd conceded to a date with her ex and had self-ishly used this annual fete hosted by the Oedipus Social Club as the one-more-shot merely so she wouldn't have to attend alone.

It had nothing to do with Graham and everything to do with looking confident and successful.

And for all of ten minutes she'd convinced herself Nick deserved another chance...until he'd shown up all tanned from a week of golf on the Gulf Coast, dressed in an Armani suit, smelling like new money, and she'd felt zero attraction. In fact, seeing him so loose, smiling and making flirty jokes made her somewhat disdainful. He kept trying with little brushes of his arm and casting meaningful glances, but the effect fell flat.

Graham had ruined her for all men...or maybe what little she and Nick had once had together had dried up like Granny B's estrogen.

"Get you something to drink, babe?" Nick said, wrapping an arm around her waist. She waited to feel warmth, some flicker of something at Nick's touch, but there was nothing.

Pulling away, she smiled. "I'll take my usual."

Nick brushed back his golden hair. "Aye-aye, Captain."

"Hey, I'm the captain around these here parts," Miles Barrow said from behind her.

Tess spun with a grin—how could she not? The man was hard to dislike. "Miles."

"Ah, Tess of the Ullos," the captain of Oedipus joked, kissing her cheek and giving her a brief squeeze. "You're looking ravishing, as usual."

"You flatterer," she murmured with a smile. Miles Barrow had been the captain and art director for Oedipus for as long as she could remember. Flamboyant, loud and slightly annoying, he loved his position of power within the super krewe, but there was something decidedly lovable about the overweight man with a gray-streaked beard.

"Of course I am, but I ain't no liar, neither, darlin'," he said, his New Orleans East accent thick as gumbo.

Nick stuck out his hand. "Miles."

"How ya been, friend?"

"Good. I'm here with Tess, aren't I?"

Miles nodded. "Damn straight. Go get you some food. We got everythin' you want. Have a ball."

Nick slipped away and headed to the bar. Tess nodded at Miles, knowing Monique expected her to help bring in his business. But he wouldn't be easy to pull away from Ullo because he was the kind of guy who respected tradition. Frank Ullo had been a friend as much as he'd been the guy building spectacular, elaborate floats with all the intricate posterboard flowers the krewe was known for. "I want to talk to you about the 2016 floats…after I snag some of those smoked oysters and do the wobble with Margaret Ann."

Miles's guffaw filled the foyer. "Ah, damn, chérie. My wife's been practicin' that dumb thing all week. You go dance with her. Will tickle her fancy, for sure. Business can wait." He waved at someone across the room and was gone in a blink just as Nick returned with a vodka tonic with a wedge of lime and offered it to her, clinking it with his own scotch and soda.

"I'm glad to be here with you, babe," he said, brushing a lock of hair off her shoulder. "It's been too long since I spent time with my Tess. I can't even remember what we fought over."

She lifted her eyebrows. "Really?"

Nick played dumb which unfortunately suited him. "Naw. What was it over? A silly Christmas present? Drinking too much at the Ullo holiday bash?"

"Merrill Wynn?"

"Merri?"

"You took her home and screwed her right after giving me that bracelet and talking about forever. Remember?" Tess said.

"Oh, yeah. I forgot. But you know she didn't mean anything. I was drunk and she was all over me."

"You don't really believe that."

"So I screwed up. I know that now. I'm ready to be the man you need." He looked down at her, so earnest, so sincere, so...freaking lying between his teeth.

"We're here as friends, Nick. That's it."

Nick smiled. "Sure. We're totally friends. And if we hook up, we hook up."

She pulled his hand from her waist and surveyed the room, wishing now she'd just come solo. Monique had urged her to bring a date, even going so far as to suggest a double date, but for some reason Tess held her off, declaring she had an appointment earlier that day. She hated lying but the thought of sitting at a table with her boss and Nick made her feel itchy.

Monique and Josh should be here by now.

Graham, too.

Her stomach did a loop-the-loop. She'd taken extra care with her appearance that evening, donning a short gold cocktail dress that clung to her hips and showed off her toned legs. The blousey crepe top showed her equally

toned arms by gathering at her shoulders and dipping low
to show the tops of her breasts. She wore diamond hoop
earrings and her hair pulled back soft against the nape of
her neck. Killer high-heeled sandals completed her look.

She'd told herself the outfit had nothing to do with Graham and everything to do with feeling confident and together—the same reason she'd brought Nick. But she lied
to herself. Rubbing the satiny lotion over her body and
sliding into her lacy underwear, her thoughts had been
of Graham. Of the way he'd loved her, made her feel like
forever was something within her grasp.

Damn it. Why couldn't she have all she wanted, including Graham? Why was everything so hard now?

"Tess, you look lovely," Monique said, sweeping alongside her.

"Oh." Tess jumped at the unexpected greeting, slosh-
ing her drink on her hand. "And you look gorgeous as always, Monique."

Monique, clad in something short, slithery and magenta,
smiled. "I see you've brought a date. Your taste is exquisite as always."

Tess made introductions for her "friend" Nick, who applied his charm with a light hand. Tess's earlier reminder
about his indiscretion must have taken the wind from his
sails. Wouldn't last long. Nick was anything if not imper-
vious to "no."

Josh bumbled up, carrying two glasses of champagne.
He handed one to his wife and turned a goofy smile on
Tess. "You clean up good, girl."

Josh wore a jaunty hat that should have looked ridiculous but somehow went perfectly with his atypically
dark, somber suit. Monique rolled her eyes at her husband's trademark joviality and got down to her trademark
sharkiness. "Graham will be here looking to get chummy
with Miles. I think I've got him in our corner, but I want

you to do a little hustling. I sent him our sketches a few days ago."

Tess smiled. "So you liked the sketches?"

Something in Monique's eyes glittered. "I sent him the best sketches. You did well, Tess."

Pleasure bloomed inside Tess at her boss's vote of confidence. She'd had to work to earn the Oedipus account and obviously it had paid off. "Float sketches are like Christmas morning to Miles. He'll get back to us soon."

"But as added insurance, don't be afraid to kiss his ass a little bit. Where is Miles, by the way?" Monique perused the room like a pro. Tess did the same and that's when she caught sight of Graham.

Her heart leaped so hard in her rib cage she pressed a hand to her chest. He looked so damn good she wanted to run and throw herself on him, maybe dropping various pieces of clothing along the way.

Tall, dark and so good-looking it should have been against the law, Graham had heads turning. The sudden feminine interest caught Monique's attention too, and she spun toward the entrance.

"Ah, the wonder boy himself. Speeding up heartbeats," Monique said under her breath.

Josh peered around Tess and gave a shrug. "Don't know why you think he would change now."

Monique patted Josh's hand as if she worried about his insecurity. "Now, Josh, being devastatingly handsome is not all it's cracked up to be."

"Bite your tongue, woman," Nick piped up, finally, turning to his good side and giving Monique one of his charming grins. Yeah, he was over the "just friends" speed bump.

Graham caught sight of them and moved their way. His stride was purposeful and naturally elegant. The same navy suit he'd worn for his interview—that had lain in her polka-dotted chair—stretched the breadth of his torso, the same classic tie lay against snowy pressed white. Same wing tips, same icy blue eyes, same response inside Tess. Shivers.

"Evening," he said, with a nod to Monique, his eye snagging on Nick who still grinned like a jackanapes. "How is Upstart this fine evening?"

Monique looked nonchalant. "We're just dandy, Mr. Naquin."

"I'm not dandy," Josh said, with a secret smile. "I'm thirsty. Grab you a beer, Graham?"

"Sure."

"I know what you like." Josh headed to the bar, looking relieved to escape.

Graham held out a hand to Nick. "I'm Graham Naquin."

Nick took his hand, a flicker of a frown marring his all-American good looks. "Nick Ashley."

And then silence so uncomfortable it might have been improved by a dog licking itself…or a kid picking his nose…or Nick saying, "I'm Tess's boyfriend."

"What?" Graham and Tess asked at the same time.

Monique raised her eyebrows.

"No, he's not," Tess clarified, smiling as if it were a joke. "He's kidding around."

"Okay, I *used* to be Tess's boyfriend," Nick said, winding his arm around Tess's waist again and tugging her against him.

Mood had gone from uncomfortable to knife-in-the-eye excruciating. Like a hound sizing up the competition over a bone, Graham eyed Nick. In fact, he looked as if he might rip Nick's arm off and beat him with it at any minute.

Aww…Graham was jealous. Warmth washed over Tess and she removed Nick's hand from her waist.

Monique studied the three of them, narrowing her eyes. "How interesting."

"Yes, but we haven't been together since last year," Tess said, searching for some other way to lighten the moment. Or maybe she should just run. "I think I'll find Josh and trade in this cocktail for something stronger."

Nick looked down at the untouched cocktail in her hand. "You haven't even taken a sip."

Tess raised the drink to her lips and took a gulp, smacking as she backed away. "Definitely not strong enough."

Graham suddenly looked—dare she think it?—hurt.

"Wait a sec." Monique clutched Tess's elbow, making her drink slosh yet again on her wrist. All three looked at the small woman who had a knowing gleam in her eye. "Did you sleep with Graham?"

IF GRAHAM HAD BEEN a lesser man, he might have gotten embarrassed at Monique's query...or cussed like a cab-driver....but he prided himself on keeping his composure. Tess, however, wasn't as composed.

"What?" she squealed, the glass in her hand slipping to shatter on the marble floor of the Yacht Club foyer. It was a scene from a bad movie. Or a soap opera.

Several people mimicked Tess's shriek, stepping away as the liquid spread. Tess dropped and tried to pick up the shattered glass, but a waiter moved quickly toward her with a towel and tray, brushing her hands away, as he made quick work of the mess.

Monique shot a knowing smile at Graham—the kind he'd always hated. "How did I miss this? You two have something going on and it's more than just business."

Graham gave her a quelling look. "Not now, Monique."

"Suddenly things are so clear."

"There's nothing clear in any situation with you, Monique. You've never been uncomplicated, and in my limited experience with your new art designer, neither is she."

Tess looked up from where she squatted, her expression something between tortured and angry. "Stop talking about me as if I'm not here. And, frankly, who I sleep with—" she glanced over to Nick "—or who I *don't* sleep with, is no one's damn business."

Monique gave a choked laugh. "Oh, dear Lord, this is so effed up it's crazy. You never change, Gray. Always find a way to needle me. Sleeping with one of my employees…really classy."

Nick, who'd stood looking slightly confused, clued in. "Wait. You're with this guy, Tess?"

Shaking her head. "I'm definitely not with him."

Tess's quiet words sank into him. He didn't want them to be true. He wanted to be with her in every way. If only…

"But you're not with me, either." Shooting Tess a look of outrage, Nick stalked off. Graham understood. Nothing like getting smacked in the face with that kind of news along with a pointed message about the night ending with a cursory "goodnight" rather than an invitation to come up for coffee.

"I know how he feels," Monique said.

"That's enough, Monique," Graham warned, giving her the hardest look he could manage.

Monique inhaled and exhaled with great show. "Please tell me this happened before you took a job with her father's company? Please tell me you didn't sleep your way into daddy's good graces because that would be low even for someone like you."

"Someone like me?" He tried to keep anger from his voice.

"A man who likes to grind his heel on everyone who stands in his way. A man who would go to work for the competition just to rub my nose in it. A man who would seduce Frank Ullo's daughter…all so he could get ahead."

"Don't you dare go there," he said, gritting his teeth, wishing Monique would shut the hell up. Things were already tenuous between him and Tess. He didn't need his ex making it look like he'd spent that night with Tess for any other reason than that she'd taken hold of him.

And it felt like she'd never let go…even during those weeks he'd convinced himself it had been a fleeting moment and nothing more. But he'd known even then that Tess was special. That she was a forever kind of girl.

"You love to hurt me." Monique jutted her sharp chin, her eyes crackling.

"I still have that power? Somehow I doubt it."

"You don't," she sniped.

Graham sighed. "Why do you always think everything is about you? What happened between me and Tess has nothing to do with Upstart or Ullo. Never had anything to do with business."

Tess edged a shoulder between him and Monique. Pointing a finger at each of them, she hissed, "Both of you, zip it. People are staring…and listening."

Monique snapped her mouth shut and glared at both of them.

He took several steps back, tossing an apologetic look at Tess. "I'm sorry, Tess. I came to say hello, not create drama."

Tess looked unconvinced. "Drama has become my stalker. I should start walking backward."

Graham gave her a tight smile. Hell, even annoyed, Tess looked spectacular. Her dress fit her to perfection, and she'd carefully applied makeup that highlighted her expressive green eyes and pouty lips. Her toned legs looked amazing in the short skirt and strappy sandals, and underlying her sultry scent was the fresh scent of apples. He wanted to whisk her away from the fake laughter and clinking glasses, wanted to go back in time to that rain-soaked night. He wanted to peel the dress from her body, kiss his way along her collarbone and make her shatter against him again and again.

What he didn't want was her standing there frowning at him. Maybe even setting more bricks in the wall they had between them.

"I'll say goodnight," he said, ducking his head in farewell.

Monique nodded. "Yeah, you should say goodnight."

Tess said nothing in his defense, so there was little left to do than walk away.

So he did.

And ran right into the main reason he'd buffed his dress shoes—Miles Barrow.

"Hey, Graham Naquin, new man about town, I've been looking for you," Miles said, extending his hand. "Gotta tell you, you've got competition with those gals over there. When we meet, I'm going to need to be dazzled."

Graham took the proffered hand. "You think Ullo isn't prepared to do that? Frank and I have worked up a deal you won't be able to refuse, but we shouldn't discuss it now. I'd love to have drinks with you this week or maybe drop by your offices. The sooner, the better."

"Call my office Monday morning and tell Jules to schedule us a liquid lunch." Miles grinned, slapping Graham on the back.

Out of the corner of his eye, Graham saw Monique and Tess watching them. The two women looked mildly concerned and he liked that. Graham wasn't going to let Monique get her stiletto in the Oedipus door...even if she had the magical Tess on her team. After the exchange with Tess on Thursday night at the soccer field, he'd dropped by to see a bedridden Frank, seeking his approval on a three-year contract with Oedipus. He knew that as CEO he didn't need Frank's permission, but it felt like the right thing to do.

Frank had been weak, but in good spirits…except when Graham had mentioned Tess. A prickly yawn still gaped between the father and daughter. But overall, he saw gratitude in Frank's eyes as they hammered out a proposal that would give the super krewe early priority in the building schedule, locked in prices and a hefty discount on tractor rental. It was a to-the-bone contract, of little benefit to Ullo, but he'd be damned if he lost this account. Oedipus, with its overindulgent floats and eye-popping fiber optics, had always been a showcase for Ullo Float Builders. Making calculated risks was part of the business, and Graham felt in his gut it would be a good gamble.

"I'll call Monday morning. Go ahead and get a bucket of ice ready for the champagne. We'll have a lot to celebrate," Graham said.

"I like your confidence, Naquin. Can't wait to see what Ullo wants to do for Oedipus next season. Now go have a good time and meet some of the other members of the krewe. They're good people who love a good time. No more business tonight—too much wine to drink and pretty girls to dance with," Miles said before melting into the crowd.

Graham couldn't resist looking back at Tess, not because he wanted to one-up her, but because he'd hated the way he'd left things between them…hated Monique's ugly words. Nothing about the way he felt about Tess had to do with Mardi Gras, floats or getting a leg up in business.

No, it had everything to do with something he'd believed couldn't exist for him.

But Tess was no longer standing in the foyer.

She was gone.

CHAPTER FIFTEEN

TESS PRESSED HERSELF into a small shadow on the balcony of the Yacht Club and wished herself away to anywhere other than where she now stood. Stock-still and breathing shallow, she wondered if she stood motionless long enough she'd turn into a statue.

God, she wished she were a statue. Then no one would expect anything of her. Wasn't there a play or something about a girl who turned into a statue…or was that about a girl who had been a statue and then fell in love with her creator?

Falling in love.

Every little girl's fairy tale. She'd cherished the wonder of that moment, imagining it as she lay on her down comforter, staring at the soccer posters on the wall of her childhood bedroom. She'd look sophisticated, holding a glass of champagne. And he would be handsome (looking like David Beckham), swooping in, kissing her hand and taking her in his arms. And she would know. Somehow she'd know this was the man for her. Love would slam into her, and happily ever after would be sitting right behind her smiling prince.

That was the way it was supposed to be.

Easy.

But nothing about what she felt for Graham was easy. She hated him. She loved him. Wanted to punch him. Wanted to kiss him. Falling in love wasn't supposed to be this confusing. Usually, she wasn't the kind of girl who looked at the glass half empty. But this particular glass from the tales of Tess Ullo's life looked cracked. No, shattered...just like the one she'd dropped minutes ago, making her look incredibly stupid in front of everyone.

Someone stepped onto the balcony and walked to the edge overlooking Lake Pontchartrain, a stark figure against the light of the full moon.

Graham.

Her flippin' prince.

Shame, embarrassment, guilt and longing throbbed inside her. The sight of Graham did nothing to relieve it. She didn't want to deal with him again so she scooted even farther into the shadows, craving some time alone before she attempted to carry out Monique's directives given mere seconds ago—mix, mingle and nail Miles down to the floor. Monique didn't seem all that affected that her newest employee had slept with her ex and rival. For Monique, it was always about the business.

But Tess needed a few minutes to compose herself.

Her furtive movement drew attention, and Graham turned, presenting her his profile.

Shit.

"Tess?" His voice was soft as the night spread before them.

No sense in playing statue anymore. She stepped forward. "How did you know it was me?"

"You're wearing gold and it catches in the moonlight," he said, moving so close she caught the scent of his cologne. The fragrance wound itself around her just like this man who had enraptured her that night long ago.

"I knew I should have worn the black dress my mother bought me on sale last spring. It was practically made for subterfuge," she cracked dryly. Wasn't like she could hop over the railing and disappear into the depths of the lake. She wore her only pair of Manolo Blahnik heels.

"You look spectacular in the one you're wearing," he said, a smile flickering at his delicious mouth. Oh, damn it all. Why was his mouth so delicious?

"You're just in suck-up mode and can't turn it off. I saw you with Miles. You both looked very chummy.... Makes me wonder what you're working up for him. Should have kept my big, fat mouth shut."

"Yeah, but I like your mouth open," he said, his eyes deepening. This man's words were silk against her skin, making her yield.

She didn't want this. Couldn't handle moonlight and seduction…not when so much was at stake. "Do you? Well, then you won't mind when I open it and tell you you're grasping at straws with Miles. He prefers quality above all else. My sketches give him that. Paired with Monique's offer, he can't resist. So save your pandering."

"Tess, I'm just doing my job."

"Which should have been my job," she muttered and immediately wished she hadn't. It was moot. Indulgent. A freaking dead horse. Her inner toddler may shout "It's not fair!" but the reality was life wasn't fair.

Suck it up, Tess, and stop dragging that hurt out into the light.

"Touché," he said, staring out at the boats anchored in the marina, bobbing in the gentle waves. He probably wondered how many times he'd have to hear about something that wasn't his fault. "I wish things were different for you, Tess. I wish I could make it better."

Something pinged inside her and made her aware of her constant harping on being usurped. "I have to move past what happened. I have to let it go."

He didn't say anything. Just stared out into the inky darkness as if he could find the answers for her there. After a minute or so, he turned. "About what Monique said. You know that's not true. That night wasn't—"

"I know. That night belongs to us. No one else. It's our memory, Graham, and I know you didn't know I was Frank Ullo's daughter."

"Monique likes to paint me as the bad guy."

Tess gulped back a laugh. "You *are* the bad guy."

He moved closer still. "Is that what you really think?"

She didn't answer. He knew she didn't think he was bad. He knew she wanted him…maybe even knew she admired the way he loved Emily, the way he stood up for Ullo.

Graham cupped her chin, raising her face to his. The moonlight cast a soft glow on his face, making his eyes soft and mystical. "I'm the bad guy? I used you?"

Still she said nothing.

"Tess?"

Swallowing hard, she closed her eyes. "No."

"No?"

She opened her eyes. "You're not a bad guy, Graham."

He lifted another hand and brushed back a tendril of her hair. "I want to be your good guy. I want things you can't imagine."

"I know you do," she whispered, longing rising within her. How did he always manage to do this? "I thought you were the right guy that night, but everything went so wrong. How could it have gone so wrong, Graham?"

Her words brought him to her. It was as if he could see she hadn't fully closed the door to him. She wanted him. She couldn't keep him out.

Wrapping an arm around her waist, Graham maneuvered them both even farther into the shadows. The touch of his body brushing against hers ignited a torrent of desire. She couldn't resist him…. She didn't even want to stop him.

Maybe just a little taste.

Couldn't hurt to have one secret moment on the balcony, maybe then she could let him go. Maybe one kiss would be enough, maybe it would be average and not at all as special as she remembered.

She lifted her face to him…and then his mouth was on hers, hungry, almost punishing.

But she didn't care. She welcomed the nip of his teeth, the tightness of his grip, the tug of her hair as he tipped her head back so he could deepen the kiss. Like a pirate in tales of old framed against the moon on the water, Graham plundered and she surrendered.

There was no other recourse.

"Tess," he groaned against her mouth, his hands sliding down to her ass, bringing her hard against his body, against his erection. Like a match dropped onto lighter fluid, lust exploded in her. Nothing average about this kiss.

"I need you, Tess. I want to—" He kissed her again… and again.

Tess anchored his head with her hands as the world fell away. There was only Graham—his hard body and hot mouth moving her to a place where nothing else mattered but a man, a woman and a deep pulsating need.

"Just one more time," she said as his head dropped and his lips moved against the pulse beating strong in her neck. She dropped her head back, brushing the weathered paint behind her, giving him what he wanted. Threading her hands in his hair, she held him to her, thrilling as his hands wandered over the backs of her thighs, rising to cup her bottom beneath the short skirt.

"Come with me," he breathed against the valley between her breasts as his fingers brushed the dampening heat gathered between her legs. One finger slid along the soft lace of her panties, drawing a half sigh, half groan. "I need you. Just once, Tess. Just one more time so I can remember forever."

His words did more than even his magic fingers, his hot mouth on her skin. She wanted that, too.

"Your car?" she panted, lifting her leg to give him room. Her body was a slave to him. She could no more stop herself than a moth could ignore a flame.

And then his mouth was back on hers, nearly frantic. "Yes, somewhere. Hurry."

Stepping back, he looked down at her, his breathing ragged, something so intense in his eyes. Tess had never seen anything so compelling. He stood in that buttoned-up suit, looking as if he might lose control. In that moment, she was certain nothing could keep him from her—she'd do anything for him. Rob a bank. Run away to Vegas. Have his babies. Whatever he wanted. Because there was nothing between them but an uncontrollable need she had to quench one more time.

Then she'd let him go.

He reached in his pocket for his keys, withdrawing them, looking around for an exit even as his other hand slid over her back and bottom.

Tess felt drugged and knew at that moment what an addict felt. She was hooked on Graham.

And that's when Tess heard Nick.

"Tess is out here somewhere. I saw her slip out when I went to the bar," Nick was saying to someone.

"I haven't seen her in forever," came the responding trill, which sounded really flirty and really drunk. "But if we don't find her, we can always find something else to do."

Nick laughed and then there was a girly squeal.

"Oh, you bad boy. I love it." She giggled.

The effect was like cold water down her back.

Good Lord. What was she doing? How easily she'd tossed all her convictions for one more time in Graham's arms.

Who had she become that she'd consider running out on her date? She'd come with Nick, and though he was a jerk, she still owed him some semblance of decency. She couldn't sneak off with another man, no matter how damn good Graham looked standing slightly rumpled, his silvery blue eyes moving over her with a hot hunger. It was, well, wrong. Even if it looked like Nick would rebound just fine with his new friend.

"Stop, Graham," she whispered. "I can't do this. It's wrong."

"Are you serious? This isn't wrong, Tess. Nothing about this is wrong," he said, drawing her back to him.

She pushed against his chest. "I'm here with Nick. I can't."

"He doesn't sound too worried about it."

"Maybe not, but I'm not that kind of girl. I'm not sneaking off with you just because I have a hard time resisting you."

He stopped stroking her, dropping his hands from a body shaking in need.

Stepping back, he gave a beleaguered sigh. "Still fighting it, huh?"

"I have to. I'll admit I want you. It's obvious you trip my control switch, but if things are complicated now, what will they be if we do this?"

"The same, but we'll feel a hell of a lot better. Jesus, Tess, I need you." The longing in his voice nearly unraveled her last shred of control.

"I—I want you, Graham. That's not the problem. It's all the other stuff."

Eyes narrowed, he said. "Because we're 'against' one another?" He made the quote marks with his fingers…his beautiful, masculine fingers…the ones she wanted on her body doing delicious things.

Tess swallowed the need clawing to get out. "Yes. Exactly."

"So because we're both hustling Miles Barrow for a

contract and because you're working for my ex and because I took over the operation of your family business and because you're here with Nick—" Graham tilted his head, his mouth sardonic even as a twinkle of amusement sparked in his eye "—those little things are keeping you from leaping the locked gate over there and getting it on in the parking lot with me?"

And in that moment, Tess's heart gave a lurch in her chest. He'd unlocked an escape hatch with a large dose of absurd humor. Tess covered her mouth to keep from almost hysterical laughter, but she sent him a thank-you with her eye. "And I'm wearing a dress and heels. Hard to scale a gate in this getup."

He held up his hands. "Hey, you can't blame me for trying. I've never been a saint, and you are pretty much the perfect girl for me…outside all of those other things."

Before she could stop herself, she snorted.

"No, it's true. You're highly uncomplicated and without any baggage. How can I resist?" More teasing, more lightness, more squeezing of her heart. He was being more than decent. He was living up to being her prince…even when she wanted him to be the pirate. To scoop her up, toss her over his shoulder and then have his wicked way with her despite her protests.

"If that's what you're looking for, then yeah, I'm your girl," she said, still wanting to kick off her heels and scale the iron gate, but glad Graham had not pressed the issue. It was not the right time or right place.

Might well never be the right time or place.

And that made her heart ache.

She moved toward the rail and Graham trailed behind her, looking casual and not so "I'm about to rip this chick's clothes off in the middle of a business mixer."

"Hey, there you are, Tess," Nick said, spotting her as she emerged from the shadows, the sequins of her dress no doubt catching in the light of the glowing orb hunkered over the gentle lake waves. "Look who I found."

Riley Ann Richard waved and spread her hands into a big hug. "Tess."

"Hey, Riley," Tess said as she was enveloped in a cloud of Vera Wang perfume. Her old teammate squeezed her hard and brushed her cheek with a kiss.

"I haven't seen you since we graduated. Isn't that crazy?" Riley said, stepping back into her towering platform shoes. The dress Riley wore was a bit too small but had gorgeous lace detail across the bodice. Her friend had blond curly hair piled on her head, bright blue eyes and a salon tan. She looked stunning as always which made Tess want to kick her.

"It is. How are you?" Tess asked.

"Good. I'm a buyer for Saks now. I'm in for Leo's wedding. Mom and Dad are over the moon to have me here for two weeks." Riley eyed Graham, who stood just over Tess's shoulder.

Tess moved back and made introductions…which seemed to make Riley's night. Her eyes ate Graham up and she cooed, flirted and basically did everything short of handing him a room key. Jealousy, like a cur catching scent of meat, raised its head inside Tess. She'd never felt that before, and she didn't like it. Had no reason to own that emotion when it came to Graham. If he wanted to take Riley up on her offer, it was none of her business.

Of course, Tess might have to rip her friend's throat out if he did. Dear Lord, she not only was jealous, she was feral.

"It's been nice meeting you, Riley," Graham said, smiling congenially, "but I need to talk to Miles before I slip out."

"Oh, I'll walk with you. I haven't seen him in forever," Riley said, shooting Tess and Nick a smile and linking her arm with Graham's. "Who knew I'd find such a hand-some escort when I showed up tonight. I didn't even want to come but Daddy begged me."

Riley gave a little ta-ta wave and dragged Graham off.

Graham glanced back and in the depths of his eyes she saw resignation. He was stuck. And she wasn't going to rescue him the way she had that night at Two-Legged Pete's. Nick gave a heavy sigh as he saw his only chance for a random hookup striding away on Graham's arm.

"That dude is ballin' with the chicks, huh?" he said, his expression hangdog.

"Really?" Tess said, shooting him an incredulous look. "An hour ago you were telling me you've changed. Don't think I didn't see you putting the moves on Riley."

Nick blinked. "I was not."

"Oh, don't give me that, Nick. I know you. That last statement was you bemoaning the fact you're not getting underneath Riley's too tight dress."

"Well, I'm not getting underneath yours, that's for sure."

Tess snapped her fingers. "You got that right, buster."

And then she stalked away, heading for the exit. Monique could kiss her ass. She cared about her job, but she had to get out of the May Madcap Mixer. Like, pronto. Like, yesterday. Like, at that second.

Before she punched Nick, ripped Riley away from Graham and had a nervous breakdown in the middle of a primo Mardi Gras krewes shindig.

Tess Ullo was finally cracking up.

And there was nothing funny about it.

GRAHAM PRIED TESS's friend's hands off his ass for the second time that evening. Seemed the woman was a veritable octopus.

"I'm feeling a little drunk," Riley trilled, grinning at him as they danced on the small dance floor set in front of a New Orleans funk band. "And you know what that means…."

"You're going to bed early?" he cracked.

"Oh, yeah. With you." She wiggled her eyebrows and grabbed his hands, moving them down to her ass.

Graham had to admit that any other time in his life, Riley would have gotten that early night. She was extremely pretty and obviously very available. But this wasn't the old Graham.

Coming to New Orleans had been about starting over, and he wasn't going back to the man who'd walked on the edge, wondering if any day he might drop down into the same pit his own father fell into. No. Conviction had grown inside him—the conviction to be a respectable businessman, an available father and a good person. No letting his goal slip through his fingers, which meant no more sleeping around with pretty, half-drunk girls.

Except when it came to a stubborn dishwater blonde with a perfect mouth, spectacular breasts and a laugh that made angels jealous. That's how you started, dude. Picking up a half-drunk girl in a bar…and falling in love with her.

Tess was the one.

Even though a gulf stretched between them, he knew deep down inside in places he pretended didn't exist that he'd fallen for Tess.

"Riley, you're a beautiful woman, but I'm not available in that way," he said as she slightly ground her pelvis into his.

A furrow gathered between her pretty eyes. She studied him for a moment before raising her eyebrows. "Ohhhh. Yeah, that's unfortunate. Uh, for me."

What did that mean?

"The good ones are always gay," she muttered, jerking his hand back up to her waist.

Graham almost laughed but controlled himself. "Yeah, we are. Sorry about that."

"That's okay. You can salvage this evening by telling me what you think about Armani's new collection. I'm a buyer for Saks and all my other gay friends are so conflicted about the new cut on the jacket. What do you think?"

"You think all gay men know fashion?" Graham asked.

"Most the ones I hang with do, but then again, I'm in the fashion industry. So give it to me from a layman's point of view," she said, looping an arm around his neck and studying him intently. "What do you think about Armani's newest line? Or Tom Ford's?"

Graham opened his mouth but couldn't figure out how to get out of this one. "Riley, I have no clue."

She studied him, this time a little longer. "You're not really gay, are you?"

"No."

"So you're unavailable because you're with someone?"

"Sort of."

She sank against him. "Well, then, do me a favor. For the next few minutes pretend like she's watching and show her what she's missing not dancing with you."

But she wasn't watching. Graham had seen Tess leave, looking as if a pack of wildebeest chased her. And he knew some of it had to do with Riley, some of it had to do with Nick but most of it had to do with what had passed between the two of them—the passion neither of them could control.

Thing was, Graham no longer wanted to control it.

He just couldn't figure out how to get from Point A to Point B. Usually that was his greatest talent. That was his freaking job. But this whole situation he and Tess had blundered into was like tiptoeing through a minefield. One wrong step and...

"Just hold me a little closer, please," Riley said, her eyes not so much drunk as...sad?

"Sure," he said, gathering her up tight against him.

"Thank you." She sighed against his lapel. "I recently split with my boyfriend of two years. It's been pretty hellacious. I shouldn't have drank so much and propositioned you that way. Thought it might help stop the freaking bleeding inside, you know?"

"It's fine, Riley," he murmured against her hair. And then he did what she suggested. He danced with the brokenhearted Riley like he meant it, holding her tight, treating her like she was the center of his world, sliding his hands against her back, even giving her a little twirl.

When the music died, he gently brushed a kiss against her cheek. "Be happy, Riley."

She looked up and smiled, still a little shaky on her feet. "Yeah, I wish I could. Things would be a whole lot easier if he wasn't already married."

"Sometimes the things that stand between two people in love are insurmountable. And sometimes we can knock down those walls...or bridge those waters."

"Yeah, but not in my case. His wife is pregnant." Riley lifted herself on her tiptoes and kissed his cheek. "Good luck with Tess, Graham."

He stood alone on the dance floor as Riley faded into the other dancers.

The woman had known him for all of half an hour and had known he was in love with Tess. That's how obvious his feelings were. But what could he do about it? How could he break down the enormous wall between them?

It would already have been there if he'd come back and she wasn't an Ullo. He'd have had to grovel, admit to her his weakness, his greatest fear of being a failure like his father. But add in the fact he'd taken the job she'd expected to get, her father's terminal illness, and the fact they were rivals scrabbling for the same accounts and that wall felt never ending. His own personal Great Wall of China.

But walls could be torn down. And he would have to figure out a way to reach the woman he wanted on the other side.

Like a knight of old, he needed a plan to breach the castle. If he wanted Tess Ullo, he'd have to do more than mope and complain.

He had to be a man of action.

CHAPTER SIXTEEN

SUNDAY DAWNED HOT for early May. Tess had struggled from bed, forced herself to go for a run, showered and journeyed to her parents early as requested by her mother.

She had thought about faking a migraine because the idea of bed and a never-ending series of Lifetime movies seemed to suit how she felt today. But duty called and she found herself entering her parents' house via the backdoor.

"Hello there, my Tess," her mother said, from her position behind the mammoth stove. "You look pretty this morning, hon. I like the way you're wearing your hair."

She'd braided it down the side. "Thanks."

"And you've lost a little weight."

Not sure if that was good or bad. Her mother was always trying to fatten her up with Italian pastries and calorie-laden pastas. "Stress takes it off me. You know that."

Her mother lifted the spoon from the red sauce, tasted it, tossed in some salt and turned to her. "Time to talk turkey, missy."

"You wanted me to come early to talk about poultry?" Of course, Tess knew this wasn't about anything as inane as food. This was about her father. Neither she nor Frank had figured out how to traverse the gulf between them, so Maggie had built the raft. Tess had dreaded this moment as much as she had craved it. She needed to be moved and her mother was the woman to kick her ass in gear.

"Turkey is fowl," her mother intoned, tossing the spoon into the sink and untying her apron. "Let's go out back."

"It's hot, Ma."

"So is the kitchen," Maggie said, grabbing a sweating glass of lemonade and shoving another one that had obviously been waiting on Tess. "Here. Follow me."

Tess had no recourse but to do as directed. Her mother wasn't a woman to be questioned—people just did whatever the diminutive drill sergeant said. Yep, Maggie had missed her calling in life. Tess sighed. "Fine."

They walked to the flagstone patio sitting near the waterfall her mother had insisted they build to cover the noise of the nearby highway. The oaks gracefully bowed, magnanimously sharing the cover of their leaves, casting pure shadow on the outdoor living room her mother had created. With the tumbling verbena and vibrant canna lilies clustered with the blooming irises, the patio looked like the cover of a gardening magazine.

"Sit down," her mother said with a gracious wave of her hand, reminding Tess of the spider opening her parlor to the fly. Suddenly Tess felt twitchy. She so should have faked a migraine.

"What's up? I'm looking for the coals you're about to rake me over but I don't see any." Tess set her glass down, plopped onto an overstuffed chair and crossed her arms. Realizing she probably looked like a sullen teenager, she uncrossed them, hooking one on the back of her chair.

"Oh, honey, you know I don't have to tell you what is up. You know what's up," Maggie said, taking a careful sip of her lemonade before setting it beside Tess's on the stone coffee table.

Tess sucked in a deep breath and tried one last-ditch effort to prevent the talk they were about to have. "Dad told everyone this is between him and me."

"Oh, no, honey. It's not." Maggie leveled her with the "mom look" she'd used on Tess her whole life. Tess refrained from doing the requisite squirm.

"I can't—"

"Oh, yes, you can. I understand your disappointment with his decision regarding the company, but he *is* your father."

Silence fell hard and the tinkling of the waterfall fountain thing might as well have been fingernails on a chalkboard. Tess already knew that. What she didn't know was how to forgive him so she could deal with his illness.

"Let me say that again, Tess. He is your *father*."

"But he didn't remember he was my father when it came time to choose his replacement. I'm his *daughter*."

"So you are," Maggie said with a sigh. "But have you ever paused to wonder if you were the one who was wrong?"

She jerked her gaze up to Maggie's. "What?"

"Have you ever examined the notion you truly aren't ready to run the company?"

Her mother's question might as well have been a bucket of cold water in the face. *Not ready?* "How can you even suggest that?"

"How can I not?"

Tess looked away, grappling with the thought her own mother didn't think she was able to run Ullo. Tess *was* capable of running the company. Sure, there would be a learning curve, just like at Upstart. But Tess knew she could do it, and that her own mother doubted her felt like a razor blade swiped across her heart.

Maggie waited.

Tess raised her gaze to the woman who'd always believed her daughter could do anything she set her mind to. "You don't think I can."

Maggie hesitated for a few minutes, seemingly looking for the right words. "I'm not sure. You know the answer to that, but you've clung to the belief it was your birthright for so long, you never stopped to consider whether it was the right place for you. I don't work for Ullo. My job is to love the man who built the company…and my job is to love you."

Tess sank back on the cushion. "I can run Ullo."

"Maybe the question is not whether you can run Ullo, but if you are ready to run it at this moment."

"Yes," Tess said, even though a flicker of doubt grew stronger within her. She'd never stopped to really think about her father's motivation for hiring Graham. Maybe it wasn't that he hadn't thought Tess capable of being the head honcho, but rather that she wasn't prepared for the task at present. Or maybe she would have never been ready to step into her father's shoes. Maybe she'd already found the shoes that fit her…and she hadn't wanted to let go of her intention. "This is what I'd been working toward. I followed in Dad's footsteps because my brothers didn't. I did this for him. For Ullo."

"Is that the right answer?" her mother asked, her expression thoughtful. Annoyingly thoughtful.

Tess wanted to slap her mother for making her think— no, doubt—all she had believed. "I've always thought it was the right answer."

"Maybe it is, but your father never made any of you feel as if you had to work for Ullo. He made sure each of his children knew they were free to find their own path and follow it. He's always been proud you chose to work in the world he loves, but he never said he'd give you the key to the company one day, did he?"

"No," Tess said, feeling a lump in her throat. Those words hurt. God, they hurt almost as much as the day her father had said them from the chair in which Graham now sat. "I always thought that's what he intended. That he had faith in me. He's never questioned my abilities."

"He does have faith in you, and he's been amazingly patient while you've figured things out," Maggie said, clasping her hands and leaning forward. "Don't you get it, sweetheart?"

Tess stared at her mother, the woman she'd expected to be on her side, the woman that she expected to cajole her to reconcile with her father…not make her doubt herself. Not make her examine herself. Tess shook her head and blinked the tears away.

Maggie gave her a small smile. "Your father wasn't slighting you or saying he didn't trust you—"

"Then why didn't he tell me about Graham to begin with?" Gone was the hurt of her mother siding with Frank, and in its stead reared aggravation. "Dad never had the conversation he should have had with me. He allowed me to think this, Mom."

"Frank never wants to hurt you," Maggie said.

"Really? 'Cause he did, Mom. He should have respected me enough to tell me I wasn't good enough."

"I'm not saying he handled this well."

"Finally, something we agree on." Tess folded her arms, feeling justified …petulant. No matter what her father believed, he should have been honest. Tess deserved as much.

"There is no black and white in this situation, Tess."

"No shit," Tess muttered.

Maggie briefly narrowed her eyes before sucking in a deep breath. "I can admit Frank made mistakes, but his frame of mind was to protect you. He's a man who has spent his entire life working hard to take care of us all, and he found out he has pancreatic cancer. Can you imagine what he felt?"

"Of course I can't imagine, but you can't use his cancer as justification for tricking me."

"Shut up," Maggie said, her eyes crackling. "Just put your outrage on hold and listen to me for a minute."

"Fine." Tess pressed her lips together.

"All our dreams of retirement are—poof—up in smoke.

And it's not just about the family he leaves behind. It's about the company with its fifty-plus employees. All of that places an enormous burden on your father. Have you thought about that?"

"You said 'leave behind,'" Tess said, her heart trembling at the thought of what might happen. No. What would likely happen. Up until this point her mother had been super positive, refusing to even think Frank could leave anyone or anything behind. The possibility of Frank not beating this cancer had never been uttered.

Maggie's eyes sheened and she looked away, blinking rapidly. "Look, I'm *not* giving up on your father, but you and I both know the percentage of people who have beaten this kind of cancer is not good. My point is, your father has a lot he's worrying about and all of this has been very tough on him. Maybe he couldn't face telling you one-on-one that he didn't think you capable of running Ullo yet. You aren't the easiest of people, Tess."

"What do you mean by that? You make me sound like I'm some kind of unreasonable diva. I'm not."

"No." Maggie paused for several seconds before turning her gaze back to Tess. "You've never taken no for an answer. It's a great quality…sometimes."

Not easy? Never take no for an answer? Her mother made her sound…spoiled. So maybe she was a little manipulative when it came to getting her way, but she wasn't a total pill. "I take no for an answer."

"But only after you've exhausted every angle. You don't make it easy."

Tess stared at her mother, disbelief gathering inside.

Maggie spread her hands. "Remember when you wanted your ears pierced? Or how about when you wanted your soccer team to wear bright green cleats? Or when you wanted the VW Bug? Or when it came to picking colleges? Or the paint color in your condo? From sleepovers to cereal choices, you wheedled and wore us down until you got what you wanted. You're not a diva, but you are a master manipulator."

"No, I'm discriminating. That doesn't mean I'm irrational or illogical…or can't accept not getting my way."

Her mother's blank stare said it all.

And Tess didn't want to admit she was right, but… "Okay, I'm slightly difficult."

"Well, your father is overloaded with difficult things at present. Maybe he was cowardly and dishonest, but he's not perfect, and neither are you."

"So you're saying it's okay to lie to me and sneak behind my back to hire a new CEO," Tess intoned, still aggravated by her mother's calling a spade a spade.

"I'm telling you your father loves you, didn't want to hurt you and has never been good at telling you no. If he'd have told you what he planned, you would have talked him out of it. You would have made him make you CEO, which in his emotional state of mind might not have been a wise decision. So he went around you."

Her mother's words found their mark, and again, pierced her. But she knew those words were true.

From early on, Tess had always been able to talk her father into anything she wanted. Case in point, he'd bought her diamond earrings when she was seven, donated lime green cleats to her eighth grade soccer team and a bright red convertible VW Bug had tooled her around the campus of the college she insisted on. Tess was accustomed to getting what she wanted…mostly because Frank Ullo had seen she got it. "You make me sound like a bad person."

Anger flashed in her mother's eyes. "Don't put words in my mouth, Tess. You know that's not what I'm doing. You are a very good person, but your father spoiled you. Quite frankly, I think he realized it when the doctor gave him the diagnosis and he had to think hard about what direction to go with his company."

Tess stood and walked to the edge of the patio. She'd held on to her anger at her father for weeks, and then when she'd found out he was gravely sick, the guilt and confusion over what she felt had blanketed her, smothering the rage she'd felt over the slight she'd perceived her father to give her. She'd never looked at it from his point of view, never wanted to even entertain the idea she couldn't slip right into the old man's shoes and run the company without a hitch.

Turning away from the beauty of the emerging cannas along the fence line, she looked at her mother. Maggie had always seemed eternally youthful, but in that moment, Tess noted how tired she looked. Her roots showed gray, and her face seemed more lined than ever. Worrying about her husband had taken its toll on her. "My emotions are so mixed up, Mom. I don't know what to do."

Maggie came to Tess and wound an arm about her waist. "You'll find a way. You always do."

"I'm still hurt, and there's no way to fix what I've done. I work for Upstart. It's like I'm not even an Ullo anymore." Emotion welled in her, choking her at the thought of what she'd done for pride's sake. What she'd given up because she couldn't accept the fact her father might have been right.

"Ah, Tess, that will never be true. You're an Ullo to your core. Your father is proud of you no matter who you work for." Maggie smiled at her. "And I am, too."

Tess had tried so hard not to cry, but tears came anyway. "This has all been so terrible, Mama. Everything in my life feels so off-kilter. How can I change that?"

Maggie wrapped her arms around Tess, and the emotion unleashed. Just like in Graham's car, grief, hurt and anger swamped Tess, rending her control, sloughing away any power she had against the feeling. For several seconds she allowed herself to cling to her mother's strength.

Finally, Maggie eased Tess away from her. "I can't fix things for you, baby. You should have learned that long ago. Or…maybe I learned it."

"That was before. When my life was golden."

"Life can't be golden every day. Having dark days makes the golden ones precious. Believe me, I've learned to bask in the light and hold tight to the memories of the sun on my shoulders during times I can't see. Nothing's perfect, Tess. You just never learned to accept that sometimes good and bad must exist together."

"I haven't had much bad in my life until recently. Now everything's turned to shit." Tess rubbed her eyes.

Maggie sighed. "Yeah, it is kind of shitty, but we'll survive as best we can, enjoying the golden moments that crop up."

For a moment, they stood quietly, each wrapped in their own thoughts.

"Mama?"

"Yeah?"

"I can't talk to Daddy yet. I need more time."

Maggie turned and measured her with astute green eyes before giving a curt nod. "Okay, you think about the words we exchanged today, but…"

Tess looked up, expecting more words of wisdom.

"…don't take too long thinking about forgiveness. Imagine a world without your father. Imagine a world in which you never break through your anger at him. Your life has always been better because your father was in it."

And then something hit Tess. A sort of understanding, heavy and dark, slammed into her. There were no words for what it was. Or maybe there were, but Tess couldn't have found them.

And it hurt like a knife stuck into her soul.

"Mom, don't say that. Don't act like he won't make it," Tess said, her voice cracking.

Her mother shook her head, waving off the tears, waving off falling apart as she'd done for all of Tess's life. "Don't. Don't make me cry."

Tess sank back against the cushions and fell silent while her mother reclaimed herself. Finally, Maggie tugged her tunic shirt down, breathed deeply and gave a small smile. "I have to get back to lunch. If I burn the sauce, your grandmother will tell everyone in Golden Oaks. Last time, I got recipe cards from three of the women there."

Tess tried to smile but the effort fell flat. "I'll be up in a minute."

Maggie nodded and walked up the stone pavers toward the grand patio sweeping across the back of the house. Well-maintained flower beds spilled beautiful blooms onto the manicured lawn. Everything was picture-perfect, the absolute best available, marred only by the cancer growing inside the walls her mother entered.

The irony soured Tess's stomach.

She closed her eyes as if doing so allowed her to close out the world she didn't want to face.

But that was the problem.

She'd stuck her head in the sand and hoped things like dealing with her father and dealing with what she felt for Graham would go away. Thing was…they hadn't.

Can't run from the world, Tess.

She'd have to face her demons, putting one foot in front of the other. The first hurdle she'd face would be her father.

The fact he'd lied to her, even by omission, still hurt. Then fresh pain tumbled in at knowing he'd tried to protect her from her own ego. He'd tried to fix her mistakes before she'd even made them, planning from his grave to take care of Tess. Something about that thought was comforting, and the other half was maddening. He hadn't had faith in her.

But maybe she'd had too much faith in herself.

She'd never considered her father might be right. So certain she could handle every situation that came up at Ullo, Tess hadn't accepted any weaknesses in her skill set. But she'd learned very quickly at the smaller Upstart, she had little experience with hammering out contracts, crunching the numbers, dealing with insurance and codes and reviewing the legalities. At Ullo, she'd always handed that stuff over to someone else. Working hard to prove herself, she'd struggled with the nuances in which Monique had expected her to be proficient...the ones Tess had never learned because she'd never had to.

Not to mention she still dealt with hostility from Cecily, blowback from the artists and delicate intrapersonal relationships with Josh and Monique. The pressure Monique placed on her to bring in new accounts pulled at her day and night.

What would things be like if she'd stayed at Ullo?

Had her pride led her to greater hardship? Had it pointed her in a direction she was never meant to travel?

She didn't know the answers to any of her own questions, and unfortunately, her mother had been right.

Tess would have to walk the path she'd hacked out of the jungle of life on her own. Any missteps would be her own. Time to own her mistakes, suck it up and move forward. There were no do-overs.

But she could move forward with a better vision, accepting exactly what her mother had said—life isn't perfect.

To recognize the good, she had to experience the bad.

Tess rose, and like her mother moments ago, straightened her shirt, took a deep breath and gave the world a tremulous smile.

FRANK ULLO FORCED HIMSELF to sit up straight at the dinner table when all he really wanted to do was lie down. Some people who underwent chemotherapy didn't feel too bad. Some did. He was in the latter category, which made him angry. The least this bastard cancer could do was leave what little he had left of life alone.

His family chattered as if it were just another Sunday. He supposed it was just another Sunday to them, but to him it was the fourteenth Sunday since he found out he was dying. Thinking about the day that way caused an incessant pricking of his conscience.

How many more Sundays did he have?

Looking down the table, Frank settled his gaze on his youngest, who'd been awfully polite and quiet during the meal. He'd seen Maggie take her out for a talk. Part of him resented his wife's interference, part of him felt relief. He and Tess had gone too long without talking.

She lifted her eyes and caught his gaze. Holding it this time, rather than looking away, her eyes filled with tears. The sight ripped at his heart. Tess dropped her eyes and shoveled her food around on her plate before looking around at her brothers and their wives assembled at the table. The kids were all in the kitchen and the meal had passed without any bickering or spilled iced tea.

Clearing her throat, Tess asked, "Do you guys think I'm difficult?"

His sons stopped eating and looked at their much younger sister.

"What do you mean?" Joseph asked. This son was always calm and reasonable, repressing the dreamer he'd once been.

"I mean, do you guys think I'm hard to deal with?"

Maggie pressed her lips together and looked at him. Frank raised his eyebrows but said nothing.

Michael laughed. "What dude has told you this?"

Tess grimaced. "This isn't about a guy. I'm just wondering."

"Hell, yeah, you're difficult," Frank, Jr. said, jabbing a fork at her. "You always have been. Remember when she was teething, Ma? And we couldn't get her to stop biting everything? She bit the poor dog every time we turned around."

"And when she decided she was going to be a chef and made us those terrible cookies and brownies every day?" Michael made a face. "That kick lasted for months."

"Or when it came to her spelling?" Joseph smiled, joining in on the fun. "Or putting sunscreen on her? Or how about when she had to take medicine?"

"She's just like Granny B," Michael concluded, lifting a finger in the classic eureka pose.

Frank watched the aggravation gather on his daughter's face. She never should have asked her brothers if she was difficult. New tears gathered in her eyes.

"I'm not like Granny B, Michael," Tess said, not huffy like she'd usually get, but rather resigned.

"Yeah, you are," Frank, Jr. said, with an emphatic nod. "You might be worse. You've still got a lot of years left on you."

"Hush," Maggie intoned. Laurie and Beth also shot looks toward their husbands.

Frank looked down at his daughter. "Tess?"

This time she didn't ignore him. "Yeah?"

"You're worth the trouble, baby. Always have been."

His words caused Tess to burst into tears.

Michael pulled away from his sister as if she were a loathsome cockroach, shooting his dad a funny expression. "Why'd you go and do that for? We haven't even gotten to dessert yet."

For the first time in weeks, Frank felt a lightness bloom within him. He looked at his baby girl crying into her napkin and knew her anger had abated. Something in the way she'd looked at him had told him all he needed to know.

Tess had forgiven him for his transgression. She'd seen things from his side of the table and had accepted in some small way that his view was valid.

Didn't mean things were healed between them.

But he could wait.

Didn't have a lot of time left in this world, but for the moment it was enough.

CHAPTER SEVENTEEN

TESS WALKED INTO her loft feeling as if she'd been washed twice and hung out to dry. Limp as a noodle, her conscience cleaner, she sank onto her couch and looked around the silent room. She'd tidied the place that morning, picking up the gold dress she'd flung on the chair the night before, scooping up the sandals tossed capriciously onto her fluffy area rug. Her cleaning service had come Friday and the apartment smelled clean. Everything in its place.

But it was lonely.

Picking herself up, she opened the fridge. Maybe she'd make supper. She closed the door. Or not.

Emptiness stared back at her when she spun around.

Her fingers seemed to reach for her phone as if they weren't even attached to her brain. Scrolling through her contacts, she found him.

Graham Naquin.

Her finger hovered over his number before she sighed and tossed the phone onto the counter.

A booty call? Really, sister, it's come to that?

So she wanted him? So she'd dreamed about him all last night? So she'd regretted not finding an immediate exit so she could get busy with him in the parking lot?

Did that mean she had to call him and—

The sound of the buzzer interrupted her personal lambasting. Probably Gigi coming over to chat her up about the amazing guy she'd hooked up with the night before.

She'd seen drunken pics on Facebook earlier. Or it could be food delivery or—

She pressed the button. "Yes?"

"Tess?"

"Graham?" A rush of pleasure, of anticipation.

"Hey, let me in."

"Not by the hair on my chinny, chin, chin," she muttered, before pressing the buzzer.

Ask and you shall receive.

Rifling through her purse, she found some breath mints. She hadn't eaten much of her mother's garlicky pasta, but she'd had a bite. After tossing a mint in her mouth, she tucked her hair behind her ears, giving her cheeks a pinch. She wished she'd had time for a shower, time to wash her face after bawling like a baby at the dinner table.

He knocked on the door.

Too late.

"Come in," she called, turning on the faucet as if she'd been about to start the...

No dishes in the sink.

Turning off the water, she grabbed a dishtowel and dried her hands, spinning toward the door as it opened.

"Hey," she said inanely, her eyes working over every inch of his body. "What are you doing here?"

He closed the door. "Breaching your walls."

"Beg your pardon?"

Graham advanced, his gaze determined, his mouth set. "I'm about to breach your walls the only way I know how."

"I'm not sure what you're talking about. In case you haven't noticed, I'm not a lady in distress, and there isn't an actual castle."

He stopped in front of her, not touching her, but close enough for her to wish she'd popped a second mint. "You're a lady in distress if there ever was one."

Point taken.

"Maybe a little distressed, but I'm working through it," she said, studying his beautiful lips. How could a man have pretty lips? But Graham did. Graham had pretty everything. He was a walking dirty sex dream.

"Are you?" he asked, his eyes equally thoughtful and sinful.

"Giving it the ol' college try," she said, sucking in some air so she didn't pitch forward and cover his body with her own. That might happen later. God, she hoped it happened later, but right now there were questions. "Seriously, what are you doing in the enemy camp?"

"Can we shelve that? I'm tired of talking about why. I'm tired of it being you against me."

"Tired of being enemies?"

"You know we aren't enemies," he said, hands now propped on his hips, legs akimbo. "We're far from that designation."

"Okay, we're not enemies, but we're not playing for the same team."

"And whose fault is that?"

Tess felt aggravation hone in on the desire that had already overtaken her. "Are you here to fight?"

"Hell, no. I'm here for the opposite," he said, grabbing her by the hips, drawing her to him. She let him because she couldn't think of a good reason not to. Okay, she could, but she wanted Graham more than she wanted her principles at that moment. She'd think about those tomorrow. Along with all the other thoughts that had tumbled about in her head that afternoon. She didn't want to talk about why, either…or anything else, for that matter.

She crooked her head and smiled. "The opposite of fighting is—"

"Loving," he said, his head dipping toward hers. "After last night, I figured there's nothing else I can do to make things up to you, nothing else I can do to make you feel better....but be your sex slave for one night."

Tess caught him by the jaw just before his lips covered hers. "Who said it was your responsibility to make anything up to me?" she whispered.

"Maybe it's not. Maybe I just want to see you smile," he said, his blue eyes nearly violet as he studied her.

Tess smiled. "Sex slave? I think that's the best offer I've received in a while."

"Good," he said, one arm going around her. "Now stop talking."

"But what about tomorrow? What about when life closes in and we're back to the real stuff?"

"To hell with tomorrow. I want this moment, Tess. I want you," he breathed as he covered her mouth with his.

A beautiful sweet hunger swept through her. Holding his head in both her hands she took from him as much as he took from her. The kiss went from sweet to hot in seconds.

Tess moved backward, tugging Graham toward her bedroom, but she ran into the counter.

"Oh, let's go—" She tried to get the words out, but she couldn't seem to stop kissing him, to stop running her hands up and down his back.

He cupped her ass and lifted her onto the cold granite. Pulling back slightly, he tugged the shoulder of her blouse to the side but met resistance.

"Here," she said, grabbing the elastic bottom and jerking the shirt over her head. She'd worn a plain white bra that day, nothing dazzling or sexy, but Graham didn't seem to mind. His hands made short work of the clasp.

"Ah," he breathed as she shimmied out of the stretchy cotton, her breasts jiggling with the effort. "I've dreamed about these."

Tess smiled and her eyes widened...and then shut as

his mouth moved down her body, capturing one breast and sucking it into the heat of his mouth. "Graham."

"Mmm" was all he said.

Boneless, Tess fell back to her elbows, knocking some papers to the floor and hitting the empty fruit bowl. Graham ignored the clatter, choosing instead to shift his attention to her other breast and tugging her pelvis tight against his, unapologetically grinding his erection against her sensitive flesh.

"The bedroom," she gasped as he continued the delicious torture. At that moment there was nothing else but Graham, his magical hands and hot mouth.

He lifted her into his arms and she wrapped her legs around his waist. Raising his head, he kissed his way up her throat to her mouth and walked to her bedroom.

Graham set her on the bed and she reached back to catch herself, unwittingly thrusting her chest forward. Legs sprawled, back arched and breasts unbound, she likely looked like a calendar girl. He stepped back and caressed her with his gaze as he slowly raised his soft T-shirt, revealing a sculpted torso. Graham wasn't freakishly muscular, but he was hot. He'd gotten some sun since she'd last seen him, and the golden flesh made Tess's mouth water.

Unbuttoning his shorts, he allowed them to slide down his legs, leaving only his tented boxers in place. It was a delightful striptease, made even humorous when he stood absolutely naked in front of her wearing only his running shoes.

"I like your look," she said with a wicked smile. "Are you jogging off somewhere as soon as we finish?"

His teeth flashed in the dimness of her room. "Ah, baby, it's going to be a long time before I leave."

Tess shimmied out of her shorts and tossed them across the room, leaving only a tiny pair of bikinis covering the area Graham's eyes zoomed to. Thankfully, she'd waxed a few days ago in anticipation of hitting the pool with Gigi. Finally, something she'd done right.

Lifting her arms, she reached for him. "Please."

He toed off his shoes, pulled off his socks and lowered himself to his knees, inching forward across the area rug toward her. "All in good time. You see, I've had these dreams, these memories of the way you feel beneath my hand. Memories of the way you smell, the way you taste, and the sound you make when you come. You can have your fun, Tess, but only after I've had mine."

With that, he gently pushed her onto her back, tugging her knees so her legs dangled off the side of the bed on either side of his body. Then he leaned forward and blew on the exact spot that throbbed for him.

"Ohhh," she said, her hips tilting toward him.

"Yeah, just like that," he said, his hands sliding down her equally smooth legs, lifting them so they draped over his shoulders. He hooked his thumbs in the waistband of her panties and peeled them off her. The smile he flashed when she lifted her head to look down at him made her shiver with anticipation.

And then Graham Naquin, the man who'd stolen her job, the man she'd tried to outwit in business, the man she'd fallen half in love with months ago made Tess scream his name.

GRAHAM RUBBED THE sweet melon-scented soap over Tess's breasts, enjoying the way the flickering candles played over her wet skin. "If we don't get out, we're going to get all wrinkly."

"Who cares?" Tess sighed, lifting her leg and using her big toe to shut off the hot water she'd turned on to warm the tepid. "I've never had a better bath. You're like a soft easy chair I can snuggle into." She wiggled against him, allowing her bottom to brush against his genitals.

When he laughed, the water sloshed over the hills and valleys of Tess's body which he liked. Clutching the soap tightly, he continued washing, lifting her arm and soaping the length of it.

She sighed again.

Best sound ever. No, second best. First was when she'd called his name and shuddered against him. He could go to his grave happy after hearing that one.

"So that's why you lured me over to your place," he teased.

Tess turned the head she had resting on his chest. "I did not lure you over. This wasn't my idea."

He made a face.

"So why did you come?" she asked, her voice suddenly serious. "Or maybe the better question is why did I let you in?"

"I'm a sure thing?" He didn't want to talk about whys. He wanted to live in the moment. He couldn't handle serious talk right now because serious talk set something between them.

"So confident," she said.

"I thought that's what you liked about me," he said, lifting her other arm and washing that one, too. Dropping it back into the soapy water, he wrapped his arms around her, locking her to him. She felt good against him. He could hold her this way forever.

"I like a lot of things about you," Tess said, laying her arms over his. "I like your confidence, I like the father you are to Emily and I like the way you fill out your running shorts."

He laughed. More water moving over her body. Beautiful. "Actually, I joked about confidence. I'm surprised that's a characteristic you like about me."

"Everyone has doubts, right?" she said.

At that moment he could see the doubts Tess carried

and knew he could put at least one of those to bed. "Yeah, but my lack of confidence is what kept me from you in the first place."

Her head tilted and a piece of the honey-streaked hair she'd piled atop her head fell loose. "What do you mean?"

"Last year was tough. I lost my job and couldn't find another one. I was either too experienced or not experienced enough. My financial situation got pretty grim. Actually, when the headhunter repping your father called me, I was on the cusp of taking a job at a local electronics store."

Tess stiffened slightly—was she shocked or disappointed? "Things are tough out there."

He wanted to say "you wouldn't know that" but bit his tongue. At the very least, he had to give Tess credit for refusing to bend to her father's will and striking out on her own. She'd done pretty damn well, taking a fair chunk of Ullo's business with her. "Yeah, it is tough which is why when I landed this job—the perfect job—I was not as much ecstatic as relieved. I didn't really want to have to hawk big-screen TVs and routers."

"Hmmm," was all she said. He didn't know what to make of her response. Was she angry? Or did she pity him?

"And that's the real reason I didn't return your call. I had every intention of calling you when I got to New Orleans, but I wanted to get set up here, get caught up on my bills. I didn't want to come to you half a man. I was too embarrassed to tell you the real reason, so I let you think it was no big deal."

Tess sat up, water sluicing off her back as she twisted to face him. In the low light, he couldn't read her eyes. Her mouth drew into an outraged line. "You think having a hard time financially makes you half a man?"

Didn't it? He didn't know one man who would blurt out "I'm over-extended and I don't have a job. Wanna go on a date?" Hell, no. Dudes wanted to show they could afford a good bottle of wine and a filet. "I wanted to be stable, able to take you out for that night on the town I'd promised you without having to calculate the cost. Frankly, my pride stood in my way. I didn't want to be the loser I'd felt like for the last six months," he shrugged and shifted his gaze away. "I wanted to be good enough for you."

"You're joking, right?"

He glanced back at her, trying to figure out if she were angry or sympathetic. "Actually I'm baring my soul to you, something that's always been hard for me."

"Wait, you didn't call because you thought you weren't worthy of me? Did you think I was that kind of girl? Was there anything in my demeanor that said I need a man with money in order to fall in love?"

Love. She'd said the word he'd danced around for the past few weeks. Falling in love should be wonderful. It shouldn't be like this—fraught with difficulty and hurt.

"I knew what kind of girl you were. It was on me. I'm the one with the insecurity." He pulled her back to him, settling her against him, stroking her side as if he could take away the insult. Maybe she needed to understand him better; maybe she'd see he was insecure because of what he'd lost so young. "You have to understand—my father spent his life chasing dreams. There was always a sure thing on the horizon. He'd sink every bit of our money into the venture and then—nothing. I spent my whole life watching my old man get beat down. Then one day, he didn't come home."

"He left you and your family?"

"He left everyone. They found him hanging from a rafter down at a shack on the lake. It was supposed to be a piece of development land he'd bought, but that had fallen through, too."

Tess covered her mouth with a hand. "Oh, my God, Graham. I'm so sorry."

"He was a loser and not brave enough to admit his failings. He checked out rather than face reality, so living through that left a mark on me. I didn't want to come to you empty-handed. I thought if I got myself together, we could start over." He gave a wry laugh. "Things didn't exactly work out, did they?"

Tess moved her hand down to capture his. "No. Who would have ever thought we'd tangle ourselves so well in a web of our own making?"

For a moment they both lay in the warm fragrant water, minds turning over the irony that had bound them together.

"What about now?" he asked, lifting her hand and kissing the tip of each finger. "Does this change anything?"

"I don't know. Professionally? No. Personally? I'm not sure. We could try to sneak around and see each other. Or maybe we could say the hell with it and make our relationship public, but what would happen? We work for rival companies and eventually there'd be suspicion. I already feel like Monique's heading that way. That's no way to start a relationship."

Graham wanted Tess so much, he didn't want to hear any argument against getting what he wanted, but deep down he knew she was right. When she was nestled in his arms in their own private world, he could believe in a tomorrow for them, but in the cold light of day, when the eyes of the world were on them, he knew it would be impossible. "So this is it? Tonight is what we have?"

Tess turned her head, her green eyes mysterious in the candlelight. "I think it has to be this way. At least for now. Nothing has changed other than...I know you." Her voice cracked a little.

He caught her lips, kissing her softly. Sadness settled around him. He'd found the perfect girl, but because he'd taken the perfect job, he couldn't have her. Bitter, bitter irony. Actual tears caught in his throat when he thought of this being the last time he held Tess.

"Life is not fair," he said, trying to keep sorrow from spoiling the time they had left.

"I'm beginning to understand that more and more. Come on. We still have tonight. I don't want to think about tomorrow." She stood and the water ran off her naked body.

And then he wasn't so sad anymore.

She was a goddess—not of the usual variety—but of the Tess variety with her trim legs, soft ass and perfect breasts. Girl next door meets Barbie. Freaking awesome.

Graham rose and pulled her against him. "Only tonight."

She kissed him. "A good policy for the moment."

Much later, after they'd made love again, Graham walked quietly out of Tess's bedroom where she lay dozing. He hadn't had supper, and after spending the last few hours quenching his hunger for Tess, he was ravenous. He rounded the bar and nearly slipped on the papers that had fallen when he'd lifted Tess onto the counter. He shuffled the papers into a haphazard stack and tossed them and the folder onto the bar before opening the fridge.

Eh, not much to be had. He grabbed a yogurt that had expired a week ago and found the silverware. In the low light, he leaned against the counter and made short work of the yogurt. Looking around Tess's Spartan kitchen, his gaze snagged on the only disorganized object—the stack of papers—and the drawings lying atop the folder he'd dropped.

He moved closer, lifting the first one so he could see it better in the light.

Stunning.

He picked up a few more and took them back to the light above the sink so he could see them better. Obviously they were the drawings done for Oedipus with their theme of

"Song of the South." Instead of large bulky props, Tess had layers of numerous smaller magnolias over the sides of the "Belle of Bourbon" with a twisting oak sprawled across the middle of the float, holding fiber optic glowing magnolias and glossy poster board leaves. The second layer resembled a huge white plantation house. The design was elegant, elaborate and…way better than what Ullo had put together.

He flipped through the other sketches: "Paddling the Mississippi," "Ain't She a Peach" and "Bayou Dreamin'." All were artistic and—

"What the hell are you doing?" Tess said from the hallway.

Graham jumped, nearly dropping the computer-generated sketches. "I was picking up the papers we'd knocked down."

She crossed her arms over the large T-shirt she'd pulled on. "Way over there?"

Tossing the sketches back upon the folder, he shrugged. "Everything fell out. I came to get something to eat and they caught my eye."

Narrowed eyes. Mistrust.

He held up his hands. "I'm only human. Those sketches are like porn to a fifteen-year-old boy. I can't not look."

"This is what I'm talking about. Competing against each other, minding our words, worrying about subconsciously sabotaging each other's work—this is why it can't work between us," she said, padding into the kitchen and stacking the drawings together before sliding them back into the folder.

"Does it help to say your proposal for Oedipus is…so good I'm breaking a sweat?"

Her head snapped around. "You're just saying that because I let you tie my hands to the bed and play Princess Leia and Han Solo a few minutes ago."

"Is that why you called me Han?" he joked, pulling her to him. "Baby, those are brilliant. Really beautiful."

"Those are the early copies, but probably won't be enough for Miles. He protects the integrity of the parade, but he's more a nuts-and-bolts guy. He'll appreciate working with you," she said, relaxing against him, even as her gaze stayed on the folder. "I don't want to talk business. I want to go back to bed with you, feel you against me. Morning will come soon, and until the first ray peeks over the sill, I need to stay in the world we've created."

Ducking his head, Graham placed a gentle kiss atop her head. He wanted that, too, but he wanted it to last past morning. But at 1:17 am, his brain was too fuzzy to figure out how to make that happen…and his body had gone from boneless to hard while holding Tess.

There were better things to do than contemplate the morrow.

Daylight would come soon enough and pop the bubble of contentment that enveloped them.

Like that Scarlett O'Hara chick, he'd think about another day.

CHAPTER EIGHTEEN

MILES BARROW'S OFFICE held a huge desk, a huge blue marlin mounted on the wall, a huge plate glass window overlooking Magazine Street and a small assistant twitching nearby like a bluejay guarding its nest.

"Julian, sit down or go fetch more coffee. You're driving me batty with your hovering," Miles said, leafing through the contract Graham had brought, his legs stretched in front of him, huge leather desk chair tilted back.

"I don't hover," Julian drawled, pressing his hands down the skin-tight chambray jacket. Slim white trousers tailored down to classic oxfords. A jaunty bowtie, moused faux hawk and dark edgy glasses completed his dapper look. "But I will go for coffee if you want. Mr. Naquin?"

"None for me, thanks," Graham said, waving a hand and trying to look at home while his gut clenched awaiting Miles's response. This deal meant the difference between a decent 2016 and a subpar one…and he'd seen what Upstart had delivered.

"I don't need the caffeine anyway," Miles muttered. "Just work on the Happy Burger case."

Julian held up a hang loose sign and then the door snicked closed, leaving Miles to continue his *hmm*s after reviewing each page.

Finally, the large man set the contracts followed by the numbered float specs on his desk and looked up at Graham. "Interesting."

"I think so, and I think it's a solid proposal. Dave Wegmann, our art director, took your vision and created something over-the-top, and we're offering you more perks than we've ever offered another krewe. Frank Ullo wants to keep you happy, Miles."

Miles nodded, making a teepee of his hands atop his large stomach. "And I like that. But this isn't brain surgery, right? I like the relationship I have with Ullo. We've always used you guys, but I gotta admit there have been some issues in the past with labor costs and parade day glitches. This new outfit Frank's daughter is working for has promised me those bumps will be smoothed out. Her floats aren't exactly what I was looking for, but sometimes the experience with prop builders is more important."

"Not what you're looking for?" Graham said, leaning forward, his emotions mixed. Something within him hitched at the thought of Miles not liking what Tess had created for Oedipus. How could anyone not appreciate the designs she'd created? "I actually saw a few of them. Too elaborate?"

Miles made a face. "Since when has an artist for a rival company ever showed her designs? And, no, that wasn't the issue. Not detailed enough, in my opinion."

Something prickled on the back of Graham's neck. "I won't comment on how, but I thought they were exquisite, detailed and, honestly, better than ours." He pressed a hand against his head and mumbled, "I probably shouldn't have said that. Stupid."

Miles chuckled. "Look, guy, this ain't Wall Street and though business is business, you know how things are run in New Orleans. I don't hold nothin' against you as long as it don't affect me."

Graham rocked back in his chair, discomfited, as Miles spun his chair. An attorney by day, krewe captain by whatever was left over after billable hours, Miles didn't seem to be the most organized of men. Which is probably why he spun back around empty-handed and pressed a button on his phone. "Julian!"

"You don't have to yell into the phone, Miles," Julian drawled like the smart-ass he obviously was.

"Get me the Upstart proposal," Miles said, ignoring Julian's tone.

"As your generation says, '10-4,' big guy," Julian responded.

Five seconds later the assistant entered and handed off the bonded proposal. He turned and winked at Graham.

"Don't mind him. Bold as the devil, but the best legal assistant I've had. He's taking the LSATs next month so I'll probably lose him," Miles said, opening the proposal. "This is what the courier brought."

He passed it to Graham who flipped through quickly. None of Tess's designs were in the proposal. Graham snapped it closed. "I'm confused."

Miles lifted his wooly eyebrows. "Why?"

"These aren't the sketches I saw."

The big man shrugged. "This is what I got."

"Hmmm," Graham said, shaking his head. Something was rotten in Denmark. He hadn't prodded Tess any further about business—they'd been busy exploring other pleasurable things, and when they'd parted this morning, they'd agreed to go back to whatever it was they had before, each agreeing it had to be over for now. Tess had given him one night, perhaps relying on their lovemaking as a time-released medication, working long enough to get her through the next few weeks. Or maybe it was merely a last-ditch effort to get him out of her system. Or maybe he didn't know what it was other than it had given him another taste of something he wanted so badly, and that would have to do him for a while.

But he had a bad feeling about what Monique had obviously done. His ex-partner and lover used Tess to bring in business, like a prized carrot dangled in front of krewe royalty. But if Monique didn't value Tess as part of her team beyond some honeyed trap, there was going to be an issue. Tess deserved to be valued as a designer…as a team member. Monique had quite deceitfully hog-tied her, subbing what he was quite certain were his ex's own designs instead of Tess's. Monique's biggest flaw had always been her hubris. Unable to let go of her need to control every aspect of Upstart, she'd submitted her own designs rather than better ones.

Here was the reason Upstart would never rise above midtier. If a CEO wasn't willing to toss his or her own pride aside and rely on the person best for the job, then all the efforts to nab new business would be for naught.

This was where Frank Ullo trumped Monique.

"Miles, if that's so, you should know Tess's designs are ten times better than what's in this proposal," Graham said, slapping the Upstart proposal on the oak desk. "And they're better than my proposal. God help me."

Miles narrowed his eyes, looking confused. "So why? If Monique wanted the Oedipus contract, why wouldn't she give her best?"

Graham licked his lips and thought how to say what needed to be said without sounding crass. "There is much to admire about Monique, but she's, how do I put this, wrapped up in herself?"

Miles nodded. "Egocentric, sure, but still. These are good sketches, nothing wrong with them, but if she knew—"

"She wouldn't. She can't look beyond her own nose. Monique likes to control every aspect of Upstart. Not a bad thing, but team player she ain't. So in her mind, she gave you what she believed were the best sketches—hers. The world revolves around Monique. That's about as nice as I can say it."

Miles sat, silent and taciturn.

"Look," Graham said, closing his eyes briefly before opening them, "I can't believe I'm saying this, but you need to call Monique and ask for Tess's set of designs. You don't have to tell her how you know what you know, but give Tess a shot at landing your business. Her design work is better. Plain and simple."

Miles Barrow hadn't been born yesterday. He shifted his gaze to a plant that needed a good watering and sat still for a moment before returning his gaze to Graham. For several seconds Miles studied him. Graham didn't like the perusal, for the man seemed to possess the uncanny ability to see within to the soul. After a moment, recognition sparked within the depths of the man's eyes. "Okay. Tess is a good girl. Things ain't been grand for her lately, so I think you're right. She deserves a shot even if I have to tangle with Monique for it to happen."

Graham didn't know whether to punch himself in the face or pat himself on the back. He'd just wrapped a ribbon around Oedipus and given it to the competition.

God, he was a fool.

Or maybe he'd righted the wrong inadvertently done to Tess Ullo.

Miles stood and offered his hand to Graham. "Damn, man, I can't say you're a good businessman."

Graham's ego shrank a bit.

"But you're a good person." Miles gave a hard squeeze. "And in the game of life that's always more important."

"Tell that to Frank."

"Frank knows. Your company is only as good as the person running it. There's a lot you can learn from Frank Ullo. He's a good businessman, and though many don't know it, he's a good person. Not everything is out for all to see, you know what I mean?"

Graham dropped Miles's hand. "I do know."

The big man came around the desk and slapped a hand on Graham's back. "I'll have a word with Monique and be in touch."

Graham gave Miles a final handshake, a wave to Julian and then stepped out of the tidy shotgun house that had been converted into an office and inhaled the humid air.

Next week he might be out on his ass, tossed there by Frank Ullo for destroying any chance the company had to revitalize the business.

But for the time being he'd cherish the idea he'd done something honorable. He'd done something brave. One step closer to his goal of being a better man…and one step closer to losing the job he loved.

TESS LOOKED OVER the notes the captain of Icarus made on the prop rotations she'd suggested and glanced at her inbox. Monique had been out of the office all afternoon and hadn't answered when Tess had texted her about the new guidelines the city had put out regarding rider-safety harnesses. She wanted to make sure Upstart had already made them on the 2015 floats because the penalties assessed for failure to comply were stiff. The krewes would expect the builders to get that right.

Spinning in her chair, she closed her eyes and sighed.

All morning she'd tried to get serious work done instead of reliving Sunday night in her mind.

Being with Graham had been good…almost healing. After weeks of feeling so alone, having him beside her connected her, gave her a glimpse of what it would feel to be in a relationship with him.

Oh, it wasn't just the sex—which was amazing, of course. Their conversations stimulated and comforted just as they had from the first time she'd met him on that barstool at Two-Legged Pete's. She wanted more than what she currently had with him which was…nothing.

Okay, they were nothing on paper, but maybe they could—

"What the hell, Tess?" Monique growled from the open doorway.

Tess spun. Oh, God. Monique knew about her and Graham. But how could she? Unless the woman had been following him around. Or maybe she'd hired a private eye or something. Sometimes women did that in custody cases... but she and Graham weren't in a custody battle, were they? "What do you mean?"

"You know exactly what I mean," Monique said, framed in the doorway, looking like she might spit fire. Tess's office masqueraded as a broom closet, so Monique stood close, her eyes snapping, her dark hair slicked back into a low ponytail. Dressed in a black minidress and fishnet stockings, she was the epitome of every Disney villainess. Sorta scary.

And right on cue, her lackey Cecily popped her head over Monique's shoulder, self-satisfied half smile on her face.

"I really don't know what you're talking about," Tess hedged, hoping it was something other than the fact she'd had sex with the competition.

Like, three times.

"Miles Barrow called me and wanted a meeting. Basically, we've landed the Oedipus contract with the stipulation you take the lead," Monique said, her eyes still narrowed to slits. For someone who should be over the moon, she was decidedly aggravated.

Tess, relieved this wasn't over Graham, made a face. "I don't understand why you're upset. That's wonderful news."

"Miles wants your float designs."

"Well, yeah." Tess couldn't grasp the conversation. She felt as if she'd fallen into some parallel dimension where bad news was good news and vice versa. "That's what we gave him."

"No."

"No?" Tess sat back in her chair. "You didn't sub my proposal? You subbed yours?"

"Exactly. But somehow he knew about yours."

Monique moved inside the office and Cecily took up her former position at the door, looking gleeful, as if she were watching an execution.

Tess gripped her chair arms, and she wasn't sure if it was because she wanted to punch Monique or needed the support. "I never talked to Miles about my designs and, frankly, I'm pissed you chose yours over mine."

"Why? It's my company. I can submit whatever I wish."

"And yours weren't better than hers anyway. You've never been told no, have you, princess?" Cecily said, with another greasy smile.

Tess stared at both the women wondering if this was a joke, and then the situation really hit her.

Monique had not given Miles Barrow the designs Tess had slaved over.

Instead the woman had submitted her own substandard float designs. Monique had allowed Tess to play at design much like she'd given Emily a made-up project to keep her occupied, never intending to use Tess's work in the first place. Fury flooded Tess. She stood.

"Wrong. My designs were the better of the two, and you know it." Tess peered over Monique's shoulder. "And your fairy godwitch knows it, too, but she's too busy with her nose in your ass to tell you the truth."

Cecily gasped but Monique laughed. "Ah, there's my tiger."

Tess hadn't expected the amusement cropping up in Monique's eyes. God, the betrayal the woman had just exercised was almost as bad as what her father had done.

Monique hadn't valued her in any way beyond her family's name. She'd used Tess and the Ullo reputation to her own advantage, lied about the designs and then had the gall to laugh about it.

Monique patted her cheek and Tess swatted at her hand. "Don't be mad, Tess. Maybe you're right. Yours might have been better, but you have to know I will always have final say," Monique said, not looking even slightly guilty.

"But you purposefully deceived me." For once Tess was glad she was bigger than Monique. She crossed her arms and became her father—cold, businesslike and pissed a person could treat an employee so shabbily.

"I merely decided at the last minute I liked the original proposal." Monique rolled her hand, very nonchalant even though in her gaze Tess could see a prickling of uncertainty. "So how did you know?"

She hadn't. And she had no idea why Miles insisted she take the lead beyond what she suspected—the man trusted her because he'd worked with her before.

Not saying a word, Tess stared at her boss, trying to make her uncomfortable with the way she'd behaved.

Monique shrugged, seemingly unaffected. "But know what? It's fine. Not a bad idea to give him choices. I just wished you'd have consulted me before proceeding with Miles. He's signed the contract stipulating we use your designs and that you oversee the production. You're his contact person and now wholly responsible for Oedipus. I'm half pissed at you and half proud of you for going after what you wanted."

Tess opened her mouth but this time nothing came out. Yeah. Speechless.

"I'll send all the information over to you. Miles wants a few adjustments on your Gulf of Mexico float, but beyond that, he trusts your vision. Congratulations." And with that, Monique left. Cecily stood openmouthed as Monique passed.

Tess sat down before her trembling knees buckled. She couldn't grasp what had just happened.

Cecily's drawn-on eyebrows rose toward her thinning hairline. "You don't get where your bread is buttered, do you?"

"Stuff it."

Cecily scoffed. "You didn't get your way so you ran off and played poor little rich girl with Miles."

"I had nothing to do with this."

"Bullshit," the woman said, her mouth curling into a half snarl that would have made Elvis jealous. "You're cut from the same cloth as your old man—you do whatever it takes."

"Don't even speak his name. Besides, I don't need the approval of a woman who stoops so low to accomplish her goals. You're pathetic. Now, don't let the door hit you in the ass when you leave," Tess said, making a shooing motion toward the older woman.

"She won't keep you on, you know. Don't think you didn't piss her off. She'll use you and then toss the accounts your name nets us to me." With that said, Her Creepiness slunk out, closing the door behind her.

Tess released the breath she'd been holding for the last few seconds and tried to center herself. Anger galloped like a stallion through her body, pounding through her blood, leaving her trembling from the sudden adrenaline rush.

How dare Monique?

Tess spun toward her computer, moving her mouse, automatically clicking on her email out of habit, while her mind raced and the anger continued its steadfast course through her body.

A little ding announced a new email as the window

popped open and there it was—all the information forwarded by Monique regarding the Oedipus account.

Un-freaking-believable.

Her bitch of a boss hadn't even submitted Tess's designs. And they were so much better. Why had she done that?

But deep down inside Tess knew. Monique had a sort of egotistical insecurity that prevented her from seeing the truth in front of her. She'd felt threatened and less important, so she'd made sure she would get the credit. Tess was fairly certain Monique needed some intensive therapy to deal with her Napoleon complex.

Monique won't keep you on, you know.

At that moment, she understood everything about Monique's intent. She didn't want a team at Upstart—it was a dictatorship. Tess was an instrument to be used...but not valued.

Here's our Tess. You know she's an Ullo, right? Works for us now because she realized her father's company was a sinking ship. Utmost quality is what we offer—even an Ullo can attest to that. Her mark is on everything we do.

Yeah, right.

More like *Here's Tess Ullo. She does nothing but smile like a moron, and we lie to her and tell her what she wants to hear because it behooves us.*

Clicking the mouse, Tess reviewed what Miles wanted, feeling only a smidge of pride at the clause stating Tess Ullo must be attached to the project as director or the contract was subject to a renegotiation of terms or a forfeit of agreement between the two parties. At least *Miles* valued her.

But how had he known?

Tess liked to sign her name to her renderings much as any artist. Perhaps Miles had glanced down at the signature and not recognized it as Tess's? She was certain she hadn't mentioned specifics at the mixer.

So how had Miles figured it out? Maybe…

Couldn't be.

Other than Monique, Graham was the only other person to see her execution for the floats, and he would have to be dog-assed stupid to mention her designs to Miles. Losing the Oedipus account would piss her father off. Sick or not, her old man wouldn't suffer the loss of Oedipus. In fact, he'd likely fire Graham for losing so much business his first month as CEO…even if he did like the man.

And with Graham out of the way…

Oh, God, Tess. What the hell are you thinking? Do you want control of Ullo Float Builders so badly, you'd wish ill-will on the man you lo—

She mentally clamped down on that thought.

No.

Deny that word. Contradict those feelings. The fact was she didn't want control of Ullo enough to stoop to Monique's tactics. If anything came of this experience, it was that Tess knew better who she was. Tess was tough, stood up for her beliefs and recognized she did indeed have weaknesses. She could sweet-talk a city inspector, she could coach a gaggle of seven-year-old future soccer stars and she could cry on someone's shoulder, allowing herself to be vulnerable.

She could also learn she was wrong.

Wasn't easy for her to admit it, but she'd been off base in thinking she'd be capable of running Ullo at present. Perhaps she could have slipped right into her father's Hush Puppies and never missed a beat, but then again, maybe those shoes wouldn't have fit. Perhaps they never would.

Maybe she'd never be part of Ullo again so all this self-discovery wouldn't matter for shit. But now she knew being at Ullo meant being part of a team—a team that affirmed her and allowed her to shine. Her family company wasn't perfect, but with failure came a chance to learn.

She'd been wrong about so much.

Rising, she grabbed her purse and looped it over her shoulder before turning back to the computer and quickly transferring the Oedipus file to her personal email account, carbon-copying it to Gigi. She'd text her friend and see if she could give her a crash course on reading through contracts. Tess didn't have much experience, always leaving legal matters to her father. He'd break it down, review it with their attorney and then report back, giving her the nuts and bolts about what each krewe expected for their floats. Another weakness Tess had discovered—she didn't know diddly poop about contract negotiations.

She flipped the light switch, prepared to tell anyone who tried to stop her to go to hell.

"Hey, Tess," the small voice came from the makeshift break area sitting outside the painting bay.

Tess turned to Emily with a forced smile. "Hey, Em."

The little girl sat at a table, eating powdered donuts, swinging her untied sneakers back and forth beneath the table. "I'm doing my homework. Just finished spelling and now I got a worksheet on subtraction. Yuck."

"Yeah, subtraction stinks," Tess said with a shrug, "but yay for finishing your spelling. Oh, and don't forget you have to work on a Ladybug chant. We have practice tomorrow."

Emily's eyes lit up. "I already got one. Dad helped me make it up. Wanna hear it?"

"Sure," Tess conceded, moving closer to Emily while eyeing the unhealthy half-filled bag of donuts.

Emily leaped from the chair and spread her arms out wide. "Fly, fly ladybug, give it all your might. Fly, fly ladybug, show 'em how we fight. Red and black dynamite, we run, kick and score. Lake End Ladybugs, hear the crowd roar!"

During the chant, the child had waved her arms, kicked

her feet and performed a little wiggle with her rump. Like a giant fan, Emily's antics cooled the ire raging inside Tess.

As she watched, trying not to giggle, something quite wonderful struck her. Here was Monique's daughter—a piece of the woman who'd so callously used Tess for her own gain. And here was Graham's daughter—a piece of a man who'd waited so patiently for Tess to find her way. Two parts of a whole.

Emily, with her lopsided bow, mouth ringed in powdered sugar and shirt too tight across her middle. She was part of those two, imperfect and wonderful all at the same time. Innocent of the machinations employed by those in her life, Emily hungered for attention and acceptance.

Just a little girl who loved her daddy and wanted to please him. Not so unlike Tess herself.

Finishing her final spin, Emily struck a pose and blinked up expectantly at Tess.

Sudden tears pricked Tess's eyes.

"Oh, man. It was terrible," Emily said, her small head tilting down.

"Are you kidding me?" Tess said, bending down and sweeping Emily into a huge hug. "It was the best cheer I've heard in forever. It was perfect."

"Really?" Emily leaned back and studied Tess's face as if she were a police detective. "You're not just saying that? Mom said it was pretty good, but Dad thought it rocked. He helped me with the motions, too, but he looked really weird doing them."

Tess laughed. "I can only imagine."

"Tess, do you like my daddy?" Emily asked, suddenly earnest. Suddenly looking older than her seven years.

"Sure I do. He's been a pretty good assistant coach. I never have to yell at him for not having our water bottles filled," Tess joked, not sure how much Emily understood about the relationship between a man and woman.

"No. I mean like love stuff. I think Daddy likes you. You know, he wants to kiss you." Emily averted her gaze, suddenly finding the ancient coffeepot fascinating.

Tess straightened. "What makes you think that?"

Emily shrugged. "A few of my fish died."

Uh, what? Tess looked at Emily with a blank expression. She had no clue. No innate mothering skill to enable her to peer into the wackiness of a child's brain. Fish and kissing. How in the hell did that relate?

The girl made a face. "When Daddy moved here, he said he wanted to be a family. He can't marry my mom. She's already married to Josh. But I'd really like a baby brother, you know."

"Uh, I'm not following the fish thing," Tess said.

"Well, I said maybe we could get a kitten to help us be more of a family, but Daddy said no. He said we have to start with fish. So we got us some, but the yellow one and two of the blue ones with the pretty tails died."

"Oh," Tess said. "Uh, I'm sorry."

"So maybe you could just marry my dad? Maybe have a baby or something? There's a swimming pool at his new place." Emily smiled encouragingly, her blue eyes half full of pleading, half full of "this is a great idea."

"People don't just get married."

"They do on TV. I watched that bachelor show once. Those girls were just happy with a hot tub. And they kissed a bunch," Emily said, nodding her head this time like she'd figured out the entire formula for falling in love.

Yeah. A hole with water inside.

Tess thought about arguing with the child, but then thought better of it. "Okay, I'll keep that in mind. You keep practicing your chant, get that math homework and lay off the donuts—you're in training."

"For what?"

"Being a Ladybug," Tess said, giving Emily a wave.

"Oh, yeah," she said, hurrying back over to her chair and folding the bag closed. "I gotta be able to run fast."

And Tess walked briskly out—proud of herself for not running.

THE GODDAMN SWEAT rolled down Frank's back as he sat like an old bullfrog on the patio out back. Maggie had gone to Peggy Garland's house to take a pound cake for the visitation. Her choir friend's mother had passed. Frank wondered if Peggy would return the favor when he passed. What was it with frickin' pound cakes anyway? In his opinion most tasted like crap. Give him a good piece of coconut cake. Maybe he'd send Peggy a note and tell her he wanted to be honored with something more than pound cake...but that might be too morbid.

Middle of May and already it was sultry. A breeze made a half-assed attempt at stirring the leaves, but it wasn't enough to stop him from sweating.

And then he felt the first mosquito.

Christ. Nothing like feeling good enough for some fresh air and then having to battle Louisiana.

He'd finally finished the last round of chemo, had a PET scan next week to see if anything had worked. The doctor had talked about some kind of surgery if there hadn't been any progress, but Frank had told him to go fly a kite. No more pain, no more puking and no more last-ditch efforts.

He craved peace.

The only thing stopping him from surrendering— No, wait, he wasn't giving up on himself or the medicine yet. But he could relax into his fate better if he and Tess could talk. Her gaze last Sunday had told him her heart had changed, but the words had not been spoken.

He and Tess had things to say.

"Dad?"

Frank snapped out of his reverie to find the very devil

he'd been thinking about standing in front of him as if his thoughts had summoned her. Tess didn't look like anyone who could bedevil with her benign honey hair and sweet face, but this one had never been an angel. Just his Tess— perfect in his eyes.

He squinted against the sun slanting in through the oak's canopy. "You okay?"

She shrugged. "Drove around for a while, looking for a spot I could breathe in. My car took me here."

Thank God. Frank patted the bench. "You can sit."

"I'm good. How are you feeling?"

"Like I've been pumped full of chemicals."

"Yeah," she said, her brow furrowing. "Mom said the doctors haven't said much."

"Gotta do a scan to check on the cells or something like that." He brushed the matter away with his hand. He didn't want to talk about being sick, but he didn't know how to bring up what sat between them.

"I'm sorry, Dad."

For what? His cancer? Quitting Ullo? Not speaking to him for over a month?

"About a lot of stuff," she clarified, looking down at her hands. Then she glanced around. "Guess our backyard has always been the go-to place when you need to talk. When you need to think. Maybe I knew I could breathe here."

Frank looked around. "And sweat. I'm about to burn slap up sitting out here and the mosquitos are eating on me. Wanna go inside to the other place where family problems are solved to have this conversation?"

"The kitchen?" Tess asked, a small smile creeping out.

Frank struggled to his feet, and Tess rushed to grab his elbow. He patted her arm. "I'm good. A little weak still, but not as bad as I was last week. This shit really did a number on me. Guess I ain't too tolerant of chemo."

Tess's face crumpled. "Dad…"

"None of that. We gotta talk about what happened, Tess. We got a lot of words to say and I can't say 'em if you start blubbering. You know what your tears do to me."

Tess managed a shaky smile. "Think that's the problem to begin with, huh?"

"A little."

Together they moved toward the back door, each with much to say, but for a moment content to feel the other's presence. Shoulder to shoulder, they walked. Father and daughter—more alike than either wanted to admit.

CHAPTER NINETEEN

TESS POURED SOME LEMONADE in a tall glass and handed it to her father, glad to have something to occupy her hands. He waved it away, sinking on a bar stool with a small sigh.

He didn't look good, but she supposed after all the rounds of chemotherapy he'd undergone, he wasn't supposed to. His body was at war, so he wasn't exactly up for running marathons. His craggy face with the large Italian nose, so dear to her, held a pall, the wrinkles more pronounced, and his salt-and-pepper hair more salt now.

She knew why she'd come. After the drama in her office with Monique…after the realization of what she'd given up, she'd come home not to lick her wounds but repair one still bleeding.

Or maybe it was more she needed to loosen the knots she'd tied around herself, but she wasn't here to ask her father to fix anything in her life. She was here to make things right.

"Mom and I had a long talk," Tess said, pulling the cool glass to her place as she sank onto the stool opposite her father.

"She told me but didn't say much else," Frank said, playing with the bobbing rooster her mother had bought at a flea market one summer. "I didn't ask her. I knew you needed some time to figure things out."

"I've had plenty of time," Tess said, in the quiet of the kitchen. "I'd graduated into avoidance. Sorry I didn't return your calls. I didn't know what to say."

Her father looked at her. "None of this has been easy, has it? I'm still trying to get my footing. Thing is, I may never be rock-solid again."

Tess put her hand over his worn, calloused one. "Don't say it like that, Daddy."

"Baby, I ain't afraid of dying. I just don't want to leave all of you behind. But the good Lord might just be ready for me up there. I've come to terms with that, Therese. I have."

"I haven't," she said. His words ripped into her, shredding her heart. She couldn't grasp the concept of her father dying. She refused to.

"I know, honey, but dying isn't as scary as living sometimes. I have faith there's a place for me, and I'll be waiting in glory for all of you. Maybe not my own mama 'cause she might not make it past St. Peter." He gave her a sad wink.

Tess managed a small smile. "She'd probably tell God how to run the joint. You know she still writes her congressman about daylight saving time?"

For a moment they both smiled through the pain.

"But I'm not just sorry about your getting sick, Daddy. I'm sorry about everything that happened when you gave Graham the position of CEO. I didn't think before I acted, and, honestly, put myself in a bad situation."

Frank shook his head. "Ah, Tess, I didn't handle it right, either. I was a coward, plain and simple. Everything in life was suddenly so hard, so scary. I knew I couldn't undergo all the procedures and chemotherapy and still run the company. It broke my heart." Her father's voice quivered and Tess couldn't stop a lone tear from trailing down her cheek. Swiping it away, she realized she'd never stopped to think about how hard handing over his company, virtually his baby, must have been for him. She'd never even considered how being given a virtual death sentence had affected her father. She'd only thought of herself.

"I didn't know, Dad."

"I know you didn't. Once I found out about the cancer, I didn't tell anyone for several days...not even your mother or Joe. This horrible thing grew inside me, twisting around this selfish need to pretend like everything was okay. At first, I planned on not telling anyone at all. Just thought I'd ride it out until the end and then cash my check. I didn't want to put anyone through all the crap that comes with the fight. But I changed my mind the day we rolled Bacchus out. You remember?"

She did. That Sunday had been perfect. Maggie had brought them a big picnic basket and she and her father had sat in the parade stand, each connected with their guys coordinating the tractors. Last-minute emergency work was handled by Red Jack and Bennie B so Tess, Dave and her father had been able to enjoy the fruits of their labor. All her brothers and their families had been there, each bringing a picnic basket full of New Orleans favorites, including a huge cinnamon-and-sugar king cake. The weather had been mild, no floats had broken down and the excitement in the air had been electric. It had been a while since Tess had enjoyed herself like that at a parade. "It was perfect."

"Yeah, the floats looked great and there were so few hiccups. I laughed for the first time since the doc sat me down with that news." Frank smiled as if sucked back into the memory. "You laughed a lot, too, and it was good to see you happy. That Nick fellow had pissed you off over Christmas and then the season hit and we were too busy to think, much less smile. I remember watching you and your mama that day, flirting for beads and dancing to the music. At the end of the parade, you laid your head on your mama's shoulder and she kissed your forehead. That was when I knew I had to fight, and I knew I'd have to make some tough decisions."

Tess dropped her gaze because it hurt to think about that moment, hurt to know the burden her father had carried.

"I've always been proud you wanted to do what I do, Tess. We make magic. We make people happy. That's a satisfying feeling. I hadn't planned on retiring this soon, and I'll be honest, I thought with a little more tempering and the right crew around you, you'd be fine running the company. But I didn't think you were ready. I'm not saying you had to have a business degree, but you didn't have a clue what I do on my end. I thought if I could find a guy—"

"Or girl?" Tess added.

"Maybe. There aren't many women in this business, Tess. Well, at least not many running the show, no how. But I wasn't against hiring a woman—I wasn't against anyone who could do a good job. I wanted to find someone who could easily do what I do and leave you to do what you do." Frank spread his hands, and Tess was able to climb over the fence and see it from his side. He hadn't wanted her stressed. He'd tried to take care of her even then.

"So when the headhunter guy called me and sent me Naquin's resume, it was like being handed a lottery ticket with the winning numbers. He was a perfect fit—young, experienced and had listed New Orleans as his ideal relocation area. I thought I was doing you a favor, keeping you from worrying so much when I wasn't around. But I also knew you'd be mad at me. And that's when I got chicken."

"But you should have told me. You should have given me the benefit of knowing before he got there, not send me off with Granny B so I wouldn't know."

"Yeah, I should have, but I think, as your mother told you, I'm not good at telling you no, baby. You've talked me into about anything you've wanted all your life. I gained five pounds one summer on those Plum Street Snoballs alone. What you wanted, you got."

She'd gotten on a Snoball kick one summer between seventh and eighth grade, wanting one after every soccer practice. Her father had dutifully driven her to get her blackberry with crème.

Frank continued. "I loved giving you things, but when you're facing a crypt down the road there—" he pointed toward the huge cemetery sitting a few miles down Metairie Road "—you start looking at things differently. You start doubting all the decisions you made, wondering if you'd given your kids and wife what they really needed all this time."

For a moment he paused. "I don't think I did that bad. I'm not perfect and, yeah, I screwed this the hell up, but when I thought about just giving you the position, it felt wrong."

A fishhook of hurt snagged inside her soul. "I wanted to be good enough."

"Ah, Tess, you know that's not it. Don't make it that. You're brilliant at what you do, but I decided as soon as you came aboard, this was a business that needed a partnership to run it. You taught me that, so I thought I'd replaced myself with a guy who could balance you out. He seemed a lot like me. Determined and smart, but not too hardass."

Tess's heart leaped at those words. A partnership with Graham.... It fit in more than just a business sense. What if her dad had seen beyond the business to who she needed in her life—a man who balanced her?

Not a pretty rich boy with little stickability like Nick. Not the half dozen other guys she'd dated—an attorney in Gigi's office, a hairstylist from the Westbank or the guy who said he was an officer in the Navy but really just worked at the base—but a guy who had a passion for doing what she did. A guy who balanced out her creativity with a nose for business. A guy who looked pretty damn spectacular in the buff, loved his own daughter above all else and wasn't as confident and capable as he portrayed. Like Tess, he wasn't perfect.

But maybe Graham was perfect for her.

"I've screwed up so badly, Dad," Tess said, emotion

snagging in her throat. She couldn't undo what she'd done. She couldn't expect her father to fix what her pride had led her to.

"Maybe not. But you landed a job on your own, and I bet you've learned more working for a smaller company than you ever did working for a bigger one. No one to hand things off to—you had to do it yourself. And Monique's an interesting woman."

"Monique is a bitch, Dad."

Frank laughed and for a moment he didn't look sick. Color bloomed into his cheeks and his eyes sparkled. "She's ambitious. I respect that about her. Personally, I never cared about her politics when it came to doing business, but I'm sure she didn't care for mine. She's broken new ground for women in this business and made a better way for you and other little girls who want to build floats and play with the big boys."

Tess nodded, still miffed over the way Monique had handled the Oedipus deal. "Fine. I'll give her that. She's definitely interesting."

"So, Tess, do you forgive me for hiring Graham?"

Tess nodded. "Yes. I've had to swallow my pride and admit I can't do all I thought I could. Working for Upstart has taught me a lot about myself. But most of all, I've learned to accept my flaws and to just keep swimming when the current gets rough. Never had to do that before."

Frank lifted his hands and beckoned her. "Come here, my Tess."

Tess swallowed the lump in her throat and walked around the end of the bar. Her father enveloped her in a strong hug and for a few seconds, Tess lay her head on the man's shoulder, inhaling the Hugo Boss cologne he'd gotten for a "song" at T.J. Maxx and the lavender fabric softener her mother used in the laundry. He smelled like her father. He smelled like all things safe. He smelled like her past and present. Like home. But he'd also given her the scent for her future.

Inhaling once again, she took the deep breath she'd been looking for and exhaled, determined to fix the other parts of her life she'd mishandled.

GRAHAM SAT AT HIS DESK and stared at the stapler. He'd chosen that particular item at random. He could have stared at the nameplate Billie had stuck on his desk the day before as if she were placing a tiara on the head of a beauty pageant winner. But he didn't want to stare at it. It seemed indefinite, like he might have to toss it in the trashcan at any minute...along with his short-lived reign as CEO of Frank Ullo Float Builders. So the stapler would have to be his focal point while he contemplated his future.

Like he did most days around the end of the workday, Dave popped his head in. "You busy?"

"No. I should be, but I'm contemplating what I'll be qualified for when Frank tosses me out like last week's Chinese."

Dave settled in the chair opposite him. "Nah, Frank has faith in you, and after your speech last week, we all have that faith in you."

Had it only been last week? Seemed long ago he'd rallied the troops around pizza and a common objective. "We lost the Oedipus account to Upstart. Miles Barrow just called me."

Dave's eyes popped wide. "Oh, well, in that case, I'll go get a box for your things."

Graham shifted his gaze back to the stapler. "Yeah, right."

Dave sighed. "That's really shitty news. Tess snaked us, huh? I taught that girl too well."

What to say to that? He didn't want to admit he'd handed over the contract to Upstart by telling Miles about Tess's designs. What stupid-ass CEO would do such a thing? Miles's kind words about his intent and about how Frank would understand did little to buffer the sting of the call he'd just received. He'd known it was likely coming, but the finality of it suckerpunched him in spite of it. "Yeah, she's good. I wish she were still here doing work for us. I tried to talk her into coming back but it did little good. Her pride was pricked and I likely wasn't the right person to persuade her."

Dave's laugh was bitter. "No kidding. But I'm impressed you went to her and asked her to come back. I like that about you. A little humbleness is welcome around here, you know?"

"All I got left is humbleness," Graham said.

"Nah, we got plenty of business. I talked to some krewes out of Houma and Lake Charles today that want new marque floats and we're working hard to keep our regular customers happy. I won't lie and say Oedipus wasn't a loss, but we'll be okay." Dave stood and perused the schedule board Graham had mounted on the wall. "Might not be the best of times to ask, but we really need someone to help me. Honestly, the part of the job Tess did as liaison with the other directors and captains was never something I wanted to do. Tess was good with them, keeping them happy, making sure the vision fit actuality, so if you could shift that job requirement over to the new guy, I'll keep the lion's share of the design work. And my pay raise."

Graham rubbed a hand over his face. "Anyone in house capable of doing the job?"

"Not really, but Billie sent an ad to some local websites, and Red Jack posted it on some NOLA message boards for artists. He's into all that crap."

Graham stood, offering his hand just as he'd done for the last few days. Having Dave on his team felt good. Billie, too. He'd finally gotten some decent coffee. "I'll pull any resumes Billie has and set up some interviews at the beginning of next week."

"Good man," Dave said, taking his leave for the day.

Graham sank back into his chair and pulled out his cellphone. Tess still hadn't called him back.

His work life might be in shambles, but, damn, Sunday night had been incredible. He'd called her earlier in the week and left a message. Then texted her right after the Oedipus meeting, hoping the magnanimous gesture of giving Miles the real skinny had lined the stars up in his favor.

But she hadn't called or returned his text.

In her eyes, they were over.

He could see her point, being rivals and all, but after the tender way they'd parted, he'd hoped she relented and considered a tenuous relationship.

Damn it all, didn't they deserve to see if what they had was the real thing? Bad blood or no, he knew she'd fit him like a latex glove—no room for anything else. Just skin on skin—the way he liked it between them.

He pressed the email icon and sighed. No email, either. *Frick.*

He picked up the desktop phone and hit the red button that would page Billie.

"What's up?" she said.

"We have any resumes for the art director gig?"

"Four."

"Can you get them to me?"

Billie sighed. "Can a woodpecker peck wood? Check your inbox in thirty seconds. No, wait. Make that a minute or two." She clicked off and Graham went through his other messages, waiting on the resumes.

Waiting on Tess.

CHAPTER TWENTY

AFTER LEAVING HER parents' house, Tess headed back into the city, phoning Gigi because she'd emailed her friend the contract terms Miles had sent Monique, hoping Gigi could do a quick look-see.

"What up, homey?" Gigi drawled into the receiver.

"I know you're super busy, but I sent you an email—"

"Already got it, and I'm charging you the usual friend rate," Gigi said, moving around some papers or something in the background.

"A night of binge drinking and then holding your hair back while you puke?"

"Exactly." Gigi laughed and it sounded like little bells tinkling. Seriously, how did someone have a magical laugh like that? "So when do you want to go out and shoot Jagermeister?"

"I could use a drink now, but I think I need a clear head this afternoon."

"You okay? You sound stopped up."

"It's been an emotional couple of days. I finally talked to my dad and got things straight with him. Now I'm facing down this whole career decision I made."

"Yeah, I feel sort of responsible for that, so I've already read through the contract. It's fairly standard stuff in regards to business contracts. But there's this huge loophole. Like, I'm talking big-as-a-cloverleaf-in-LA huge."

"About my being the project manager?" Tess switched lanes and headed deeper into the city.

"Exactly."

"So if I quit Upstart…"

"Let's start with the contract I drew between you and Upstart in regards to your employment. See, when you and Monique agreed upon the three-month provision, I intentionally left the language loose. That's not to say you take any business you score for Upstart with you if you part ways, but I made sure you own your work and that it becomes the property of Upstart while you work for them. Intellectual rights stuff can get pretty complex, so I won't wade into that."

"My head's getting muddled just thinking about it," Tess said.

"So if you were to, say, leave Upstart, you would not be able to take any of the designs you created for Upstart with you. They would belong to the company because you were employed by the company. You dig?"

"Yeah. Sort of."

"Okay, so this Oedipus deal is different. Miles Barrow is sharp as a pressed suit. In the contract he signed with Upstart, he designated that you, Tess Ullo, must be attached to the project in order for the contract to be valid. In other words, if you walk, he walks with you. In a roundabout way, he signed a contract with you, but because you work for Upstart, they get the krewe's business."

Tess hit a pothole and her teeth banged together, even as something radical bloomed within her. "So I'm the key to Oedipus?"

"Pretty much."

"Why would Monique agree to these terms knowing I could leave Upstart during my interim period without any repercussions, taking Miles Barrow's business with me?"

"It's risky, sure, but you said her ego is as big as Dallas, so maybe she's hedging her bets. After all, she believes you're out for revenge against your father. She might feel secure in the idea you won't leave a perfectly good job. Besides, I'm pretty sure she owns your designs. In other words, you can leave and take Oedipus with you, but you can't take the designs because those belong to Upstart."

"But those weren't the original designs submitted by Upstart," Tess grumbled, disappointed that her best work belonged to Monique...and the woman hadn't even appreciated it enough to send it out.

Gigi's lawyer signal kicked in. "What do you mean?"

Tess went over what she'd learned about the original proposal subbed to Upstart.

"So how did Miles know the designs weren't yours? Do you have some sort of trademark design I don't know about?"

"No. The only thing I could think of is that Miles saw the signatures or something on the designs Monique submitted that told him they weren't mine. He knew I had worked the account because I told him as much at the mixer."

"Hmmm..." Gigi said, her wheels obviously spinning. "My advice is to call Miles and see what's up."

"Is that official legal advice?"

"Yeah, totally free as long as you invite me to Sunday dinner when your ma makes Bolognese sauce."

Tess smiled. "Will do."

Clicking off with Gigi, Tess had pulled over to Cuppa Joe's, her mind reeling with this new information. Something in her was exhilarated at the thought of having Monique by the balls. She'd call Miles from the coffee shop and grab a cup of soothing tea to calm her shot nerves.

The place wasn't too busy and she quickly found a table and gave Miles a call. Of course, he wasn't available.

"Well, this is important, so I'd really appreciate it if you would give him my cell number and have him call me ASAP."

"All his calls are important, so you'll just have to hold on to your britches," Julian said.

"Julian, this is Tess Ullo. I sent you the gift certificate to Emeril's last year. This is me calling in my favor."

"Missy miss," Julian said, and Tess could picture him rolling his eyes. Probably clad in poplin and a bow tie. "I'll have him call you. Don't have a hissy."

Tess grumbled an "okay" and then hung up. Settling back to wait, she watched the people coming in and out of the coffee shop. Her city was such a diverse one—the doors swung open to a teen girl with piercings and a tattoo wrapped around her neck, a soccer mom in Lululemon, a businessman barking into his Bluetooth and a gaggle of kids who'd obviously been tap-dancing in the quarter after school. They paid in wadded up dollars and change, counting it out carefully and sucking down the sweet, icy coffees.

Finally, her phone rang.

"Ma chère," Miles crowed into the receiver. "I've made you a happy woman, eh?"

"Yes, Miles. I appreciate your liking my designs so much," Tess said, cradling the dainty cup she always requested for her tea.

"Good, good. So why the frantic call? You had Julian doing flips trying to get me off a conference call with a disgruntled, and might I add, burned, employee of Happy Burger."

"Sorry, I had a few questions," Tess said, unsure as to how to basically ask if he were aware her boss double-crossed her. "The first proposal Monique submitted wasn't mine."

"I know," he said, with a smile in his voice. "That's why I called her and asked her to take a meeting with me. I didn't understand why she would hire the best float designer in town with the best name in Mardi Gras and not use her the way God intended."

Because Monique couldn't give up the slightest bit of power to anyone? Because she was scared? Because she was a bitch? Because she was a blooming idiot? Pick one. Any one.

Tess didn't say that, of course. "How did you know the design wasn't mine?"

"I didn't. The first proposal was fine, but to be honest, I had decided to continue with your dad's company. I've been with Ullo a long time and what Monique gave me wasn't enough to make me want to switch. They were very competent and professional, but I needed fantastic to make that switch, you know? So this morning, I met with Graham Naquin and prepared to sign on the dotted line."

Graham again.

The man popped up everywhere—in her thoughts, dreams...her life.

"So..." she prompted.

"Well, in the course of my conversation with Naquin this morning, he said something about your design that didn't mesh."

"He talked about my design?" Something not so warm climbed within her. He'd been poking through her things, had seen her designs, giving himself a leg up on what the competition planned.

But then the rational part of her remembered who Graham was. He wouldn't have trashed her. Wouldn't have good reason to mention her at all.

"In a good way. He said something to the effect of having seen your designs and sweating our contract negotiations. Something about that didn't sit right with me."

Another long stretch of silence.

"Miles?"

"Yeah. Okay, here's the deal. You know I'm a man of my word and you know I'm not underhanded in the slightest. Well, at least not much. But I showed Graham the designs Upstart had submitted. Now, don't you go telling Monique. I don't need her riding my back, implying I'm unethical. I've never done nothing like that before, but I can smell when something ain't right.

"So, I hand over the proposal to Graham and he gets this funny look on his face. Finally, he tosses the proposal on my desk and says it isn't your work."

Tess sat back so hard in her chair she scared the man reading the paper sitting behind her. "What? He…uh… I can't—"

"Yeah, I couldn't believe it, either, but he said they weren't yours, and that I couldn't ask him how he knew, but he knew. Then he did the damnedest thing I ever saw in the business world."

Tess knew what Miles was going to say before he said it. "He told you my designs were better than his."

Miles laughed. "Yeah, the bastard did. He said I should call Monique and tell her to send your stuff over. He said you deserved a shot at my business."

Tess dropped her head to her chest as a huge wave of mixed emotion washed over her—guilt, shame, pleasure, gratitude and love were only a few of them. "Why would he do that?"

"I don't know. He's either the most honest man in the world, or he had a really good reason. But he was right. Your designs are better than any of the others I've received. I don't understand why Monique didn't sub them. Well, I've met her a few times and actually I do."

Tess couldn't comprehend what Graham had done. Why had he destroyed his chance to secure the krewe of Oedipus's business? It didn't make sense for him to hand over the golden apple, a very lucrative, point-of-pride golden apple. Integrity was one thing, being stupid in business another.

Maybe her father had been wrong.

Or maybe Graham had a different motivation. Maybe Graham was more like her father than what she wanted to admit.

"Okay," Tess said, nodding her head though only the man who'd gotten up and moved to another table could see her. "That's what I wanted to know."

"Hey, Tess," Miles said, his tone growing more serious. "I'm not saying anything against Monique, but I will note this. I don't like she didn't present your work over the proposal she sent over. Any fool could see your design was better, but I gathered she thought her design work should stand before yours. A good business owner never lets her ego get in the way of doing what is best for the company. The only reason why I signed on with Upstart, for one year only I might add, was because of your designs. Monique wasn't overly happy with contract terms."

"Yeah, so I gather," Tess said, walking toward the bar and sliding her cup over to the barista. "I thank you for being forthcoming with me, Miles."

"See ya, Tess."

Tess hung up, took a deep coffee-scented breath and pushed back out into the humid New Orleans air.

Finally the pieces of her life were snapping into place. She had learned more about her boss in ten minutes than she had the entire time working for her. Tess wasn't cavalier enough to overlook the blatant lack of professionalism her boss had displayed. Nor was she willing to play backup to Cecily. She'd made peace with her father, and in doing so, made peace with her own faults. And finally, she'd come face-to-face with Graham's selflessness. Maybe not the shark her father had hoped for, but the man had a heart of gold and an undeniable sense of honor.

Her pride had brought her to where she now stood, but love would take her where she belonged.

Tess climbed in her car and drove straight to Upstart.

At the office, the workday had wound down, but Monique still sat at her desk, phone to ear, fingers clicking on her keyboard.

Josh wasn't lounging around anywhere, and Emily didn't seem to be around, either.

Perfect time to quit her job.

Tess didn't belong at Upstart…and never would.

Monique sat the phone in the cradle, not bothering to meet Tess's gaze. She said, "What's up?"

"Can I talk to you?"

"You are talking to me," Monique drawled, the glow of the computer illuminating her perfect features.

Yeah. And there was the whole "make Tess feel stupid" thing Monique had going.

"I'm not going to stay."

Monique's brow furrowed and still she didn't look at Tess. "You don't have to. I'm not checking your hours. I trust you."

"Wow, that's unexpected," Tess said, placing the copy of her contract on the desk. "But what I'm trying to say is that I don't think my job here at Upstart is going to work out."

Monique finally looked at her before slamming her hands onto the desk. "No. Unacceptable."

"I can't stay, Monique."

"Is this because of what happened earlier? It was a disagreement, Tess. Please don't tell me your skin is that thin."

"It's not just about today. It's about realizing I will never belong here."

Eyes blazing, Monique leaned back. "I guess you're not the woman I thought you were."

"I guess I'm not," Tess said. "But you can't deny I don't fit here. I've learned a lot from you, but I think it's better if I don't continue."

Looking down at the contract, Monique sighed. "I knew

I shouldn't have agreed to that ninety-day trial period. Damn it."

Tess sank onto the same chair she'd sat in over a month ago. "I don't think you're happy with me, either. You're accustomed to running things, and I am, too. This was the first clash we've had, but it wouldn't be the last. Upstart is a good company, and you were doing fine without me."

"We're doing better with you," she said.

Tess nodded. "Maybe for a while, but the Ullo name only does so much, Monique."

"Is this about Graham?"

Tess jolted at the thought of Monique seeing so easily through her. "A little, but mostly it's about me. This past month I've had to take a hard look at myself. I left my father's company because of arrogance. I took this job because I wanted to punish him. None of those were good enough reasons. From the beginning I knew I'd made a mistake, but I was too stubborn, too prideful to admit it."

"Nothing wrong with being tenacious or having self-respect."

"Maybe not," Tess said, looking around Monique's office, seeing nothing of a personal nature. Not even a drawing by Emily or a photo of Josh. Nothing. Empty. "Can I say something to you that might be a little out of line?"

Monique snorted before rolling her eyes. "I know what you're going to say. I'm a bitch. I'm underhanded, merciless, sneaky. Go ahead. I've heard it all before."

"That's not what I was going to say," Tess said, with a small smile. "I wanted to tell you how talented you are, and how much I admire your determination to make it in this business."

"But…?"

"I think you're scared."

Monique flinched. "I'm not scared."

"You conduct business like you're scared. Like you're

afraid someone won't think you're good enough. That's what that whole sketch thing was about—control and ego."

"That's ridiculous."

Tess shrugged. "Maybe, but you're only as good as the people around you. My father taught me that. I hadn't even realized it. And it's not just your employees, it's Josh. It's that wonderful, funny little girl who draws you pictures every day." Tess looked around the austere office again and arched an eyebrow at Monique.

Monique pulled out a plastic container of drawings from a drawer. She took the top one, a picture of what looked to be a person playing soccer. "This one is of you, I think." She passed it over.

Tess took the drawing and smiled at the little girl's interpretation of the soccer field and the overly long prongs on the soccer cleats.

"Whatever anyone may think about me, I love my daughter." Her tone wasn't defensive. It was sad.

Tess nodded. "I know you do."

"I'm good at running this place. I'm just not good at being a mom." Not knowing what to say, Tess handed the drawing back.

"It was easier when she was a baby. Feed her, change her, rock her. I didn't worry about messing up, but as she grew, I felt more and more helpless. Josh is actually better with her than I am." Monique snapped the lid closed and placed the box back in her drawer. "I'm sorry. I shouldn't have even gone there. I guess I didn't want you to think I'm some unfeeling monster."

"I don't think that, Monique."

"Well, I feel that way sometimes," she said with a sigh.

"My dad built Ullo from nothing, just like you, but it's easier for a man. He had my mother at home taking care of carpool, homework, snacks—the stuff all parents have to deal with. He worked hard to build Ullo but he never put his business before his family. Never. I think that's a good policy."

Monique twisted her mouth and shifted her gaze, seemingly thinking about what Tess said. "Maybe so."

"My father's dying, and in these final months, he's let Ullo go…but he's gathered the people he loves to him. It's not about contracts—" Tess tapped the paper "—or specifications. It's about people."

Tugging the contract from beneath Tess's finger, Monique tossed it in the trash. "Okay. There. I'll start with you."

Tess gave her a puzzled look.

"I'm not going to read over the fine print, talk badly about you for changing your mind or pitch a fit over the Oedipus bid. I'm going to let it go so I can go home early and watch Josh and Emily kick balls into the net Graham bought her. The thing takes up our whole backyard." Monique gave her a shrug and a slight smile. "I don't want to lose you, Tess, but I'm not going to stop you. Hell, I can't stop you anyway. I agreed to that damn waiting period."

"Thank you," Tess said, standing and extending a hand. "And I'm sorry if I got preachy on you."

"Maybe I needed a little preaching. Maybe I need to quit trying so damn hard. Miles actually said something like that to me, too." Monique took her hand.

Miles and Oedipus. The conversation between her and Monique had taken a turn off course, and Tess hadn't addressed the contract clause Miles had placed in the agreement with Upstart. "You need to talk to Miles and renegotiate the contract. I'm not staying, but my Oedipus designs belong to you."

Monique released her hand. "I'll call him."

Tess turned and started for the door.

"Hey, Tess," Monique said.

Tess turned around. "Yeah?"

"I never said I was sorry, but I am. I shouldn't have allowed Cecily to tell me my stuff was better when it obviously wasn't. You're right about my issue with control and wanting affirmation. I need to deal better with that. I don't want you to leave Upstart, but I understand about belonging."

"Thank you for the apology. I learned a lot about myself working here."

"Like what not to do?" Monique lifted one corner of her mouth.

"I learned it's okay to fail, to be wrong and to accept who I am." Tess gave Monique a smile and then walked out of Upstart. When she got to her car, she dialed the number she hadn't dialed in almost two months.

"Hey, Billie, it's Tess. I'm wondering if Mr. Naquin has filled my old position yet."

She listened for several seconds, covering the mouthpiece to keep from laughing in relief.

"In that case, I'd like to make an appointment for next week."

CHAPTER TWENTY-ONE

THE FOLLOWING MONDAY came with little relief from the now summerlike heat or the ache in Graham's heart. He had seen Tess Thursday at Ladybug soccer practice, where she treated him with polite professionalism.

Hell, he'd rather she rubbed in the fact she'd scored the Oedipus floats for 2016 than treat him as if he were just another parent. He'd gotten the message last Monday when they'd parted—they'd had one more night of magic together and then it was business as usual. He didn't like it at all.

The entire time he watched her work with the little girls on the soccer team, he kept thinking, "She's mine."

But she wasn't and likely never would be.

She'd never responded to his call or text, and now he knew how she'd felt months ago. Made him feel used and not worth bothering with.

Pair all that with the fact he'd lost the Oedipus account and the shipment of industrial foam was on back order and today was about as shitty as they came. The only upside was that Emily had stopped bugging him about a kitten. Of course, she'd replaced it with wanting him to get married and get her a baby brother, so it really was lose-lose.

"Hey," Billie said, knocking then immediately popping her head in. "Your first applicant for the art director position is here. Where are you planning to hold the meeting?"

Graham closed his eyes for a moment and rubbed a hand

across his face. A dull headache pounded behind his eyes. Cracking open an eye, he saw the clock read 10:00 a.m. Still had a long way to go to finish the day, which would end with a meeting at Frank's house.

"Uh, I suppose we can do it here."

"Okay. I put the applicant in Frank's office, but I can—"

"Nah, that's fine. His office is nicer. Now which one is this? The one from Mobile?"

"Oh, I don't think I gave you the file on this one. I'll grab it and bring it to you," Billie said.

Graham waited for ten minutes, buzzing Billie intermittently, but she didn't answer or return with the folder. Damn it.

He didn't like to keep people waiting. He'd certainly never appreciated such tactics when he was being interviewed, so he didn't like to do the same with others.

Rising, he peered out into the recesses of the outer office. Billie wasn't at her desk and Dave's door was closed.

"Hell," he breathed under his breath, walking toward Frank's office. He'd have to wing it. No other recourse.

Opening the door, he donned a polite smile. "Hi, I'm sorry to keep you waiting." As he shut the door all he could see of the person waiting for him was the top of her bun.

Rounding the desk, he focused on the blotter to see if perhaps Billie had left the applicant's file for him before she disappeared. "I'm sorry I'm a bit late. I'm afraid I don't—"

"That's okay," the applicant said.

Graham snapped his head up. "Tess?"

She smiled politely, humor tipping the corners of her mouth as she extended her hand. "I'm Therese Ullo."

If the door had blown down and he'd found himself surrounded by a legion of gladiators he wouldn't have been more shocked than he was now.

What in the hell was she doing there?

"What in the hell are you doing here?"

She arched an eyebrow. "We have a ten o'clock appointment. An interview for the Head of Operations position."

"An interview? Head of Operations? I don't think—"

"Yes. I saw the ad on the NOLA artist forum. It said you were looking for an assistant art director, but when I called I was told it had changed to Head of Operations with art direction being only part of the tasks involved. Don't worry. I'm qualified for both." She folded her hands in her lap and looked at him expectantly.

Graham sat in her father's chair a little too hard. For several seconds he stared at her, trying to figure out if this was for real.

She looked the part of interviewee in a crisp white blouse, knotted at the neck with a huge bow and a tight black skirt that went to midcalf. Her shoes were low-heeled and conservative, as was the honey-brown hair she'd pulled into a knot.

"You're here to interview for a job?" he asked again.

"Yes," she said with an emphatic nod.

"Because you don't have one?"

"Right."

Graham stared at the historical float plans which Frank had hung on his walls, trying to figure out what was happening. "Okay then, let's get started. So, tell me a little about yourself, Miss Ullo. Wait, it *is* Miss, correct?"

"Yes, I'm unmarried. In other words, I'm single."

"Good," he said.

"I'm twenty-seven years old, turning twenty-eight in August, and I have worked in the float building industry all my life. I have a bachelor's degree in industrial design from Carnegie-Mellon and almost ten years' experience working in the field, starting with my first job in high school. I'm a former employee of this company and most recently Upstart."

"Former employee of Upstart?"

"Yes, former. Unfortunately, I found I wasn't a good fit there."

"May I ask why you chose to leave your former position?"

Tess shifted her gaze from his and studied the same stapler he'd studied a week ago. "Creative differences were part of it, but also, in the course of working for that company, I learned enough about myself to figure out where I belong."

"And that is…?"

"The reason I'm interviewing for this job." She smoothed her hair and rubbed her delicious lips together. "I find I'm more suitable for a company that emphasizes teamwork."

Graham wanted to laugh. He wanted to round the desk, clasp her to him and spin her around. But it was a job interview so he had to be professional. "I see. So tell me why I should hire you, Miss Ullo."

"I'm punctual—" she raised her eyebrows as if to point out his tardiness for the interview "—and I play well with others."

"Do you, now?"

Her smile was pure siren. "Oh, yes. I have a particular skill set. Never had complaints before. I'm highly imaginative in the office…and out. I'm confident, but I've also learned over the past few months, I'm not always right. Hmm…guess that means I'm flexible. In the office…and out."

Graham grew aroused thinking about her flexibility and particular skill set. Thank goodness he was behind the desk. "You sound like an interesting candidate, especially the flexible part."

Tess lifted one shoulder in a sexy shrug. "I'd be happy to prove it to you, um, that is, if I get the opportunity."

Graham swallowed and looked at his hands. "How soon would you be able to start?"

"When do you want me?"

Morning, night and day. He cleared his throat. "As soon as you're ready."

Tess's eyes deepened. "I'm ready now."

His heart literally started beating faster. Was this merely about working for Ullo, or was this about something more? With him? God, please let it be about more than a job.

"Good," he said, rising slightly and offering his hand.

She rose and placed her hand in his. Perfect fit. "So does this mean I have a future here?"

"I believe it does."

She rubbed her glossy lips together again. "Do you have an office policy on employees dating?"

"You'll need to fill out a disclosure statement. We like to be aboveboard here." His thumb stroked the curve of her finger.

Tess jerked her hand away. "Good to know." Then she turned, shouldered her attaché case and walked to the door.

Graham dropped his hand. "I'm guessing you think the interview is over?"

She spun around. "I was simply locking the door."

Graham laughed.

Tess shook her head. "I'm kidding, of course. Another one of my good qualities—a good sense of humor."

"You were kidding?" Graham didn't want to look so confused, but he knew he must have.

"This is a job interview. Business only." Tess looked at him like he was stupid.

Something in his stomach sank. "Right."

"But I was hoping you could recommend a place for

drinks. I'm thinking I want something local...and close by," she said with a Tess-like twinkle in her eye.

Graham couldn't stop the bubble of happiness that sprang to life inside of him. "Well, there's this place called Two-Legged Pete's—"

"Two-Legged?" she cracked.

"Yeah, the guy who owns it has a sense of humor, I guess. It's not far from here and I hear they have great stuffed mushrooms and will turn the TV to baseball if you ask nicely."

She tilted her head. "I love baseball. Think I'll stop by there around—" she looked at her wrist where her Cookie Monster watch popped out from beneath her blouse "—five-thirty?"

"That's a great time to go to Two-Legged Pete's. I met the woman of my dreams there once."

"You don't say," she said, a smile creeping over her face. "Well, then I'm definitely going so I can meet the man of my dreams."

Graham grinned like a goober, but he didn't care. "He'll be there."

"That's what I'm hoping for."

AFTER LUNCH WITH GIGI—where Tess bought all the drinks—and an afternoon of finding the perfect black dress and killer pumps covered in black lace, Tess walked into Two-Legged Pete's. She looked about as good as she ever had. The dress was tight, classy and made her legs look awesome. Or maybe it was the shoes that did that. She'd sprung for a manicure and the technician had even applied her makeup after suggesting a few things to do with her eyes.

As a result, Tess knew she didn't look like the girl Graham had met at Two-Legged Pete's that Monday night months ago.

"Hot damn, you look good, girl," Ron declared from behind the bar where a string of customers lined up. The place was busier than usual, but Tess found Graham immediately. He'd turned and watched her as she entered the bar, a beautiful smile on his gorgeous face.

"I try sometimes," Tess said, with a flirty smile. As usual Ron ate it up as he reached for the gin. "How's that little one?"

Ron set down the Hendrick's and reached into his back pocket. Tess pointed toward where Graham sat and Ron raised his eyebrows. "Okay, then. I'll show you later."

Tess made her way down to the very end of the bar where sitting right next to the trivia machine was her new boss.

And, God willing and the creek didn't rise, her new man.

Graham hooked his foot around a stool against the wall and pulled it over close. "Would the lady like a seat?"

"She would," Tess said, sitting.

Graham smiled at her and she remembered the last time they'd sat in this very bar. There had been an aura of mystery, of excitement, of crazy attraction. All of that was still there, but joining those feelings was a certainty she'd found the right man for her.

Finally.

Ron set the drink in front of her and slid Graham another of what he was having. "I suppose you two want to watch baseball," he said with disgust.

Graham hadn't taken his eyes off her. "Nah, man. We're good."

"So I see. What started months ago seems to have ended," Ron joked, and swaggered off to wait on more customers and drive up the tips for him and his new family.

"He's wrong," Graham said softly.

"Oh?" Tess asked.

"It's a new beginning. The one we should have had after that night."

"Well, I'm wearing my black dress."

"Very well, too, I might add," Graham said, his eyes sliding down her body. "Very, very well."

She wanted to say so much to him, and yet at the same time she wanted to say nothing at all. She was so tired of all the drama. Complicated was so overrated. "I'm sorry."

"I'm sorry, too."

"I want to start over—with a clean slate. No more grudges, blame or wounded pride. No more embarrassment over who we are." Tess reached out and touched the rugged hand cupping the sweating tumbler.

Graham turned his hand over and clasped hers. "Agreed. I'm ready to start clean."

"And I'd also like to say thank you."

He arched a dark eyebrow. "For what? Telling Miles the truth? For hiring you? Everything I did was aboveboard. You're deserving of all those things."

"No, though those things are nice." She swallowed the anxiety that cropped up. She needed to just say it. Do what she'd said she would do when she told Monique she couldn't work for Upstart…when she'd strolled into the warehouse she'd vowed never to step into again months ago. "I wanted to thank you for loving me in spite of my being a complete asshole."

Graham started laughing.

Tess gulped. "I mean, I love you. I shouldn't necessarily presume you—"

His mouth shut her up.

Tess swallowed the stupid words and kissed him, her heart breaking apart and knitting back together at the sheer rightness of this man kissing away her fears.

Pulling away slightly, he smiled at her. "You can shut up now."

"Is that all you have to say?"

"No, I got tons to say, but I'm only going to say two key things. Are you ready?"

She nodded.

"First, tonight we are going to have a real date. I'm going to take you out for a nice dinner, we're going to drink wine, maybe dance beneath the stars then go to your place and make love until the sun comes up."

"Sounds good," Tess said. "But I need to remind you, I have a new job to start tomorrow."

"Sleeping with the boss has benefits," he joked, before becoming serious. "I'm not really your boss, you know."

"I know. You're my partner. My dad ordered you up for me. I just didn't realize it."

Graham kissed her hard and fast.

"Now, two." He held up two fingers, making sure she focused on him.

"I'm listening."

"Therese Ullo, I want to spend the rest of my life loving you. I'm not talking about a fling. I'm talking about forever. My partner in every way. I love you."

Tess's heart burst and she tried not to cry because she didn't want to mess up her makeup. It really looked good for once. Sweeping her bottom lash with a finger, she stopped the tear from falling. "You do?"

Graham grasped her face between both hands and kissed her before looking deep into her eyes. "You make me crazy, but I love it. This is a forever thing."

Tess smiled. "You don't know how good that sounds."

"You don't know how good it feels."

They smiled at one another, laughing as they heard Ron tell someone how he'd brought them together one rainy night months ago. And how he totally knew they were meant to be when he saw them together. And about how he was certain his daughter would be just old enough to be a flower girl when they wed.

"He's got plans for us," Tess said.

"They sound like good ones," Graham said.

And then she kissed her forever guy again.

EPILOGUE

Three months later

GRAHAM PROPPED HIS FOOT on the ottoman holding a stack of *Glamour* magazines and moved his arm so it wouldn't go numb. Tess sighed in her sleep and shifted so her head dropped into his lap.

Her tear-streaked face was slack and peaceful in the late-afternoon sun streaking in the loft windows. Across the room Emily, also asleep, curled in an armchair with her new kitten's head tucked against her.

Frank's funeral was held earlier and they were all worn out from the grief. Frank had passed peacefully three days ago with the family gathered around him—a family that now included Graham. Tess's father had been at home and in good spirits, his hospice nurse close by, rolling her eyes at Frank's bad jokes and monitoring his pain.

At one point when everyone had gone to the kitchen for tea and cookies or whatever else Maggie had baked, Graham borrowed a moment alone with Frank.

"Frank, can I talk to you a sec?"

"Quick. That's all I got," Frank cracked, gaunt and pale in his bed, but smiling nevertheless.

"Bad joke."

"I'm full of 'em," he said. "Is this about business? 'Cause if it is, I want you to know I trust you."

"No, it's about Tess." Graham swallowed the sudden

tears that pricked in his eyes. "I wanted to ask your permission to marry your daughter."

Frank smiled. "Oh. My Tess, huh?"

"I love her."

"I know you do. I can see it in your eyes. Just the way I've always looked at Mags. It's precious, you know. Love. So many people let it die, allow their pride to stand in the way. They allow the world to interfere, to tell them what love should or shouldn't be. Bah. What does the world know?"

He drifted a bit, wincing and sucking in air.

"Frank?"

"Still breathing," he muttered and opened his eyes again. "I knew there was something about you. Didn't know this was about my girl. Thought it was just about business, but the good Lord knew. He sent you here for a reason."

"Yes," Graham agreed, easing a hand onto Frank's shoulder.

Frank covered Graham's hand with his own. "Can't think of a better son to add to this family. Marry her, have babies, name your first son Frank."

Graham laughed. "Thank you. I will treasure her always."

"I know you will," Frank said. "You're a good man."

And at that moment, Graham finally believed he was a good man. In that reverent moment, Frank had given him something his own father never had—a sense of belonging.

Tess moved against his arm now, opening her eyes, drawing him to the present.

Yawning, Tess sat up. "I fell asleep."

"You're tired," he said, brushing a hand over her head. "It's been a long day."

"We did him justice, didn't we?" she asked, her voice soft in the quiet of the room.

"He was there the entire time. In every conversation, bigger than life—"

"And very pleased no one brought pound cake," Tess said with a smile.

"Yeah, and he's still here now. He'll always be with you. He'll always be with us." Graham gathered her against him.

"It's such a sad day but it was beautiful, too. All those flowers and the way the sun shone like Daddy was already in heaven, maybe even organizing some parades."

"I got something for you," Graham said, digging in his pocket.

He brought out a small tin that looked like a pillbox.

Tess took it from him. "What is it?"

"It was your Grandmother Bella's. Your father kept it in his sock drawer."

Tess made a face. "How did you get it?"

"He made me get it out about a week ago…when I asked him for your hand in marriage."

"Marriage?" Her eyes widened as she looked at the box. Then she lifted her eyes to his. "You asked my daddy?"

Smiling, Graham brushed her lips with his and then slid to the floor. "Today we buried your father, Tess, but he and I talked. He loved you beyond anything imaginable. The way I love her." Graham glanced over at Emily.

"Oh, God, Graham." Tess breathed, dampness gathering in her eyes. "I can't cry anymore. Please don't make me cry. I'm empty."

"No more tears. Today isn't just about sorrow. It's about love. Your father wanted you to have this as your engagement ring." Graham laughed. "He said he had to steal it from your grandmother's safety deposit box so you can't wear it around her."

Tess jerked her head up, eyes widening.

"He was kidding. You know your dad."

That made her smile.

"So Therese Ullo, will you do me the honor of becoming my wife?"

He opened the box displaying a beautiful silver filigree ring with a small diamond winking within the lacy design.

"Oh." Tess brushed her finger over the antique ring. "It's beautiful."

"Just like you."

Then she kissed him, pulling back only to say clearly, "Just try and get rid of me."

And in the moment, Graham knew he'd finally come home.

* * * * *

A sneaky peek at next month...

Cherish™

ROMANCE TO MELT THE HEART EVERY TIME

My wish list for next month's titles...

In stores from 21st February 2014:

❏ The Returning Hero – Soraya Lane

& Road Trip With the Eligible Bachelor – Michelle Douglas

❏ Lassoed by Fortune – Marie Ferrarella

& Celebration's Family – Nancy Robards Thompson

In stores from 7th March 2014:

❏ Safe in the Tycoon's Arms – Jennifer Faye

& The Secrets of Her Past – Emilie Rose

❏ Awakened By His Touch – Nikki Logan

& Finding Family...and Forever? – Teresa Southwick

Available at WHSmith, Tesco, Asda, Eason, Amazon and Apple

Just can't wait?

Visit us Online

You can buy our books online a month before they hit the shops! **www.millsandboon.co.uk**

0214/23

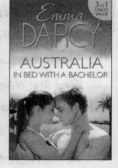

Join the Mills & Boon Book Club

Want to read more **Cherish**™ books?
We're offering you **2 more** absolutely **FREE**!

We'll also treat you to these fabulous extras:

- 🌹 Exclusive offers and much more!
- 🌹 FREE home delivery
- 🌹 FREE books and gifts with our special rewards scheme

Get your free books now!

visit www.millsandboon.co.uk/bookclub
or call Customer Relations on 020 8288 2888

Discover more romance at

www.millsandboon.co.uk

❤ WIN great prizes in our exclusive competitions

❤ BUY new titles before they hit the shops

❤ BROWSE new books and REVIEW your favourites

❤ SAVE on new books with the Mills & Boon® Bookclub™

❤ DISCOVER new authors

PLUS, to chat about your favourite reads, get the latest news and find special offers:

⬛ Find us on facebook.com/millsandboon

🐦 Follow us on twitter.com/millsandboonuk

❤ Sign up to our newsletter at millsandboon.co.uk

WEB_SD